Dom... dark ... skin. ...re..., he ...ught, he looked exactly like the photos of himself his mother kept in the family album. He looked like a Bonelli.

But it was impossible. A coincidence. *This boy was not his son....*

From *Mother at Heart* by Joan Elliott Pickart

She could handle anything. Certainly taking care of one little baby alone couldn't be as hard as any of the backbreaking, bone-wrenching work she'd done on the ranch. Could it?

Even if it were, she could do it. But what if her ex-husband, her once-beloved Ash, had come to Elk Creek to be with her? Could it be that she wasn't as alone as she'd thought?

Beth didn't dare to hope....

From *Baby My Baby* by Victoria Pade

JOAN ELLIOTT PICKART

is the author of over eighty-five novels. She is a
two-time Romance Writers of America RITA® Award
finalist. When she isn't writing, she has tea parties,
reads stories, plays dress-up—and the list goes
on—with her young daughter, Autumn. Joan also
has three grown daughters and three wonderful
little grandchildren. Joan and Autumn live in a
small town in the high pine country of Arizona.

VICTORIA PADE

is a bestselling author of both historical and
contemporary romance fiction, and mother of
two energetic daughters, Cori and Erin. Although
she enjoys her chosen career as a novelist, she
occasionally laments that she has never traveled
farther from her Colorado home than Disneyland,
instead spending all her spare time plugging away
at her computer. She takes breaks from writing by
indulging in her favorite hobby—eating chocolate.

Baby

JOAN ELLIOTT PICKART

VICTORIA PADE

Love

Silhouette Books

Published by Silhouette Books

America's Publisher of Contemporary Romance

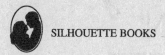

SILHOUETTE BOOKS

ISBN 0-373-23012-5

by Request

BABY LOVE

Copyright © 2003 by Harlequin Books S.A.

The publisher acknowledges the copyright holders
of the individual works as follows:

MOTHER AT HEART
Copyright © 1995 by Joan Elliott Pickart

BABY MY BABY
Copyright © 1995 by Victoria Pade

Visit Silhouette at www.eHarlequin.com

Printed in U.S.A.

CONTENTS

Dear Reader,

When I wrote *Mother at Heart* years ago I felt
a special bond with Tessa Russell and understood
how much she loved her precious son, Jason. She
had adopted Jason after her sister died shortly after
giving birth to him. While Jason was not a child of
her body, in her heart she was his mother and she
would do anything to protect him from harm's way.
I think perhaps I related to Tessa so completely
because I have four adopted daughters of my own.
Babies of my heart.

For those of you who are meeting Tessa, Jason and
the handsome Dominic for the first time, I hope you
enjoy sharing their journey toward everlasting love.

If you are reading this story again after so many
years, I hope you enjoy the memories.

Thanks to all of you for your continued support
and for the wonderful letters you write to me.

Warmest regards,

Joan Elliott Pickart

MOTHER AT HEART
Joan Elliott Pickart

For my mother, Olive Elliott,
for all and everything....
Thanks, Mom.

Prologue

Abby Thatcher laid her head on her folded arms and tried not to cry. Winthrop had hated tears, though God knew he'd handled enough weeping women during the forty years he'd practiced law in this small office in downtown Phoenix.

Exhaustion, combined with sorrow, had her feeling numb. But the numbness didn't make the ache in her heart go away. She raised her head and, taking a deep breath, straightened her thin shoulders and patted her salt-and-pepper hair. Indulging her grief wouldn't get the work done, and now, on top of everything else, she had to deal with the ineptitude of the temporary help she'd just dismissed. In two days, the silly woman hadn't been able to follow the simplest directions.

It had been only three days since Winthrop's funeral, but with all Abby had had to cope with since his fatal heart attack last week, it seemed more like three years.

She opened a file on her always-organized desk, wishing instead she could give way to her grief for the man she had loved for over four decades, the man who'd seen her only as his dedicated, organized and ever-so dependable secretary. There had never been any hope for her. Winthrop Ames, Esq., had been married to the law.

Her last official duty would be to close his office. Before she could, she had to make arrangements for his pending cases and dispose of a lifetime's accumulation of files, since he had no partners.

The half-dozen cartons along the oak-paneled wall of the small library would be picked up this afternoon by a messenger from the law firm one of Winthrop's clients had asked to assume his case. Yesterday, she'd directed the temp to mail several real estate files. Abby was still waiting to hear from other people she'd spoken with regarding their cases, and had letters to write to Winthrop's remaining clients.

But before another sheet of paper left the office, she needed to tend to the special files—those that had been so dear to Winthrop's heart.

With a sense of purpose, she crossed the room to the cartons she'd filled herself. Large manila envelopes, along with a stack of typing paper the temp had failed to put away after mailing the real estate files, were on the desk next to them.

Abby stopped in front of a yellow carton. A small smile touched her lips as she looked fondly at the folders inside.

The babies, she thought, a rush of warmth suffusing her.

Winthrop's practice had been varied, but his favorite cases were the adoptions. He'd loved little children. Three cases in particular had been special to Winthrop: Shaw, Russell and Parker.

It was with that thought that she noticed the first folder

wasn't the one she'd placed there yesterday. She was certain she'd left the Shaw file in front. She specifically remembered putting it there after instructing the temp to mail everything in the carton next to it.

Perplexed, she removed the box of stationery and mailing labels the woman had left on the box and searched through the remaining folders. The Parker and Russell files were there, but where was Shaw?

She went through the box again slowly, carefully checking each folder. Fifteen minutes later, she admitted defeat. The Shaw file was nowhere to be found. Deeply troubled, she picked up the Russell file.

Russell, Janice, she thought, reading the name on the folder tab. She frowned as she glanced through the papers. She'd never approved of Janice Russell's decision. It just wasn't right that the young man had never been told he was a father. He should know he had a child.

Abby reached for a mailing envelope.

Chapter One

Five Years Ago

As Tessa Russell entered the hospital, she was only vaguely aware of the bustling people, the bright lights, the faint odor of antiseptic.

She felt strange, disoriented, as though she were standing outside of herself, watching what she was doing from afar.

A part of her mind realized that she was in a state of semishock, and that it was imperative that she get a grip on herself in order to be prepared for what she was about to face.

Another part of her preferred to stay in her other-world fog, where it was possible to postpone dealing with the harsh truths of reality.

The touch of a hand on her arm caused her to stop and

look around at the attorney who had brought her here, the man who had been the cause of her life being suddenly turned upside down.

"Yes, Mr. Ames?" she said, her voice unsteady.

Winthrop Ames, Esq., was a short, round, balding man in his early sixties, who was dressed in a three-piece suit, complete with the old-fashioned touch of a watch chain. He had a surprisingly dynamic voice for someone of his small stature, and it must have served him well during his many years in the courtroom.

It was his eyes that Tessa sought, needing the gentleness and compassion evident there.

"Are you all right, Ms. Russell?" Winthrop asked.

"Yes. No." She shook her head. "I'm sorry. I'm not behaving very well. I know I must be strong, but it's just so much to comprehend." She drew a deep breath, then lifted her chin. "I'll be fine. You've been so kind, so caring, and I appreciate all you're doing."

"You're quite welcome."

She managed a small smile. "Attorneys, I'm afraid, have a reputation for being rather coldhearted and money-hungry, more often than not. You're a refreshing exception to the rule, Mr. Ames."

He chuckled. "That may be why I drive a ten-year-old car, and wear a suit every bit as ancient." His smile faded. "I deal in people, not cases, not clients given a number on a file folder, but human beings. I haven't been highly successful in the practice of law on a monetary level, Ms. Russell, but I sleep with an inner peace at night, and that's extremely important to me. I'm able to live with myself with a clear conscience."

Tessa nodded.

"Are you ready to go upstairs now, Ms. Russell?"

"Please, call me Tessa."

"Yes, all right, Tessa. Your sister is on the maternity floor, but is in a private room where her heart can be continually monitored, as well as a close watch kept on the condition of the baby."

"Janice," Tessa whispered, struggling against threatening tears. "It's been so many years since she ran away from the foster home where we were placed when our parents were killed. She was so unhappy and angry. Her world had been destroyed at twelve years old, and at fourteen, she disappeared during the night."

An errant tear slid down one cheek, and she dashed it away.

"For the past nine years, I didn't know if she was alive or dead, or what had happened to her," Tessa said. "And now? Dear God, she's about to give birth to a baby."

"Tessa," Winthrop said gently, "you must remember that Janice is extremely ill. The life-style she was caught up in, the drugs, alcohol... The toll on her heart has been devastating. The doctors have said that the chances of Janice surviving the birth of her child are very slim. She's aware of that fact, and she requested that I find you. You can be assured that she took excellent care of herself during her pregnancy for the sake of the child, and try to find solace in that."

"Yes. Yes, I will. Let's go upstairs, Mr. Ames. I want to see my sister."

Winthrop looked directly at her for long moment, then nodded.

Tessa stood next to the bed, gripping the top rung of the safety rail so tightly, her knuckles were white. Several machines nearby made strange beeping noises, and had wires trailing under the blanket covering Janice.

Tessa stared down at her sleeping sister, her heart aching and tears once again misting her eyes.

Janice was two years younger than Tessa, but appeared ten years older. She was pale and gaunt, with purple smudges beneath her closed eyes. Her short hair was tangled and dull, with no natural sheen.

She looked so small, so fragile, as though the slightest breeze could fling her into oblivion.

Janice was dying.

"Dear God," Tessa said, pressing the fingertips of one hand to her lips to stifle a sob.

She forced herself to shift her tormented gaze to the mound that was Janice's stomach pressing against the light green blanket.

A baby, Tessa thought. A miracle. Somehow, for the sake of her own sanity, she had to concentrate on the life, not the pending death, within her view.

Winthrop Ames had explained that Janice had first approached him to assist her with plans to place the baby for adoption. She'd refused to name the father.

As the months passed, Janice had changed her mind, deciding to keep the baby so she would have someone to love, someone to love her.

Winthrop had finally convinced Janice that as a single parent, she owed it to her baby to name a guardian in the event that something should happen to her, the child's mother.

He'd also persuaded her to identify the father in case a unique and life-threatening medical problem arose with the child. The biological father's blood or bone marrow might mean the difference between life and death. Janice had reluctantly agreed. Tessa Russell was to be the baby's legal guardian.

Oh, Janice, Tessa thought, *why didn't you come to me*

years ago? Janice had told Winthrop that Tessa was living in Tucson, and she had even known the address and telephone number. She was too ashamed of how she'd lived her life, she'd told the attorney, to contact her older sister.

Tessa shook her head. She wouldn't have stood in judgment of Janice. She would have been overjoyed to have welcomed her into her life and home. But now it was too late. Too late.

Janice stirred and opened her eyes.

"Tessa?" she said, her voice weak.

"I'm here. Oh, Janice, I..." Tears choked off Tessa's words.

"Don't cry. Please, Tessa, there isn't time for tears, for sorrow. We have to think of the baby. Listen to me, please?"

"Yes, I'm listening. Don't tire yourself."

"I'm not important now. I know I'm dying, Tessa, but my baby is alive and healthy." She smiled. "It's a boy. They told me after one of my tests. A little boy."

"That's wonderful," Tessa said, managing to smile through her tears. "What would you like to name him?"

Janice's smile faded. "*You* decide on his name. You're going to be his mother." She paused and her eyes widened. "Oh, God, Tessa, you *will* take my baby, won't you? Please? Oh, please, Tessa?"

Tessa covered one of Janice's hands with her own. "Shh, calm down. You mustn't upset yourself like this. Of course I'll love him as my own, and raise him the very best I can." Tears spilled onto her cheeks. "I'm sorry, but this is so difficult. I've missed you, Janice, so very much."

"Forgive me for causing you such pain. That's all I can say...please forgive me, because there isn't time to explain how I felt during those years, how angry and confused I was. It doesn't matter now."

Tessa nodded as she swept the tears away.

"Tessa, you must promise me that you won't contact the baby's father. Mr. Ames convinced me to have his name on file in case of a medical emergency. If that occurs, God forbid, then... But otherwise, the father isn't to be told. Will you promise me that?"

"Why, Janice? You obviously feel very strongly about this, but why?"

Janice sighed wearily. "It was a fling, a party, nothing more. I was living in Las Vegas, and he came with friends to celebrate the opening of his own law practice in Tucson. All he thinks about is money. He's cold, hard and places money at the top of his list of importance. Oh, he's very handsome, and he's a fantastic lover, I'll give him that. *But the man has no soul.* Keep him away from my baby, Tessa. *Please.*"

"Don't excite yourself, Janice."

"Promise me!"

"Yes, yes, I promise."

"Thank you. Thank you. I knew you lived in Tucson, and I moved here to Phoenix when I discovered I was pregnant so I would feel closer to you. But I couldn't face you, I just couldn't." Her eyes drifted closed. "I'm so tired, so tired. I love you very much, Tessa."

"I love you, too, Janice," she whispered.

Tessa covered her face with her hands and wept softly.

Jason Robert Russell came into the world with a lusty wail and a fluffy cap of black hair. He weighed seven pounds, seven ounces, and was declared to be perfectly healthy. Tessa named him Jason as a male version of Janice, and Robert for his deceased grandfather, Janice and Tessa's father.

* * *

Janice Russell died peacefully in her sleep less than an hour after the birth.

Forty-eight hours later, following a memorial service for her sister, Tessa Russell took the precious baby home.

Chapter Two

The Present

Dominic Bonelli replaced the receiver of the telephone, then rotated his head back and forth in an attempt to loosen the tightened muscles in his neck and shoulders.

He'd been talking on the telephone for almost two hours in a tough negotiating session with the attorney representing the principals wanting to purchase the company that Dominic's client wished to sell.

Four additional clauses of the complicated contract had been ironed out, line by line, some even word by word.

There was a lot of work yet to do, Dominic knew, but the deal was steadily moving forward. The concessions he'd had to make had been few, and if things continued as they were, his client would be extremely pleased.

There was no if about it, he decided. The final contract

would lean heavily in his client's favor. Dominic would have won the disputed issues of importance, and given in on only minor details. While the attorney for the buyer was crowing over Dominic's defeats, the seller would have everything Dominic had set out to gain.

He nodded in satisfaction. Each new deal he undertook was a challenge, with strategies to be planned after hours spent studying the facts down to the most minute detail. It was a game of sorts, that required knowing the opposition every bit as well as his own client.

His reputation in Tucson—in fact, across the state—for being a sharp, aggressive corporate attorney, who hammered away at contracts until they were letter-perfect, was growing. The ever-increasing number of clients coming through the door was evidence of his expertise.

Dominic Bonelli, attorney-at-law, was on his way to the top at only thirty-five years old. Nothing, and no one, would keep him from reaching his career goals.

A light tap on his office door brought him from his pleasant reverie, and he answered the summons with an automatic, ''Come in.''

A woman in her early fifties entered the large room. Gladys Weber was short, rather plump, wore her gray hair in a bun at the nape of her neck and had a smile always at the ready.

She looked, Dominic had once told her, like someone who should be home baking cookies for her grandchildren. Her grandkids, she'd retorted, ate store-bought cookies at her house. She was a top-notch administrative assistant, thank you very much, and Dominic would do well to remember that. His reply had been a grin.

''You'll have to speak up, Gladys,'' Dominic said as she stopped in front of his enormous desk. ''My ear died.''

''I don't doubt it. You were certainly on the phone a

long time. I thought that little red light on my console was never going to blink off. Half the morning is gone.'' She deposited a stack of material in front of him. ''Your mail, master, and the messages from everyone who tried to reach you for the past two hours.'' She paused. ''I assume the negotiations are going well?''

''They are,'' he said with a decisive nod.

''Of course. Oh, there's an envelope in that stack marked personal that I didn't open. It's that legal-size one on the bottom. Are you taking calls yet?''

''No, give me about fifteen minutes to clear my head and go through this mail, then I'll be back on duty.''

''Got it.'' She turned and briskly walked from the room, closing the door behind her as she left.

Gladys was a gem, Dominic mused, staring at the closed door. She'd agreed to work for him when he'd started his own practice over five years before, gambling on the fact that he wasn't going to fall flat on his face.

They'd weathered the early days, the ones that had been financially lean despite the nest egg he'd been putting aside for years while eagerly anticipating the opening of his own firm. Then they'd cheered together as the client list grew. There were now two paralegals under Gladys's command, who respected and sincerely liked her.

She was a prize, no doubt about it. She put up with his dark moods, his intensity, his perfectionism. She even took his eccentricities in stride, such as his directive that his office door was to remain closed at all times.

Dominic leaned back in the butter-soft leather chair, resting his head against the high back and staring at the ceiling.

The sense of privacy the closed door afforded him was important. It continually reaffirmed where he was now, compared to where he had come from.

He lifted his head to sweep his gaze over the spacious, expensively decorated office. The furniture was gleaming mahogany, the thick carpeting was chocolate brown. The color scheme was dark blue with varying shades of browns and tans, lightening to off-white.

A grouping of easy chairs surrounding a low, round table was on the far side of the room, and two chairs were placed in front of his desk. The mahogany filing cabinets along one wall had been custom-built.

The room was masculine and richly appointed. The exact message he wished to convey to those entering was that of command and wealth.

Dominic's glance fell on the pile of mail in front of him, and he forced himself to end his mental ramblings. Curiosity rose to the fore, and he pulled free the unopened envelope Gladys had spoken of.

There was no return address, he noted, nor was there a typed mailing label. The writing was wobbly, as though the person's hand had been shaking.

He slit the top of the envelope with a letter opener, and withdrew a manila file folder. The tab on the side read: Russell, Janice.

Pushing the remaining mail to one side, he placed the file in front of him, and flipped it open. Within moments, a deep frown knitted his eyebrows.

"What in the hell," he muttered, then read further.

Rising fury caused his heartbeat to quicken, and every muscle in his body to tighten. As he finished reading the last document, he smacked the papers with the palm of one hand, and lunged to his feet.

Moving from behind his desk, he began to pace the floor with heavy, anger-induced steps.

He'd never heard of Janice or Tessa Russell, nor had he

had any contact with a Phoenix attorney named Winthrop Ames.

The documents were dated over five years ago. Janice Russell had met with Winthrop Ames to discuss placing her then-unborn child for adoption upon its birth. She later changed her mind, having decided to keep the child.

A copy of Janice's death certificate was in the file, along with a copy of a birth certificate for Jason Robert Russell. The birth certificate had *unknown* in the space allotted for naming the father.

But, Dominic fumed, still pacing the floor, a separate sheet of paper was a legal form naming Dominic Bonelli as the father of the child. Tessa Russell, the deceased mother's sister, was the guardian of Jason Robert Russell, and had taken him from the hospital to her Tucson home at an address given.

What was the game plan? If these people were intent on slapping him with a phony paternity suit for child support, why wait five years? It was really stupid, because with the sophisticated tests available now, he could prove in an instant that he wasn't the father. If someone was attempting to instigate a con, they should at least have a modicum of brains.

"Hell," Dominic said with a snort of disgust.

He should ignore the whole thing. It wasn't worth his valuable time and energy to even acknowledge the arrival of the file.

He stopped and narrowed his eyes as he stared at the folder on the desk.

No, by damn, he decided, he wasn't going to let Winthrop Ames and Tessa Russell off that easily. They would come to know that they'd made a big mistake by trying to pull a scam on him. He'd hit them with a lawsuit that would have them running for cover.

Moving closer to the desk, Dominic pressed the button on the intercom.

"Gladys, find out everything you can on a Phoenix attorney named Winthrop Ames and report back to me right away."

"Roger. You're welcome."

"Thank you," he muttered.

He sat down in his chair and began to sort through the remaining mail, instantly realizing he was too furious to concentrate. He drummed the fingers of one hand impatiently on the top of the desk as he waited for the information from Gladys.

The intercom buzzed and he hit the button with more force than necessary.

"Yes?" he said.

"Winthrop Ames," Gladys said, "passed away about two weeks ago. He had no partners, and his practice is in the process of being disbanded."

"Thank you," Dominic said absently, his mind racing.

He sank back in the chair, laced his hands behind his head and glowered at the ceiling.

Interesting, he mused, *and very strange.* Winthrop Ames was out of the picture, leaving the spotlight on Tessa Russell. How had she gotten her hands on that folder?

He nodded.

Money. She'd approached whoever was shutting down Ames's practice and bought the damn file. Fine. He'd slap a suit on the seller, too. Tessa Russell had then doctored the documents, either alone or with the help of the seller, to include the one naming him as the father of Janice Russell's child. Clever to a point, but ridiculous considering present-day DNA tests.

Tessa Russell was going to regret having put her nasty little scheme in motion.

He looked at his appointment calendar, then pressed the intercom button again.

"Gladys, I'm going to keep my lunch date with Baxter because he's only down from Flagstaff for the day, but please reschedule my afternoon appointments. I'll be out of the office."

"Oh?"

"Don't get nosy."

"I'm not nosy, I'm efficient. Will I be able to reach you anywhere this afternoon?"

"No. I'll call in for my messages, or swing back by here, but I don't know what time."

"What if there's an emergency or…"

"Goodbye, Gladys."

It was after two o'clock before Dominic was able to end the luncheon appointment with Mr. Baxter. The Flagstaff client was retired, his time was his own and he seemed to derive a great deal of pleasure from going over every detail of the various buying-and-selling of properties that Dominic was handling for him.

At last free, Dominic consulted a city map, then drove out of the restaurant parking lot. The address given in the file for Tessa Russell was on the east side of town by the Rincon Mountains. He had to cross the city with its bumper-to-bumper traffic, and the going was slow.

Great, he thought as he stopped at yet another red light. He was getting a stress headache. He'd better chill out, as one of his nephews would say. Tensing with anger to the point of subjecting himself to painfully throbbing temples wasn't going to make the traffic move any faster so that he could confront Tessa Russell.

Taking a deep breath, he let it out slowly, then forced himself to shift mental gears.

The weather. That was an innocuous subject. September was a perfect time of year in Tucson. The daily rains of the summer monsoons were over, and the desert was a lush expanse of vivid colors displayed by scrub grass and wildflowers. The days were warm and the nights were cool enough for retrieving blankets from the closet shelf.

The three mountain ranges edging the city, the Santa Catalinas, the Rincons and the Tucsons, stood out in sharp relief against a brilliant blue sky dotted with fluffy white clouds.

"Very nice day," he said aloud, then rolled his eyes heavenward.

Finally, the traffic began to thin as Dominic drove farther away from town. He pressed harder on the gas pedal of his silver BMW, relishing the feel of the powerful vehicle responding to his command.

The paved road soon turned to dirt, creating a cloud of dust that left a coating on Dominic's sparkling clean car. His frame of mind *definitely* did not improve.

Consulting the map he'd placed next to him on the plush seat, he at last turned onto a side road, immediately slowing as he hit a pothole.

"Hell," he said as he saw that the road had more ruts than smooth surfaces.

The narrow road curved and Dominic drove on, seeing a house that was situated, in his opinion, in the middle of nowhere. The majestic Rincon Mountains were in the distance, desert stretched as far as the eye could see and there was the house, appearing as though it had been plunked down there as an afterthought.

He pressed on the brake at the end of a driveway leading to the structure, and checked the number on the mailbox mounted on a post.

Nodding as he saw that the number matched the one

shown in the file, he folded his arms on top of the steering wheel and scrutinized the house, which was about two hundred yards away.

It was an old, two-story wooden house badly in need of paint. A porch stretched across the entire front, displaying a bench swing suspended by chains and several white wicker chairs.

Mounted just above the steps was a multicolored sign that read: Rainbow's End Day-Care Center. A chain-link fence was on one side of the house, creating an area where children were playing on a variety of equipment.

So, Dominic mused, Tessa Russell ran a baby-sitting service in a house that looked as though it might be blown away by a gust of wind. Well, it wasn't going to be *his* money that would spruce up this dump.

"Nice try, Tessa," he said under his breath. "But no cigar."

He drove to the front of the house, the driveway even bumpier than the road leading to it. He parked the vehicle. Grabbing his briefcase, he left the car and went up the rickety steps. Hesitating a moment, he decided it wasn't necessary to knock on the door of a business. He entered the house, a tinkling bell above the door announcing his arrival.

Sweeping his gaze quickly over the room, he mentally cataloged the worn carpeting and furniture. Against one wall was a wooden creation of connected, open square boxes, each with a name printed on cardboard above the opening. Another unit had shelves with toys and books. A neat stack of small throw rugs was in a corner beyond a flight of stairs that no doubt led to the second floor.

Everything was extremely shabby, he thought. The inside needed painting as badly as the exterior, but at least it was clean.

He sniffed the air, finally identifying the faint aroma as cinnamon.

"I'll be right with you," a woman called from somewhere in the distance.

Dominic buttoned his suit coat, straightened his shoulders and waited.

Tessa slid the last snickerdoodle off the cookie sheet, then quickly removed the hot-pad mitts. Straightening the waistband of her royal blue T-shirt over her faded jeans, she blew a puff of air upward in a futile attempt to create a semblance of order to her naturally curly bangs. She hurried from the kitchen to greet whoever had entered the house.

As she went into the living room, she slowed her step to enable herself to take a quick mental inventory of the man standing by the front door.

Tall, dark and handsome, she thought. Whoever had invented the cliché must have had someone like this in mind. He appeared to be about six feet tall, was around thirty-five and drop-dead gorgeous.

Hair...dark as night. Eyes...ebony pools surrounded by long eyelashes a woman would die for. Physique... perfectly proportioned, with wide shoulders, narrow hips, long legs, all of which were displayed to perfection in what was obviously a custom-tailored suit. Features...strong and rugged, extremely masculine rather than pretty-boy smooth. Tanned, but then, maybe not. He looked Italian, or perhaps Greek, so the bronzed glow of his skin was one of nature's gifts of his heritage.

And, darn it, he was carrying a briefcase. Mr. Scrumptious was a salesman, albeit a very impressive-looking one. So, okay, she was now in her polite, but firm, no-I-don't-want-to-buy-any-insurance mode.

She stopped ten feet in front of him.

"Hello," she said pleasantly. "I'm Tessa Russell, the owner of Rainbow's End. How may I help you?"

Dominic narrowed his eyes slightly.

So, this was the con artist, he mused. She certainly didn't look the part. She was tall, slender but not skinny, had short, curly, strawberry-blond hair, and the biggest brown eyes he'd ever seen.

She was close to thirty, he supposed, but appeared younger in a refreshing, no-makeup way. She could be a wholesome-model candidate for a box of cornflakes.

But he knew better. He had her number. While he wasn't a trial lawyer, he'd spent enough time in the courthouse to be aware that the less-than-savory came in all shapes, sizes and ages. Tessa Russell was a crook-in-training.

"Sir?" Tessa said, frowning slightly.

Dominic brought his thoughts to an abrupt halt and looked directly into Tessa's eyes.

"I'm here," he said, his voice ominously low, "in re sponse to the information I received from you in the mail today, Ms. Russell."

Tessa's frown deepened. "I'm afraid I don't understand. I mailed you something? An insurance payment or… Excuse me, because I don't mean to be rude, but who are you?"

A pulse began to beat wildly in Dominic's temple as his anger soared once again.

"Dominic Bonelli."

The knot that tightened instantly in Tessa's stomach was so painful, she instinctively wrapped her hands around her elbows in a protective gesture. She could actually feel the color draining from her face.

Dear God, no! her mind screamed. She used to have a

bone-chilling fear that Dominic Bonelli would somehow learn of his son's existence, and arrive like an evil demon in the night to snatch her Jason.

But as the years passed, she'd calmed that terrifying thought until it was finally gone, flung into oblivion for all time.

And now? He was there, standing no more than a few feet away. He was big, strong, and because he was an attorney, he was also very powerful in the arena of the law.

Please. No. This couldn't be happening. But it was. *Dominic Bonelli was here.*

"My, my, Ms. Russell," Dominic said, sarcasm ringing in his voice, "you seem shaken. Surely you expected me to respond to what you sent me."

Tessa reached deep within herself for all the emotional strength she possessed. Her life was at stake.

"I'm not upset in the least, Mr. Bonelli," she said, lifting her chin. "I didn't have time for lunch today, and felt light-headed for a moment." She attempted a smile that failed to materialize. "Now then, let's clear up this matter, shall we? I'm very busy. I did *not* send anything to you through the mail. I don't even know you."

"Nor do I know you, or your deceased sister, Janice."

Tessa's eyes widened. "Janice?"

"Do you have an office where we can discuss this?"

"Yes, I have an office, but there's nothing to discuss. My sister died over five years ago. I can't imagine what you received pertaining to her, but it's obviously a mistake."

"Oh, yes, indeed," he said, nodding. She'd chosen the wrong man to attempt to fleece. Ms. Russell was in a great deal of trouble. "It was a very big mistake on your part."

"You're talking in riddles, and I've had quite enough

of your veiled threats. I'd like you to leave my home immediately.''

"You live here?" he said, glancing around. "How quaint."

"Goodbye, Mr. Bonelli."

"I think not. You've apparently gotten cold feet now that we're face-to-face, but I have every intention of pursuing the matter and filing charges against you."

"For what?" she said, nearly shrieking.

"Try extortion, libel, defamation of character, mental duress, for starters."

"You're out of your mind."

"*You* were, to think you could pull this off. I have in my possession the file you mailed me. You remember the file, don't you? It's the one with the phony document naming me as the father of Janice Russell's child, the boy you became legal guardian of when your sister died."

"That's impossible. Winthrop Ames would never have—"

"Winthrop Ames has been dead for two weeks. You managed to get your hands on the file, added the form naming me as the baby's father and set your plan in motion. I'm curious... Why me? Did you simply turn to the page in the telephone directory listing attorneys and pick one, figuring lawyers made enough money to serve your purpose?"

"I repeat, Mr. Bonelli," Tessa said, her voice trembling, "you're out of your mind. Yes, my sister died the day her baby was born. And, yes, I'm his guardian, which is not a fact anyone knows besides myself, Mr. Ames and the court. The baby's birth certificate states that the father is unknown.

"I wasn't aware that Mr. Ames had passed away. I have no idea who sent you that file, or why they added the document you're speaking of. What I *do* know is that it wasn't me.''

Doubt flickered through Dominic's mind. Had he acted too hastily? Had the mailing of the file been step one, with contact to follow from whoever was behind the scam? Was it possible that Tessa Russell was innocent of any wrong-doing?

''You've spoken of pressing charges against me,'' Tessa said coolly. ''Well, I'm in a position to file a complaint against you, sir. This is an invasion of my privacy, and is placing the mental well-being of a child at risk. I've chosen to allow him to believe that I'm his natural mother until he is of an age to comprehend the truth. He will be told, at some point in the future, in accordance with my sister's wishes, that his father is unknown.

''Someone, Mr. Bonelli, is trying to extort money from you. Quite frankly, that is *your* problem. However, if one word of my true relationship to the child in question becomes public knowledge while you're dealing with this situation, I'll sue you. Count on it.''

''Nicely said, Ms. Russell, but I have further questions to ask you. I want to know the names of everyone who worked in Winthrop Ames's office. I want to know if Ames or your sister ever referred to me in any manner. I want to know—''

''I have nothing more to say to you,'' Tessa interrupted. ''Leave my home. Now.''

Dominic studied her pale face for a long moment before speaking.

''All right,'' he said finally. ''I'll leave. If you're as innocent as you claim, I'll be contacted by the culprit very soon, I imagine. If that occurs, I'll inform you of that fact, and apologize for distressing you. I will also guarantee you of my silence regarding your relationship with the child by requesting that the complaint I register against whoever is behind this is heard in judge's chambers.''

"Fine."

"However, if I am *not* contacted, I'll be back, Ms. Russell. The cast of players will have narrowed down to one. You. Only you."

"Goodbye, Mr. Bonelli."

Dominic turned and started toward the door.

Go, Tessa mentally pleaded. Go, and never come back. Three more steps, and Dominic Bonelli would be out of her life. Jason would be safe again, with her, where he belonged. Three more steps. Two. One. Just one more.

As Dominic reached for the knob, the door burst open and a small boy ran in, carrying a paper cup he was covering with one hand.

"Mom," he yelled. "Mommy, guess what? I caught a lizard. It's here in this cup. Wanna see? He's cool, Mom. Can I keep him?"

Dominic stared at the boy, seeing his black hair, dark eyes with long lashes, the tawny hue of his skin.

Dear Lord, he thought, he looked exactly like himself in the photos his mother kept in the family album. The boy looked like his nephews had, too, at around five years old. He looked like a Bonelli.

No, damn it. It was impossible. The whole situation was so infuriating, he wasn't thinking clearly. He was allowing his imagination to run away with him.

Perhaps Janice Russell's lover had looked like him. It was a strange coincidence, nothing more. But he'd never heard of Janice Russell, and was not the father of her child. *This boy was not his son.*

"Hi," the boy said, turning to Dominic. "Wanna see my lizard?"

"Another time, perhaps," Dominic said. "Aren't you going to introduce me to this young man, Ms. Russell?"

"Mr. Bonelli," Tessa said, her voice now strong and steady, "this is Jason Robert Russell. *My son.*"

Chapter Three

The remainder of the workday seemed endless to Tessa. She performed by rote, having the strange sensation of being detached from herself as she watched her interaction with the children.

Each time she replayed in her mind the scene with Dominic Bonelli, she was consumed by chilling fear. She wanted to snatch up Jason and run as far away as possible as quickly as she could.

After Dominic had left the house, she'd admonished herself for having admitted that she was Jason's legal guardian due to Janice's death. And by telling Dominic that Jason was not aware of the truth, she'd given the threatening man the power to make her dance to his tune in exchange for his silence.

Many years before, she'd vowed to never again relinquish control of her life. After the nightmare of losing her parents, and being at the mercy of the foster-home system, she was determined that no one would ever dictate to her again.

She'd been furious with herself for so readily admitting her true relationship with Jason. But as the hours passed, she'd realized that she'd had no choice.

Dominic Bonelli had the file from Winthrop Ames's office. If Dominic chose to verify the authenticity of the death and birth certificates, it would be a simple task to accomplish. To deny that Janice had been Jason's natural mother would have been foolish.

She'd taken the only viable stand, she'd finally decided. It was true that she had no idea who had mailed the file to Dominic. But she had to adamantly maintain that the document naming Dominic as Jason's father was false. It was a mistake, or hoax, or an attempt to extort money from Dominic. Whatever the reason, she knew nothing about it.

Dominic Bonelli must never know that Jason was his son.

During the tedious afternoon, both of Tessa's employees, Patty and Emma, had asked her if she was all right. She'd pleaded a headache, managed to smile and continued with her duties.

Jason had been reluctantly convinced that the tiny lizard would be happier if allowed to go free to scamper along the desert floor.

Each time Tessa had looked at Jason, her heart quickened in terror. Dominic Bonelli possessed the power to take her son away from her. The court would lean heavily in favor of custody being given to a natural father over an aunt named as legal guardian.

Oh, God, no! her mind had hammered over and over. Jason was *her* baby, *her* beloved son.

At nine o'clock that night, Tessa stood next to Jason's bed, watching him sleep. In the glow of the night-light, she could see him clearly. His dark hair was a silky tumble, his long lashes lay like delicate fans on his cheeks.

He was so beautiful, she mused. He was a healthy, happy little boy. From the moment he'd been placed in her arms, she'd been filled with a love of such intensity, it was nearly painful.

When she'd left the foster home, she'd had a dream. She would someday have her own business. *She* would be in charge, in control. *She* would command her destiny.

The arrival of Jason into her life had been her call to action. She'd saved every penny she could during the years she'd worked as a waitress, and taken endless courses in business management, accounting, business law and taxes.

Her sudden and unexpected role as a single mother had given her the solution to the yet unanswered question of what type of business she wished to have. A day-care center. It was perfect. She could raise Jason herself, and still provide for their welfare.

For five blissful years, everything had been wonderful. There was very little money left over for extras after paying expenses, but Rainbow's End was holding its own. She even had a waiting list of those wishing to bring their children here, despite the location's being off the beaten track.

She was proud of what she'd accomplished in the past five years. And each morning as parents dropped off their children, she still felt a rush of joy that she didn't have to leave Jason.

They'd been a team, mother and son, since he was born. Laughter had echoed within the walls of the old house. Jason had cut his first tooth here, taken his first steps, spoken his first words. It was their home, where Tessa could close the door against the world. It was their safe haven.

Until now.

Until Dominic Bonelli had entered that house and threatened all that Tessa held dear. He had the power to shatter her existence.

With a ragged sigh that held a hint of a sob, she leaned over and kissed Jason gently on the forehead. She left the bedroom and went into the living room.

As she sank onto the worn sofa, crushing exhaustion overcame her. Tears filled her eyes and she lacked the energy to struggle against them.

What would happen next? she wondered frantically. She'd managed to instill doubt in Dominic's mind, but even though he'd backed off, he was not convinced that she was blameless.

Who had mailed him the file? And why? The culprit wasn't after him for child support. Did someone actually believe in these modern times that a prominent attorney would feel his reputation was at risk because he'd fathered a child out of wedlock? That was nonsense. Whoever had mailed the file was not in touch with reality. Dominic would deny that he was Jason's father, Tessa would concur and the extortionist would be left high and dry.

But if that person came to his senses and didn't contact Dominic further, the lawyer would come back to Rainbow's End. He wouldn't view the situation as a potential blackmailer having second thoughts. Oh, no, he'd made it clear that if he didn't hear from another source, then the nasty scheme had been Tessa's brainstorm.

And he would be back.

"Dear God," she whispered as a chill swept through her.

Shaking her head in despair, she gave way to the tears, and cried.

* * *

An entire week passed with no word from Dominic Bonelli. As each day went by, Tessa's hope that she would never hear from him again grew stronger.

A part of her mind registered the urge to look up his telephone number in the directory and call him, to get some kind of emotional closure of the situation. She needed something, anything, to reassure herself that Dominic was truly no longer a threat to her and Jason.

Another section of her brain refused to allow her to contact Dominic. Clichés such as *No news is good news* and *Let sleeping dogs lie* flickered in her mind, and she finally dismissed the idea of calling him.

She *did,* however, dial Information to ask for the number of Winthrop Ames's office. The kind and compassionate attorney had passed away, but perhaps there was someone still in his office who might have a clue as to how the confidential file had come to be mailed to Dominic. The operator informed her that the number was no longer in service.

Another day of blessed silence, Tessa thought as she waved goodbye to the last child leaving Rainbow's End. Another day without hearing from Dominic Bonelli.

"I'm off," Patty said, bringing Tessa from her thoughts.

"Me, too," Emma said. "It was a typical exhausting Monday. The kids are so rambunctious after the weekend. I swear, they must spend every Saturday and Sunday eating nothing but sweets. They're so wired on Mondays, like bouncing kangaroos."

Tessa laughed. "That's a perfect description of our little darlings on a Monday."

"Tomorrow will be better," Patty said. "Good night, Tessa. Have a nice evening, and go to bed early. You looked so tired all of last week, and the weekend didn't erase those dark smudges under your eyes."

"Yes, I'll go to bed early," Tessa said, smiling.

"I should hope so," Emma said.

Tessa stood at the door and watched as the two women went to their cars.

They were wonderful, she thought, both of them. They were in their early fifties and their grandchildren lived in other states. Rainbow's End gave them a chance to be with children, as well as the opportunity to earn some money. She was fortunate to have them.

"Mom?"

Tessa looked down at a frowning Jason. "Yes, sir?" she said, smiling at him. "You rang?"

"I'm hungry."

She ruffled his silky black hair. "You're always hungry. This time, your tummy is on schedule. I'll fix dinner pronto, Tonto. You can set the table."

"Can I make airplane napkins?"

"Sure. I think it's very classy to have a napkin by my plate that's folded into an airplane."

"Okay," he said, then ran toward the kitchen.

The upstairs of the house had three bedrooms and a bathroom. Tessa had furnished one of the bedrooms as a living room, with a sofa, a small easy chair, coffee and end tables. A television was set on top of a low bookcase.

It was in that cozy room that she and Jason spent their evenings. After they ate dinner, she would prepare fresh juice and snacks for the children for the next day, then she and Jason would "go home." The telephone was wired to ring in the kitchen, as well as the living room above.

Shortly after eight o'clock, Tessa finished reading Jason his nightly story, then kissed him on the forehead. He pulled the covers to beneath his chin, and wiggled into a comfortable position in his bed.

"Good night, good night," Tessa said. "Don't let the bedbugs bite."

Jason giggled.

"I love you, Jason Robert," she said.

"I love you, too, Mom," he said. "Whole bunches."

Tessa kissed him once more, this time on the tip of his nose, then left the room, knowing he would be asleep within minutes.

Jason went at full speed all day, she mused, going back into the living room. He was a bundle of energy, a healthy, joyful little boy. He *was* always hungry, it seemed, and was growing like a weed. He was probably going to be a tall man like his father.

She stopped statue-still by the sofa.

Dear heaven, where had that thought come from? She wanted no connection between Jason and Dominic, not even in her mind.

She sank onto one of the rather lumpy cushions of the sofa.

It was going to be more difficult now that she'd actually seen Dominic Bonelli. Ever since Jason was born, the man who had fathered him had been nothing more than a shadowy figure with no substance or form. He'd had a name, that was all.

But now? The resemblance between Jason and Dominic was uncanny. Jason was a miniature Dominic, with no visible trace of Janice.

Why hadn't Dominic seen the mirror image of himself when he'd looked at Jason? She'd been terrified when Jason had come dashing in the door the day Dominic had been here. He'd insisted on being introduced to the little boy, but there had been no shock, or wonder, in his expression when he'd said hello to Jason.

She should count her blessings that Dominic hadn't seen

the carbon copy of himself in Jason. She was positive that if Emma or Patty had seen the pair together, they would have had questions as to the relationship between the two.

Had Dominic been too angry to really see the evidence before his eyes? Yes, that was a distinct possibility. That, along with the fact that he had no recollection of knowing Janice, had probably caused him to dismiss Jason out of hand.

On another, calmer occasion, Dominic might take a closer look at Jason and *see* the small duplicate of himself.

Hopefully, she would never hear from Dominic Bonelli again. But if she did, she must make very certain that he didn't come in contact with Jason.

The shrill ringing of the telephone caused Tessa to jerk in surprise at the sudden noise in the quiet room. She picked up the receiver.

"Hello?"

"Ms. Russell? This is Dominic Bonelli."

Dear heaven, Tessa's mind screamed. *I've conjured him up by thinking about him.* No, that was ridiculous. She had to get a grip on herself. *Now.*

"Ms. Russell?"

"Yes, I'm here."

"I waited until this hour to call in hopes that the boy would be asleep so we could speak privately."

"Oh?"

"I've not been contacted by anyone regarding the file, Ms. Russell. I decided to allow one week to go by before taking further action. Is the boy in bed?"

"Yes."

"Fine. I'm leaving here now, and should arrive at your house in half an hour, or so."

"Now wait just a minute. This is my home. You have no right to simply announce that you're coming here."

"I have every right. Thirty minutes. You and I are going to have what I predict will be a very interesting and revealing chat."

"No, I—" Tessa stopped speaking when she realized she was speaking to the dial tone.

She slammed the receiver into place and got to her feet, only to sink back onto the sofa an instant later as her trembling legs refused to support her.

Thirty minutes, her mind echoed. She had half an hour to prepare for the arrival of the man who held the power to destroy her life.

Chapter Four

Tessa entertained the idea of changing her clothes, then rejected the thought. Jeans, a shell-pink knit top and tennis shoes were just fine. She didn't wish to impress Dominic Bonelli, she just wanted him out of her life.

Should she offer him refreshments? she wondered, pacing restlessly around the living room. No, forget it. This was definitely not a social call.

She'd prefer to meet with him in her small office off of the kitchen downstairs, rather than have him upstairs in her home. But she had no choice but to bring him up; she wouldn't be comfortable leaving Jason all alone in their living quarters. He rarely awakened once he was asleep for the night, but when he had, she'd always been there for him.

She was, Tessa suddenly realized, bouncing back and forth between the emotions of fear and anger.

She was terrified of Dominic Bonelli and what he might do if he realized that Jason was indeed his son.

And she was mad as blue blazes at Dominic's over-bearing attitude, the way he snapped orders, and his threats of filing charges against her. He was brash, arrogant and extremely rude.

Dominic was obviously quite accustomed to being in control and command, having things done his way with no questions asked.

Well, she had news for Mr. Bonelli. She wasn't going to bow three times, then jump to carry out his directives. She'd stand firm. She'd continue to state that she'd never heard of him, she'd maintain that the form in the file naming him as Jason's father was some kind of error that she knew nothing about and that there was nothing for him to gain by harassing her further.

Fine, she thought, walking to the window. She was no longer shifting between fear and anger. She was solidly set on *mad as hell*, which would serve her very well.

Brushing back the curtains, she saw the bobbing headlights of an approaching vehicle. It probably irritated the mighty Dominic Bonelli no end to have his fancy car jarred and covered in dust on the road leading to Rainbow's End. Good. It served him right for insisting on coming here again and invading her privacy.

Tessa waited until the car turned into the driveway, then went downstairs. There was a night-light in the front room, and she decided not to turn on any other lights. It might be taken as a welcoming gesture.

The bell rang, Tessa counted slowly to thirty, then opened the door.

''Come in,'' she said coolly, unlatching the screen.

Suit, tie and briefcase, she thought as Dominic moved

past her. Did he ever remove his attorney uniform? He probably slept in it.

"Ms. Russell," Dominic said with a slight nod.

"This way," she said, not acknowledging his brisk greeting.

When she crossed the room and started up the stairs with Dominic following her, she was suddenly aware that he was getting an eyeful of her bottom encased as they were in her snug jeans.

So what? He wasn't a man, he was a menace. That he was one of the best-looking men she'd ever encountered meant nothing to her, and she couldn't care less what he thought of her as a woman.

She wouldn't be remotely close to being his type, anyway. He no doubt dated classy, sophisticated women from the high-society, wealthy set.

Unless he was married.

Tessa stumbled slightly at the unexpected thought. It had never occurred to her that Dominic Bonelli might be married. If he was, surely his wife wouldn't be overjoyed at learning he'd fathered a child five years ago, and now intended to gain custody of his son and bring him into their family.

Fantastic, she thought, renewed hope surging through her. She'd stay on alert to await just the right moment to hit him with the ramifications of taking Jason from her. Perhaps he was still so angry, he hadn't projected any of his actions into the future.

With any luck at all, though, things wouldn't get that far. She had to stay calm and cool, and keep repeating like a broken record that the form in the file was erroneous.

When they entered the living room, Tessa waved one hand toward the easy chair, knowing it was lumpier than the sofa.

"Have a seat," she said, settling onto the sofa.

Dominic sat down, resisted the urge to immediately stand up again as he felt a spring poke his backside, then leaned his briefcase against the side of the chair. He swept his gaze around the small room.

It was like the lower level of the house, he thought. Clean, but shabby.

"Please get on with whatever it is you came here to say," Tessa told him, looking somewhere over his right shoulder. "I get up very early in the morning, so I don't stay up late at night. Therefore, I'd appreciate your speaking your piece and leaving as quickly as possible."

Well, well, Dominic thought, surprised that he had to suppress a smile. Ms. Russell was in a feisty mood tonight. There was a determined lift to her chin, and a flush on her cheeks. She really was quite attractive, and certainly filled out tight jeans nicely. She was not his type, of course, but she was definitely capable of turning heads when she entered a room.

What would she look like in a stunning evening dress, instead of faded jeans? Even more, what would she look like wearing nothing at all?

Lord, Bonelli, he admonished himself, knock it off. Tessa Russell wasn't a woman, she was a nuisance.

"Mr. Bonelli?"

"You know why I'm here," he said, pulling his thoughts back to the moment at hand. "I told you when we first met that if I wasn't contacted by anyone else, the cast of players would be narrowed down to you. That's precisely what has happened. I presume your intentions were to extort a large sum of money from me?"

"This is the last time I'm going to say this, Mr. Bonelli. I have no idea how that file came to be in your possession, nor do I know who prepared the false document naming you as my son's father. I want nothing from you, except for you to leave me alone. Jason is mine, he has nothing whatsoever to do with you, and that is that.

"I'm willing to sign an affidavit stating that I have not contacted you in the past, nor will I ever contact you in regard to Jason, in exchange for a document from you guaranteeing your silence about my being Jason's aunt, rather than his natural mother. That should cover everything quite nicely."

"No, I don't believe it will."

Tessa got to her feet. "What on earth is the matter with you? Have you considered the damage you could do to others by pursuing this nonsense? Have you thought of anyone other than yourself?"

This was it, she decided. This was the time to play her ace.

"What about your own family, your wife and children?" she went on. "If Jason was your son—which he isn't—do you think your wife would be thrilled to make a home for him if you gained custody?

"So, fine, Jason isn't yours. But what kind of distress do you think it would cause your wife if she discovered there was a document stating that he was? Have you thought further than your own anger? Don't you care about the people you love?"

"I have never been married."

Oh, hell, Tessa thought, sinking back onto the sofa.

Dominic studied her face for a long moment as he sifted and sorted the data in his mind.

"Perhaps you're right, Ms. Russell," he finally said slowly. "I may not be thinking past my anger. If you wanted money, this would be the time to demand it. You've either gotten cold feet, or you're actually as innocent as you profess to be."

"Cold feet?" Tessa said, her voice rising. "I really resent—"

"Yes, all right," he interrupted, raising both hands. "I'll give consideration to the affidavits you proposed, and contact you in the next few days." He got to his feet. "I…"

Dominic stopped speaking and frowned as the telephone suddenly began to make strange noises, sounding almost like a quacking duck. Tessa was paying absolutely no attention to the intrusive noise.

"What's wrong with your telephone?" he said.

"My phone?" she said, momentarily confused by his abrupt change of subject. "I don't even hear that nonsense anymore. Sometimes it just squeaks, squawks, whatever you want to call it."

"It quacks," he said, his frown deepening. "Have you told the telephone company about this?"

"Yes." She shrugged. "They can't figure it out, either. It doesn't do it very often, and there's no pattern to it, so I just ignore it. Jason loves it. He says it's E.T. trying to phone *our* home."

Dominic crossed the room and picked up the receiver, giving it a sharp shake. It quacked.

"Ridiculous," he said. "Hold down the button on the base to cut off the dial tone." He began to unscrew the mouthpiece. "The button?"

Tessa got to her feet and moved around him to do as instructed.

He certainly was pushy, she thought, considering the fact it was *her* telephone that was "quacking," to quote Mr. Bonelli. Well, at least his mind had shifted to something other than the reason for his being here.

"Hold this," he said, extending the mouthpiece toward her.

As Tessa took the round piece of plastic from Dominic,

their hands brushed in a light, fleeting motion that seemed to her to encompass minutes instead of seconds. A flutter of heat skittered along her spine.

She snapped her head up to look at him, only to find that he was staring directly at her. As though they'd both been delivered the message at the same time that they were standing so close together their bodies were nearly touching, they each took a step backward.

Dominic cleared his throat, directed his attention to the telephone, and began to fiddle with some wires. A few minutes later, he retrieved the mouthpiece from Tessa's outstretched palm, and twisted it into place. He returned the receiver to the base of the telephone.

"That should take care of it," he said. "There was a loose connection inside. I would have thought a telephone company repairman would have seen it easily enough. Well, it's fixed now."

He started across the room to where he'd left his brief-case.

The telephone quacked.

A bubble of laughter escaped from Tessa's lips.

Dominic spun around and glowered at the telephone, glaring at Tessa for good measure.

"If I were you," she said, unable to curb her smile, "I wouldn't moonlight as a telephone repairman."

"Yes, well," he said, then ran a restless hand down his tie. "Forget it. Let's get back to the subject at hand, shall we?"

Tessa's smile instantly disappeared.

"I may never get to the bottom of *who* did this," Dominic said, "or *why* they did it. My time is too valuable to devote much more energy to the situation. It's probably best to put it to rest."

Tessa's heart began to pound and she had the near-hysterical urge to let out a loud cheer. This nightmare was almost over!

"Mommy?"

Tessa jumped to her feet at the sound of Jason's voice.

Dear heaven, no. Not again. Jason had entered the house just as Dominic was leaving the first time. Now it was happening again. *Oh, Jason, why did you wake up?*

"Mommy, I heard yelling."

"I'm sorry, sweetheart," she said, hurrying to him. "We didn't mean to disturb you. Let's get you tucked back into bed."

"Wait," Dominic said, his voice ringing with tension.

Tessa turned to look at him, and saw to her horror that he was staring intently at Jason.

My God, Dominic thought, this child had been fathered by a Bonelli. Jason Russell had a slight dip on the very top of his right ear that every Bonelli had had for generations. It was not that noticeable, and was easily covered by hair, but he could see it now in Jason's tousled state.

Tessa glared at Dominic, then ushered Jason from the room. After seeing him back into bed, she returned to the living room.

"I'll walk you to the front door, Mr. Bonelli," she said.

"No, I..." He dragged one hand through his hair. "This changes everything."

"What do you mean?"

"The boy's right ear, Ms. Russell. He has a slight dip on the top."

"So?"

"So, every Bonelli for generations has had that dip. As each of my nieces and nephews were born, we all said we could pick them out through the nursery window by looking at their right ear, no matter how many Italian babies might be on display."

"But..."

Dominic swept back the thick hair over his right ear. A chill coursed through Tessa as she saw the tiny dip that was exactly like Jason's. Dominic finger-combed his hair back into place.

"I rest my case," he said. "That boy is a Bonelli."

"That boy has a name," Tessa said, her voice quivering. "He's a living, breathing child. You spit out the word 'boy' as if it's distasteful to you. He is Jason Robert Russell." She fought against threatening tears. "*He is my son.* I swear to God that if you attempt to take him away from me, I'll fight you with every breath in my body."

"Take him away from you? Attempt to gain legal custody of him? Believe me, that is the last thing I'd do. You were right in saying that attention needs to be paid to the ramifications of this situation, the lives that could be irrevocably damaged." He paused. "Do you know where the boy...where Jason...was conceived?"

"I don't see what that has to do—"

"Where?" Dominic snapped.

"Las Vegas," she retorted.

"Damn it," he said, staring up at the ceiling. "Over five years ago in Las Vegas. It fits. Damn it, it fits." He looked at Tessa again. "Silence, Ms. Russell, is the word here. You and I are going to reach an agreement of absolute silence regarding *your* son's existence."

"You're confusing me," she said, shaking her head. "You're going on and on, and I don't understand."

"It's painfully clear. A little more than five years ago, I finally opened my own law firm. For the first time in my life, the very first, I decided to celebrate and have some fun. Well, there's obviously going to be a higher price to pay than just the tab I picked up for all of us."

"All of who?" she said, throwing up her hands in a gesture of frustration. "You're talking in riddles."

"Jason was conceived in Las Vegas during a wild and undisciplined celebration. He is, without a doubt, a Bonelli. Jason's father is a married man with children, and this would be extremely destructive to his marriage."

"But you said you've never been married."

"Not me," he said, splaying out one hand on his chest. "I would never behave in such an irresponsible manner. Oh, no, Ms. Russell, not me. Jason's father is one of my four brothers."

Chapter Five

Tessa opened her mouth, then immediately snapped it closed.

Without realizing she had done it, she pressed her fingertips to her lips, as though ensuring that no words of protest would escape. She stared at Dominic with wide eyes, her mind racing.

Dominic was wrong! She knew he was Jason's father, without a flicker of doubt. Janice had had no reason not to tell the truth when she'd reluctantly agreed to Winthrop Ames's pleas to name the father of her baby as a safeguard in the event of a medical emergency.

Even more, Janice had told her that the man had been celebrating the opening of his *own* law practice.

Dominic Bonelli was Jason's father.

Why, dear heaven, why was he shifting the responsibility to one of his brothers? The direction he was taking suited her just fine, though. There would be no fight for custody, no more danger of her losing her precious son.

But why was he doing this? It just didn't make sense.

Think, Tessa, she told herself. What else had Janice said about Dominic? It was so long ago, and her emotions had been in such turmoil that day.

Think.

Yes, wait, it was coming back to her now. Janice had said that Dominic considered money the most important thing in his life. He was handsome, a great lover, but he was hard, cold.

Janice had said that Dominic Bonelli had no soul.

"Ms. Russell?" Dominic said, snapping her back to attention. "Are you listening to me?"

"What? Oh, yes, of course I am. I can truthfully say, Mr. Bonelli, that I was *not* cognizant of the fact that one of your brothers fathered Jason."

"Yes, all right," he said, a weary quality to his voice, "I'll go with that, with reservations." He shook his head. "Damn, what a mess. Look, could we sit back down and discuss this?"

Good idea, Tessa thought, moving to the sofa. Her legs were trembling so badly, she felt as if she were about to topple over onto her nose.

Dominic sat down in the chair, then leaned forward, resting his elbows on his knees and making a steeple of his long fingers.

Las Vegas, his mind hammered. It had been a wild bash. He'd never engaged in such a reckless event before, nor since, that weekend. The details were fuzzy, which was understandable due to its having taken place over five years ago.

He'd been drinking, but not to excess, he was certain. *That* he would never do, no matter what the circumstances.

He'd never turn the control of himself over to liquor. His brothers, however, had really been putting away the booze.

His brothers. One of them had obviously picked up Janice Russell and taken her to bed. None of the four cheated on their wives, but when drunk as a skunk, sound reason and decent values must have been drowned in the alcohol.

Which one was it? Frank, Vince, Benny or Joe? He'd like to wring his neck, whoever it was, that was for damn sure.

Well, the situation was now good old Dominic's to deal with. He was the head of the family, and had been since he was fourteen years old. He made the decisions, provided the guidance, had supported his mother, two sisters and four brothers, until each was able to stand on their own. He continued to provide for Delores, his mother, whom he respected more than he could say.

Come on, Bonelli, he admonished himself. *Your mind is wandering.* He was chasing around well-known facts to postpone having to address the next imperative issue at hand—the guarantee of Tessa Russell's silence.

"Well," he said, straightening and leaning back in the chair, "it would appear, Ms. Russell, that the ball is now in your court. How much money do you want in exchange for not divulging the fact that Jason's father is a Bonelli?"

Fury rose in Tessa like a building storm, gaining momentum with every beat of her heart.

"Get out of my house," she said, her voice shaking from anger. "Get out, don't ever come back and never contact me again. Go. Now."

Dominic sighed. "Let's cut to the chase, shall we? I'm really not in the mood to play games. I'll prepare a document for you to sign that will state that you will never divulge the identity of Jason's father. I realize it could be any one of four men, so it will be worded to say you won't reveal that a Bonelli is the father.

"The fake document in the file makes perfect sense, because while my brothers earn good money, I have far more than they do. Whether it was you, or someone you have no knowledge of who prepared the form, is now immaterial. I haven't been contacted, so it's between the two of us."

"You don't feel that a man has the right to know he has a son?" Tessa felt she had to ask, though she knew such a question was strange coming from someone with so much to lose.

"Under the circumstances? No."

"Who appointed you master over people's lives?" Tessa said, her voice rising.

"Fate. I've been the head of my family since our father died when I was fourteen. My authority isn't questioned. *I* have decided how this will be handled, and that's the way it will be. I repeat, Ms. Russell, how much money do you want?"

Tessa got to her feet. "Leave my home!"

"I almost believe you don't want to be paid off," he said, retrieving his briefcase and getting to his feet. "Almost." He glanced around the room. "I'm quite sure you'll come up with a sizable figure in a few days. That's fine. The boy is a part of my family, therefore I feel a sense of responsibility toward him. Bonellis don't live like this, not anymore. Some money could do wonders for this place."

"You are the most despicable man I've ever had the misfortune to meet," she said, wrapping her hands around her elbows.

"Despicable? Yes, I've been told that a time or two." He crossed the room to the door, then turned to look at her. "You *are* going to follow me downstairs, aren't you? Lock the door behind me? After all, you have a Bonelli in your safekeeping, a fact I won't idly stand by and allow you to take lightly."

Trembling with anger, Tessa followed Dominic from the room and down the stairs. A thousand scathing words tumbled through her mind, but she was unable to speak due to her rage.

At the door, Dominic looked at her once again. "While I'm preparing the document you're to sign, I'll be waiting to hear from you regarding your price." He left the house.

Tessa fumbled with the lock with shaking hands, then finally clicked it into place. She made her way to the stairs, then sank onto the bottom step, resting her forehead on her knees.

Janice's voice echoed in her mind.

The man has no soul.

The man has no soul.

"Dear God," she whispered to the night, "Janice was right."

During the next two weeks, Dominic was aware that his level of tension was building steadily. His temper was on a short fuse, and Gladys had threatened to quit on four occasions.

His stress was due, he knew, to the lack of communication from Tessa Russell. He'd stayed late at the office one night to personally prepare the document for her to sign, not wishing anyone else to know of its existence. There was, however, a blank space on the form for the amount of money to be paid to Tessa in exchange for her silence.

In the middle of the morning that marked two weeks and three days since he'd last seen Tessa, Dominic tossed his pen onto the open file on his desk. He muttered an earthy expletive and got to his feet.

Walking to the sparkling-clean floor-to-ceiling windows, he shoved his hands into his pockets and stared unseeing at the view before him.

Why, he wondered for the umpteenth time, hadn't Tessa made her move? Until money changed hands and the document was signed, she was a threat. She had control of the situation by keeping him on tenterhooks.

He narrowed his eyes in anger.

Dominic Bonelli, he inwardly fumed, was not controlled by anyone, or anything. *Enough was enough.* Tessa Russell was obviously playing some sort of game, and he'd reached the end of his patience. He was taking the ball back into *his* court.

He strode to his chair, sat down and began to drum a rhythm on the top of the desk.

As a plan began to take shape in his mind, he nodded in satisfaction. It was risky, but a helluva lot better than enduring Tessa's silence. The type of compensation he was now contemplating could be money down the drain if she ultimately refused to sign the document. But by going with the new program, he'd have leverage, something tangible to help apply pressure for her signature.

Besides, he mused, he'd meant what he'd said. Tessa's house was clean, but shabby. Bonellis did not now, nor would they ever again, live with threadbare furniture and peeling paint.

Two objectives could be accomplished, hopefully, with his new idea.

With his jaw set in a determined line, he reached for the receiver.

Tessa turned the book around to show the brightly colored picture to the dozen children before her. They were sitting on the floor, each on a throw rug, watching her with rapt attention where she was perched on a low stool.

"Wow," a little girl said. "I'd like to live in a big castle like that."

"You have to be a princess, or queen, or something, Sarah," a boy said. "That's the rules of castles."

"I can live there if I wanna," Sarah said. "You don't know everything, Jeremiah."

"I know castle stuff," he said.

Tessa smiled, deciding to allow the debate to continue for a bit. Story hour was scheduled for after lunch each day. It provided time for the children's meals to settle, plus, more often than not, some of the kids curled up on their fluffy rugs and fell asleep.

To declare that it was nap time, Tessa had discovered early on, created an instant fuss and a chorus of objections. The way she did it now, those in need of sleep would drift off, and the others listened to the story.

Patty and Emma were tending to cleaning the kitchen from lunch, while Tessa had taken charge of story hour, her favorite time of the day.

"Maybe," another little girl said, "if you move into a castle, that makes you a princess right now, 'cause you live there."

"That's dumb," Jeremiah said.

"Is not," Sarah said.

Tessa's mind wandered as more voices joined the castle controversy.

Two weeks and three days, counting this one, she thought. That's how long it had been since Dominic Bonelli had paid his late-night visit. Surely he was intelligent enough to have deduced by now that she had no intention of asking him for money. She wanted nothing from him, *nothing*, except to be left alone.

She'd sign his damnable document guaranteeing her silence if he insisted upon it, but he'd have to come to her and ask for the coveted signature. He was no longer a threat to her and Jason.

What she didn't know, would probably never understand, was why Dominic had so quickly placed the responsibility of Jason's paternity onto one of his brothers. He'd strongly stated that *he* would never act in such an irresponsible manner, yet she knew he had. Perhaps Dominic was not capable of admitting a human weakness of any kind.

He was so cold, hard, aloof. It was, she supposed, totally unacceptable to him to acknowledge an error in judgment. But, dear heaven, when that slip in control had resulted in a beautiful child like Jason, how could Dominic deny the truth as he was doing? *Jason was his son.*

Because the man has no soul, she thought. It was incredibly sad. How empty Dominic Bonelli's life must be. He'd spoken of having been responsible for his large family from an early age. *Responsible.* That was admirable; he'd taken on a tremendous burden at fourteen years old. But did he *feel* anything toward that family except a sense of responsibility? Did he love them?

For Pete's sake, Tessa, she admonished herself, who cared? She was wasting mental energy wondering about the depth of Dominic Bonelli's emotions. Ridiculous. His outer shell was handsome, compelling, but within he was empty. That was *his* problem.

"Tessa, Tessa," Jeremiah yelled. "Aren't you gonna read the story?"

"What?" she said. "Oh, of course."

She turned the book back around, placed it on her knees and began to read.

An hour later, Patty and Emma took the children to the play area outside, while Tessa prepared the afternoon snack. As she was slicing an apple, the doorbell rang. She hurried from the kitchen to answer the summons.

On the other side of the locked screen door was a man appearing to be in his mid-twenties and who had blond hair, blue eyes and freckles. He was wearing jeans, a T-shirt and a smile.

"Hello," Tessa said, matching his smile. "How may I help you?"

As the man opened his mouth to reply, Tessa glanced over his shoulder and read the name of the company painted on the door of the truck parked beyond the front walkway.

"I'm Jeff, from—"

"Bonelli Painting and Restoration," Tessa said, in unison with him.

"Yes, ma'am," Jeff said.

"Bonelli Painting and Restoration?" Tessa repeated, her voice rising. "What in heaven's name are you doing here?"

Jeff's smile slid off his chin and he frowned. "I came to inspect your house, top to bottom, inside and out. You know, gather data on what needs to be done to make this place shipshape." He smiled again. "Okay?"

Tessa planted her hands on her hips and narrowed her eyes. "No, it is *not* okay. I didn't ask for an inspection of that sort, nor do I want one. You can march right back to town, and inform Mr. Bonelli of that fact."

"Oh," Jeff said, rubbing one hand over his chin. "Which one?"

"Tucson, of course."

"No, no, not which town, which Mr. Bonelli? I mean, it was Frank who told me to come out here, but maybe Vince told *him.* I don't know where the original order came from. It could have been Benny or Joe Bonelli. All four own Bonelli Painting and Restoration. So, who do you want me to go back and holler at?"

"Pick one," Tessa yelled. "Just make it clear that I don't want anybody from that company on my property."

"Yes, ma'am," Jeff said, raising both hands and backing up. "You betcha. No problem. I'm outta here." He turned and sprinted to the truck.

Tessa didn't move until the vehicle disappeared in a cloud of dust, then she stomped back into the kitchen. She picked up an apple and began to slice it with more force than was necessary.

Dominic Bonelli was behind this insulting maneuver, she fumed. He'd made several derogatory remarks about the condition of her house, tossing in the tidbit that Bonellis didn't live like this anymore.

Since she hadn't contacted him regarding the amount of money he expected her to demand in exchange for her silence, Dominic had apparently decided to take it upon himself to make improvements to the home where the *secret* Bonelli offspring lived.

"Oh-h-h, the nerve of that man," she said under her breath.

Well, she'd set him straight quickly enough. Once Jeff returned with her message, the whole group of Bonellis would know that Tessa Russell didn't want any part of them.

What had Dominic told his brothers? she wondered, as she made banana-fingers. What explanation had he given for requesting an inspection of Rainbow's End? Knowing him, he'd probably just barked the order, and his four brothers had clicked their heels and saluted, no questions asked.

Oh, who cared? She wasn't wasting one more minute thinking about the arrogant, pushy, drop-dead gorgeous Dominic.

With a decisive nod, she reached for a cluster of green grapes.

"That's the scoop, Dom," Frank Bonelli said. The receiver to the telephone was propped between his head and shoulder. "Tessa Russell ran Jeff off."

Dominic's hold on the receiver tightened. "Damn it, that woman is driving me crazy."

"What's going on?" Frank said. "I didn't think anything of it when you told me to get a thorough inspection done at this Rainbow's End place. You send work our way all the time. But that woman obviously doesn't want any part of it, or us. Did you get your signals crossed?"

"Look, I'll take care of Tessa Russell. Have Jeff go back out there tomorrow morning. I'll meet him at Rainbow's End at nine o'clock."

"Whatever," Frank said. "This sure doesn't make sense, Dom."

"Don't worry about it," Dominic said. "Goodbye, Frank."

Dominic slammed down the receiver and got to his feet. In the next instant, he sank back onto his chair, deciding that Tessa Russell wasn't going to cause him to pace the floor of his office again.

Frank had asked him if he'd gotten his signals crossed. Hell, he didn't know. He couldn't even begin to figure out the woman. And he had absolutely no idea why she hadn't contacted him to name her price.

He'd gotten so frustrated while waiting to hear from her, he'd decided to regain control of the situation by spending the damn money *for* her, in the manner *he* felt most appropriate.

Jason was a Bonelli, and the house where he was being raised needed a vast number of improvements. Tessa's silence would be bought, and Jason would be living in a proper environment.

It was a clever plan, an excellent plan. He'd be secure in the knowledge that the hush money wasn't being spent on frivolous things, and that the ultimate recipient would be the son of one of his brothers. Yes, it was very clever, indeed.

Until, Dominic thought, his temper flaring again, Tessa Russell had pitched her fit when Jeff had arrived at her house. Lord, she was difficult to deal with. He just couldn't get a handle on what made her tick, and he didn't like that, not one damn bit.

Well, as of nine o'clock tomorrow morning, Ms. Russell was going to start doing things *his* way.

"Get off of my porch," Tessa said through the screen door. "Get off of my entire property. If you don't leave within the next three seconds, I'm going to call the police."

"I'm gone," Jeff said.

"Don't move, Jeff," Dominic said, his jaw clenched. "There's been a small misunderstanding, that's all. Ms. Russell and I will have this straightened out in a few minutes."

"We certainly will not," she said, "because I refuse to discuss it with you. Three seconds, Mr. Bonelli."

"Tessa," Dominic said, "I can't believe that you'd want the children in your care telling their parents that an argument took place here, would you? The mothers and fathers might question whether this is a calm, peaceful environment for their children.''

''You're despicable,'' she said.

''*You* are stubborn. Open the door and let me in so we can talk privately, with no little ears to hear and little mouths to carry tales.''

Tessa glowered at Dominic for a long moment, then unlocked the door. As Dominic entered, leaving Jeff on the porch, Tessa spun around and marched across the living room, through the kitchen, and into the small office beyond.

She sat down behind the narrow desk, clutched her hands on the top and nodded toward a chair.

''Sit,'' she said. ''Speak. Fast.''

Dominic settled onto the chair. ''Do you want me to roll over? Play dead?''

''Be my guest,'' she said ever so sweetly.

''You're being very difficult, Tessa.''

''Ms. Russell to you...*Dominic*. Let me make this clear for the last time. I do not want any of your money. I do not want *anything* from you. I'll sign your document saying I won't divulge the identity of Jason's father. All right? In return, you are to assure me that you and the entire Bonelli clan never contact me again. In short, you can take your money, your paint, your restoration—and stuff it!''

Dominic planted his elbows on the worn arms of the chair and made a steeple of his fingers. He stared at Tessa over the top of his fingers.

She meant it, he thought incredulously. She honestly didn't want money from him. He had never met anyone like Tessa Russell before. She was incredibly naive, and obviously didn't realize that money was the key to unlocking the doors a person wished to pass through. It was the ace in the hole that could win the hand holding power and control.

He shook his head.

"Well," he said, "you may, or may not, learn the true facts of life in the years to come, but that's not my problem. I accept your decision to sign the affidavit with no monetary compensation. I'll draft a new document."

"Agreed. Goodbye."

"Not so fast," he said, raising one hand. "There is Jason to consider here. Your son, Tessa."

"It's Ms. Russell. I'm very aware that Jason is my son."

"He's also a Bonelli."

"Which is of no importance."

"Ah, but it is. I feel responsible for Jason because his father is one of my brothers. That responsibility includes seeing that Jason is living in a proper home, and receiving proper care."

"Are you insinuating that—"

"Hold it. Don't go off on one of your rips. I'm not questioning your care of the boy, Tessa," he said quietly. "It's obvious to me, and would be to anyone who might observe you, that you're a wonderful mother who is devoted to her son. I admire and respect that."

"Oh," she said, feeling a warm flush on her cheeks. How absurd. She was registering a sense of pride and pleasure at hearing that Dominic approved of how she was raising Jason. "Well, thank you."

"However," he went on, "this house is falling down around your ears."

"It is not. It's a tad old, that's all."

"Did the roof leak during the monsoons?"

"Not much, just here and there," she said, folding her arms across her breasts. "It's really none of your business."

"It is when a Bonelli is under that roof. Are you going to deny your son a better home because of your stubbornness? And this place needs painting. Aren't you being a little selfish?"

"Do you think money and your clinical sense of responsibility is the answer to everything?"

"It certainly is in this case. Jason is being offered comforts that you're not allowing him to have. I've provided these types of things for all the Bonellis over the years. Jason has a right to have them, too."

"And how would you suggest I explain the sudden financial windfall that enabled me to fix up my house?"

"We'll think of something. You won a contest and the prize was a new roof and some painting. That's a small glitch, and easily solved. The major issue here is my responsibility for a Bonelli, and your being willing to allow your son a more comfortable home."

"Damn you," Tessa said.

Dominic got to his feet. "I'll take that as your having seen the light. Jeff will begin the inspection immediately. Goodbye, Tessa." He left the room.

"It's Ms. Russell," she said wearily.

Chapter Six

During the remainder of that day and the major portion of the next, Friday, Jeff conducted his inspection of Rainbow's End.

Tessa gritted her teeth and ignored him, even though he seemed to pop up wherever she was at the moment. He carried a clipboard with some sort of form attached, where he continually made notations.

Jeff whistled while he worked, which grated on Tessa's nerves. Even more unsettling were the mumbled comments she'd hear him make, such as "geez," "whew," "grim," "not good, not good," and "holy smokes."

On Saturday morning, Tessa announced to Jason that they were going to town. Her need to get away from the house was overwhelming.

They had a marvelous day, going to the zoo, having lunch at a fast-food restaurant and shopping for new tennis shoes for Jason.

Sunday, she dipped into the budgeted emergency fund and took Jason to Old Tucson, a replica of a turn-of-the-century western town where a movie was presently being filmed.

In addition to enjoying the added attraction of the Hollywood film crew, they watched the regularly scheduled performance of the shoot-out between the good guys and bad guys, with stuntmen making dramatic plunges off rooftops and from the backs of galloping horses.

By Sunday evening, after an exhausted and happy Jason was tucked into bed for the night, Tessa felt more like herself, her frazzled nerves calmed. She was pleasantly tired, knew she'd sleep well and had precious memories of the events shared with Jason.

Settled on the sofa with a thick book; she jerked in surprise when the telephone rang. She narrowed her eyes as she reached for the receiver, deciding it better not be Dominic disturbing her peace of mind again.

"Hello?" she said, into the receiver.

"Dominic Bonelli."

Tessa pursed her lips and counted slowly to ten.

"Tessa?"

"This is Ms. Russell. What do you want?"

Dominic chuckled, and a strange and unexpected tingle danced along Tessa's spine as she heard the rich, masculine sound.

"A bit testy tonight, are we?" Dominic said, amusement evident in his voice. "Perhaps I should apologize for disturbing you."

"Perhaps you should," she said coolly.

"All right, Ms. Russell, I apologize for interrupting your quiet evening at home."

"Oh." She was, she realized, rather flustered that Dominic had actually apologized. "Well, I... Was there something important you wished to discuss with me?"

"Several things, as a matter of fact. First up, I'd like to suggest we call a truce on this name business. You're Tessa and I'm Dominic. After all, there's no need for the formality of the Ms. and Mr. Agreed?"

Tessa smiled in spite of herself. There was something different about Dominic tonight. The brisk and arrogant edge to his voice was gone, replaced by a more relaxed tone. She had the distinct impression that he was still smiling after having executed that sexy chuckle.

"Yes, all right," she said. "I agree."

"Good." He paused. "Did you have a nice weekend? How's the boy? No, erase that. How's *Jason?*"

"Oh, he's fine. We had a marvelous weekend because I took him to... You don't really want to know all this."

"Actually," he said slowly, "I do. I'd like to hear about your outings."

Tessa moved the receiver from her ear and stared at it for a moment with the irrational thought that she might be able to peer into Dominic's brain.

He was acting so unlike himself—at least, unlike the Dominic she knew. There was even a warmth in his voice she'd never heard before.

Oh, Tessa, don't be silly, she admonished herself, placing the receiver back to her ear. She was thinking the way someone might who had known Dominic Bonelli for a long time, and who was suddenly aware of a change in his demeanor. In actuality, she didn't know him at all.

Then again, that wasn't entirely true. He had, in fact, had a shadowy place in her life for over five years, ever since she'd signed the guardianship document so she could bring Jason home from the hospital, and had seen the information in the file naming Dominic as Jason's father.

But *this* Dominic? The one speaking to her now? He really wanted to hear about a trip to the zoo? This was a facet of him she hadn't encountered before.

"Tessa?"

She mentally shrugged. "Well, okay, you asked for it. On Saturday…"

As Tessa related the events of the weekend, she realized she was enjoying chatting with Dominic. He was a wonderful listener. He made comments in appropriate places, asked questions and laughed several times at Jason's antics.

While Dominic's chuckle had caused a tingling sensation to course through her, the deep timbre of his laughter created a heat, a swirling, churning heat, low within her.

It was disconcerting and unsettling, to say the least. And enough was enough.

"And there you have it," she said. "A synopsis of a weekend in the fast lane."

"Delightful, but you must be exhausted."

"Totally. Jason was asleep the minute his head touched the pillow."

"Thank you for sharing all that with me, Tessa," Dominic said quietly. "I enjoyed it."

"You're welcome," she said, still a bit surprised.

A silence fell that was charged with a current of sexuality. Even though they were only talking on the telephone, it was there, a nearly palpable entity.

Dominic finally cleared his throat, breaking the eerie and sensuous spell.

"Well, I'll only keep you a moment longer," he said, "so you can get some rest. I wanted to let you know that a crew will be arriving at Rainbow's End first thing in the morning to begin work on repairing the roof.

"Since I'll be writing the checks to my brothers' company, I simply told them I'm the executor of an estate that had a will stipulating that the spending of funds bequeathed to you be controlled and approved by me."

Tessa frowned. *Back to reality, Ms. Russell,* she told herself. Dominic had just put on his attorney uniform again.

"I see," she said.

"I can't dictate who is to be part of the work crew without raising questions. Therefore, if any of my brothers show up there, be certain that Jason doesn't have any direct contact with them. I don't want them to notice the Bonelli ear, for lack of a better thing to call it."

"Nor do I," she said. Damn the man, he was still doing it. He was denying that he was Jason's father, pushing the role onto one of his brothers. *This* was the Dominic she knew—cold, commanding, unwilling to admit he had any human weaknesses. "I assure you that Jason won't be any more visible than the rest of the children."

"Fine."

"Have you prepared the document you wish me to sign?"

"Not entirely. Once all the improvements and repairs have been completed at Rainbow's End, I'll be able to make a detailed list of what you received in exchange for your silence."

"Regarding the fact that one of your brothers is Jason's father."

"As I told you, the wording will stipulate that you won't name *any* Bonelli as the boy's father, since we don't know which of my brothers was involved with your sister."

"I'll sign whatever you wish," Tessa said wearily. "Do remember to include the clause that no Bonelli is to contact me in the future about this, or any other matter."

"Of course. That's settled then. Good night, Tessa. Sleep well."

"Good night."

She replaced the receiver and picked up the novel. Several minutes later, she realized she'd read the same paragraph three times and had no idea what it had said.

Smacking the book onto the sofa cushion, she glowered at the telephone, and decided to go to bed.

Dominic lost track of time as he stared at the receiver long after he'd put it back in place. As seconds ticked into countless minutes, the frown knitting his dark eyebrows deepened.

What in the hell had come over him? he fumed. He'd called Tessa Russell with the intention of telling her to keep Jason away from any of his brothers who might be part of the crew working on her roof. That was to be the full extent of the purpose of the call—short and sweet.

So where had all the chitchat come from? And if that wasn't ridiculous enough, he'd urged her to tell him about her weekend spent with a five-year-old kid!

He lunged to his feet and began to pace the large expanse of his expensively furnished living room.

The worst part was that he'd *enjoyed* every bit of the inane conversation.

Dominic stopped his trek and ran one hand over the back of his neck. The remembrance of Tessa's femininely lilting voice and the wind-chime delicacy of her laughter echoed in his head, causing an uncomfortable tightening low in his body.

He slouched back into the high-backed leather chair, and shook his head.

Bonelli, he admonished himself, *you're losing it.* Tessa was a problem he was in the process of solving. That she happened to be an attractive, refreshingly honest woman, was incidental.

His behavior on the telephone was ludicrous. Tessa wasn't even his type, damn it. He dated sophisticated career women who were single, independent and had every intention of remaining so. They weren't interested in marriage, babies or hearth and home. He slept with some, no strings attached, and a good time was had by all.

But Tessa? Sophisticated? Not even close. Maybe she dated, but as far as he knew, she operated in a narrow existence centered on Jason and Rainbow's End. Oh, she had a temper, and could spit fire when pushed too far, but there was an innocence about her that caused a man to want to protect her from...well, from men like himself.

"Oh, hell," he said.

Did he need a vacation? he wondered. He'd been working long hours, and had spent the weekend buried in legal files.

Yes, that was it. He'd have gladly listened to a lengthy dissertation about the weather, if only to mentally escape from legalese for a while. Hence, he'd allowed himself to get caught up in a tale of trips to the zoo and Old Tucson. Fine. That was now perfectly understandable.

With a satisfied nod, Dominic reached for the file on the end table. He flipped it open, then stared into space.

It had sounded as though Tessa and Jason had really enjoyed their outings. After having been to Old Tucson, Jason would no doubt spend the next several days, or even weeks, pretending he was a rough-tough cowboy. Did he have a pint-size Stetson? Some cowboy boots? Had he ever had a ride on a real horse?

"What difference does it make?" Dominic said aloud. "Who cares?"

He didn't know if his own nieces and nephews had ever

been on a horse. He'd never asked, because being the entertainment chairman for the Bonelli clan wasn't part of his job description.

His responsibility was to be certain that everyone in the family had what they needed to succeed; all the material necessities while pursuing their individual goals.

And now? There was another Bonelli suddenly on the scene—Jason Robert Russell. He was faced with the responsibility of bringing Jason's standard of living up to the proper level. As usual, he was proceeding with the program, the situation was under his command.

Would a horse frighten a little kid like Jason? Perhaps it would be better to have him ride a pony instead. Did Tessa realize that? Surely she wouldn't put Jason on a huge horse and scare the living daylights out of him, would she? Maybe he should speak to her about that....

"A Fix-Up-Your-House contest?" Patty said to Tessa. "And you won?"

"Sure did," Tessa said, not looking directly at Patty or Emma. "Isn't that something?" Her nose was going to grow. It was probably written all over her face that she was making up the whole thing. "Lucky me, huh?"

"That's wonderful," Emma said. "I won a frozen pizza once, but this is the big time."

Patty laughed. "Not only do you get a new roof, Tessa, but we get to ogle some very nice masculine bodies. Did you see the physiques on those guys outside? There are...what? Four of them? Five? And every one is built like a dream."

"Shame on you, Patty," Tessa said, smiling.

"I may be fifty-four, but I'm not dead," she said. "There's no harm in looking. You, Tessa Russell, would do well to be friendly to those hunks. You need a social life, some dates. Jason is a sweetheart, but there should be more in a woman's existence than working and taking care of her son.''

"I'm perfectly happy the way I am," Tessa said, raising both hands.

"You just *think* you are," Patty said, folding her arms over her ample bosom. "Right, Emma? Our girl needs a man."

"Absolutely," Emma said, nodding. "And there's a splendid selection working on your roof even as we speak."

"Oh, good grief," Tessa said, rolling her eyes heavenward. "I'm going to go prepare the morning snack. There are a dozen little demons awaiting your attention in the play yard, ladies. Goodbye." She spun around and headed for the kitchen.

Tessa performed her task by rote as her mind drifted back in time, colliding with painful memories.

She'd *had* a man in her life once, and had ended up with a broken heart and shattered dreams.

Cliff had eaten regularly at the restaurant where she worked as a waitress. He was good-looking, friendly and very charming. Although initially she had refused his invitations to various outings, she finally relented, and they began to date steadily.

She hadn't realized how alone and lonely she'd been until Cliff had become part of her life, a *very* important part. She'd fallen in love with him, eagerly surrendered her virginity at twenty years old, and daydreamed about being married to Cliff, having his baby, being part of a real family again.

Then after six months, Cliff had casually informed her that his *wife* was becoming suspicious of the many hours he was away from home, and he couldn't see Tessa again. *Thanks for the fun, sugar. See ya.*

"Wife," Tessa muttered, as she sliced an orange. "The creep had a wife."

When the pain of Cliff's betrayal had dimmed enough to enable her not to cry herself to sleep each night, anger had set in.

It was rip-roaring, mad-as-hell anger.

At herself.

When her parents had been killed, her life had been placed in the control of other people. She had had no say, no choices. She could only do as she was told, like an obedient robot.

Savoring her freedom when she'd gone out on her own at eighteen, she'd been determined to take charge of her existence. She'd been doing just fine, until Cliff. Then, foolish and gullible idiot that she'd been, she'd placed her happiness in his hands for safekeeping, and he'd crushed it without a second thought.

Never again, she'd vowed. Never again would she relinquish control of her life, allow anyone to dictate whether she laughed with joy, or sobbed in sorrow.

"No, Patty, Emma," Tessa said aloud, to the empty room. "I most definitely do *not* need a man in my life."

A sudden, unexpected, and unwelcomed image of Dominic flickered in Tessa's mental vision.

She narrowed her eyes.

And at the top of the Most *Un*wanted List, would be Dominic Bonelli!

Chapter Seven

A few minutes later, Tessa jerked in surprise as a ladder suddenly appeared outside the kitchen window, then thudded against the house. She rinsed her hands, dried them quickly and headed out the back door.

A man was by the ladder, operating the mechanism that would extend it to its full height, allowing him access to the roof of the two-story house.

And the man was a Bonelli.

Tessa stopped and scrutinized him. He was dressed in jeans, a T-shirt and was wearing a baseball cap. He wasn't quite as tall as Dominic, nor were his shoulders as wide, but his rough-hewn features, even in profile, shouted the fact that this was one of Dominic's brothers. He had the same straight nose, square jaw, tawny skin and the hair she could see at the edges of the cap was thick and black.

Which one of the four was he? she wondered. And how would he feel if he knew that his authoritative older brother was placing the responsibility of fathering Jason on him, or one of the other three brothers?

Dominic's refusal to acknowledge his own son was so wrong, so unbelievably wrong. Granted, it meant that the threat to her and Jason was removed from their existence, but how could a man do such a coldhearted thing?

Shaking her head, Tessa walked to where the man was still fiddling with the ladder.

"I'd like to talk to you," she said, deciding to omit a pleasant greeting. She didn't want these people here, and she had no intention of pretending that she did.

The man turned to look at her, a wide smile on his face.

There were the dark eyes and long lashes, Tessa noticed. He was good-looking but not quite as ruggedly handsome as Dominic. And there, clear as day, was the small dip on the top of his right ear.

"Good morning, ma'am," he said. "I'm Frank Bonelli. You must be Tessa Russell."

"Yes, I am," she said, folding her arms over her breasts. There was no hint of a smile on her face. "I have some concerns regarding this project, Mr. Bonelli."

Frank took off his cap, shoved his hand through his hair and settled the cap back into place. His smile never wavered.

"Well, now, we can't have you worrying about anything, ma'am. Oh, and call me Frank. We Bonellis are a friendly bunch."

Oh, ha! Tessa thought. Dominic Bonelli was *not* friendly. He was arrogant, pushy and rude. Of course, he *had* been extremely nice during the majority of that strange telephone conversation last night.

"Yes, well, Frank," she said coolly, "it occurs to me that in order to put a new roof on a house, the old roof has to come off. Therefore, the worn shingles have to get from there—'' she pointed heavenward ''—to here.'' She pointed to the ground. ''I have a dozen children playing in the side yard. I can't have shingles flying all over the place. So, let's just cancel this job, shall we?''

Frank frowned. ''I've never had anyone try to talk me out of fixing their roof before. Most people are glad to know that they won't be running a bucket brigade inside the house the next time it rains.''

''I'm not most people. I think it would be best if you and your crew just packed up and left. The safety of these children is far more important than any inconvenience I might experience during a rainstorm.''

''Now, Tessa... May I call you Tessa? That is sure a pretty name. Tessa, you come along with me, and I'll show you why you don't have a thing to worry about.'' He moved past her. ''Come on.''

''But,'' she started, then hurried after him.

At the opposite side of the house from the play yard, four men were busily hammering together large sheets of plywood.

''Yo!'' Frank yelled.

The four men stopped and looked at him questioningly.

Two more Bonellis, Tessa realized. Goodness, a person certainly could pick them out of a crowd. They wore their hair shorter than Dominic, just as Frank did, and the dips in their ears were clearly visible.

Even without the telltale ear, the family resemblance was remarkable. Yet, again, these two weren't quite as tall, or well built, or as handsome as Dominic. She couldn't quite put her finger on exactly what Dominic had that the others didn't, but it was *something*.

''Guys,'' Frank said, ''this is Tessa, the lady of the house. Tessa, you know Jeff. Those two uglies are my brothers, Benny and Vince, and that weird-looking fella is Clyde. No kiddin', his mother actually named him Clyde.''

"Hello," Tessa said, nodding slightly.

She was answered with hellos, pleased to meet yous, pleasure, ma'am and broad smiles.

Tessa smiled in spite of herself, deciding it was impossible to stay totally grumpy when surrounded by such cheerful, friendly people.

"Now then, Jeff," Frank said, "you explain to Tessa what you guys are doing there. She's worried about shingles flying around and maybe hurting some of the kids." He looked at Tessa. "We sent Jeff to school for talking lessons, so he could explain stuff to folks." He chuckled and winked at her.

Jeff cleared his throat and smoothed his T-shirt over his chest as though he were about to deliver the inaugural address.

Tessa laughed softly, mentally admitting defeat of her attempt to be stern.

"We are presently building," Jeff commenced, "a large pen where the old shingles will be placed. We'll construct a slide, of sorts, out of heavy tarps from the roof to here so we can zoom the old stuff down right where we want them. You don't have to fret one iota about your kiddies."

"Oh," Tessa said.

"Go back to sleep, Jeff," Frank said, then turned to Tessa. "You have two layers of shingles on your roof. City code says you can have up to three layers. Thing is, at the first sign of trouble down the road, everything has to come off and started fresh. Dom said to do a tear-off…that's going down to the sheathing under all the shingles…now. He wants a whole new roof, first layer."

"Oh," Tessa said again. "What if it rains while it's torn down to that sheathing?"

"No problem," Frank said. "We do it in sections. Tear off, replace, tear off, replace. We never leave at the end of the day with the roof in a condition that would be a disaster if it rained. Okay?"

"Yes, thank you. I appreciate your time, patience and information. Goodbye." She spun around and hurried away.

Back in the kitchen, she rolled her eyes heavenward.

Great, she inwardly fumed, she'd just made a complete fool of herself. She'd marched outside like Miss High-and-Mighty, her nose in the air, and told Frank Bonelli to take his shingles and go away. She'd come across as a total idiot.

Well, now wait a minute. Maybe she hadn't appeared as dumb as all that. Frank, and his whole crew, as a matter of fact, had been friendly, warm and outgoing. They'd reacted as though her concern for the safety of the children in regard to zooming shingles was perfectly reasonable. They'd addressed the question with a delightful dose of humor, and everything was fine.

The Bonelli brothers, as well as Jeff and Clyde, obviously had a special bond. There was an easiness amongst them, as well as respect for one another, a family feeling.

And Dominic? she wondered. When he was with his brothers, was he as relaxed and ready to smile as they were? Did he let down his authoritative guard, change out of his attorney uniform and become one of the boys? Surely he realized how fortunate he was to be surrounded by a large and loving family. Didn't he?

Tessa shook her head and resumed the task of preparing the children's snack.

What difference did it make to her whether or not Dominic had enough sense and sensitivity to appreciate his family? None, absolutely none. She didn't even like the man, for Pete's sake.

So why was she wasting her time thinking about him? Good question, and she had no idea what the answer was.

With a cluck of self-disgust, she headed for the play yard to round up the children for their morning snack.

Just before seven o'clock that evening, Tessa sat on the bench swing on the front porch, pushing it gently back and forth. She smiled as she watched Jason playing in the yard. He was using a straw broom as a horse and was galloping around. He'd been in a cowboy mode ever since the trip to Old Tucson.

Tessa sighed in contentment. It was a beautiful evening. There was a cool breeze whispering along the porch, and a gorgeous sunset was beginning to streak across the heavens with vibrant colors, each shade melting into the next like softening butter.

Jason was yipping, yelling and occasionally whinnying, leading her to believe he was alternating between being a horse and a cowboy.

What an enchanting world of innocence and imagination little boys existed in, she mused. These were such precious years, so special. All too soon, Jason would grow up and be forced to face the complexities, stresses and pressures of adulthood.

Her youth had ended abruptly when she was fourteen, due to her parents being killed, and soon after, Janice had been lost to her, too.

Dominic had had his boyhood cut short, as well, at the same age she had been when she had found herself confronting cold reality. While she had felt abandoned and so terribly alone, he had been placed in a position of responsibility far greater than any fourteen-year-old boy should have to assume.

He apparently had achieved his goals of providing for his family. He, himself, was a prominent attorney, and his brothers had their own business, which was no small accomplishment. Were there sisters, too? A mother?

And now there was Jason, another Bonelli, whom Dominic felt responsible for. Would he ever acknowledge that Jason was his son?

A part of her hoped and prayed that he wouldn't, as the threat of his seeking custody of Jason would once again haunt her.

But another section of her mind was registering sorrow that Jason would never be allowed to interact with his father, have a male influence in his life. And there, too, was a flicker of sadness that Dominic wouldn't experience the exquisite joy of having his son wrap his little arms around Dominic's neck and say, "I love you, Daddy."

Her mind, Tessa decided, was playing push-me-pull-me. For her and Jason's future security, she *never* wanted Dominic to admit that Jason was his. Yet, for Dominic's sake, she—

Tessa's jumbled thoughts were cut off by the sound of an approaching vehicle and the billowing dust it was stirring up. A few minutes later, the car was close enough for her to recognize who was coming to Rainbow's End.

"Dominic," she whispered.

She started to rise, then settled back onto the swing, deciding she wasn't going to snap to attention just because the almighty Mr. Bonelli was gracing them with his arrogant presence. This was *her* home, he had not been invited, so let him come to her where she sat on the swing.

Tessa, you have an attitude, she admonished herself, laughing softly. The evening was too lovely to disrupt with hostility. She'd keep an open mind and discover the purpose of Dominic's visit. She was not, however, going to jump to her feet to greet him.

Dominic parked in front of the house, got out of the car, then reached back onto the seat for something Tessa couldn't see.

As he came around the front of the vehicle and into full view, carrying a shopping bag, her breath caught and a funny flutter danced along her spine.

Dominic was wearing faded jeans and a black knit shirt. The soft, nearly-white-in-places jeans hugged his narrow hips and accentuated the length and power of his legs. The shirt clung to his wide shoulders, broad chest, and the short sleeves circled muscled biceps.

While he had been drop-dead gorgeous in his attorney uniform, he was absolutely magnificent in casual clothes.

Tessa, she ordered herself, *get a grip.*

"Hello, Jason," Dominic said, strolling up the front walk. "Do you remember me?" He stopped and looked at the little boy.

"Whoa," Jason said, pulling back on the broom. He cocked his head to one side and studied Dominic. "You were here today doin' stuff to our roof."

Dominic laughed. The funny flutter Tessa had felt earlier reappeared within her, low and deep, at the sound of the rich, masculine laughter.

"No, those were my brothers," Dominic said. "We all look alike."

Not quite, Tessa thought. Dominic was a cut above the rest for some unexplainable reason.

"Oh," Jason said. "I wish I had a brother."

Tessa stiffened and frowned.

Jason wanted a brother? He'd never said anything like

that to *her*. In fact, he'd never questioned the fact that he didn't have a father.

"Maybe someday you'll have a brother," Dominic said, "or a sister. I have two sisters."

"I don't think I'd like having a sister," Jason said. "They play with dolls and junk. I'm a cowboy."

"I thought you might be," Dominic said, nodding. "That's a great horse."

"Yep," Jason said, then turned and galloped across the yard.

As Dominic continued on his way to the porch, Tessa smiled at a spot above his right shoulder, deciding it was not a terrific idea to spend any more time staring at his physique displayed to perfection in those clothes.

"Good evening, Tessa," Dominic said, stepping onto the porch.

"Hello," she said pleasantly. "What brings you way out here? Would you care to sit down?" She gestured to one of the wicker chairs.

"Thank you," he said, then proceeded to settle next to her on the swing. He set the shopping bag on the porch at the end of the swing.

Tessa's eyes widened in surprise. She opened her mouth to object to his choice of seating, decided she'd sound like a prude, and snapped her mouth closed again.

So, fine, she thought, they'd share the swing. It was no big deal. It was just that she'd never realized before that it was so small. When Jason sat on the swing with her, his leg didn't press against hers as Dominic's was doing. But, no problem, she could handle this.

Maybe.

There was such incredible *heat* traveling from Dominic's leg into hers, then through her entire body. The heat swirled, then began to thrum in a steady pulse low within her.

Think about something else, she directed herself.

"My, my," she said, instantly realizing there was an odd, breathless quality to her voice. "Isn't this a lovely evening? The weather is so nice this time of year." She folded her hands in her lap.

Dominic spread one arm along the top of the swing, then set the swing in motion, moving it gently back and forth.

"Yes," he said, nodding. "Very nice."

A long, silent minute ticked by. Tessa slid a glance at Dominic, seeing his relaxed demeanor and the relaxed expression on his face as he looked at the sunset.

He was calm, cool and collected, she thought dismally, and she was rapidly becoming a nervous wreck. Not only did she have his leg to contend with, but now he'd added an arm that she was *extremely* aware of. What was Dominic up to? Why was he here?

"Why are you here?" she said, turning her head to look at him. That had sounded rude, but tough. She hadn't invited him, he hadn't called before coming, so she deserved to know what he wanted. "Dominic?"

"What?" He met her gaze. "I'm sorry. Between the rhythm of the swing and the spectacular sunset, I sort of mellowed out, I guess. I can't remember when I've taken the time to enjoy a sunset. Do you sit out here like this often?"

"Yes, every evening once it cools down from the summer heat. Despite his busy day, Jason still has a lot of energy left after dinner, and he likes to play in the yard." She laughed. "He talks me into playing catch with him, which is usually a disaster. I spend a great deal of time chasing after the balls I didn't manage to catch. I'm getting a reprieve tonight because he's a cowboy at the moment."

Dominic smiled. "When you told me you'd taken him to Old Tucson, I thought he'd probably be a cowboy for a while. Has he even been on a real horse?"

"He rode a pony around in a circle at one of those pony-ride things at the zoo. I don't think he's quite big enough for a full-size horse yet."

"Oh? Well, that's what I thought, too. You know, a pony ride would be fine, but a horse might frighten him."

Tessa frowned slightly. "You were thinking about Jason riding a pony?"

"It crossed my mind."

Why? Tessa wondered. Why would Dominic be using his mental energy on a topic so mundane as whether Jason should ride a horse or a pony?

"You still haven't said what brought you out here," she said.

"Well, there are a couple of reasons. First up, I wanted to make certain that everything went all right with the roof. I spoke with Frank, and he said you'd had some concerns, which he'd addressed, and everything had proceeded on schedule."

"Yes."

"I'm just double-checking," he said. Which was nuts. If Frank said things were fine, they were fine. Why was he here? Because he'd wanted to come, a fact he'd decided not to analyze.

"All is well," Tessa said, shrugging. "It's a tad noisy with the men hammering on the roof, but it's not that bad." She paused. "Your brothers are very nice. I met Frank, Benny and Vince. They're warm and friendly. Jeff and Clyde are pleasant, too."

Warm and friendly, Dominic mentally repeated. He had a sneaking suspicion that no one had ever used those words to describe *him*. Fine. He didn't have time for such things. But Vince, Benny and Frank were warm and friendly?

"I imagine you'll meet my brother Joe before the work is completed."

"Is he friendly, too?" Tessa asked, smiling.

"Damned if I know," he said gruffly. "I suppose he is. I've never thought about it."

"You don't know your own brothers' personality traits?"

"No. Yes. Like I said, I haven't given it much thought."

"Oh."

Another silent minute passed, then Dominic cleared his throat.

"Tessa, the other reason I came is that I want to officially apologize for having accused you of sending me the file about Jason. I was talking to an attorney friend of mine today, and he said that the closing of Winthrop Ames's law practice wasn't handled very well."

"Oh?"

"Apparently, his secretary had been with him for many years and was extremely upset by his death. Due to her emotional state, she didn't use proper judgment regarding some of the case files. An inventory list showed she'd mailed several files directly to people who should never have had them. I'm assuming Janice's file was one of those."

"I see," Tessa said slowly. "Well, that solves the mystery, at least. That poor woman must have been consumed by grief."

"Will you accept my apology?"

"Yes, of course. It wasn't necessary for you to drive all the way out here, Dominic." She smiled. "I accept apologies over the phone."

"Yes, well, there's a third item on my agenda. I figured

Jason was a cowboy because of your outing and…what I mean is… Hell.''

Tessa stared at him, her eyes widening slightly.

Dominic Bonelli, she thought incredulously, *was nervous.* This was yet another side to Dominic, one she'd never expected to see. There was a sudden vulnerability about him that was very human and *very* endearing.

''Dominic,'' she said, smiling softly, ''what are you trying to say?''

He cleared his throat again. ''I bought Jason a cowboy suit. It has a hat, shirt, pants, boots, but no guns. I didn't know how you felt about his having play-guns.'' He was talking too fast, damn it, blithering like an idiot. ''I've never bought clothes for a kid before. For their birthdays and at Christmas, I give my nieces and nephews checks to go into their education funds. I hope the suit fits Jason. I thought I should ask you first, though, if it's all right for him to have it.''

A sensation of warmth seemed to tiptoe around Tessa's heart, encircling it with a lovely caress.

''It's wonderful,'' she said, smiling. ''He'll be so thrilled. Thank you, Dominic. Thank you very much. Why don't you call him up here and give him the surprise yourself?'' She paused. ''Well, I've now officially included you on the list of Bonellis who are warm and friendly.''

Chapter Eight

With an earthy expletive, Dominic threw back the blankets and left the bed. He strode naked across the thick carpeting covering the floor of the large bedroom to one of the windows on the far wall.

Shoving aside a panel of the drapes, he stared out at the peaceful night, oblivious to the breathtaking spectacle of millions of stars glittering like diamonds in the sky.

On Monday, he fumed, he'd visited Tessa at Rainbow's End. This was Wednesday. This was also the third night in a row that he hadn't been able to sleep for more than snatches at a time.

Because of Tessa Russell.

"Damn it," he said, dropping the drape back into place.

He returned to the bed, stretched out, laced his hands beneath his head and glowered at a ceiling he couldn't see in the darkness.

Tessa Russell was driving him crazy. She'd taken up

residence in his mind, refused to budge, and he'd had enough of this nonsense.

He'd *never* been preoccupied by lingering thoughts and images of a woman. *Never.*

So what in the hell was the matter with him?

All right, Bonelli, he thought, get your act together. He'd attack this situation as he would a complex legal matter. He'd mentally spread it out, examine the data, then analyze the conclusions he'd drawn.

Fine.

He'd gone to Rainbow's End on Monday evening on impulse, which was extremely out of character for him.

And as if that wasn't unsettling enough, he'd taken Jason a cowboy outfit that he'd shopped for himself. He'd actually done that; gone into the kids' section of a department store for the first time in his life, and spent an incredible amount of time selecting the clothes, as though they were the most important purchases he'd ever made.

"Hell," he said with a snort of self-disgust.

In the next instant, as if of its own volition, a smile tugged at his lips.

Man, oh, man, Jason had been so excited about that cowboy suit, it was a wonder he hadn't floated right off the porch. He'd been hopping around, shouting and clapping his hands. It had really been something to witness so much pure happiness bubbling out of such a little kid.

It had taken both Tessa and himself to peel off Jason's clothes and stuff him into the cowboy garb because the boy was wiggling around so much and urging them to hurry.

Then Tessa had insisted that Jason stand still long enough to properly thank Mr. Bonelli for his wonderful gift.

"Thank you, Mr. Bonelli," Jason had said, "a whole bunch. This is the bestis surprise I *ever* had."

"You're welcome, Jason. If it's all right with your mom, I'd like you to call me Dominic."

"Mom?"

"That's fine," Tessa said, nodding.

Jason cocked his head to one side and looked at Dominic.

"Are you my friend?" the little boy asked.

A strange tightness gripped Dominic's throat, and it was a long moment before he could answer.

"Yes, Jason," he had finally said, "I'm your friend." He'd extended his hand. "And *you* are *my* friend. Let's shake on it."

Dominic pulled his hands from beneath his head and curled the fingers of his right hand into a loose fist.

He could still remember the feel of Jason's small hand in his. It was so tiny, warm, soft, delivering a message of trust. He'd never shaken hands with a child before, and he'd been moved by the gesture. He had been reluctant to release Jason's hand.

"Can I go ride my horse now?" Jason had said, jumping up and down.

"Do it," Dominic said, laughing.

Jason dashed off, and Tessa's laughter mingled with Dominic's, seeming to fill the porch, the entire yard, with joyous sound.

"Oh, Dominic," she said, placing a hand on his arm. "Thank you from the bottom of my heart. I'll always treasure the memory of the look on Jason's face when he peered into that shopping bag. Did you see his eyes? They were actually sparkling. Thank you."

Dominic covered her hand with his own.

"You're welcome," he said, smiling. "It was my pleasure, believe me, although I'm thoroughly exhausted from trying to dress a human pogo stick. That is one charged-up little kid.''

"That's a *happy* little kid because of your thoughtfulness.''

Their smiles slowly faded as each became suddenly acutely aware of how close together they were on the swing, and of the feel of their hands meshed on Dominic's arm.

They looked directly into each other's eyes, not certain of what they saw there, not knowing what they *wished* to see.

Had seconds passed? Minutes? Neither knew. It was a moment out of time, with an otherworldly quality to it.

It had been Tessa who had broken the spell by pulling her hand and gaze free of Dominic's hold....

Dominic rolled onto his stomach in the rumpled bed, then shifted onto his back again in a restless surge of energy.

Face it, Bonelli, he told himself. He'd wanted to kiss Tessa. It had taken every ounce of willpower he possessed to not slide his hand to the nape of her neck, then capture her enticing lips with his.

Heat rocketed through him as he remembered that moment, as he recalled the white-hot desire that had consumed him.

Oh, yes, he'd wanted to kiss Tessa. He'd wanted to kiss, caress, explore every inch of her. He'd wanted to make love to her through the entire night.

And he didn't like the truth of that data, not one damn bit. Tessa and Jason had done tricky things to his mind and emotions. How and why they were capable of doing it, he didn't know. What he *was* certain of was that it wasn't going to happen again.

With a groan of fatigue, he finally drifted off to sleep. And dreamed of Tessa.

On Thursday morning, Tessa stood in front of the stove stirring scrambled eggs in a frying pan. She pressed the fingertips of her free hand to her forehead, willing the nagging headache she'd awakened with to disappear.

Not a chance, she thought glumly. She'd gone to bed the night before with the headache, and it had still been there to greet her when she'd opened her eyes at dawn's light, just as it had been on Tuesday and Wednesday morning.

Well, what did she expect? When a person wasn't getting enough sleep night after night, the end result would be a fatigue-induced headache.

She was so angry at herself she could scream. The cause of her insomnia was perfectly clear to her, and it was ridiculous. She hadn't succumbed to such nonsense when she'd been an adolescent, and her behavior certainly wasn't becoming in a woman of nearly thirty years old.

"Absurd," she muttered, spooning the eggs onto two plates. "Silly. Disgusting. Asinine. And really, really dumb."

Her sleepless nights, damn the man, were caused by Dominic Bonelli.

She added bacon and toast to the plates, carried them to the table, then went to the bottom of the stairs.

"Jason," she called, "breakfast is ready. Lickety-split, kiddo. It's on the table."

"'Kay," Jason yelled. "Comin'."

Tessa returned to the kitchen, poured herself a cup of coffee, Jason a glass of milk, then sank onto a chair at the table with a weary sigh.

Dominic, her mind echoed. His unexpected visit of

Monday evening had totally unsettled her. Every detail of the time spent with him on the porch kept repeating in her mental vision like a movie playing over and over.

She could see Dominic so clearly it was as though he were sitting across the table from her at that very moment. His aroma of soap, spicy after-shave and fresh air was there, as was the sound of his deep, masculine laughter.

She saw him nervous, endearingly unsure of himself, as he explained his purchase of the cowboy outfit for Jason. The beautiful image of Jason's small hand being held in Dominic's large and strong hand, haunted her with its poignancy.

And then? Dear heaven, something strange and sensual had happened when she and Dominic had looked into each other's eyes. She could still feel the heat that had thrummed through her body, and the increased tempo of her heart.

Dominic's dark, compelling eyes had held her immobile. She'd been so incredibly *aware* of him as a man, as well as experiencing a near-painful heightened acknowledgment of her own femininity. Her breasts had become heavy, aching for a soothing touch, and even her skin had tingled.

It had been unsettling, to say the least. She'd vowed years before to never again fall prey to a man's charm or masculine magnetism. The heartbreaking lesson she'd learned from her affair with Cliff had held her in good stead, enabling her to keep the occasional men she met at arm's length. *She* was in control of her feelings, emotions, her life.

Until now.

Until Dominic Bonelli.

"Oh, Tessa," she said, shaking her head.

Her slumbering womanliness was being awakened by

the last man on earth she'd wish to have anything to do with. Well, she was going to put her femininity back to sleep, thank you very much. Somehow.

Tessa was pulled from her reverie as Jason came running into the room, then slid onto his chair.

She inwardly groaned as she once again saw the cowboy suit Dominic had given Jason, just as she had every morning since the child had received it. *That* was not helping her mental muddle one iota.

"Jason," she said, "you own other clothes, you know. You're going to wear that suit out."

"I love it, Mom," he said, beaming. "You washed it again for me, so I put it on."

"I had no choice but to wash it. You're a dusty, dirty cowpoke by the end of the day."

Jason frowned. "Are you mad at me 'cause I wore it again?"

"No, sweetheart," she said, smiling, "of course I'm not. I'm glad you like it, and you look wonderful in it."

"It's great," he said, then shoveled in a forkful of eggs.

Tessa forced herself to eat, hoping the nourishment would ease her headache at least a little.

"Dominic sure is nice," Jason said. "Right, Mom?"

"What? Oh, yes, it was very nice of him to give you such a marvelous surprise."

"Yep, but he's nice because he's my friend, too. I've never had a grown-up man as my friend before. He said he's my friend, so he is. That's cool."

"Yes," she said softly.

Oh, Jason, Jason. It was becoming painfully apparent that he missed having a male influence in his life. He'd never said a word on the subject, but his reaction to Dominic's offered friendship was speaking volumes. How shattering it would be to her son if he knew that his new hero was in actuality his father—and that Dominic refused to acknowledge that fact.

"I betcha Dominic will come to see me again," Jason said.

No! Tessa thought. She didn't want Dominic to come near her *or* Jason. Not *ever* again.

"Friends do that, you know," Jason rambled on. "They visit each other. I could show him how high I can go on the swing in the play yard."

"Honey, Dominic is a very busy man. You mustn't count on his having time to spend here."

"He'll come to see me," Jason said. "I know he will." He paused. "Is he your friend, too? Did you shake hands and stuff? That would be good, Mom, 'cause then he could visit you, too. Neato."

"Jason, please don't expect Dominic to visit. I don't want you to be disappointed or sad."

"Will *you* be sad if he doesn't come see us?"

"No."

"Don't you like him?"

"Jason, eat your breakfast. The kids will start arriving any minute now, and you know I like to have the kitchen cleaned up before they get here."

"Mommy, don't you like Dominic?"

Tessa sighed. "Yes, okay, I like Dominic."

"Good."

"Eat."

"Yep. I'm going to grow up to be as big and tall as Dominic is, and have muscles like him." He took a bite of toast.

Oh, Lord, spare me, Tessa thought. Everything was getting so out of control. It was a nightmare, all of it.

A knock at the front door brought Tessa to her feet.

"Chew," she said to Jason as she left the kitchen.

As she crossed the living room, she could see a man beyond the screen door.

"Hi," he said, when she got to the door. "I'm Joe Bonelli."

Why not? Tessa thought dryly. Heaven forbid she should miss out on meeting one of the Bonelli brothers. This one, too, looked like the others. And this one, too, drat it all, wasn't quite as tall, or handsome, or as well built as Dominic.

"What can I do for you, Joe?" she said, managing a small smile.

"I'm plumbing. The others will be along soon to finish up the roof today. I'm going to start on your plumbing problems. Nothing major is wrong. You've just got some rusty pipes that I'm going to replace. It won't cause you any inconvenience. Well, not a lot, anyway. Jeff's report says you have turn-offs by each unit, so I won't have to shut down the water to the entire house."

"Whatever," she said, throwing up her hands in a gesture of submission. "Make yourself at home, Joe." She unlatched the screen. "I'd appreciate your letting me know where you'll be working at what time, so I can reroute the children to another bathroom."

"Sure thing."

"Oh, and I need the kitchen operational at the lunch hour."

Jason came running into the room.

"Dominic?" he yelled, racing to the door. He stopped and frowned. "Oh, I thought I heard Dominic."

Joe smiled at him through the screen. "Nope. I'm Joe. People get the Bonelli boys mixed up all the time. You know Dom?"

"Dominic is my friend," Jason said, puffing out his

chest. "We shook hands and said we'd be friends. He gave me this cowboy suit."

Joe's eyes widened. "Dom...Dominic Bonelli, my brother...gave you that outfit?"

"Yep."

Wake up, Tessa, she told herself. She was supposed to keep Jason away from any one-on-one contact with Dominic's brothers. Those had been His Majesty's orders.

"Jason, please go carry your plate to the sink," she said.

"I did."

"Oh."

"When did Dom give you that outfit?" Joe asked Jason.

"The other night," Jason said, "when he came to visit. He sat on the porch swing with my mom while I was riding my broom horse, and they talked a lot, and she just told me that she likes him, and—"

"Jason," Tessa interrupted, feeling a warm flush on her cheeks, "Joe has to get to work on the plumbing now. Oh, look, here comes Jeremiah."

"Dom actually sat on that swing?" Joe said, pointing to it. "Just chilled-out, laid-back and relaxed? Dominic Bonelli?"

Tessa rolled her eyes heavenward. "We're not talking about a major miracle here."

"But close," Joe said, chuckling. "Very close. Dom doesn't do leisure time. He just works, works, works." He looked at the swing, Tessa, then slid his gaze over Jason's outfit. "This is interesting. Very, *very* interesting."

Before Tessa could think of anything to say to defuse Joe's obviously busy mind, Jeremiah hit the front porch with a bounce, and a yelp of glee at seeing Jason.

The day at Rainbow's End had officially begun.

Tessa pressed one hand to her forehead in a silent plea to her headache to vanish, then mentally counted off the hours left until the day ahead would be blessedly over.

Chapter Nine

Murphy's Law, Tessa decided in the late afternoon, was working overtime at Rainbow's End. Everything that could have gone wrong that day, had gone wrong, with a few extras thrown in for good measure.

There had not been any major crises, just an ongoing series of little upsets that had increased the intensity of Tessa's headache and the frazzled state of her nerves.

Two of the children had suffered slightly skinned knees in the play yard, resulting in sonic-boom volume levels of wails, and the need for Mickey Mouse bandages and lots of hugs.

Jeremiah had no sooner finished eating his lunch then he upchucked it onto the kitchen floor. The pale little boy had been tucked beneath a fluffy blanket on the cot in Tessa's office, where he promptly fell asleep.

A wheel had been broken off a plastic truck; a tug-of-war between two girls had amputated an arm and a leg from a doll; and Jason had spilled orange juice down the front of his western shirt.

To add to all the confusion, Joe had seemed to be constantly in the wrong place at the worst time.

When Patty started singing "Happy Days Are Here Again" at the top of her lungs, Tessa shot her a look that could have curdled milk.

"Oops," Patty said, laughing. "I was just trying to cheer things up around here. Has this been a day, or has this been a day?"

"This has been a day," Tessa said with a sigh, "*not* to remember. I just checked on Jeremiah again. He's awake, but is content to stay put. He's sure feeling punk, the poor little guy."

"Did you call his mother?"

"Yes, right after he redistributed his lunch. I told her I'd keep him quiet, and she said she'd try to leave work early, if possible, to come pick him up, but I guess she has a heartless boss. There's no telling what nasty bug Jeremiah has that he's no doubt shared with the others."

"Time will tell," Patty said in a singsong voice. "Ah, I hear a car. The mighty moms are beginning to arrive. This day is nearly history, Tessa."

"Amen," she said wearily.

"Tessa," a whiny voice said, "I gots polka dots on my tummy."

"Oh, good grief," she said.

She hurried across the kitchen to where Jeremiah stood in the doorway of the office. Joe passed her on his way to the kitchen sink. She knelt in front of Jeremiah and lifted his shirt.

"Chicken pox," she said with a moan. "Oh, sweetheart, you've got a full-blown case of chicken pox."

Jeremiah burst into tears. "I don't wanna be a chicken. I'm a boy. Don't make me be a chicken, Tessa."

Tessa scooped him up and settled onto a chair by the table, holding him on her lap.

"You're not going to turn into a chicken, Jeremiah. I promise you won't. That's just the silly name someone gave those kinds of spots on your tummy. You'll stay a boy, honest you will."

"Guaranteed," Joe said, looking over at them. "Hey, Jeremiah, chicken pox are cool. Your mom will put pink lotion on you, and you'll look like a birthday cake. No foolin', my two kids had chicken pox last year and they looked good enough to eat."

"Really?" Jeremiah said, dashing the tears from his cheeks. He pulled up his shirt to peer at his tummy. "A birthday cake?"

"Yep," Joe said, then his head and shoulders disappeared under the kitchen sink.

"Thank you, Joe," Tessa said to the general direction of his rear end.

"No problem," came a muffled reply.

The next forty-five minutes was a bustle of activity. Each mother that arrived to collect her child was informed that their darling had been exposed to chicken pox. Tessa passed out the sheets given to her by the health department regarding the disease. Reactions were varied, depending on whether their son or daughter had already suffered through the miserable, itchy, childhood malady.

Jason, Tessa thought glumly, had *not* had chicken pox. Jason was *going* to get chicken pox in approximately two to three weeks. *She* was not in the mood to have Jason get chicken pox. Darn and damn.

The last child had been picked up, Emma and Patty waved rather listless farewells and Tessa sighed with relief.

In the next moment, she frowned and glanced quickly around the main room.

Where was Jason? she wondered, hurrying toward the kitchen.

Once there, she stopped in her tracks. Jason's small bottom was poking in the air next to Joe's larger one, their upper halves under the sink.

Great, she thought. She was supposed to keep Jason away from the Bonelli brothers. Well, tough. She was exhausted and needed five minutes to catch her breath. If Joe didn't mind having Jason in the way under the sink, so be it.

She sank onto a chair at the table, propped up her elbows and massaged her aching temples.

"Whoa!" Joe yelled suddenly.

"Yeow!" Jason hollered.

"Oh, good Lord," Tessa said, jumping to her feet.

Water sprayed from beneath the sink as Jason and Joe scrambled backward, soaking wet. Joe dived back under the sink and the water stopped shooting out over the kitchen.

"Whew," Joe said. "The turn-off knob was stripped. It held for a bit, then let go. Are you okay, Jason? The water was cold, and we sure are wet, aren't we, pal?"

Tessa's horrified gaze swept over the dripping wet stove, refrigerator, cupboards and floor.

"Wet," was all she managed to say.

"I'll clean it up," Joe said. "Don't worry about a thing."

"Whatever," she said, sinking back onto the chair. "That's one way to get Jason's cowboy suit clean." She paused. "I think I'm hysterical."

"That was pretty scary," Jason said, smiling, "but I'm a brave cowboy."

"You betcha," Joe said. He whipped a huge calico-print handkerchief out of his back pocket. "This is dry. We're in business."

As Joe dried Jason's face, then began to ruffle the boy's wet hair with the handkerchief, resulting in Jason's giggling in delight, it slowly dawned on Tessa what was taking place.

No! her mind screamed. He mustn't tousle Jason's hair. *Joe Bonelli must not see Jason's right ear!*

She got to her feet, feeling as though she were moving in slow motion, the pair on the floor seeming a mile away. Her demand that Joe stop what he was doing caught in her throat, with only a near sob escaping her lips.

"This isn't all bad, you know," Joe was saying to Jason. "When your mom tells you to hit the tub tonight, you can tell her you already had a bath *and* your hair washed. Your hair sure is soaked, though. I think we're going to need..." His voice trailed off and his hands stilled in midair. "A towel."

Joe's head snapped up and his eyes collided with Tessa's. She was standing ramrod-stiff, trembling fingertips pressed to her lips.

One second ticked into two, three, then four.

"Somethin' the matter, Joe?" Jason said.

"What?" Joe tore his gaze from Tessa's and looked at Jason. "No. No, nothing is wrong. This handkerchief just isn't big enough to get the job done, that's all." He got to his feet, and Jason scrambled to his. "You go on upstairs, dry off and change your clothes on your own. Hit the trail, cowboy."

"Yep." Jason ran from the room.

Joe ripped a paper towel from the roll in the holder mounted beneath a cupboard. He dragged the paper over his wet face, wadded the paper into a tight ball, then looked at Tessa, no hint of a smile on his face.

"What in the hell is going on here?" he said.

"I...I don't know what you mean," Tessa said, her voice unsteady.

Joe flung the paper towel into the sink.

"Knock it off, Tessa," he said, a rough edge to his voice. "Your son is a Bonelli. There's no mistaking the Bonelli ear. I saw it, the little nitch in Jason's right ear. I also now realize that he looks just like my son did at that age. Hell, like *I* looked at five years old, like all the Bonelli males looked as young boys. I didn't catch it at first because I wasn't thinking along those lines. But now? That kid's father is a Bonelli."

"Oh, God," Tessa whispered. She sank back onto the chair as her legs refused to hold her for another instant.

Joe crossed the room and gripped the top of another chair, leaning slightly forward.

"Talk to me," he said, "or I'll be forced to draw my own conclusions."

Tessa shook her head.

"Damn it." He straightened and shoved his hands through his wet hair. "Okay, we'll do this your way. Actually, it's clear as a bell. Dom isn't the executor of some screwy will that says he's to oversee how your inheritance is spent. *He's* paying for this work on your house because he's Jason's father.

"You and Dom had a fling, or affair, or whatever, about six years ago, and the result was Jason. What I can't figure out is why you waited all this time to tell Dom he has a son. It's obvious he didn't know until now, because he wouldn't have stood by and allowed his son to live in a place that was falling apart. Dom is really big on responsibility."

"You don't understand."

"You've got that straight. I don't know what your game is. I'm not real thrilled with Dominic at the moment, either. He apparently didn't intend for the family to know about his son. That stinks. Jason is a Bonelli, just like the rest of us. We have the right to know that he exists. Bonellis are Bonellis, all of us, no matter what."

"Joe…"

"I'll clean up your kitchen," he said, turning and starting back toward the sink. "Then I'm going to round up the family, and we're all going to have a little chat with Dom."

Tessa jumped to her feet. "No. Joe, please, no, don't do that. I promised Dominic that I'd keep Jason away from you and your brothers while you were working here. You mustn't tell him what you've discovered. Oh, Joe, please, listen to me. This is far more complicated than you think. Leave it alone. *Please, Joe, leave it alone.*"

He turned to look at her, his voice quiet and gentle when he spoke again.

"I can't do that, Tessa. We are an old-fashioned, close-knit family. We have a code of honor that must be followed to enable us to be true to who we are, what we stand for and believe in.

"Dom is breaking the rules. He's accustomed to being in charge, since he's the head of the family. But this time, by God, he's out of line and he's accountable for that."

"Joe, please, think about Jason. He's just an innocent child. He doesn't deserve to have his world turned upside down."

"I *am* thinking about Jason," he said, splaying out one hand on his chest. "What he deserves is to have what's due him as a Bonelli. Jason has a grandmother with enough love in her heart for a million kids. He has aunts, uncles and cousins. He has a big family, Tessa, that will be there for him through good times and bad.

"And do you know what else? You're Jason's mother, and that means the family is yours, too. I don't give a tinker's damn what Dom says about that. You and Jason are part of us, all of us. I've never before crossed swords with Dom, none of us have, but there's a first time for everything."

"But I'm *not* Jason's mother." She sat back down, covered her face with her hands and shook her head. "This is a nightmare. I just want to be left alone with my son to raise him, love him, as I've always done. We were doing fine, just the two of us. He's Jason Robert Russell, my baby." A sob caught in her throat. "I wish I'd never heard of the Bonellis, any of you."

"I'm sorry I upset you. But I don't understand. One minute you're saying you're not Jason's mother, the next second you're calling him your son. You're not going to start crying, are you?"

Tessa dropped her hands and glared at him.

"A crying jag is not going to solve this, Joe Bonelli. What will, is your keeping your damn mouth shut. I don't give a hoot in hell about your Bonelli code of honor. I have a voice in this matter, mister. I intend to protect my son from you, all of you. Get out of my house." She got to her feet. *"Now!"*

"Whew," Joe said, grinning at her. "You're really something when you get on a rip. I do believe, ma'am, that Dominic Bonelli has met his match."

"Mom," Jason called, running into the kitchen. "Will you help me get my boots back on? They didn't get wet."

"What's the magic word, sport?" Joe said.

"Please," Jason said.

"That's the one," Joe said, nodding. "That's the magic

word for my kids, too." He looked directly at Tessa. "For *all* the Bonellis, as a matter of fact."

"Joe…"

"I have to do what I have to do, Tessa," he said. "I'm sorry."

"Mom? Joe?" Jason said, his eyes darting back and forth between them. "What's wrong? Mommy?"

"Nothing, sweetheart," she said, managing a small smile. "I'll help you with your boots. There's nothing wrong, Jason."

"No, Jason, nothing is wrong," Joe said. "Things that are long overdue are going to be set to rights."

Several hours later, Tessa sat on the swing on the front porch, willing the tranquillity of the peaceful desert night to ease her inner turmoil.

The evening was a blur in her mind, the activities and conversations shared with Jason having been performed by rote.

She'd gone to bed an hour after Jason had been read a story and tucked in, but despite her bone-weary fatigue, she had been unable to sleep.

Her world was falling apart, and everything she held dear was being threatened. Despite the vow she'd made years before to be in charge of her life, that control was slipping through her hands like grains of sand.

Miles away, somewhere in the city, the Bonellis were no doubt having a family meeting, and Dominic was probably being confronted with the fact that the existence of his son had been discovered.

Dear heaven, what was going to happen?

If forced to acknowledge Jason as his, would Dominic then seek custody of his son?

Was she going to lose her beloved Jason?

Chapter Ten

Dominic glanced at his watch, then pressed harder on the gas pedal. The traffic was heavy, and a moment later he was forced to reduce his speed again. He swore under his breath, then mentally ordered himself to relax.

A family meeting, he thought, frowning. It had been a couple of years since one of these had been organized. There'd been a stretch of time when the family had gathered regularly: formulating plans for Bonelli Painting and Restoration, seeing to the proper training of his brothers, arranging loans to enable the business to be launched.

There had been meetings called, he remembered, by his sisters, as well, as they made decisions regarding their futures. Carmen had requested and received a loan to attend art school. About a year later, Maria had rallied the troops to announce that she was getting married and planned to have a dozen babies.

So now what? he wondered. Everyone and everything

was under control, as far as he knew. His brothers' business was thriving, Carmen was getting ongoing excellent reviews on her oil paintings and Maria was happily expecting her third child.

Was someone ill? Did his brothers want to expand their business even more, perhaps by purchasing additional vehicles or equipment? If a new house or car was being contemplated, it didn't take a family meeting to discuss it.

Hell, he didn't know what was on the agenda. What he *was* aware of was that he wasn't in the mood for this. He'd had a grueling day, was rushing to his mother's house directly from the office and he was starving. He wanted his dinner.

Joe had left a message with Gladys regarding the family meeting to be held that night at seven o'clock at, as per tradition, their mother's house. He had not, the secretary had related, asked to speak directly with Dominic.

Whatever, he thought with a mental shrug. He knew from experience that the person telephoning wasn't necessarily the one who'd requested the gathering. Usually, though, several days' notice was given. But not this time. Well, this had better be important, that was for damn sure.

Dominic's frown and clenched jaw disappeared as he left the busy main road and drove slowly through the exclusive neighborhood where his mother now lived.

Knowing that she had the lovely, large home that she deserved never failed to bring him a sense of inner peace. It had been a long hard journey from the poverty of his youth to the quality of life his family now enjoyed. It was his responsibility to care for his family, and he was satisfied with what he had accomplished thus far.

He turned at one more corner, then pulled in next to the last of the many vehicles parked in front of the big two-story house.

Entering without knocking, he went down the Spanish-tiled entry hall to the sunken living room off to the left. As he entered the room, the buzz of conversation stopped, and all eyes were on him.

"Hello," he said, pulling the knot of his tie down several inches. "No kids? You all got baby-sitters on short notice." He crossed the room and dropped a kiss on his mother's cheek. "Hi, beautiful. How's my best girl in the whole world?"

"You look tired, Dom," Delores Bonelli said, scrutinizing his face.

She was short, plump and wore her salt-and-pepper hair in a bun at the nape of her neck. When she smiled, her eyes danced with merriment.

"I'm beat," Dominic said. He swept his gaze over the group, noting that everyone was there—husbands, wives, the entire family. And not one of them was smiling. "So? What's up? Who called for this?"

Joe got to his feet. "*I* did."

Dominic sat down in a high-backed leather chair, slouched a bit, undid the two top buttons on his shirt, then laced his fingers loosely on his chest.

"Okay, Joe," he said. "Go for it."

Joe took a deep breath, cleared his throat, then squared his shoulders.

"Everyone knows why we're here," he said. "I thought it best to allow a bit of time to digest this."

"Everyone except me," Dominic said. "Gladys said you didn't even ask to speak to me. Is there a reason for that, Joe?"

"I didn't want to get into this with you on the phone. It's too important, Dom."

"Well, you all look like you've come from a funeral,"

Dominic said. "Spit it out, Joe. What's the subject matter of this meeting?"

"Jason Robert Russell," Joe said quietly. "Jason Robert Russell...Bonelli."

Dominic lunged to his feet so quickly that Joe took a step backward.

"Are you out of your mind?" Dominic said, a steely edge to his voice. His eyes darted around the room, then centered on Joe again. "Do you realize what you're doing?"

"Yes," Joe said, then forced more strength into his voice. "Yes, I know exactly what I'm doing. It's long overdue, but I'm acknowledging the truth. Jason Russell is a Bonelli."

"The truth? At what cost?" Dominic roared. He swept one arm through the air. "Which family in this room do you plan to destroy, Joe?" He laughed, but it was a short, humorless bark of sound. "Well, one thing is clear. It wasn't you who... You're an idiot, but not a complete fool, I guess. This is really a rotten shot you're pulling on Vince, Benny or Frank."

"Now wait a minute, Dom," Joe said.

"What's wrong with you guys?" Dominic raged, as though Joe hadn't spoken. "Joe said you all knew what this meeting was about. Why didn't one of you stop him? More precisely, the man who's responsible for this mess should never have allowed this meeting to take place."

"The man responsible didn't know what the meeting was about, damn it," Joe yelled.

"What in the hell are you saying, Joe?" Dominic snapped.

"Come off it, Dom," Joe said. "You're so used to being in charge you've begun to believe you can change facts to suit you.

"Well, not this time, big brother. You're not going to pretend that Jason doesn't exist. Fixing up the house where he lives isn't enough, not even close. He deserves to be part of this family, and so does his mother, Tessa. And that, Dominic, is the way it's going to be."

Dominic narrowed his eyes and looked at each of his brothers in turn.

"Very clever," he said coldly. "You got together and planned a 'safety in numbers' routine. You're all trying to protect your marriages." He nodded. "Nice try, but I was with you in Las Vegas, remember? I assume you know that's where Jason was conceived, during the celebration of the opening of my firm.

"Tessa, by the way, is Jason's *aunt,* not his mother, although the boy doesn't know that. Oh, you celebrated big time, drank like there was no tomorrow. One of you picked up Janice Russell and went to bed with her. I was keeping Jason's existence a secret to protect whichever one of you it was so your marriage wouldn't be in jeopardy. I made Jason *my* responsibility."

"With just cause, Dom," Joe said quietly. "Jason is *your* son."

"Ah, hell, that's enough of this garbage," Dominic said, starting across the room. "I'm tired and I'm not playing this game."

"It's no game, Dom," Frank said. "You're Jason's father."

Dominic stopped and spun around. "Don't push me, Frank. I know you guys are trying to protect what you have but you can't use me to do it."

"Shut up," Frank said. He got to his feet and crossed the room to stand directly in front of Dominic. "For once in your life, just shut the hell up and listen."

"Good Lord," Carmen muttered. "Frankie has a death wish."

"Jason was conceived in Las Vegas? Then that really cinches it," Frank said. "Yeah, we drank in Vegas, but so did you, Dom. We all saw you relax, actually unbend, become…become human. It was good to see. You're always so closed, always thinking, thinking, thinking about your responsibilities. But that weekend? Man, you kicked back and went with it. We were topping off your drinks, Dom. You were totally smashed."

"What?" Dominic said, his voice a hoarse whisper. "You topped off my drinks?"

"We didn't do it *to* you," Frank went on. "We did it *for* you. You'd worked so hard for all of us. You deserved to have a great time. When the party girl approached you, we figured, hell, why not? This is Dom's celebration. Let him do what he wants. *You* spent the night with the woman, Dominic. It wasn't one of us. It was you, I swear to God it was. *Jason Russell is your son!*"

Mental images never before seen, slammed against Dominic's mind like hammering blows.

A tall, slender woman hanging on his arm, whispering in his ear…a glass of liquor that was never empty… drinking, drinking…a room, a bed, the woman laughing, beckoning him to the erotic round bed…talking, telling her that money was power, money was the key to the door of success, of having finally made it big…then falling into an abyss of dark, dreamless sleep…

Dominic dragged both hands down his face.

"My God," he whispered, "I didn't remember." He shook his head in an attempt to shake away the haunting pictures. "I really thought that one of you guys had…" He stopped speaking and stared up at the ceiling.

Jason was his son, he thought incredulously. *His.* That

funny little kid, who had nearly popped a seam because he was so excited about having a cowboy suit, was his son. That boy, who had looked at him with such innocence, so vulnerable and trusting, and asked if Dominic was his friend, was his child, born of his seed.

Dominic shifted his gaze to his right hand, staring at it, remembering the feel of Jason's small hand in his. Then he suddenly saw Tessa's smile, heard her say that he was now officially a Bonelli who was warm and friendly.

No one in the room spoke. All eyes were on Dominic. Frank and Joe returned to their seats, each reaching for their wife's hand.

Dominic dropped his hand to his side, his eyes darting around the room.

Damn it, he fumed inwardly. He felt as though he were on trial and being stripped bare by judgments passed on him by a family *he* was the head of. What was next? They'd give him a list of *their* instructions regarding what he should do about Jason Russell? Not in this lifetime. He was in charge here.

"I'm leaving now," he said gruffly. "Good night, family."

"Dom," Delores said.

"Yes?" he said, looking at his mother.

"This woman in Las Vegas," she said. "Where is she now?"

"She died," Dominic said wearily, suddenly thoroughly exhausted. "Her sister, Tessa, has raised Jason alone from the day he was born. He's five years old."

"How is it," Delores said, "that you only now know he exists?"

"I received a legal file in the mail. I guess there was a snafu when the office of the attorney who handled the whole thing was closed after he passed away. I thought at first that Tessa was pulling a scam, but I've since concluded that isn't true.

"I'd like to know, though, Joe, how *you* suddenly came to be aware that Jason was a Bonelli."

"It was a fluke," Joe said, "so don't blame Tessa. Jason got wet and I was drying his face and hair. She asked me…hell, she begged me…not to pursue this when I discovered Jason's identity. I told her I couldn't do that."

"You saw his ear," Dominic said, sighing.

"Yeah, Dom, I saw it, and I knew. I also realized that you intended to keep Jason's existence a secret, and I couldn't stand by and allow that to happen."

"Dom," his mother said gently, "do you believe that this child is yours?"

Dominic sighed again. "Yes, I guess so. Yes, all right, he's mine." He narrowed his eyes. "He's *my* responsibility. I'm already seeing to his needs and doing what has to be done. I'm having the house repaired, I'll set up a trust fund for his education, I'll convince Tessa to accept monthly support money. End of story."

"Tessa Russell sounds like a strong, courageous woman," Delores said. "She has raised her sister's child as though he were her own, and she's done it all alone. Is that correct? There's no other family?"

"No, no family," Dominic said. "Tessa will have it easier from here on out because I'll provide the money to make that possible. There's no more to be said on the subject. This meeting is over."

Delores got to her feet. "No, Dom, this family meeting is *not* over, and you are not leaving yet."

A collective gasp went up from the group, then a heavy silence fell over the room as mother and eldest son stared at each other.

Delores lifted her chin. "You have been the head of this

family for many, many years, Dom. It broke my heart to see such a young boy take on so many responsibilities, but I had no choice other than to let you do it. I had little ones to care for, and with your father gone, I turned to you.

"All of us have leaned on you through the years, looked to you for guidance, for strength, direction. You were forced into the role of a man and were robbed of your childhood. I'll always regret that, yet be grateful for what you've done."

"Mother—"

"No, Dom, hear me out. We have never questioned your role as the head of the Bonelli family. Never. Your word was law, your decisions final and you've provided well for all of us."

"Your point?" Dominic said, a muscle jumping in his jaw.

"My point, my son," Delores said, lifting her chin another notch, "is that this time you are wrong. This time, things are not going to be done the way you decree. This time *I* am making decisions and *I'm* in charge."

"I don't believe this," Carmen said.

"Shh," Maria said. "Oh, dear heaven, I don't believe this, either."

"Shh," Maria's husband said.

"I don't mean to be rude, Mother," Dominic said tightly, "but—"

"Then don't be," Delores interrupted. "Just listen. Dominic, you have a son. It's not enough that you give him money, a fine home, an education. Yes, as his father, those things are your responsibility to provide, but what of love, Dominic? Responsibility doesn't equal love. Money isn't love.

"I fear for you, Dom, for what's in your heart, your mind, your very soul. Even more, what *isn't* there. Have we done this to you by leaning on you so heavily all these years? Are we the cause of your not knowing the difference between love and responsibility? Dear God, forgive me if that's true.''

''That's enough,'' Dominic said. ''I'm not on trial here. I've provided for all of you the way my father would have wanted me to. You've got no complaints, any of you. I'll see to Jason's needs, too. He's my *responsibility* and I don't want, nor will I tolerate, interference from any of you. Is that clear?''

''Dominic,'' Delores said, ''Jason is my grandson. Tessa, in my mind, is his mother. They're part of this family, and welcome in my home. I intend to hug Jason to my breast, just as I do all my grandchildren. Tessa and Jason will eat at my table, share in the lives and love of all the Bonellis because they *are* Bonellis.''

''Damn it, you have no right to—''

''I have every right. *I* am the mother of this family. You may see yourself as the one in charge of responsibility, but *I* am in charge of family love. Tessa and Jason will have what they deserve from our hearts. None of us will tell Jason that you are his father. That is for you and Tessa to work out. We'll have another explanation for the little one as to where we all came from, if that's what you want.''

''I have no intention of informing Jason Robert Russell that he's my son!''

''So be it,'' Delores said. ''We'll respect that decision.''

''Thanks a helluva lot,'' he said, his tone sarcastic. ''You're letting me know that Tessa and Jason will be here at family celebrations, having a grand old time. The hell with how I might feel about *that*. Well, go for it, family. Include them in everything, for all I care. But count *me* out. I'm not going to interact with them because I was told to at a family meeting. Not a chance. You don't dictate to me. Not ever.''

Dominic turned and strode from the room. A few moments later, everyone cringed as the front door slammed.

Chapter Eleven

No news, Tessa decided on Sunday morning, is not always good news. Silence is *not* always golden—and whatever other clichés might be available to misapply to the nerve-racking situation, Tessa added.

She'd had a telephone call on Friday morning from the secretary at Bonelli Painting and Restoration informing her that the roof and plumbing projects were completed at Rainbow's End. The men were scheduled to be on another job that day, but would return on Monday to begin work on the outside of the house.

"Oh? Just what exactly are they going to do to it?" Tessa had asked.

"You don't know?" the secretary said.

"Not really." Tessa paused. "The woman is always the last to know." She sighed dramatically, then rolled her eyes in self-disgust. "Forget it. Do you have even a hint of what they plan to do to the outside of the house?"

"Sure. I'm looking at the work order. They'll scrape off all the old paint, then put on fresh paint. Great, huh? There's a note here that says you're to pick the color you want."

"Really? How nice," Tessa said dryly. "Well, I think I'll have it done in multicolored stripes. I mean, jeez, this *is* Rainbow's End. Why not have a house that looks like a rainbow? Good idea, don't you think?"

"Well…um…yes, that sounds…interesting. You bet. Whatever you want, Ms. Russell. Shall I write that on the work order?"

"No! Good grief, I was kidding. I'll think about the color. Okay?"

"Super idea. You think about it. The guys will show you sample charts so you can choose what will look the best. Bye for now."

"Bye," she'd said wearily.

As she replaced the receiver, she'd continued an imaginary conversation with the secretary.

Say, honey bun, you didn't happen to hear what went on at the Bonelli family meeting, did you? Is Dominic planning to murder me? Did he shoot any of his brothers? Did his brothers shoot him? *Should I snatch up my son and leave town?*

"Tessa Russell," she said aloud, "you're definitely losing it."

By early afternoon on Sunday, she was toying with the idea of taking Jason into town, when Jeremiah's mother called and asked if Jason could come play. Since Jason had already been exposed to the chicken pox, would Tessa allow him to spend the afternoon and evening with a very bored Jeremiah?

Jason thought the idea was "cool," and a polka-dot Jeremiah and his mother drove out to pick him up. Jason was, of course, wearing his cowboy suit.

Tessa wandered aimlessly around the house, scolded herself with a cliché about idle hands, which she couldn't remember in its entirety, then settled behind her desk in the small office to get caught up on the paperwork for Rainbow's End.

She really enjoyed the accounting side of the day-care center, she mused. There was a satisfying orderliness about the ledger and a mental hooray when the columns balanced. How wonderful it would be if she could so easily bring her life back under her command.

Just after four o'clock, the telephone on the desk rang, and she jerked in surprise as the shrill sound shattered the silence in the small room. She picked up the receiver halfway through the second ring.

"Hello?"

"It's Dominic. I'd like to come out there and talk to you."

No! "Yes, all right. When?" *Never!*

"I'm leaving now. Goodbye."

The dial tone buzzed in her ear before she could echo Dominic's goodbye, and she replaced the receiver slowly, realizing her hand was trembling.

This is it, she thought, getting to her feet.

She hadn't been able to gauge Dominic's mood from the extremely brief call, but she was certain that Joe had followed through on his plan to have a family meeting. So Dominic had been confronted with Jason's existence. Had he been forced to acknowledge what she already knew, that Jason was *his* son?

Yes, of course, he had, because his brothers would stand united with the truth: it had been Dominic who had gone off with Janice in Las Vegas.

Would Dominic tell *her* that he was Jason's father? Or would he attempt to continue the charade of stating that one of his brothers was responsible for Jason's conception?

He'd had many hours since that gathering on Thursday night to formulate a plan of action regarding his son. He held in his hands the power to control her entire future happiness.

"Damn it, no," she said.

This wasn't going to happen to her again. She was *not* going to be treated like a marionette whose strings were being maneuvered by someone other than herself. She'd been dictated to too many times in her life by outside forces.

Well, not this time, by heaven.

Tessa stomped up the stairs, combed her hair, freshened her lipstick and tucked a bright blue cotton blouse into her jeans.

She settled onto the swing on the porch, narrowed her eyes, pursed her lips and waited for Dominic Bonelli.

As Dominic drove toward Rainbow's End, he was aware of his bone-deep fatigue. It had been so long since he'd had an energy-restoring solid night's sleep, he'd forgotten what one felt like.

He hadn't seen, nor spoken to, any member of his family since the meeting Thursday night. He'd had no desire to communicate with them, and no Bonelli had left any messages for him with Gladys, or on his answering machine at home. So be it.

He'd needed the time to think, to digest what he'd learned from his brothers and to contemplate his options regarding the fact that Jason Robert Russell was his son.

Dear God, Jason was his son.

That truth had hammered against his brain unmercifully.

Jason was his son. He'd struggled unsuccessfully to move past that echoing message, to get in touch with himself to discover exactly how he felt about it.

But his mind refused to travel forward. It simply repeated over and over that Jason was his son.

Why was he going to Rainbow's End? Hell, he didn't know. He'd been pacing his living room like a caged lion for hours, then had snatched up the receiver to the telephone on impulse and called Tessa.

He was, he supposed, hoping that by seeing Tessa and Jason, he would feel centered again. The emotional isolation he'd felt since leaving his mother's house had created the sensation of being the only person on earth, alone with his tangled thoughts.

So, yes, all right, he was, perhaps, running to a woman for comfort, which was not a welcome realization, but at least Tessa would never know.

Seeing her, the boy, the house, would reaffirm his sense of responsibility, get him back on the right track.

The boy.

Jason.

His son.

"Damn it," he said, smacking the steering wheel with the palm of his hand.

He didn't *want* a son. Or a wife. He'd been the head of the Bonelli family for years, and now enjoyed and protected his freedom. His role in Jason's life would go no further than his providing for the child's material needs.

Responsibility doesn't equal love. Money isn't love.

Delores's words suddenly slammed against Dominic's mind.

Are we the cause of your not knowing the difference between love and responsibility? Dear God, forgive me if that's true.

His mother, he reasoned, was endearingly naive and saw hugs and kisses as the solution to all that might be wrong.

Even though Delores Bonelli had suffered through years of poverty after her husband's death, she had still managed to emerge from that era wearing rose-colored glasses with which to view the world. She simply didn't understand the intensity of the responsibility that Dominic had taken on, he decided.

Responsibility doesn't equal love. Money isn't love.

Dominic shook his head.

Delores was operating on a different plane than he was. What would have become of them all if he hadn't been willing to step in and take charge of the family? He didn't expect a brass band and flowery testimonials for his deeds. He'd done what was needed at the time, pure and simple.

But he sure as hell wasn't going to start questioning himself, his values, his mode of conduct now that everyone was provided for and things were running smoothly.

As much as he sincerely loved his mother, he felt that she had no right to use her definition of love as a measuring stick against his. No.

If Delores intended to welcome Tessa and Jason into the Bonelli family, so be it. *He* wasn't having any part of that. He would see to Jason's financial and material welfare. He would meet his responsibility for the boy head-on.

His son.

"Ah, hell," Dominic said aloud.

He gripped the steering wheel more tightly, pressed harder on the gas pedal and scowled.

By the time Tessa saw the billowing dust in the distance from Dominic's approaching car, she'd worked herself into a frenzied combination of anger and fear.

She was furious at the loss of control over her life.

She was terrified that Dominic was coming to announce that he planned to seek custody of Jason.

When Dominic parked in front of the house, then started up the front walkway, she absently registered the fact that he looked fantastic in dark slacks and a yellow dress shirt open at the neck.

She got to her feet, and as he stepped onto the porch, she curled her hands into tight fists at her sides.

"Hello, Tessa," Dominic said, not smiling. "I came here to—"

"Dominic," she interrupted, "I did the best I could keeping Jason away from your brothers while they were working here. Therefore I refuse to apologize for what happened with Jason and Joe. It just happened, that's all.

"I don't know what took place at the family meeting Joe intended to organize, and I don't really care. Why? Because no matter what was divulged during that gathering, the fact remains that Jason is my son. *Mine.*"

"Tessa—"

"Shut up. You denied being Jason's father from the onset and tried to dump the whole business on one of your brothers. That stinks, Bonelli, it really does. You don't deserve Jason. You refused to acknowledge the fact that he's yours. Well, he's *not* yours, he's mine, and I'll fight you with everything I have—"

Sudden tears filled Tessa's eyes and her voice began to tremble.

"I won't let you have my baby. I won't. I won't." A sob caught in her throat.

"Ah, Tessa," Dominic said.

Before he realized he had done it, he reached for her, pulling her into his arms, holding her close.

And Tessa cried.

She wrapped her arms around Dominic, splaying her

hands across his back, buried her face in his shirt and wept. The emotions that had been tormenting her had been too overwhelming, for too long. She was exhausted in mind and body, and to her, Dominic felt strong, powerful and solid, a safe haven where she could rest.

And so she cried.

Dominic tightened his hold on Tessa even more, feeling her pain as though it were his own, her sobs causing his heart to ache for her. His need to comfort, soothe, assure her that all was well, was like nothing he'd experienced before.

He wanted to slay the foe that was causing her unhappiness, all the while knowing the enemy was himself.

He lowered his head to inhale the clean, feminine aroma of her silken curls, and was suddenly aware of the exquisite feel of her breasts crushed to his chest, her slender, soft form molded to his rugged body. She was delicate, fragile, and instead of protecting her as a man should, he was causing her to cry as though her heart were breaking.

"Tessa," he said, not realizing he'd spoken her name aloud. "Tessa."

In her haze of misery, Tessa vaguely heard her name, then it came again, clearer, louder. She slowly registered the fact that she was weeping while being held in Dominic Bonelli's strong arms, and had no idea how she had gotten there.

She stiffened, then attempted to remove her arms unobtrusively from around Dominic, with the irrational hope that he wouldn't have noticed they had ever been there.

She stared straight ahead, appalled by the wet spots on his shirt caused by her tears, along with a smudge of lipstick. As she eased farther away, she realized that he was not releasing her.

"Tessa?"

She snapped her head up to look at him, then inwardly groaned as she remembered how puffy her eyes became when she cried, how blotchy her skin, and how red her nose must be. She was *not* a "pretty crier."

"I'm sorry," Dominic said quietly. "I'm terribly sorry that I upset you like this."

Of all the things that Dominic might have said at that moment, an apology was the last thing that Tessa had expected to hear. She opened her mouth to reply, then closed it, realizing she didn't know what to say.

She should, she told herself, tell him to remove his arms...those strong, nicely muscled arms...from her person. And she would. In a minute.

Her own arms were now hanging uselessly by her sides. Not only was she speechless, but she had no idea what to do with her hands. She felt like a gawky adolescent.

"Your nose is pink," Dominic said, smiling slightly.

"Yes, well..."

His smile faded. "Tessa, listen to me for a minute." He still didn't release her. "I know it wasn't your fault that Joe discovered that Jason is a Bonelli. Okay? You said I tried to dump the paternity of Jason onto one of my brothers."

"*Dump* wasn't a very nice word to use, I guess," she said, now staring at a button on his shirt.

Tessa, she ordered herself, *move away. You're still being held fast by a man you don't even like.* But it felt so good to be encased in strength, to not have to be so incredibly strong on her own, alone. She was so tired and drained. She needed to lean, just for a moment.

That Dominic was the cause of her distress was somehow not important right now. She was going to give herself this time as a gift.

"Tessa, look at me," Dominic said.

When she slowly shifted her gaze from the button to the obsidian depths of his eyes, her breath caught. He was looking at her with tenderness, a gentleness that she'd not seen before. And there, too, was a flicker of...yes, a haunting pain.

She knew with a surprising sureness that Dominic would not want her to see that pain, that a man of control such as he would be angry at himself for revealing any weakness, any hint of vulnerability.

A warmth suffused her that was born of compassion combined with a glowing ember of desire that she wished to deny, but knew she couldn't.

"Yes?" she said, hearing the thread of breathlessness in her voice.

"Tessa," he said, then cleared his throat. "Tessa, I honestly believed that one of my brothers was responsible for fathering Jason. That trip to Las Vegas was many years ago, and my memories of it were dimmed by time. Or so I thought.

"What I now know is that the blur of details was caused by my brothers topping off my drinks so I would really celebrate the event of opening my own firm. They did it *for* me, Frank said, not *to* me, feeling I'd earned the right to have a great time."

"And?" she said, hardly breathing.

"Because of what I learned at the family meeting, I've acknowledged the fact that Jason is...Jason is my son."

"Oh, God, you're not going to demand custody of him, are you? Dominic?" Fresh tears filled her eyes. Without realizing it, Tessa raised her hands to rest flat on Dominic's damp shirt. "You're not going to take my baby, are you? Oh, please, please, no."

Tessa's anguish ripped through Dominic like a burning spear, tearing at him.

He was the cause of her torment.

Only *he* could comfort her.

Two tears slid down Tessa's cheeks.

A moan rumbled in Dominic's chest, then he lowered his head, and kissed her.

And he was lost.

He pulled her close to his body, parted her lips to delve his tongue into the darkness of her mouth and drank of her sweetness. Desire, hot and instantaneous, coiled low and tight within him.

How long had he been waiting for this kiss? he wondered in a haze of passion. Forever, it seemed, as he filled his senses with the taste, the feel, the tantalizingly feminine aroma of Tessa.

Tessa was swept away. She returned Dominic's kiss in a total abandon that was a confused mixture of shock at her behavior, along with a wondrous feeling of rightness.

She was awash with desire, the glowing ember bursting into licking flames. Her breasts were crushed to the hard wall of his muscled chest in a strangely exquisite pain. She met his tongue boldly with her own, stroking, dueling, glorying in the existence of his arousal pressing heavily against her.

The kiss went on and on—and it was ecstasy.

Dominic slid his hands over the gentle slope of her buttocks, urging her closer yet. She encircled his neck with her hands, inching her fingertips into the thick depths of his hair.

He raised his head to draw a quick, ragged breath, then sought her lips once more, hungry, urgent, and Tessa answered his ardor in kind.

Time lost meaning. They could only feel, savor, heated desire raging like a brush fire out of control.

Then slowly, Tessa registered a sensation like insidious

fingers tapping, tapping, demanding attention, accompanied by a whispered message she couldn't decipher. It gained volume, shouting at her louder and louder.

Jason! Jason! Jason!

She tore her mouth from Dominic's and stepped back so quickly, he was forced to release her. She staggered slightly, wrapped her hands around her elbows in a protective gesture, then took a shuddering breath.

"Dear heaven, what am I doing?" she said.

"Tessa," he said, reaching for her. His voice was raspy, husky with passion.

"No," she said, moving farther back. "This is wrong. It should never have happened."

"Oh, no, Tessa, it was right. Very, *very* right."

"No! You didn't answer my question, Dominic," she said, a frantic tone creeping into her voice. "What about Jason? Tell me, damn you, are you going to try to take my son from me? Are you, Dominic?"

He stared at the floor of the porch, seeing the distance now separating him from Tessa. A feeling like nothing he'd ever experienced before washed over him in a chilling wave. He felt empty, hollow, like a shell with nothing within.

He was totally alone and for the first time in his life, he was lonely.

"No," he said, his voice low and flat. "No, Tessa, I won't seek custody of Jason. He's the child of your heart. He's my son by virtue of biology, a fact he's never to know. I'll see to his financial and material needs. I won't take your baby from you. He'll be to me just one more responsibility."

Chapter Twelve

The rush of relief and joy that swept through Tessa caused her knees to tremble. She reached out toward the swing that suddenly appeared terribly far away. She could feel the color draining from her face, and black dots danced before her eyes.

"Hey, whoa," Dominic said as she teetered unsteadily on her feet.

He stepped forward, lifted her into his arms as though she weighed hardly more than a feather pillow, then sat down on the swing with her on his lap. He kept one arm around her just below her breasts, the other across the top of her knees.

Tessa took a deep breath, let it out, shook her head slightly, then blinked.

"I'm all right," she said, not looking at Dominic. "I was just dizzy for a moment. I've been very stressed-out lately, very worried. Well, I'm just fine now, no problem.

So! If you'll unhand me, sir, I'll get off of your lap, because there's no reason for me to be here.''

''Isn't there?''

Dominic's voice was so low and rumbly, so incredibly *male*, that Tessa shivered. She was acutely aware of the rock-hardness of his thighs and the strength of his arms. The heat emanating from him was weaving through her, and her pale cheeks became flushed.

There were definite reasons that she *shouldn't* be perched on Dominic's lap. He was dangerous, very dangerous. The passion he'd evoked in her was like nothing she had ever known before. He was too powerful, not just physically, but in his ability to throw her totally off kilter.

''Tessa?''

She turned her head slowly to meet his gaze, and saw the smoky hue of desire still evident in his dark eyes. He was so close to her, so close. She had only to lean slightly forward to capture his lips and once again experience the ecstasy of his kiss....

''Kissing you was *not* wrong, Tessa. It was right, for both of us. You gave as much as you received.''

''I don't want to talk about it, Dominic.''

He looked directly into her eyes for a long moment.

''All right. We won't discuss it further. Now. You can *think* about it, instead.''

Oh, thanks, she thought crossly.

She picked up Dominic's arm that was across her knees and moved it away. Shooting him a quick glare, she scooted off his lap to stand in front of the swing. She fiddled with straightening her blouse, then looked at him, lifting her chin.

''I want to thank you,'' she said, ''for relieving my greatest fear that you might seek custody of Jason. There aren't words enough to tell you how much...'' Her voice trailed off and she threw up her hands in a gesture of frustration. "See? I hope you know how grateful I am."

"He's your child, Tessa. I wouldn't take him from you." He paused. "I should prepare you for the fact that my family intends to welcome you into the fold. They'll be inviting you and Jason to take part in an event of some sort very soon, I would imagine."

"Oh," she said, her mind racing. She wrapped her hands around her elbows. "What do they plan to say? I mean, how do I explain all this to Jason?"

Dominic shrugged. "That's up to you. They won't tell him who his father is, that much I know. They're determined to make Jason and you members of the clan. They realize you're Jason's aunt, that he doesn't know that, and it won't be divulged. In their minds, you're his mother. You two are to reap the rewards of a large extended family. My wishes on the subject didn't come into play."

Tessa sat down on the swing, angled so she could see Dominic clearly.

"You don't want us there," she said, "with your family?"

Dominic frowned and dragged a restless hand through his hair.

"I wasn't given time to even think about it, was simply *told* how things were going to be. I don't like being dictated to, Tessa, about anything. I haven't spoken to anyone in my family since that meeting Thursday night."

"I see," she said quietly.

He *didn't* want her and Jason interacting with his family, she thought. There was a painful knot in her stomach. That realization hurt her, which was ridiculous. Why should she care if Dominic did, or did not, want her underfoot? It didn't matter one way or another.

But Jason? He didn't even wish to witness his son being

a part of the Bonelli family? He now acknowledged that Jason was his child. Didn't that mean anything to him? He had said he'd view Jason as one more responsibility. Dear heaven, how cold and empty that sounded. What about love? Hadn't Dominic even considered that he might come to love his son?

Tessa, stop it, she told herself. She should count her blessings and be eternally grateful that Dominic had no intention of exploring any deeper emotions regarding Jason. A "responsibility" was a nonentity, a "thing" he had to tend to. It was safer in the long run for her and Jason if Dominic stayed emotionally detached.

But how could a man do that with his own son?

A part of her wanted to shout with joy that Jason was hers, the threat of losing him gone. Yet, she was also sad that Dominic refused to interact as a father with Jason, give his child a father's love.

Her mind was becoming a muddled maze once more. As of that moment, she refused to think about *anything*.

"Where's Jason?" Dominic said, bringing Tessa from her tangled thoughts.

"What? Oh." She glanced at the sky, seeing the last streaks of the sunset beginning to fade in the gathering dusk. "He should be home soon. He's in town playing with Jeremiah. Poor little Jeremiah has chicken pox and was so bored. His mother drove out and—"

Dominic lunged to his feet to tower over Tessa. His sudden motion caused the swing to wiggle wildly. She shifted against the back, and looked up at him in shock.

"You allowed Jason to spend time with a child who has chicken pox?" Dominic said none too quietly. "I assume Jason has already had them."

"Well, no, he hasn't but—"

"Then what in the hell is he doing playing with this

Jeremiah kid? Good Lord, Tessa, where was your common sense?''

Tessa jumped to her feet and curled her hands into fists planted on her hips.

''You just hold it right there, mister,'' she said, matching his volume. ''Don't you dare question my decisions as Jason's mother. Not ever.''

''We're talking about a contagious disease, lady!''

''Oh, shut up, Bonelli. I have enough brains to know that chicken pox are contagious. Jeremiah shared them with everyone at Rainbow's End. Jason has been exposed and I fully expect him to be a polka-dot cowboy in a couple of weeks. The damage is done. There's absolutely no harm in his being near Jeremiah now.''

She pointed one finger in the air.

''And another thing. It has been medically proven, Mr. Bonelli, that childhood diseases are best dealt with *as* a child. If Jason has chicken pox at five, he won't miss school later, *and* he won't run the risk of getting them as an adult and perhaps being seriously ill.''

''Oh. Well, how was I supposed to know all that?''

''Why should you care?''

''Damn it, he's my son!''

A sudden heavy silence fell as the impact of Dominic's statement hung in the air. They stared at each other, expressions of confusion on both of their faces.

Dominic finally exhaled a pent-up breath that puffed out his cheeks, then dragged both hands down his face.

''Man,'' he said quietly, ''I'm a mess. My mind is spaghetti.'' He chuckled, and then shook his head. Tessa sure was on a rip. ''You're something, Tessa Russell, you really are,'' he said, matching her smile. In the next instant, he was serious again. ''This whole thing blindsided me. I'll get a handle on it, though. But I don't want you to worry further that I might seek custody of Jason. I won't. I just need some time to adjust to the fact that he's my son.

"I never intended to have a wife and children because I've had the responsibility of a large family since I was fourteen years old. And I'm *still* responsible for them, always will be, I guess. Don't worry, I'll get Jason's existence into perspective."

"Just another Bonelli in a long line of Bonellis," Tessa said, frowning.

"Well, no, not quite. I have an even greater sense of responsibility toward Jason. When I thought he was the son of one of my brothers, I wanted him, as a Bonelli, to live in a house that was sound, in proper repair."

Tessa opened her mouth to retort, but Dominic raised one hand to silence her.

"Don't spin into a tizzy. When you get that temper of yours going, you're a handful, and I'm one exhausted man."

"Mmm," she said with an indignant little sniff.

"Believe me, Tessa, I respect what you've done with your life and the way you've provided for Jason. You're to be commended for starting Rainbow's End from scratch, devising a means whereby you could be with Jason on a daily basis and still earn a living. You've carried a helluva load on your shoulders."

"Oh, well..." She shrugged.

"I'm not diminishing anything you've done. If you view this from a practical standpoint, it's very simple. I'm in a position to smooth out the rough edges, such as a leaky roof, faulty plumbing, a coat of paint here and there.

"Jason deserves that, and so do you, as a matter of fact. I can provide those things, and I intend to do it. I'll also set up a trust fund for his college education, and give you monthly support payments."

"No."

"Yes. Jason is not just another Bonelli in a long line of Bonellis. He *is* my son. Therefore, my responsibility for him is greater than it is for my sisters, brothers, nieces and nephews. Does this make sense to you?"

It was all so cold, so clinical, Tessa thought. She was really getting tired of hearing Dominic say the word "responsibility."

"Does it?" he said.

Tessa sighed. "I suppose so."

"Good. Well, I'd better shove off."

Then Tessa glanced up and saw a cloud of dust in the distance, along with the bobbing headlights of a car.

"Dominic, wait. I'm fairly certain that's Jeremiah's mother driving this way. Jason has talked about his friend Dominic coming to visit him. I tried to explain that you're very busy and might not be able to come out here, but he was adamant, convinced you would. It would mean a lot to him if you could stay a few minutes to say hello."

Dominic looked in the direction of the approaching vehicle.

"Sure," he said. "No problem."

Then why, he wondered, was his heart suddenly thudding like a bongo drum? Dumb question. Easy answer. This would be the first time he'd seen Jason since learning that the boy was his son. Well, fine. That was the reason he'd come all the way out here...to see Jason and put him in the proper slot in his mind.

He had *not* driven to Rainbow's End with the intention of kissing Tessa Russell. But kiss her he had, and it was not going to be easily forgotten. He hadn't wanted to *stop* kissing her. The bottom line? He'd wanted to make love with her, had ached with that need.

Crazy. It was really crazy. She wasn't his type. She

didn't play the fast-lane game of no commitments, no to-morrows. Tessa was hearth, home and motherhood, the kind of woman he stayed a hundred miles away from.

But, oh, how he'd wanted her.

Understandable, he assured himself. He was emotionally drained and her tears had caught him off guard. Plus, she was an attractive, sensuous, *very sensuous,* woman who had responded completely to his kisses. There was an ex-tremely passionate female within the fresh-air-and-sunshine, jean-clad exterior of Tessa Russell.

Fine. He'd figured out why she'd been capable of tying him in knots, why he'd wanted her with an intensity far beyond anything he could remember experiencing before. And that was that.

The car stopped in front of the house, Jason got out and hollered "'Bye" as he slammed the door. Jeremiah's mother tooted the horn and waved at Tessa before turning the car around and driving away.

Even in the rapidly falling darkness, Dominic could clearly see Jason as he ran up the front walkway.

My son, his mind hammered. *This child is my son.*

"Dominic," Jason yelled. "You came to see me. I knew you would. I told you, Mom. Dominic is here."

Jason barreled up the steps and virtually launched him-self at Dominic. Out of pure reflex, Dominic opened his arms to catch the human missile. In the next instant, Jason had his legs wrapped around Dominic's waist and his little arms encircling his neck.

"You came to see me," Jason said, beaming.

"Yeah," Dominic said, unable to keep from smiling. "Yeah, I came." He paused. "Whew. You're quite a load, sport. I've never held a five-year-old cowboy before."

He hadn't? Tessa thought, staring at the pair. What did

he do with his nieces and nephews? Pat them on the head as though they were cute puppies?

"My gosh, Jason," Dominic said, "you've sure put some miles on your cowboy suit. It *was* bright red, but it's two shades lighter now. The white fringe is missing in spots, too. Been riding the range a lot?"

"Yep," Jason said.

"No joke," Tessa said, laughing. "It's been worn and washed every day since you gave it to him. I mean it, he has *not* worn anything other than that suit."

"No kidding?" Dominic said. "That's great, really great. I'm glad you like it, Jason."

"It's my bestis thing in the whole wide world."

"Fantastic," Dominic said.

Oh, look at them, Tessa thought. Even as dark as it was becoming, she could see the mirror images of father and son. The shape of their heads, the tawny skin, the outline of their features, on and on the list went. And the quirky little matching nitches in their ears were there, she knew, hidden beneath the silky thickness of their black hair.

They were beautiful. Both of them.

"Mom," Jason said, "can Dominic have ice cream with us? Please?"

"Oh, honey, Dominic has to leave. He was waiting to say hello to you, but he really has to go back into town now."

"I've got time for a dish of ice cream," Dominic said. *He did?* she thought in surprise. "You do?"

"Yippee!" Jason yelled.

"No," Dominic said. "Correct that. I have time for a dish of *gelato*."

"What?" Jason said.

"*Gelato* is ice cream," Dominic said. "It's time you learned some Italian, kiddo, and *gelato* is a good place to start."

Chapter Thirteen

"*Gelato!*"

Jason accented his holler with a jump into the kitchen, landing with a loud thud on both feet.

"*Gelato!*" Jump. "*Gelato!*" Jump.

"Jason, enough," Tessa yelled.

"I can say *gelato*, Mom," he said, sliding onto his chair at the table.

"No kidding," she said dryly, placing a plate of scrambled eggs and bacon in front of him. "Eat your breakfast. It's a new day, a new week, and you can start it off right by cleaning your plate."

Jason shoveled in a forkful of eggs. Tessa sat down across from him with a mug of coffee and a plate containing two slices of raisin toast.

"Don't you think it was really cool of Dominic to teach me how to say *gelato?*" Jason said.

"*Gelato* is cool," she said, then paused. "That's a joke,

Jason. *Gelato* is ice cream, which is cold, as in *cool*. Get it?''

"Oh," he said, nodding. "Yeah. Dominic said he'd see me again soon."

"Yes," she said wearily. "I heard him tell you that last night."

What she'd heard and observed during Dominic's extended stay to have a dish of ice cream—forever to be known as *gelato* apparently—had simply added to her state of confusion.

Dominic, she mused, *was a walking, talking contradiction.* He'd firmly declared that Jason was to be nothing more to him than a financial responsibility.

Then he'd turned right around and joined them for a snack, laughing and talking with Jason as though they were best buddies. And if that wasn't muddling enough, Dominic had decided that it was time Jason learned some Italian, for Pete's sake.

Tessa sighed, then nibbled absently on a corner of toast.

She'd dreamed about Dominic. She'd realized that the moment she'd opened her eyes this morning. The dreams had been vivid and sensual. They'd been kissing, touching, reaching for each other time and again.

The backgrounds had shifted, one into the next. They'd been on the porch, then in a vast field of wildflowers. Her jeans and blouse had suddenly been replaced by a gorgeous full-length, pale blue dress that swirled around her like gossamer wings. She'd been so beautiful, Dominic so handsome in a tuxedo, and they'd been dancing in a huge, crowded ballroom.

He'd kissed her again, a searing, heated, hungry kiss that had consumed her with passion. Then...

"Mom?"

Tessa blinked and stared at Jason for a moment as she came back to earth. ''What can I do for you, sir?''

''You look weird, or somethin'. You gots a funny smile on your face.''

''I do? I did? Oh, well, I was thinking about something funny. Eat your eggs.''

Funny? she mentally repeated. *Not even close. Dangerous was the word that applied.* When Dominic had touched her, kissed her, held her, she'd melted, simply dissolved. The remembrance of it all, even the mere memories, caused desire to thrum within her, low and hot. The man was a masculine menace, and she wasn't getting within ten feet of him again.

''Mom,'' Jason said, ''somebody's at the door.''

''Oh.'' She got to her feet, then looked at Jason. ''Eggs, mister.''

''Gelato!'' Jason said as she left the room.

''Give me strength,'' Tessa muttered.

At the door, she greeted Joe Bonelli pleasantly, then invited him in.

''How are you?'' he said, a serious expression on his face.

''Never better,'' she said, breezily waving a hand through the air.

''Then why aren't you smiling?''

''I'm *not* smiling?'' She plastered a bright smile onto her face. ''There.''

''Nice try, no cigar. Have you heard from Dom?''

''Oh, my, yes. The man in question was here last evening. He told me about the Bonelli family meeting, how you all shoved Jason and me down his throat, as far as informing him we were to be invited to outings and what have you, and that no one will divulge the truth to Jason.

''Dominic plans to be financially responsible for his son,

but not acknowledge him.'' *And Dominic Bonelli had kissed her senseless.* ''That's that.''

''Dom was furious at that meeting,'' Joe said. ''Man, was he hot. I was wondering if my best suit needed to go to the cleaners before I was buried in it. You should have seen my mother, Tessa. She stood toe to toe with Dom, and told him the way it was going to be. That was something to behold.''

''Really?'' Tessa said, a genuine smile now appearing. ''Oh, I would have loved to have seen that discussion.''

Joe chuckled. ''It was something, all right. Frank and I were shaking in our shorts. We're staying clear of Dom until he cools off.''

''Hi, Joe,'' Jason said, running into the room. ''Wanna hear me say *gelato?*''

''No,'' Tessa said.

''*Gelato!*'' Jason boomed.

''I may never eat ice cream again,'' Tessa said, rolling her eyes heavenward.

''*Gelato,* huh?'' Joe said, smiling at Jason. ''Who taught you how to say ice cream in Italian?''

''Dominic. He's my friend. He said I should learn Italian stuff. I couldn't wear my cowboy suit today 'cause it was too late for my mom to wash it. Can you say Italian stuff?''

''*Sì,*'' Joe said, nodding. He held out his right hand. *''Diventare amici.''*

''What's that? What's that?'' Jason said, hopping up and down.

''To make friends,'' Joe said, ''or to be friends. Shake on it, pal.''

''Cool,'' Jason said, pumping Joe's hand. ''Italian stuff is so neato. Cool, cool, cool. I'm going to tell all the kids how to say *gelato.*''

''Oh, dandy,'' Tessa said.

"Hey, Joe," a man called from outside. "Are we doing this, or taking a nap?"

"Get started," Joe hollered over his shoulder. "I'll be right there." He looked at Tessa again. "We're going to start stripping the paint off your house today. We'll be using a heat gun to blister up the old paint to make it easier to scrape off, with less mess. You won't have to worry about the kids because we don't let the debris fly around."

"Yes, all right," Tessa said.

"I'll bring in some charts so you can pick the color you want. Hey, Jason, what color do you want your house painted?"

"Red. Just like my cowboy suit."

"No," Tessa said, laughing. "Oh, good grief, no."

An hour later, Tessa told Joe the number of the little box on the chart that showed the color she'd chosen for the exterior of the house.

An hour after that, she realized she'd picked the same pale blue shade of the beautiful dress she'd worn in her dream about Dominic.

That evening, Tessa had just returned to the living room after reading a story to Jason and tucking him in bed, when the telephone rang. She sat down on the sofa at the same time as she picked up the receiver.

"Hello?"

"Tessa? This is Delores Bonelli."

Oh, my goodness, Tessa thought with a flicker of panic. *Dominic's mother.*

"Hello, Mrs. Bonelli," she said, hoping her voice was steady.

"No, no, call me Delores." She paused. "Tessa, I would have preferred to have this conversation in person, but Joe explained that you're very busy during the day at your Rainbow's End, and your evenings must be spent tending to Jason.''

"Yes. Yes, I am busy through the day, and Jason just went to bed.''

"So this call will just have to do for now. I'm so eager to meet you and Jason. We're planning a family barbecue here at my home Sunday afternoon at three, and I'm hoping you'll agree to come.''

"Well, I don't know, Mrs.... Delores. Dominic isn't pleased in the least with your plans to include me and Jason in your family activities.''

"*Your* family, Tessa. Yours and Jason's. I realize that Dominic is being difficult, but I'm ignoring him for the moment. I'll invite him to the barbecue, but I doubt he'll attend. You've met my other sons, so we won't *all* be strangers to you. When you first arrive, you can tell me quietly what you've said to Jason regarding who we are, and I'll let the others know.

"You can be assured that your wishes will be respected. None of us will tell Jason who his father is, either. Will you join us?''

Tessa took a steadying breath before she answered.

"Yes, Jason and I will be delighted to attend. Is it potluck? Shall I bring something?''

"Yes, it *is* potluck. Since you're a member of our family and not a guest, how about bringing a dessert?''

"That will be fine.''

"Would you like someone to pick you up?''

"No, I'll drive in if you'll give me directions to your house.''

A few minutes later, Tessa replaced the receiver, then pressed her hands to her cheeks.

Dear heaven, had she done the right thing? She could

have politely refused Delores's invitation, making it clear that she and Jason were *not* going to be swept up into the Bonelli family.

But she knew deep within her heart that that wouldn't be fair to Jason. There was no reason for him to grow up with only her as his family, when a loving group of people were ready and willing to welcome him into their embrace.

Okay, Tessa, she told herself, *admit it. She* wanted to be part of a large family, too. She'd been so alone for such a long time, and the image in her mind of the Bonelli clan brought an instant smile to her lips.

And Dominic? Oh, heavens, what about Dominic? He was confusing her in so many ways. He said one thing about his responsibility-only relationship with Jason, then turned right around and did just the opposite. Jason was enthralled with his new friend; he thought Dominic was wonderful. He had definitely made an impression on Jason.

"What about you, madam?" she said aloud.

Impression was too lightweight a word for the impact Dominic Bonelli had had on *her*. The man had thrown her totally off kilter and awakened her femininity. He had evoked a desire within her that continued to smolder like a glowing ember.

Well, she was aware of it and, therefore, was in control of it. She'd interact with Dominic just as she did with all the other Bonellis. She'd be chatty, friendly—just another member of the family.

As for the barbecue on Sunday, Delores had said she didn't expect Dominic to even be there. Fine. The first gathering with the Bonellis would be less stressful without Dominic there.

Yes, everything was under control. *Her* control.

The imperative thing to concentrate on now was how to explain to Jason who the Bonellis were. It was so important for her son's emotional well-being that she handle this in the correct manner. She'd use the time available to her between now and Sunday to carefully outline what she would tell him.

And she would not spend one minute dwelling on Dominic Bonelli.

Early Sunday afternoon, Tessa smoothed chocolate icing over the two-layer chocolate cake she'd baked. Jason sat at the table, busily licking a chocolate-coated spatula.

The outside of the house was now painted the lovely shade of pale blue that Tessa had chosen. The crew had returned yesterday to paint the porch and trim white so it would have time to dry before the children returned to Rainbow's End on Monday. She and Jason were using the back door during the weekend.

She finished the cake, placed it carefully in a carrier, tended to the dishes, then sat down opposite Jason at the table.

"Jason," she said, "I'd like to talk to you."

"'Kay," he said, still licking the spatula.

"There's not a speck of chocolate left on there." She reached over and took the spatula from his hands. "You'd best quit licking before I don't have a spatula."

"That was yummy," he said.

"Good. Sweetheart, do you remember the story we read sometimes about the lonely little bunny?"

"Sure. That's Buddy Bunny."

"Why was he lonely?"

"'Cause he didn't have a family like the other bunnies, 'cause he lost them when he was a baby bunny, but he didn't know that, 'cause babies don't 'member stuff good."

"Right. Then he met a bunny who *did* remember Buddy's family, and he took him to meet them."

"And he was happy, happy, happy. Can I have some *gelato?*"

"No, not now. That spatula of icing was your snack. Jason, sometimes *people* have a family they didn't know about."

"Like Buddy?"

"Yes, just like Buddy."

"That would be cool."

"Well, that's exactly what has happened to you, to us. I have you, you have me, but now there are others in our family, too. It's all too confusing to explain to you, but what it means is that you have a grandmother, aunts, uncles and cousins." *And a father, Jason. You have a father but, God help me, I can't tell you that.* "We have a big family, Jason, who are very excited about meeting you."

Jason's eyes widened and he sat up straighter in the chair.

"Really, Mom? Really for honest?"

"Really for honest," she said, nodding. She smiled at him warmly.

"Who are they? Where do they live? Can we go see them?" He jumped off the chair and grabbed her hand. "Come on, Mom, let's go get them."

"We'll go this afternoon. We'll have bubble baths, change our clothes, then it will be time to go."

"Wow. Neato. Who are they?"

"The...the Bonellis, Jason." She lifted him onto her lap. "The Bonellis are our family."

"Dominic? Dominic is my family?"

"Honey, listen. We're going to a picnic, a barbecue. Joe, Frank, Vince and Benny will be there, and lots of other Bonellis. Dominic won't be able to come, though."

Jason frowned. "Why not? Doesn't he want to see me find my lost family like Buddy Bunny did?"

"Of course he does, but he's very busy. You like Joe and the others you've already met, and there are more for you to get to know. There will be kids for you to play with, too. Those are your cousins. It's going to be wonderful, you'll see. That's why I baked the cake. We're taking it to the picnic."

"*Buono!*" Jason yelled, sliding off her lap. "That means 'good.' Joe taught me that. Can I wear my cowboy suit?"

"No, not this time. It's worse for wear, you know. I'd like you to look very nice."

"Oh. Well, okay. This is *buono,* Mom. We gots a family. A family, Mommy. Don't you think this is super, really neato?"

"Yes." *I hope so, Jason. Oh, dear Lord, I hope I'm doing the right thing.* "Now, off to the bathtub. You can go first."

Jason started toward the door, then stopped, turning to look at Tessa again.

"Mommy?"

"Yes, honey?"

"Now that we found our family, they won't get lost again, will they? Buddy Bunny got to keep his family when he found them. Can we be with the Bonellis forever, Mom?"

The achy sensation of threatening tears clutched Tessa's throat.

"Forever, Jason," she whispered. "I promise. We won't lose our family now that we've found them. We won't lose them ever again."

Chapter Fourteen

Just after five o'clock, Dominic parked next to the last car in the row of vehicles in front of his mother's house. As he turned off the ignition, he could hear the mingled sounds of children's laughter and the shouts of adult voices in the distance, reaching him through the open windows of his car.

He folded his arms over the top of the steering wheel, leaning forward as he stared out the front window.

In his mind's eye, he could clearly envision the scene taking place in the large yard behind the house. He'd attended gatherings such as this countless times in the past, although he'd made only quick, token appearances on numerous occasions.

On the thick carpet of green grass, a volleyball game would be in progress between the adults of the clan interested in taking part in the strenuous sport. Others would be sitting in lawn chairs in the shade of the tall mulberry trees, keeping watch over the children as they played.

A long picnic table that Frank and Benny had built years before would be covered in the traditional red-and-white-checked vinyl cloth. His brothers had constructed the table so that as the family grew in numbers and added space was needed, another section could be easily attached.

There would be high chairs, playpens, a multitude of toys and a group of diaper bags. The half-dozen barbecues would be standing in a row, the coals now beginning to glow, at the ready to receive the towers of thick steaks piled on platters.

Yes, he mused, he knew exactly what was happening beyond his view behind the house. Only this time, there was a major difference.

Tessa was there.

And so was Jason.

His son.

Dominic sighed and sank back in the plush seat.

Why had he come? He'd had no intention of attending this barbecue. That decision had been firmly in place when he'd awakened that morning, but as the hours of the day crept slowly by, his solid resolve had begun to crumble, chipped away by the silence and solitude within the walls of his house.

Images of Tessa had taunted him, and the remembrance of the kisses shared with her had caused heat to coil low and aching in his body.

When he'd forced his thoughts away from Tessa, they fell on Jason. Jason, with his sparkling dark eyes, excited laughter, and the memory of how incredible it had been to hold the little boy in his arms.

Then Tessa would nudge her way back into his mental

vision. He'd see her crying, her pain his own. He'd see her smiling. He'd see her lips moist from his kisses, and her expressive brown eyes smoky with desire, with the want of him.

Back and forth, his mind had gone. Back and forth. Tessa. Jason. Tessa. Jason.

Unable to bear the infuriating torment another moment, he'd stormed out of the house in a rage.

And here he was, he thought dryly, hiding in his car like an intimidated kid. Why was he hesitating? Why didn't he just march into the backyard as he normally would?

Was it because he'd taken the stand that the family would not now, nor ever, tell him what to do? Did he feel he'd be losing face, diminish his role as head of the Bonellis by making an appearance at an event *they'd* dictated would take place, without asking for his approval or opinion?

No, damn it, that wasn't it. One Sunday afternoon barbecue couldn't erase the many years of his being in charge, the one responsible for all of them, the one they turned to for advice and guidance.

He was sitting in his car like an idiot because of Tessa, and because of Jason Robert Russell...Bonelli.

"Hell," he said, smacking the steering wheel with the palm of one hand.

He got out of the car, started to slam the door, then closed it with a quiet click followed by a snort of self-disgust.

With heavy steps, he strode along the paved walkway at the side of the house, coming to a halt at the five-foot high, redwood gate. His gaze swept over the yard, seeing everything as he'd imagined it.

He ignored the sudden increased tempo of his heart as

he sought, then found, Tessa. She was playing volleyball. There was a bright smile on her face and a vibrant aura of carefree happiness emanating from her as she jumped high to strike the ball.

"Way to go, Tessa," Carmen yelled. "Our point. Our point. We're clobbering you do-nothings."

"It ain't over till it's over, Miss Mouth," Vince called, from the other side of the net.

"One more point and it's over," Tessa said, laughing. "Our serve. Joe, do your stuff."

As the players rotated their positions, Dominic blinked in surprise as he realized he was smiling. He replaced the expression with a frown as he ran one hand over the back of his neck.

Damn, Tessa looked so...so *right* in the midst of his family. She was obviously having fun. She deserved it, and he was sincerely pleased that she was reaping the rewards of being welcomed into the warm embrace of the Bonelli clan.

And Jason? How was he doing? Dominic wondered, his eyes darting around the expanse. Yes, there he was. Lord, he looked so much like the other Bonelli kids, it had been difficult to pinpoint him for a moment.

The older children were playing "wheelbarrow," with Frank's nine-year-old son, Tony, holding up Jason's feet as the boy scrambled on his hands. He was giggling so hard, he lost his balance and toppled forward, rolling around in the grass and laughing.

"*Buono!*" Jason yelled. "That was *buono*. Let's do it again, Tony."

"We won!" Carmen shouted. "Ho-ho, we beat the socks off you guys!"

Delores suddenly swung a brass bell in the air that was a replica of one used to call students into school in frontier days. Everyone stopped immediately and looked in her direction.

"Attention, attention," she said, beaming. "You all know your assignments. There are little ones needing their hands washed, the food is to be brought out and you boys decide among you who's to barbecue the steaks. We'll need three cooks, per usual. Tessa, you can help bring the food from the house. Jason, *bambino,* go with the others and wash your hands. *Óra di colazione!"*

"Wow," Jason said to Tony. "Nana talks Italian stuff really great. What did she say?"

"It's lunchtime, dinnertime, whatever," Tony said with a shrug. "You know, time to eat. Come on, Jason, I'll race you to the house."

As everyone moved to follow Delores's directives, Dominic stepped back out of view, leaning against the house and closing his eyes.

A chill of loneliness, of total isolation, swept over him with such intensity that he shivered. He opened his eyes and stared up at the heavens.

His family, he thought, didn't need him for anything.

Of course an event as simple as a Sunday barbecue could take place without his supervision. Delores was in her drill-sergeant mode, everyone snapped to attention and loved it. But it went deeper than that. He'd absently realized the other night that it had been a couple of years since a family meeting had been called. That fact hadn't meant anything to him at the time.

But now? The truth hit him like punishing blows. Everyone was set, taken care of, getting on well with their lives. They were making their own decisions. They were *responsible* for themselves.

They didn't need him anymore.

He dragged both hands down his face and drew a shuddering breath.

And Tessa? Jason? Hell, they were obviously doing fine, were comfortable in the midst of the clan and had been accepted as part of the family. Except for sprucing up her house and providing extra money each month, he had no place in Tessa's life, either.

Damn it, Bonelli, he fumed. *What in the blue blazes is the matter with you?* He should be relieved to know that the role he'd had since he was fourteen was at an end. He was free to live his own life, really live it, without looking over his shoulder all the time to determine which family member needed what.

He should feel as though a tremendous weight had been lifted from his shoulders. Yes, he was free to live.

And love?

Dominic stiffened and frowned.

And love? Where had that bizarre thought come from? Love, as in fall in love with a special woman, marry, have children? Join the rank and file of upwardly mobile yuppies with a checklist of hearth, home and two-point-five kids?

Hell, no!

There was no room for that malarkey in his life. He had all he could handle being responsible for the multitude of Bonellis, who looked to him for...

Nothing.

"Jason," Tessa yelled, "don't roll around in the grass or you'll have to wash your hands again. Come sit down, sweetheart."

"Can I sit by Tony?"

"You sure can," Frank said. "You two look so much alike, though, I'd better be careful I don't take the wrong boy home."

"I'm bigger than Jason, Dad," Tony said.

Frank laughed. "That you are, son."

"I'm getting bigger," Jason said. "When I grow up, I'm going to be tall and have muscles like my friend Dominic."

"Dominic's your friend, huh?" Frank said.

"Yep," Jason said.

Dominic narrowed his eyes. *I'm his father!*

Before he realized he'd moved, Dominic pushed off from the side of the house, opened the gate and entered the yard, slamming the gate closed behind him. The noise caused all heads to turn in his direction, and he stopped dead in his tracks, now acutely aware of what he'd done.

"Dominic!" Jason yelled, running toward him. "You came."

As Jason flung himself at Dominic, he lifted the boy, holding him close.

"Yeah, I came," he said quietly. He didn't know why. He didn't even know if he really wanted to be there but... "I'm here."

"Know what?" Jason said, wrapping his arms around Dominic's neck. "Me and my mom gots a family now. We're Bonellis, sort of, 'cause we found our family we didn't know we had 'cause they were lost and... It's like Buddy Bunny. Isn't that neato? You're my friend *and* my family, Dominic. Don't you think that's cool?"

"Very cool," Dominic said, setting Jason back on his feet.

He straightened and swept his gaze over the throng, feeling like a bug under a microscope as everyone continued to stare at him. His eyes collided with Tessa's, and she smiled at him tentatively.

She moved around the table to walk slowly toward him.

Her smile grew, the warmth of it reaching the depths of her brown eyes.

"Hello, Dominic," she said, stopping in front of him. "It's nice to see you. Jason and I are having a marvelous time with your wonderful family."

"Say *ciao* 'stead of 'hello,'" Jason told her. "That's Italian. Mom, they're our family, too. That's what you told me."

"Yes," she said, still looking directly into Dominic's eyes. "They're our family, too."

Tessa, Dominic's mind hummed. She was so pretty. She was wearing jeans and a pink string-sweater, her face was flushed with a healthy glow from the exertion of the volleyball game, her hair was a fetching disarray of silky, strawberry-blond curls.

He wanted to kiss her, hold her, feel her feminine softness nestled against him. Heat was coiling low in his body and his heart was beating a rapid tattoo.

Oh, hello, Dominic, ciao, Tessa mused. In jeans and a burgundy-colored knit shirt, he looked tall and massive, so strong, so male. She had the nearly uncontrollable urge to fling herself into his arms and capture his lips with hers to savor the ecstasy of his kiss.

"Who's cooking steaks?" Delores said, breaking the silence in the yard.

Dominic's head snapped up as he tore his gaze from Tessa's.

"I am," he said. "I've never done it before, but how tough can it be?"

"Dom's going to barbecue?" Maria whispered to Carmen, and Frank's wife, Lydia. "Is that weird?"

"I think," Carmen said thoughtfully, "that's Tessa."

"Huh?" Maria said.

"Shh," Carmen said.

"Interesting," Joe said.

"You've got that straight, big brother," Carmen said.

"Huh?" Maria said.

"Shh," Carmen, Joe and Lydia said in unison.

The beehive of activity resumed, along with the volume-on-high chatter. Delores watched Dominic stride across the yard to the row of barbecues, with Jason close on his heels. Dominic hunkered down to speak to Jason, explaining that it wasn't safe for little boys to be near the fires.

"Oh," Jason said. "'Kay. Will you sit by me when we eat? I'm by Tony, and you can be with us."

"What about your mom?" Dominic said.

"She can be by us, too. 'Kay?"

"'Kay," he said, ruffling Jason's hair. "Now scoot, sport."

Jason dashed off and Dominic stepped closer to the barbecues.

"You burn it," Joe said, "you eat it."

Dominic laughed and Delores smiled, looking as if her heart were nearly bursting with love as she gazed at her eldest son.

"*Buono*, my Dom," she whispered. "*Buono.*"

When Dominic sat down next to Tessa to begin the meal, she fully expected to become tense within moments and unable to eat any of the vast selection of delicious food.

To her own amazement, her nerves stayed steady. She was, admittedly, acutely aware of Dominic's proximity, but there was a strange feeling of rightness to his being by her side.

Jason was next to Dominic, then Tony. Carmen sat on Tessa's left. When Dominic reached over to cut Jason's meat into bite-size pieces, Tessa and Carmen exchanged surprised glances, ending with Carmen winking at her.

Everyone managed to eat and talk at the same time. Dominic was kidded good-naturedly about his lack of barbecuing skills, with Frank telling him not to quit his day job, nor to think about becoming a chef.

Tessa had difficulty keeping track of the buzz of topics being discussed, deciding it must take practice to interact with so many people at once.

"Rainbow's End," Carmen said, gaining Tessa's full attention. "I love the name of your day-care center. Do you have a main room where the kids gather?"

"Yes," Tessa said.

"Well, I was thinking it would be fun to paint a big rainbow on one wall. There could be fluffy clouds, and birds, too."

"Oh, that sounds fantastic, Carmen."

"Hold it," Dominic said.

The two women turned to look at him, Tessa surprised he'd heard what Carmen had said as he'd appeared to be listening to Vince.

"You can do the rainbow," Dominic said, "after the interior of the house has been painted. It's going to be done top to bottom. It'll be easier to paint the wall first, than have to go around a rainbow and other stuff. You'll have to wait a week or so, Carmen."

"Paint the interior?" Tessa said.

"That's fine, Dom," Carmen said. "Maybe we'll pick a pale blue for that wall. You know, like a sky, then I can come in and add the clouds, birds and rainbow."

"Paint the interior?" Tessa repeated, but no one paid any attention to her.

"Good plan," Frank said from farther down the table. "We don't want to dink around having to paint the edges of little birds. We'll slap on the sky color, *then* you can go nuts, Carmen.''

''Yep,'' Benny said from another direction. ''That's the plan. It's a done deal.''

''But,'' Tessa said.

Carmen patted her hand and smiled. ''Go with the flow, Tessa. You'll get used to us. You'll come to love us, if we don't drive you crazy first.''

Tessa laughed. ''Whatever,'' she said, rolling her eyes heavenward.

You'll come to love us, her mind echoed.

You'll come to love us, Dominic mentally repeated.

They looked at each other at the same time, as though the matching messages in their minds had been heard by the other. Their expressions were questioning, accompanied by slight frowns of confusion. An instant later, they averted their eyes, then feigned interest in a debate taking place on a movie currently receiving mixed reviews.

The desserts were consumed, then moans and groans followed, with laments of having eaten too much, and the inability to move for a week. Delores announced they could hibernate like well-fed bears *after* the table was cleared.

Darkness was inching its way across the sky, chasing the vibrant sunset to the horizon, as fussing babies were lifted into soothing arms and belongings were gathered.

Lydia approached Tessa, speaking to her in a quiet voice.

''Tessa,'' she said, ''Tony would like Jason to spend the night with us next Saturday. I didn't want to ask in front of Jason. Despite the difference in their ages, they get along great. What do you think?''

''Jason's never spent a night away from home. I can't

guarantee he won't change his mind in the middle of the night.''

Lydia shrugged. ''No problem. I can handle that.''

''Well, then I guess it would be fine if he wants to.'' Tessa paused. ''Oh, wait a minute. Jason was exposed to chicken pox about ten days ago. Add another week to that and he's liable to be a speckled cowboy.''

''My kids have had chicken pox,'' Lydia said. ''If Jason is still feeling all right, he's welcome to come. If the nasty little spots pop out while he's with us, so be it.''

Tessa laughed. ''You're a brave soul, Lydia.'' She Glanced around. ''Jason, come here please.''

As Jason ran across the yard, Dominic finished helping Benny dump the ashes from the barbecues into a metal pail, then strolled toward Tessa. He heard Tessa explain to Jason the invitation for the following Saturday.

''Wow,'' Jason said. ''Can I go to Tony's, Mom? Can I? Please?''

''If you want to.''

''Yes, yes, yes,'' he said, hopping up and down. ''Hey, Tony, guess what?'' He took off at a run to find his new friend.

''Hi, Dom,'' Lydia said, glancing up at him as he joined them. ''How do you like barbecuing steaks?''

He chuckled. ''My technique needs work.''

''Lydia,'' Frank called, ''let's hit the road, babe.''

''I'll call you this week, Tessa,'' Lydia said, ''to iron out the details for Jason's sleep-over. It was so wonderful to meet you and your son.'' She gave Tessa a quick hug. ''Bye for now.''

''Goodbye and thank you,'' Tessa said, then watched Lydia hurry away. ''Well, I'd better round up my cowpoke and head for the hills.''

''Tessa, wait,'' Dominic said quietly.

"Yes?"

"Jason is going to be at Lydia and Frank's Saturday night, so that solves your babysitting problem. I was wondering if you'd like to go out to dinner? How does seven o'clock sound?"

Tessa cocked her head slightly to one side, studied Dominic's face and frowned.

"Why?" she said.

"Why?" he repeated, obviously startled by her response.

She folded her arms over her breasts. "Yes. It's a reasonable question. Why do you want to take me to dinner? To discuss additional plans for my house? That would be a novelty. So far, I've been the last to know what's going to be done. Or will you have your briefcase in hand, ready to produce the document I'm supposed to sign? Or—"

"Damn it," Dominic interrupted, none too quietly "I'm inviting you out to dinner because I want to be with you. Is that simple enough for you, Ms. Russell?"

"Sounds plain to me," Carmen said from somewhere in the distance.

"Me, too," Joe added.

"Dinner and dancing," Maria said wistfully. "I remember dancing. That was back when I could see my feet. Pick a place that has a band, Dom."

"Oh, good Lord," he said, dropping his chin to his chest. "In my next life, I'm going to be an only child, I swear it."

"Tessa," Delores said, "Dominic is getting grumpy. Answer his question."

"Dominic Bonelli," Tessa shouted, then burst into laughter, "I'd be delighted to have dinner with you at seven o'clock on Saturday night!" She dissolved in a fit of giggles.

A cheer went up from the Bonelli clan.

Chapter Fifteen

When the alarm clock rang early the next morning, Tessa shut it off, then stretched lazily while deciding to indulge in an extra five minutes in bed.

She had, she realized, as she became fully awake, a new sense of anticipation about the day. In fact, the entire week held a nice appeal.

It wasn't as though she was accustomed to starting each day in a gloomy mood. During the past five years, she'd considered herself a happy, contented, upbeat person.

But now? Today? Well, there was just so much more in her life than had been there before. The work crew consisting of the warm, fun and friendly Bonellis would be descending again to begin painting the interior of the house. They were part of her and Jason's ''sort of'' family and were delightful.

Then, later in the week, perhaps, Carmen would come to paint the rainbow, fluffy clouds and the birds on the wall. The children would love it, and she was looking forward to seeing Carmen again.

There was more depth to her existence, a richer, deeper texture made up of wonderful people. Jason, too, was reaping the rewards of having been welcomed into the Bonelli family and she was thrilled for her son.

And to top off the hustle and bustle of the week was her dinner date with Dominic.

"Oh," she said aloud. A frown replaced the smile that had appeared as if of its own volition. "Oh, dear," she added as she remembered.

She'd acted a tad out of character by hollering to the heavens her acceptance of Dominic's invitation. Laughing her head off hadn't been a terrific thing to do, either.

It was just that she'd had such a fantastic time at the barbecue, and Dominic had been a good sport as he'd interacted with his family. He'd actually lightened up. She'd witnessed yet another layer of him and had liked it very, very much.

So, when he'd gotten crabby and slipped back into his ever-so-serious mode, she'd decided not to allow him to dim her happy frame of mind. It was a wonder the man hadn't strangled her on the spot.

Tessa threw back the blankets, left the bed and began to gather clean clothes.

She had a dinner date with Dominic Bonelli on Saturday night, she mentally repeated. How did she *really* feel about that? Dominic had said that he was inviting her out to dinner because he wanted to be with her.

Fancy that, she mused, heading for the bathroom. Well, she wanted to be with *him,* too. The unanswered question that was causing a little curl of fear in the pit of her stomach was whether or not she *should* be going out with Dominic.

She turned on the water in the bathtub, added a scoop of fragrant crystals, then watched the bubbles instantly begin to appear, filling the small room with the delicate aroma of wildflowers. She brushed her teeth, then minutes later sank with a sigh of pleasure into the warm, bubbly water.

Dominic. He was dangerous, no doubt about it. He caused her to lose control of her common sense. When held in his strong arms, she could only feel, savor the ecstasy of his kiss, the awareness of his blatant masculinity.

It was so risky to be near him. She'd vowed to never again relinquish command of her mind, body or heart, and be at the mercy of another's whims.

So, break the dinner date, she told herself.

She sighed as she pulled the stopper free to release the water, and stepped out of the tub, reaching for a towel.

Canceling the date was what she *should* do, but wasn't *going* to do. She *wanted* to go out with Dominic, be the recipient of his charm and undivided attention. She *wanted* to feel pretty and womanly, if even for a few stolen hours. She *wanted* Dominic to kiss her good-night at her door, allow desire to hum through her in a heated current, making her feel alive, vital and feminine.

"Remember that, Ms. Russell," she muttered as she tugged jeans over her bikini panties. "Say goodbye at the door. On the porch. If you invite the man inside when he brings you home, I'll wring your silly neck."

She woke a grumbling Jason, then went downstairs to cook breakfast. As she was whipping pancake batter in a bowl, her hand suddenly stilled.

"Oh, good grief," she said to the lumpy batter. "I don't have a thing to wear Saturday night. Cinderella did *not* wear jeans to the ball."

Just as she and Jason were finishing breakfast, Frank knocked on the screen door. He was his usual cheery self, and once Jason's request to have his bedroom painted red like his cowboy suit was rejected, Tessa chose a soft white for the interior of the house. The wall to receive Carmen's mural would be the same shade of blue as the exterior.

The color, Tessa mused, of the beautiful dress she'd worn in that not-to-be-forgotten dream she'd had about Dominic.

Greetings were exchanged with the other Bonellis, then they tromped up the stairs with a variety of equipment. Joe drove back into town to get more paint, enough being in the truck to get started.

The day progressed in the normal routine, but all the while, Tessa was aware that the Bonelli brothers were busily at work on the upper level of her home.

She liked that realization, she admitted. She and Jason were, indeed, part of a family. The only void in the cozy thought was the lack of Dominic's presence.

Lydia telephoned in midafternoon to confirm Jason's visit, providing he wasn't feeling ill due to approaching chicken pox.

"I'll drive Jason into town on Saturday," Tessa said. "I have some shopping to do." How embarrassing it would be if Lydia knew Tessa didn't own a dress pretty enough for a dinner date. "What time should I have him at your house?"

"Oh, early afternoon is fine," Lydia said. "I hope you find exactly what you're looking for."

"Pardon me?"

"You're going shopping for a dress for your date with Dominic. Right? Think really sexy, Tessa. Knock him for a loop."

"Oh, well, I..." Her voice trailed off as she felt a flush on her cheeks.

"We're all buzzing about Dominic showing up at the barbecue. Not only that, but the way he acted... You know, laughing, chatting, paying attention to Jason and the other kids. That's not the Dominic we're used to seeing. You're good for him, Tessa, you really are.

"You, Dominic and Jason look so right together. We're all hoping... Well, as Mama Bonelli says, 'Time holds all the answers.' Delores is a very wise and wonderful woman." Lydia paused. "Now then, let me give you directions to our house for Saturday afternoon. We'll drive Jason home after dinner Sunday evening." She laughed. "Ah, chicken pox. Time holds the answer to them, too."

The following days passed quickly.

Tessa was thoroughly delighted with the fresh, clean appearance of the living area upstairs. Jason declared his room to be *buono*.

The sky-blue wall in the main room downstairs was painted on Wednesday, and Carmen called to say she'd drive out Friday to add the rainbow, clouds and birds.

To Tessa's amazement, the Bonelli brothers managed to work around her as they painted the kitchen. They simply took a break when she needed to prepare snacks or lunches, the men never showing the least bit of irritation or impatience when they had to step out of the way.

The big, old house was full of people, noise, confusion, ongoing activity and seemingly endless laughter. The sound of deep masculine laughter combined with that of Tessa's, Emma's and Patty's, topped off by the gleeful giggles of happy children.

It was as though, Tessa reflected, her home had awakened from a quiet slumber that had been peaceful when only she and Jason were there. But now the house was overflowing with sunshine, was vitally alive during the day, while still offering a safe haven at night. It was perfect.

Carmen arrived bright and early on Friday morning with a smile, a hug for Tessa and Jason and an intriguing array of art supplies.

The children begged to be allowed to watch Carmen paint the rainbow instead of going to the play yard, and Tessa agreed, lining up toy blocks as the barrier they were not to cross while Carmen painted. With awe and wonder on their little faces, the children didn't budge as Carmen worked her magic.

Tessa, Patty and Emma shrugged, sat on the floor behind the children and enjoyed the reprieve from chasing the busy kids.

"Oh, my," Tessa whispered as the rainbow began to take shape. "Isn't that glorious?"

"Carmen is a very talented young lady," Emma said. "She's doing that freehand, just swish and there it is. She's a Bonelli, too?"

Tessa nodded.

"They're quite a family," Emma said. "I like them, all of them."

"So do I," Patty said. "They're so… Oh, what word do I want?" She paused. "*Real.* Yes, that's it. They're real, down-to-earth people. As the teenagers say, 'What you see is what you get.'"

Not quite, Tessa thought, frowning slightly. Dominic Bonelli was a lot different. He had many sides to him, layers that were being slowly revealed to her.

Suddenly, Janice's words spoken so many years before slammed against Tessa's mind.

The man has no soul.

A smile formed on Tessa's lips, a gentle smile, a warm, womanly smile.

The man has no soul. No, that wasn't true. Oh, she'd wholeheartedly agreed with the statement at first. When she'd first met him, he'd seemed a cold, hard, controlling man. He'd barked orders and expected them to be carried out to the letter. He'd worn his attorney uniform like a suit of armor and was prepared to battle for victory against anyone who didn't follow his dictates.

But that was then, this was now.

Dominic most definitely had a soul and a heart. He knew how to smile, laugh, demonstrate honest affection and give of himself beyond what his checkbook provided.

He stood, as she did, behind a protective wall. He moved, as she did, tentatively, cautiously from that shield, like a child taking unsteady steps. He'd been robbed, as she had, of childhood and was trying on greater depths of living like a coat never worn before.

Dominic was warm, fun and friendly, just as his brothers were.

Dominic Bonelli was lovable.

Tessa blinked and stiffened, glancing quickly at Emma and Patty to be certain they hadn't somehow read her mind.

Lovable? she mentally repeated. As in, a man a woman could love, fall in love with, be in love with for all time? A man a woman could envision as a husband and the father of her children. *That* kind of lovable?

Yes.

Not that she was the woman in the equation, she quickly told herself. She wasn't remotely interested in marrying. She had no intention of placing her heart and happiness in a man's safekeeping ever again.

Tessa frowned as the image of a faceless woman being

held in Dominic's strong arms flitted across her mind's eye.

Oh, dear, she thought, she didn't like that, not one little bit. That was *not* a picture she cared to dwell on, thank you very much.

She had been the recipient of Dominic's exquisite kisses while being held in his gentle but powerful embrace.

She had seen the heated passion in his dark eyes, that spoke of his desire for *her*.

She was the one who had a dinner date with the man in question on Saturday night, by gum, not some nameless bimbo from the high-society, monied arena Dominic no doubt traveled in.

So there!

Tessa Russell, she admonished herself, *stop it*. Shame on you. She sounded about as mature as Jason when he was throwing a tantrum. She was also making mental noises like a jealous, possessive woman, who considered Dominic exclusively hers.

Absurd. Ridiculous. It was a toss-up between whether she should be sent to her room, or carted off to the funny farm.

But, oh, mercy, the mere thought of Dominic caused desire to thrum within her—hot, so hot. The memory of his kiss, touch, aroma, the sound of his rich laughter, caused a tantalizing shiver to course through her.

And if she went an imaginary step further, inched toward the fantasy of making love with Dominic Bonelli, her heart, her mind, her very soul, seemed to nearly burst with the realization that it would be wonderful, beautiful, glorious...

And so very, *very* right.

No, no, Tessa, please, no, she silently begged. She mustn't do this to herself. She mustn't succumb to Dominic's magnetism. She had to run like the devil back behind her protective wall and remain there, safe from harm's way and the risk of being shattered into a million pieces.

"Ladies and gentlemen," Carmen said. Tessa jerked in surprise as she was jarred from her thoughts. "I hereby present you with your very own rainbow, complete with fluffy clouds and pretty birds."

The children applauded, then jumped to their feet. Tessa, Emma and Patty moved quickly to the front of the room to be certain none of the excited children crossed the toy-block line.

"Children, the paint is wet," Tessa said. "You can have a closer look later." She turned to the artist. "Oh, Carmen, it's fantastic, absolutely incredible."

Emma clapped her hands. "Okay, little guys, let's wash up for lunch. What do you say to Carmen?"

A chorus of "Thank you, Carmen" went up from the pint-size throng, with Jason's *gràzie* thrown in for Italian good measure. The children lined up and marched away with Patty and Emma as Carmen began to pack her equipment. Tessa stared transfixed at the wall.

"Thank you so much, Carmen," she said. "This is such a special gift. I hardly know what to say."

"It was fun. All my critics should be as easily pleased as your gang." Carmen laughed. "If you decide to sell this place, I'll have a Bonelli brother cover my handiwork. I don't think many people would go for a rainbow in their living room."

"I'm not selling this house. It's my home. I'll be here until I'm old and creaky."

"Oh, you never know, Tessa. Life is just full of surprises."

"Well, I can't argue with that. The past weeks have

turned my world upside down. I've definitely had a major dose of surprises lately.''

''Yep. All set for your dinner date with Dominic tomorrow night?''

''Oh, sure,'' she said, breezily waving one hand in the air. ''It's just a simple let's-go-out-to-dinner thing, you know.''

''Right,'' Carmen said, laughing. ''Whatever you say.''

''It is!''

''You bet,'' Carmen said, her smile firmly in place. ''I have a date tomorrow night myself, but mine is with a starving artist I somehow got conned into cooking for. Have a quiet moment of sympathetic thoughts for me while you're doing the town with my cost-is-no-obstacle brother.''

''Dinner is dinner,'' Tessa said, shrugging.

''Mmm,'' Carmen said, stifling another burst of laughter. She snapped closed a metal box containing jars of paint. ''Tessa, I want to show you something on the wall,'' she went on, her tone and expression now serious. ''Come here.''

Tessa stepped closer, obviously confused, then looked at the mural where Carmen was pointing. At the base of the rainbow was a tiny, shiny black, old-fashioned pot with handles painted on each side.

''This is your home and your business,'' Carmen said quietly, ''and you named it Rainbow's End. The tradition is to find a pot of gold at the end of the rainbow. But this one is yours, all of it. Only *you* know what you want, what your hopes and dreams are. That's why I left the pot empty. It's yours to fill, not mine.''

''Oh, my,'' Tessa said. ''What a lovely thing to do, to say.''

''Think carefully, Tessa, about what you'll put in that

little pot, about what you truly want to find at the end of your rainbow.''

As Carmen left the house, Tessa wrapped her hands around her elbows and stared at the empty pot at the base of the rainbow.

A gasp escaped from her lips as a swirling, blurry shape suddenly seemed to hover above the opening of the pot, then settled with crystal clarity into place.

''Dear heaven,'' she said, taking a step backward.

Her eyes widened as she stood statue-still, her heart racing. Dominic Bonelli was her pot of gold.

Chapter Sixteen

As Dominic drove toward Rainbow's End on Saturday evening, he told himself he'd left home with plenty of time to spare to allow for potentially heavy traffic.

A moment later, he mentally threw up his hands in defeat and admitted he was ahead of schedule because he'd been restless and edgy, had been staring at a clock in his living room that seemed to stubbornly refuse to move forward.

Lord, he thought, he was like a kid who was nervous about picking up his date for the senior prom. Well, since he hadn't had the money while in high school to attend any proms, maybe he was going through a second childhood. Oh, hell, whatever.

It had been a strange week that had seemed more like a month, he mused. He'd been extremely busy at the office, which wasn't unusual; it had been the events taking place around the perimeter of his existence that were out of the ordinary.

He had, for the first time he could remember, relived the events of a family barbecue. In the past, the gatherings were forgotten by the time he reached home, his mind focused on what awaited him on his desk the next day.

But not this time.

One of the conclusions he'd come to about the barbecue was that he'd had a good time, had actually enjoyed himself. He was a lousy cook, that was for sure, but he'd get the hang of it in the future.

Another fact he'd realized to be true was that Tessa had been right about his brothers. They *were* warm and friendly. They were nice guys.

Their wives were pleasant, Maria's husband was obviously devoted to her and the zillion kids were as cute as a button—buttons who all looked alike. They'd accepted Jason with no question, just as the adults had welcomed Tessa.

Tessa. Jason. Tessa. Jason.

There his mind went again, doing its Ping-Pong ball routine. Back and forth. Back and forth.

Tessa Russell was driving him nuts.

Tessa Russell had taken up residence in his brain and refused to budge.

Tessa Russell was a nuisance.

And he was looking forward so much to the hours ahead that he would spend with her, it was ridiculous.

"Bonelli," he said aloud, "your mind is mud."

He'd invited his mother out to lunch on Wednesday and officially apologized for his less-than-polite behavior at the family meeting. He'd also, striving for a casual tone of voice he hadn't quite pulled off, told her the barbecue had been rather fun. When Delores had raised her eyebrows at his comment, he'd rolled his eyes heavenward.

"Okay, okay, Mother, I had a good time, really enjoyed myself."

"*Buono,*" she said. "I know you did. I was waiting to see if you'd admit it. Tessa and Jason seemed to enjoy themselves, too. They're wonderful, both of them." She paused. "So! You're taking Tessa out to dinner Saturday night."

Dominic chuckled. "That's no secret. She yelled it so loudly, she might as well have announced it on the ten o'clock news."

"Well, you weren't exactly quiet about the fact, either, Dom."

"I know. She gets to me sometimes, and I lose it. Did you notice that her emotions are telegraphed on her face, in her eyes? She couldn't hide what she's feeling if she tried, which she probably wouldn't do because she's open and honest."

"Mmm," Delores said, nodding.

"She's not my type, of course, but she's lovely, quite beautiful in a wholesome, fresh-air-and-sunshine sort of way. She's a great mother. Jason is a lucky little kid."

"Yes."

"Tessa has done a helluva fine job with her life, especially considering she's all alone. I really respect that. Did you hear her laugh? It's infectious, makes a person smile whether they intended to or not. Her laughter reminds me of wind chimes and—" He stopped speaking and frowned. "Who put the nickel in me? I'm blithering on like an idiot."

Delores covered one of his hands with hers on the top of the table and smiled at him gently.

"No, Dom, you're not blithering on. You're changing,

and it's long overdue. It's time for you to live *your* life, instead of concentrating on the needs of your family. We're all fine, doing well.

"I can't give you back the years we took from you, but my heart will sing with joy if you really start living for yourself now."

"Right," he said gruffly, pulling his hand free. "I've already figured out that I'm not needed in my role as the head of the family anymore. You don't have to beat me over the head with that fact."

"Oh, Dominic, don't get angry. We're all so very grateful for what you've done for us. But, my *bambino,* it's your turn to have what *you* want as your first priority. The important thing now is for you to get in touch with yourself and discover what you really do want. Think about it, please, Dom. What do you want?"

Dominic turned off the main road and slowed his speed as he headed out of town toward Rainbow's End.

What do you want?

His mother's words had haunted him since that luncheon with her. When he'd managed to push Tessa and Jason from his thoughts, there would be Delores Bonelli tapping him on the shoulder.

What do you want?

The maddening part was, before he could concentrate on the nagging question, Tessa would be there, front-row center in his mind's eye, cluttering up his thought processes.

Damn that woman. What was it about her that made it so hard for him to shake loose of her image, of the remembrance of the kisses he'd shared with her, of how sensational she'd felt in his arms?

Hell, he didn't know.

He just didn't know.

This dinner date tonight, he decided, was a good idea. He'd blurted out the invitation on impulse and hadn't been quite certain afterward if he was pleased with himself or not.

But now, as of this moment, the evening ahead had a definite purpose. Without Jason around, he could view Tessa strictly as a woman with no connection to his son. He'd realize in spades that she wasn't his type, and that would be that.

"Excellent," he said, pressing harder on the gas pedal. "By the end of this date, everything will be under control again. *My* control."

Dominic glanced at the sky.

The days were getting shorter, he realized. Autumn was in full swing. *Changes.* That seemed to be the operative word lately regarding his life. There were just so damn many changes.

Tessa stood in her bedroom with her back to the full-length mirror hanging on the inside of her closet door. She pressed both hands on her stomach, willing the swarm of butterflies to still.

She'd tried the dress on in the store but had been in a cubbyhole-size room in her bare feet. This was truth time.

Light makeup had been applied, a half-slip, panty hose and evening sandals put on, her hair was washed and the curls brushed until they shone. The delicate scent of wildflower cologne had been sprayed on her throat and wrists.

Then she'd floated the dress over her head...and frozen, unable to gather the courage to turn around and look at herself in the mirror.

Oh, this dress, she thought, glancing down. She'd found it in the third store she'd entered, as though it had been waiting for her, calling her name.

It was blue. It was the exact shade of the dress she'd worn in the dream about Dominic, the same color as the outside of the house and the sky on the wall where Carmen had created her magical mural. Beautiful, beautiful blue.

She took a deep breath, let it out, then turned slowly to face the mirror.

"Oh," she whispered. "Oh, my."

She was beautiful.

The dress fell to midcalf in soft folds of chiffon and had a camisole top with tiny straps.

She stepped closer to the mirror and narrowed her eyes as she peered at herself.

Had the top been cut that low when she'd modeled it in the store? Had the narrow white-lace inserts in the bodice been that transparent? Had she been so...so bare?

Of course, dolt, she scolded herself. The creation hadn't been altered by cute little mice as had been done for Cinderella.

She turned one way, then the other, delighting in the feel and look of the skirt as it swung gently, then fell back into place. She made no attempt to curb the smile that formed on her lips as she indulged in continuing to gaze at her own reflection.

She'd never owned such a lovely dress, had never felt so...well, so beautiful. There was just no other word for it. Every inch of her was a declaration of her womanliness, her femininity.

No wonder Cinderella hadn't wanted to leave the ball, she reflected. Grubby Cindy had been transformed into a glorious woman for her stolen night on the town.

With her Prince Charming.

"Oh." Tessa blinked and pulled herself back to reality from the dreamy place she'd drifted to.

Cindy had Prince Charming, she thought. Tessa was going out with Dominic. So, fine, no problem. She'd covered all that in her mind. She was going to have a marvelous evening in the company of an extremely handsome man. The important thing to remember was the plan to bid him adieu on the front porch. *Outside, Tessa.*

"Got that?" she asked her reflection.

With a decisive nod, she picked up a small clutch purse and a white shawl, then left the room, turning off the light as she went.

She was ready.

She was woman.

She was beautiful!

Tessa Russell, Dominic thought, as he entered the house, was exquisite. *Tessa was beautiful.*

"You look sensational, Tessa," he said, not pleased with the raspy quality of his voice. "Very lovely. Very beautiful."

"Thank you," she said, smiling. "You're rather smashing yourself."

Gorgeous, she decided. The man was simply gorgeous. Charcoal gray suit tailored to perfection, crisp white shirt, paisley tie in shades of gray and burgundy, and a silk burgundy handkerchief visible in the top pocket of the jacket. It all added up to gorgeous, accentuating his physique, the tawny hue of his skin, the night darkness of his hair and eyes.

Was she going to survive this man? Maybe not, but what a fantastic way to dissolve into a puddle and die.

Tessa, she ordered herself, *get a grip.*

"Shall we go?" she said. Darn it, she'd been trying for a cool, sophisticated "Shall we go." What she'd actually produced was a squeaky-sounding "Shall we go" that could have been uttered by one of Cinderella's cute mice. "Well, Dominic?"

As if of their own volition, Dominic's hands raised to frame Tessa's face. His heart was beating so rapidly, he could hear the thudding echo roaring in his ears.

He wanted, he *needed,* he thought hazily, to kiss Tessa now, *right now.* It seemed like an eternity since he'd tasted the nectar of her mouth, felt her feminine curves pressed to his body, inhaled her aroma of wildflowers.

She was a vision of loveliness in that pale blue dress. She looked sexy and sensuous and just gazing at her had the blood pounding wildly through his veins.

Dominic lowered his head and his mouth melted over Tessa's, his tongue parting her lips to delve within, savoring the sweetness.

Yes, his mind hammered.

He dropped his hands to encircle her with his arms, nestling her to his heated body. His arousal was instantaneous, heavy and aching.

Tessa's purse and shawl fell unnoticed to the floor as her arms floated upward to entwine Dominic's neck. She returned his searing kiss in total abandon.

Oh, yes, her mind hummed.

Desire thrummed within her, swirling in a hot current that pulsed low and deep. Her senses were heightened as never before, making her acutely and wondrously aware of her own femininity and Dominic's rugged masculinity.

The kiss was ecstasy, she thought dreamily. Dominic tasted so good, smelled so good, like soap and musky after-shave.

Slowly, reluctantly, Dominic raised his head to meet Tessa's smoky gaze.

"You cast spells over me, Tessa," he said, his voice

husky with passion. "I don't behave true to form when I'm with you."

"Nor do I when I'm with you, Dominic. It's all so strange and...and rather frightening."

His hold on her tightened slightly and he frowned. "Are you afraid of me? Lord, Tessa, I never meant to frighten you in any way."

"No, no, I'm not *physically* afraid of you. If I asked you to drop your arms right now and let me go, I know you would."

"Guaranteed."

"What frightens me is that I don't seem capable of thinking straight when I'm with you. There are new emotions involved that I don't understand." She paused. "Dominic, I was hurt very badly in a relationship years ago, and I have no intention of ever allowing that to happen to me again.

"A part of me says I should put as much distance between us as possible, and yet..." She shook her head. "I don't know. It's all so confusing."

"You've got that straight," he said, managing a small smile. "Look, we're all right. I don't want a serious relationship, either. I've waited too long to be free of so many responsibilities. I've faced the fact that my family doesn't need me as they once did. My life is finally my own to live as I please.

"We're very attracted to each other, Tessa, and we set off sexual sparks when we're together. As long as we keep a clear understanding in our minds of what we *don't* want, we can go as far as we mutually agree upon with what we *do* want. Agree?"

"I...I guess so," she said quietly. "No strings, no commitments, no tomorrows, just the now of the moment we're in."

"Exactly. So, are you ready to go to dinner?"

"Yes."

He released her, then picked up the purse and shawl and handed them to her. As she was about to walk out the door, she turned to glance at the far wall and the empty pot at the end of the rainbow.

As they drove into town, Dominic tuned the radio to an easy-listening station, and soothing music drifted through the car.

Everything was going according to plan, Dominic thought. He was in control, the situation with Tessa was now clearly defined, the boundaries firmly in place. Fine. Great.

Then why in the hell did he feel as though a dark, gloomy cloud was hovering over him?

Tessa looked out the side window, appalled by the realization that tears were prickling at the back of her eyes.

What on earth was the matter with her? she wondered frantically. She and Dominic had *communicated,* just as magazine articles said two people should. They were on the same wavelength regarding the fact that they did *not* want any kind of serious involvement. They could enjoy each other's company. No one would get hurt.

Then why did she feel as though she were about to burst into tears and weep for a week?

Chapter Seventeen

She now *thoroughly* understood, Tessa thought, why Cinderella had wanted to stay at the ball.

The restaurant Dominic had chosen was one of Tucson's finest. The moment they entered the plush establishment, Tessa's strange and confusing gloomy mood dissipated into thin air.

They were led to a small, cloth-covered table. A candle in the center in a hurricane lamp cast a rosy glow. Even though the restaurant was crowded, the seating arrangement had been skillfully planned to afford diners a sense of privacy.

The waiters, to Tessa's wide-eyed amazement, were dressed in tuxedos, and the menus they were handed were oversize, with a flocked front and back and parchment paper inside.

It was the fanciest, most incredible place she'd ever been in, Tessa thought, looking around to savor every de-

tail. Just being here made a person feel special and...
beautiful.

"Oh, Dominic," she said, leaning slightly toward him,
"this is wonderful. It's like something out of a movie, a
make-believe setting."

Dominic smiled, instantly realizing it was a genuine
smile and that the dark cloud was no longer hovering over
him.

Tessa was enchanting, he thought. Her eyes were sparkling with excitement, and there was an endearing child-
like quality to her at the moment as she drank in the atmo-
sphere.

He'd eaten here on many occasions in the past, but this
was the first time he'd really *seen* it. Tessa's awe and
wonder was delightfully infectious.

There were so many things he took for granted: dining
in restaurants such as this one, attending concerts and
plays, being invited to private, invitation-only showings at
art galleries. Seeing those things and more through Tessa's
eyes, fresh, new, as though for the very first time, held
great appeal.

She *deserved* the finest and he was in the position to
provide it for her. She'd made do with too little for too
long. Well, that was going to change as of this very night.
Tessa was *his* now.

Dominic stiffened and frowned.

Tessa was his now?

Where in the hell had that bizarre thought come from?
She wasn't *his*. They'd just discussed the rules of their
seeing each other. There would be no commitments, certainly no possessiveness, no nonsense of "I am yours, you
are mine."

Tessa was his now.

Bonelli, he told himself, *knock it off.*

They ordered, and their tuxedo-clad waiter had, to Tessa's total delight, a very British accent. Dominic selected, tasted, then approved a fine wine. Salads were placed in front of them on wafer-thin china plates edged in gold trim.

"Thank you for bringing me here, Dominic," Tessa said, smiling. "If I was attempting to be ultrasophisticated, I'd try to pretend I was accustomed to places like this. But that would be silly, because it isn't remotely close to being true. This is glorious and I'll never forget it." She laughed. "Cinderella and I really have a great deal in common."

"Only to a point," he said, matching her smile. "Your evening doesn't have to end at midnight. My car, your coach, isn't going to turn into a pumpkin. I hope. I'd never able to explain *that* to my insurance agent."

Tessa laughed in delight and the wind-chime sound caused a shaft of heat to rocket through Dominic. As she began to eat the salad, he continued to gaze at her, his own plate forgotten.

She was lovely in the glow of candlelight, he thought. Her skin looked like a soft peach, and her hair shone like silken threads. That dress was seductive, alluring, hinting at the feminine bounty beneath.

Tessa was his now.

With a shake of his head in self-disgust, he picked up his fork and began to eat.

Conversation between them flowed easily through the delicious meal. They discussed movies, books, the political scene in Tucson.

Dominic related some humorous tales of Bonelli antics when his brothers and sisters were young.

Tessa then shared some endearing stories from Jason's toddler years.

"You have some wonderful memories of events shared with Jason, don't you?" Dominic said quietly.

"Yes. Yes, I do." She paused and looked directly into Dominic's dark eyes. "He's only five years old, Dominic. There are years of memories yet to come before he's ready to leave home. You created a memory with him the evening you gave him the cowboy suit. It's yours, that memory. Are you going to keep it?"

He frowned slightly. "That's an unusual way to put it, but…" He nodded. "Yes, I'm going to keep it."

"Good. I'm glad."

They smiled at each other warmly, then their smiles disappeared as they were held immobile, unable to move, or hardly breathe. The muted sounds of voices and clinking dishes faded into oblivion, as did the room itself.

They were aware, acutely aware, only of each other. Messages of desire were sent and received with no words spoken. Heat thrummed within them and the sensuality weaving around and through them was nearly palpable.

"Coffee?"

The sudden sound of the waiter's voice caused both Tessa and Dominic to jerk in surprise.

"Oh," Dominic said, "yes, that would be fine. Tessa, would you care for some dessert?"

"No, just coffee," she said, then drew a steadying breath. "Thank you."

Their cups were filled from a sterling silver pot, then the waiter moved on.

Tessa busied herself adding cream and sugar to the steaming liquid, then devoted her entire attention to the process of stirring. She willed her racing heart to resume a normal rhythm, and hoped to the heavens that the raw desire she'd seen in Dominic's eyes hadn't been visible to him in her own.

"Tessa," Dominic said quietly.

"Hmm?" she said, still concentrating on stirring the coffee.

"You said at your house that you were badly hurt in a relationship years ago."

Tessa's head snapped up and she looked at Dominic, a frown on her face.

"Where did that come from?" she said.

"Well, it occurs to me that by protecting yourself against *all* men because of what *one* did isn't fair, not to men *or* you. Something special, rare, could pass you by because you're too wary to run the risk of loving again. You're young, beautiful and you have a lot to offer. Don't you want to spend your life with someone? Rather than being alone?"

Tessa leaned forward, nearly bumping the coffee cup.

"Dominic," she said, "do you honestly believe that is any of your business?"

Yes! his mind yelled.

Tessa was his now.

No! Damn it, what was he doing? Her attitude suited him perfectly, and there he sat doing a hard sell on putting the past behind her and being open, receptive, to love in the present. Was he nuts? Yes, that was it. He'd slipped over the edge into insanity.

"Dominic?"

"I… That is, being a single parent is very difficult. If your mind wasn't so closed against men, Jason might very well have a father."

Tessa straightened and narrowed her eyes. "He *has* a father." She pushed back her chair. "Excuse me. I'm going to the powder room." Shooting him a dark glare, she got to her feet, then hurried away.

Dominic slouched back in his chair and watched her go.

Tessa was mad as hell, he thought, and he didn't blame her. He'd made it sound as though he'd be delighted if she'd get off the stick and find a man to raise his son.

That was *not* remotely close to what he wanted. The idea of Jason calling another man *Daddy* caused a knot to tighten in his gut.

That same faceless man would be Tessa's husband, would kiss, hold, caress her, reach for her in the night and... The hell he would!

Tessa was his now.

Oh, man, he thought, running one hand over the back of his neck. His mind was a maze of confusion. If he didn't know better, he might begin to believe that he was falling in love with Tessa Russell. That was absurd.

He glanced up and saw Tessa crossing the room to return to the table, seeing several men give her appreciative scrutiny.

So lovely, he mused, his gaze riveted on her. The skirt of her dress swung provocatively, accentuating her nicely shaped legs and the gentle slope of her hips. She held herself straight and tall, emphasizing her elegance and grace.

He knew her to be fun and funny, warm, intelligent, a devoted mother, a savvy businesswoman, and she had a temper that could go off like a bomb when she was provoked.

She was everything, and more, that any man would hope to discover in his life's partner.

Was he falling in love with Tessa?

Maybe, just maybe he was. But even if that proved to be true, he wouldn't pursue it. He wanted no part of the multitude of responsibilities that being a husband and father on a daily basis entailed. He'd tend to Jason's material needs from the edge of the boy's existence.

And Tessa?

If his heart overruled the orders from his brain and he *did* fall in love with her, he'd exit stage left from her life immediately.

Bonelli, he thought, with a decisive nod, *you're back under control.*

He got to his feet when Tessa reached the table.

"Would you like to go into the ballroom and dance?" he said. "They have an excellent combo here."

Tessa opened her mouth to decline, having decided during her exodus to ask to go home. She'd been angered and strangely hurt by Dominic's urgings to find herself a husband, and provide Jason with a father at the same time.

"I…" Her voice trailed off.

"Forget what I said just before you left the table, Tessa. I didn't mean it like it sounded. Rather than sit here and dissect it for the next hour, let's just erase what I said and enjoy the rest of the evening." He extended one hand to her. "May I have this dance, Cinderella?" He smiled.

The man, Tessa thought, placing her hand in his, did *not* play fair.

The large ballroom was lighted by a dozen crystal chandeliers that had been dimmed to a soft glow. Small tables with chairs edged the gleaming dance floor, and a combo was playing a dreamy waltz when Tessa and Dominic entered. She placed her purse and shawl on one of the tables, then they moved onto the fairly crowded floor.

Dominic drew Tessa into his arms and began to dance with smooth expertise.

Cinderella, Tessa's mind whispered as the lingering shadows of her anger and hurt fled. *Oh, yes, she was Cinderella at the ball.* Being held in Dominic's arms, swaying to the dreamy music, was heavenly. This was *her* night, and she was going to allow nothing to mar its splendor. She was beautiful, Dominic was beautiful, *everything* was beautiful.

She sighed with pleasure and nestled closer to Dominic.

Dominic nearly groaned aloud as Tessa pressed against him. Coming into the ballroom to dance, he'd decided, would defuse her anger. What he hadn't taken into consideration was the torture it would be to have Tessa in his arms, close, so close, to his heated, aroused body.

He inhaled her aroma of wildflowers, shutting his eyes for a moment to fully savor the delicate, feminine scent. Her breasts were crushed with exquisite softness to his chest, and he could feel the sensuous curve of her lower back where his hand rested.

He was going up in flames.

The song ended and another began. Dominic cleared his throat and eased Tessa away from him just enough to cause her to tilt her head to look at him questioningly.

"Great band," he said, instantly deciding that had been a lame thing to say.

"Yes. You're an excellent dancer, very easy to follow." She smiled. "That's a good thing, because I'm very rusty when it comes to dancing."

"You do very well, Tessa. You sort of…float." He shook his head. "This is a dumb conversation. We sound like strangers struggling to find something to talk about."

"Well…"

"We are *not* strangers. In fact, I feel as though I've known you for a very long time."

"Oh?" she said, laughing softly. "Are you bored yet?"

"Ms. Russell, there is no way on earth that a man could ever be bored around you. There are so many layers, facets to you, that really keep a guy on his toes."

"You're not exactly uncomplicated yourself, Mr. Bonelli."

"So you're not bored, either?"

"Not even close."

They smiled at each other, then Dominic pulled her to him again. They danced on and on, lost in the magic of the Cinderella night.

Much later, the last song was played, and with Tessa tucked next to him, Dominic led her from the restaurant to the car. By unspoken agreement, she snuggled close to him as they drove toward Rainbow's End.

The sensual spell that had been weaving around and through them during the hours of the evening seemed to fill the car to overflowing.

Once out of the surging traffic, Dominic slowed his speed, wishing to delay the end of the time spent with Tessa. They didn't speak, yet the silence was welcome, leaving them free to savor the crackling awareness of each other.

As her house came into view, the light she'd left on downstairs glowed like a beacon in the darkness, and a niggling little voice began to sound in Tessa's hazy mind. It whispered to her, nudging her to remember her earlier vow to bid Dominic good-night on the porch.

Her heart did a funny flip-flop as he maneuvered the car onto the road that would bring them in just minutes to the house.

Well, Cinderella, she thought. *It's pumpkin time.* The glorious hours were over, the last song had been played. She'd step inside that big old house alone, climb the stairs alone, get ready for bed and sleep—*alone.*

Suddenly, the image of the rainbow Carmen had painted flitted before Tessa's eyes. She saw the empty pot, and remembered Carmen's dictate that it was up to Tessa to fill it with *her* hopes and dreams.

Dominic.

Oh, dear heaven, was she falling in love with Dominic Bonelli?

The thought of his turning from the porch and walking away caused a cold fist to grip her heart. On this night, *her* night, the house loomed too big, empty, too lonely, without Dominic's magnificent presence within its walls.

She wanted him with her, holding, kissing, caressing her, bringing her vitally alive and glorying in her womanliness.

She wanted to make love with Dominic.

But was she falling *in* love with him?

She didn't know. She just didn't know.

Dominic stopped the car, turned off the ignition and opened the door. After getting out, he leaned down to extend his hand to Tessa, indicating she should slide beneath the steering wheel to leave the vehicle on his side.

The instant she stood, he dropped her hand, wrapped his arms around her and kissed her deeply. She parted her lips to receive his questing tongue as she encircled his neck with her hands.

The kiss was urgent, hungry, evidence of the mutual passion that had built within them during the hours they'd danced. Dominic lifted his head, then slanted his mouth the other way, drinking in her sweetness, savoring the taste. His arousal was heavy, hot, the ache for Tessa, the need and want of her, overpowering rational thought.

He tore his mouth from hers.

"Tessa," he said, his voice raspy, "I want to make love with you. You can feel what you're doing to me, I know you can. I think...I think I'd better see you to the door. Now."

He brushed his lips over hers, then released her. Reaching back into the car, he produced her purse and shawl, then closed the door. With one of his arms across her shoulders, they started up the walkway to the porch.

This was it, Tessa thought. In a couple of seconds, she had to make a decision that would have a tremendous impact on her life.

Her hands were trembling slightly as she took the house key from her purse. They crossed the porch to stop by the door.

In her mental vision, she once again saw the pot at the base of the rainbow; the empty pot that only she, Tessa, could fill.

Oh, Tessa, she thought frantically, *think.* Whatever decision she made tonight, she would have to square off against at dawn's light tomorrow. *Think.*

"Your key, Cinderella?" Dominic said, holding out his hand.

Cinderella, her mind hummed. *Yes.* This was *her* night, her glorious night to fill the rainbow's pot with *her* hopes and dreams. She'd face tomorrow when it came. *Tonight was hers.*

"Dominic," she said, her voice hushed, "would you like to come in?"

"Ahh, Tessa," he said, drawing one thumb over her lips, "if I come in, I won't be leaving tonight. If I walk through that door, we'll make love."

She looked at the door, seeing in her mind's eye the pot and the rainbow. The pot suddenly began to glow with a golden light.

"Rainbow's end," she whispered.

"Tessa? Do you understand what I'm saying? It's up to you, it has to be. Do you want me to stay?"

She looked up at him and said one word that caused a

warm-fuzzy feeling to tiptoe around her heart and a lovely smile to form on her lips.

Just one little word.

''Yes.''

Chapter Eighteen

The small lamp on the nightstand next to the double bed cast a soft glow over the room, and over Tessa and Dominic, who stood naked before each other.

They had entered the house, gone up the stairs and into the bedroom, with an easiness that bespoke an inner knowledge that what was taking place was very right.

In Tessa's room, Dominic had drawn her close and kissed her deeply, causing her to tremble in his arms. Moments later, she'd flipped back the blankets to reveal pristine white sheets.

They'd removed their clothes, then stood statue-still, eyes meeting, then roaming, over the other, savoring all within their view. It was as though there were no world beyond this room. It was a magical night, a Cinderella night, and they were the only two people in the universe.

"You're lovely, Tessa," Dominic said, then extended one hand to her.

She smiled, marveling at her calmness, at the serene sense of knowing who she was and what she wanted. Placing her hand in Dominic's, she stepped into his embrace, relishing the feel of the dark, curly hair on his board chest brushing against the soft flesh of her breasts.

As his mouth captured hers, she drank in his taste while inhaling the aroma that was uniquely his. His strong arms encircled her, held her fast, power tempered with gentleness.

The kiss intensified and heated desire thrummed within them, pulsing, causing hearts to race.

Dominic broke the kiss and lifted Tessa into his arms, placing her on the cool sheets. He reached on the floor for his pants and took a foil packet from his wallet. When he was prepared, he turned to look at her. She lifted her arms to welcome him.

"So beautiful," he murmured, then stretched out next to her, resting on one forearm.

"Dominic," Tessa said, her voice hushed, "it's been so long. My experience is very limited, you see, and I—"

"Shh," he said, then brushed his lips over hers. "Everything will be fine, wonderful."

And it was.

It was a journey of discovery, of touching, kissing, glorying in revealing the mysteries each of the other, rejoicing in the exquisite differences between woman and man, anticipating with ever-growing passion what each would give and receive.

Dominic paid homage to one of Tessa's breasts, then the other, drawing the sweetness deep into his mouth. She purred in pure feminine pleasure.

Her hands were never still as they skimmed over him, feeling the taut muscles beneath her palms. He groaned low in his chest.

Where hands had traveled, lips followed, tongues flicking, tantalizing, heightening desires to a fever pitch of need.

"Oh, Dominic," Tessa whispered.

"I want you, Tessa," he said, his voice gritty.

"Yes."

He filled her with all he was as a man, and she received him joyously with all she was as a woman. In the rhythm ancient as Time itself, yet theirs alone in their special world, the dance of lovers began.

Dominic increased the tempo, and Tessa matched his pace in perfect synchronization. Tension build within them; tighter, hotter, coiling. They were reaching for the summit, going higher, faster, the rhythm now a pounding cadence.

"Dominic!"

Tessa was flung into a place where she had never gone before as she clung to Dominic, calling his name over and over. Rainbow colors burst into glorious pieces like sparkling diamonds.

Moments later, Dominic joined her there, flinging his head back and closing his eyes.

"Tessa."

They stayed in their other-world for moments, or was it forever? Time had no meaning, reality was ecstasy. They were one entity, so totally meshed that in their hearts, minds and souls, there was no discerning one from the other.

It was glorious.

It was beyond anything either of them had ever known before.

Then slowly, quietly, they drifted back, sated, contented, awed by what they'd shared.

Dominic moved off of Tessa, pulled the blankets over

them, then nestled her close to his side, one arm wrapped around her waist.

She sighed. "Oh, Dominic, I don't know what to say."

He kissed her on the forehead. "It was incredible. It was... I don't know what to say, either."

"Mmm. I'm so sleepy."

"Then sleep. I'll hold you right here in my arms."

"Yes."

As Tessa drifted off into blissful slumber, Dominic frowned.

He felt strange, shaken, unsettled. Making love with Tessa had touched him in a place deep within that he hadn't known existed, nor did he understand what it was. The exquisite physical release was overshadowed by the intensity of emotions very foreign and new, having no names, no identities.

Was this love? Falling in love? How was a man to know? Had this delicate woman sleeping so peacefully in his arms captured his heart? Why did he, a man of experience and intelligence, not know the answers to these questions?

Tessa stirred and he tightened his hold on her, wanting her close to him...where she belonged.

Tessa was his now.

With an earthy expletive, he willed himself to blank his mind, *to not think,* not now. He kissed Tessa gently, then slept.

Hours later, as though in a dream, they awakened, reaching for the other, eagerly, urgently. Without speaking, they joined. Without speaking, they traveled yet again to the splendor of the rainbow colors. Without speaking, they savored it all, then allowed sleep to claim them once more.

* * *

Tessa opened her eyes, blinked against the bright sunlight that filled the room, then frowned in confusion as she realized she smelled coffee.

"Good morning, Sleeping Beauty," Dominic said.

She turned her head to see him sitting on the edge of the bed.

"Sleeping Beauty?" she said, smiling. "From Cinderella to Sleeping Beauty? I hope my next identity isn't Snow White. I'd really blow my food budget trying to feed those seven guys she hangs out with."

Dominic chuckled, then reached over to the nightstand for one of the two mugs sitting there.

"Coffee?" he said. "I hope you don't mind my making myself at home and fixing a pot."

"Then bringing me a mug in bed? No, I certainly don't mind." She propped her pillow against the headboard, then sat up, tucking the sheet beneath her arms to cover her bare breasts. Accepting the mug from Dominic, she took a sip. "Delicious. Thank you."

Dominic picked up the other mug, then looked directly at Tessa.

"No regrets?" he said, no hint of a smile on his face.

"Oh, no, Dominic, none at all," she said. He looked so ruggedly handsome this morning. He needed a shave, and he was wearing his slacks. He'd slipped on his shirt, but had left it open and hanging free of his pants. The enticing glimpse of his bare chest that was still revealed, caused a frisson of heat to whisper through her. "Do you? Have any regrets?"

"No," he said, then took a swallow of coffee. He could live without the tangled maze of confusion in his weary mind, but he'd tackle that later. "No, Tessa."

Their eyes met again, and the ember of desire still smoldering deep within them burst into flames. Dominic tore his gaze from Tessa's and glanced at the clock.

"It's after nine," he said.

"You're kidding. Goodness, I can't remember when I've slept so late. Little boys are human alarm clocks, even on weekends."

"Jason isn't coming home until this evening, is he?"

"No."

"Well, I thought we could spend the day shopping for furniture."

Tessa frowned. "Furniture?"

"Yes. It may take more than one outing to redo this place, but we could get started on it. What room do you want to do first?"

Tessa reached over and placed her mug on the nightstand. Her frown was very much in evidence when she looked at Dominic again.

"I don't recall a discussion regarding new furniture," she said.

"I'm sure I mentioned it." He shrugged. "Maybe not, though. It doesn't matter. It goes with the package of fixing up your house. Things are progressing nicely so far, but there's still furniture and carpeting to do. I'm considering having the road leading in here blacktopped. It's murder on vehicles the way it is. Do you think Jason would like to have bunk beds so he could have a friend sleep over?"

"Wait a minute, Dominic," Tessa said. She raised one hand in a halting gesture, then quickly dropped it as the sheet began to slip. "I don't want new furniture. What I have isn't very expensive, but I saved for each piece, bought it used, then painted, scrubbed, fixed everything up. I'm proud of my purchases."

"What you've done is very admirable, Tessa, but that

was then, and this is now. Jason is my son. I want him to have…well, better than this. It's my responsibility."

A cold fist tightened in Tessa's stomach, and she could feel the color drain from her face.

"Responsibility?" she said. "Dear heaven, we're back to responsibility? Or was I wrong to assume that being with Jason, with me, had moved you away from that arena into one of caring?"

Dominic matched her frown. "What I may feel has nothing to do with the fact that I intend to replace your furniture. I don't understand what you're getting upset about."

"No, I realize you have no idea what's bothering me," she said, her voice rising. "Good Lord, I'm sick of hearing you talk about your responsibility. How do you think I feel right now, right this minute, Dominic?"

"Tessa, what in the hell is the matter with you?"

"I'll be only too happy to tell you, Mr. Bonelli. You just spent the night in my bed, remember? We made love. Or did we? Maybe that was just plain old sex, a roll in the hay. It would certainly seem so, because in the light of the new day, you're ready to whip out your checkbook and buy me new furniture."

Dominic thudded his mug onto the nightstand and got to his feet.

"One has nothing to do with the other," he said, matching her volume. "What we shared here—" he swept one arm in the direction of the bed "—is separate and apart from my responsibility for my son. A Bonelli does *not* live in a house with shabby furniture. You're twisting things around, Tessa. You're looking for trouble that isn't there. Being with you has nothing to do with providing material possessions for you and Jason."

"How can you do that? How can you separate your

emotions into compartments to suit your fancy? Jason and I aren't robots who need sprucing up. You can't deal with us the way you would when you have your car washed.''

"Tessa, stop it. You're being ridiculous. We agreed on this project of fixing your home long before you and I became lovers. One has nothing to do with the other.''

Tessa scrambled to her knees, dragging the sheet with her to keep herself covered. Unwelcome tears filled her eyes, but she ignored them.

"You're wrong, Dominic Bonelli. You're so hung up on responsibility, you don't have room for anything else, any other emotions. You actually believe you can interact with me and my son, *my son,* take whatever you want from us, then chalk us up as responsibilities and write a check to cover it.''

"Now look—"

"No, you look *and* listen, for a change. I've had enough of your controlling my life, marching in here and barking orders about what will be done to make *my* home meet *your* standards. Jason adores you and I love you and, by damn, you're not going to deal with our existence for one second longer with your crummy money.''

"You what?'' he said, his voice suddenly very low and very quiet. "You love me?''

"No! Don't be an idiot. I never said…'' Tessa voice trailed off, and her eyes widened in horror. "Oh, merciful saints,'' she whispered.

She *had* said it…well, yelled it. She'd declared her love for Dominic because…because it was true. She *was* in love with him. Oh, darn. Oh, damn. What a stupid thing to have gone and done.

"Tessa?''

"Forget it,'' she said, shaking her head. "Just forget it. It's not important. That's not the issue here. We're discussing your lamebrain attitude of thinking that your money, your sense of *responsibility,* is all you need to be part of people's lives. That may work with some, but not with me and, by God, not with my son.''

Two tears spilled onto her pale cheeks.

"Get out of my house, *my home,* Dominic Bonelli. You can't possibly be comfortable here, anyway, surrounded by such shabby furniture. Stay away from me, and don't you dare come near Jason again. He honestly believes that you're his friend, that you care about him. Little does he know that your caring is measured in dollars and cents. I won't allow you to break that child's heart. Go. Now!''

Dominic opened his mouth to retort, then snapped it closed again, clenching his jaw in anger. He gathered his remaining clothes, and strode toward the door. He stopped in the doorway and turned to look at Tessa.

"You can't keep me from my son, Tessa," he said. "If I decide to see Jason, I will. No one tells me what I can, or can't do. *No one.* I *do* have a responsibility toward Jason, and I'll see it through to its proper end. Whether that suits your concept of how I should conduct myself is of no importance to me. You can pass judgment on me from here to Sunday, Tessa Russell, but don't expect me to give a tinker's damn one way or another.''

He turned again and left the room, his heavy footsteps on the stairs echoing through the house moments later.

"Dominic?" Tessa said to the empty room. A sob caught in her throat.

Trembling, she shifted to curl beneath the blankets, her fingertips pressed to her lips.

He was gone. She'd sent him away. In the same moment she'd discovered she'd fallen in love with him, she'd ordered him out of her house and her life.

Why couldn't Dominic see that money wasn't the an-

swer to everything? That responsibility wasn't synony-
mous with love?

Oh, what difference did it make? He didn't love her. He
didn't love Jason. They were simply items on a list to be
tended to.

She was a foolish, foolish woman. She'd let down her
guard, stepped from behind her protective walls, and
would now pay the price with a shattered heart. Once
again, she'd fallen in love with the wrong man.

Chapter Nineteen

On Monday afternoon, Dominic stood in his office staring out the window. His hands were shoved into his pockets, and a deep frown knit his eyebrows.

He was, yet again, replaying in his mind everything that had taken place at Tessa's on Sunday morning.

No, that wasn't quite accurate. He was also, despite his attempts to the contrary, reliving Saturday night, as well. The memory of the hours at the restaurant, then the incredible lovemaking shared with Tessa, haunted him, and were now intertwined with the horrendous blowup they'd had.

"Damn," he muttered.

How was it possible that a man could get into so much trouble by suggesting an outing as simple as shopping to buy new furniture? When dealing with a woman, that was how. Tessa had been irrational and stubborn. She had refused to listen to reason; she had twisted things around in every direction except the one that was right.

Man, oh, man, she'd been furious.

And sad.

Dominic stared up at the ceiling, seeing in his mind's eye the tears glistening in Tessa's eyes, then slipping down her pale cheeks.

Surely she knew that their lovemaking had been exactly that…*making love*. It hadn't been remotely close to being casual sex—a roll in the hay, as she'd put it. It had, in fact, been more meaningful than anything he'd experienced before.

Damn it, why couldn't she get a handle on the facts as they stood, as he'd explained them to her? His sense of responsibility toward Jason, toward Tessa herself, were far removed from what he and Tessa shared. What was so difficult to comprehend about that concept? It made perfect sense to *him*.

You're so hung up on responsibility, you don't have room for anything else, any other emotions.

Tessa's words hammered against Dominic's mind as he shifted his gaze to stare once again out the window. A painful headache began to throb in his temples.

Suddenly, he heard the echo of what his mother had said at that fateful family meeting, and later, when he'd taken her to lunch.

Responsibility isn't love. Money isn't love. Are we the cause of your not knowing the difference between love and responsibility?

What do you want?

What do you want?

Dominic ran one hand over the back of his neck.

As long as he was going straight out of his mind, he

might as well do it up royally, pull out all the stops, square off against what he'd been trying to ignore.

Tessa Russell loved him.

Emotions slammed against him with such intensity that he took a sharp breath. But the emotions were a tangled maze, twisting and turning, making it impossible to decipher one from the next. Nothing was clear. *Nothing.*

A light knock sounded at the door, then Gladys entered. Dominic turned, grateful for the distraction, for the chance to escape from his own tormented thoughts.

"These letters are ready for your autograph," Gladys said.

He moved behind his desk, sat down and began to sign his name to the pile of letters.

"You're very quiet today," Gladys said.

"I have a lot on my mind."

"Do you want to talk about it?"

"No."

"You never do, Dominic. It can help to talk things through, put it out where you can see it more clearly."

"That wouldn't solve anything in this case, Gladys, but I appreciate the offer." He handed her the letters. "There you go. Thank you."

"You're welcome." She started toward the door.

"Gladys."

She stopped and looked at him over one shoulder. "Yes?"

"Would you leave the door open, please?"

She marched back to stand in front of his desk.

"That corks it," she said. "You've gone over the edge. Leave the door *open?* Dominic, talk to me. You're not a well man. Either that, or you're not Dominic Bonelli at all. Your body has been invaded by alien creatures.

"You *never* want your office door left open. You hold the world at bay with the symbolism of that closed door, as well as providing a private place for yourself where you control who enters."

"I never said any of that," he said, frowning up at her.

"I figured it out for myself because I'm an extremely intelligent woman. Are you going to try to tell me I'm wrong?"

He opened his mouth to do exactly that, then snapped it closed, shook his head and sighed.

"No," he said wearily, "I'm not, because you're right."

"And now?" she said gently. "Is it finally time to allow some of that world out there into your life?"

"Maybe. I don't know, Gladys, but…maybe."

"I hope so, Dominic, I truly do."

He leaned back in his chair and laced his fingers behind his head.

"Gladys, humor me. If you had to give a definition of the difference between love and responsibility, what would you say?"

"That's easy enough. Love comes from the heart, responsibility from the mind."

"Don't you think it's more complicated than that?"

"Nope. Would you like an example?"

He nodded.

"Okay. Suppose it's my birthday. If someone buys me a gift out of a sense of responsibility—you know, with an attitude of *this is something I should do*—then that gift wouldn't be worth much to me. But if it's given out of love, then it's very, very precious."

"Oh."

"My phone is ringing." She hurried from the room, leaving the door *open*.

"Love comes from the heart," Dominic said aloud, "responsibility from the mind. It can't be that simple." He paused. "Can it?"

He was an attorney who dealt in concrete facts, proven data. A theory had now been placed in front of him for his consideration. Well, a thought, opinion, idea, *anything* would be an improvement over the tangled maze of confusion in his brain.

Love comes from the heart, responsibility from the mind.
Tessa Russell loved him.
What do you want?

Dominic lunged to his feet.

Enough. He was going crazy. He *had* to find answers to the questions plaguing him, and he'd better do a damn good job of it.

Because he knew, just somehow knew that the conclusions he came to were going to have a tremendous impact on his future.

A half hour later, Dominic stood in a florist shop being smiled at by a grandmotherly-type woman.

"How may I help you, sir?" the grandmother-type said.

"I'd like to send a bouquet of fresh flowers to my mother."

"Certainly. Did you have something particular in mind? Is it a special occasion?"

"No, it's not," he said, leaning slightly toward her to more clearly analyze her reaction. "That's the point. I'm sending her flowers simply because I want to, because I feel like it."

"Oh-h-h," the woman said, beaming. "What a loving thing to do."

Dominic straightened and blinked. "It is?" He nodded, then smiled, appearing rather pleased with himself. "Well, yes, I guess it is."

The next morning, Carmen opened the door to her studio to find Dominic standing in front of her.

"Dominic?" she said. "What's wrong? Why are you here?"

He frowned. "May I come in?"

"Oh, yes, of course." She stepped back to allow him to enter, then closed the door after him. "Now tell me what's wrong."

He flung out his arms. "Why does something have to be wrong for me to have come here?"

She planted her hands on her hips and glared at him. "Because you don't make social calls on members of your family, big brother. You never have, so why would you start now?"

"Oh," he said, running one hand over the back of his neck. "You're right. I don't just drop by to see how you are, do I?"

"No."

"I certainly am a nice guy," he said dryly.

Carmen cocked her head to one side and studied him. "Are you feeling okay?"

"No, as a matter of fact, I'm not." He paused. "Would you answer a question for me?"

"Sure."

"Why did you paint the rainbow on Tessa's wall?"

"Huh?"

"The rainbow, Carmen, why did you paint it? You took time out from your busy schedule, used expensive supplies, the whole nine yards. Why?"

She shrugged. "Because I like Tessa very much, and

Jason is a heart-stealer. I thought they'd enjoy seeing the rainbow every day. It was something I could do for them that might bring some pleasure to their lives.''

"I see. Were you registering a sense of responsibility toward them? You know, they're part of the family now so you should do something for them?"

"Responsibility? Heavens no, it never crossed my mind." She splayed one hand across her heart. "I did it because it felt right."

"Man, oh, man, that is really incredible." He gave her a quick kiss on the forehead. "Thanks, Carmen. Bye." He hurried out the door.

Carmen pressed one fingertip to the spot on her forehead where Dominic had kissed her.

"How am I going to break it to our mother," she said aloud, "that her oldest son is no longer playing with a full deck?"

The next evening after work, Dominic stood in the department store where he'd purchased Jason's cowboy suit. He stared at the rack of similar outfits, having told two different saleswomen that he was just browsing.

He mentally took himself back in time to when he'd gotten the bright red suit for Jason.

Why had he done it? It had been on impulse, not something he'd thought through before taking action, which was definitely out of character for him.

How had he felt when he'd given the gift to Jason? Sensational. He'd never forget how that little boy's face had lit up, the way his dark eyes had sparkled with excitement. What a job he and Tessa had had trying to get Jason to stand still long enough to change his clothes. Oh, yes, he was keeping that memory he'd shared with his son.

He'd bought Jason the cowboy suit with a sense of caring...of love. Responsibility hadn't entered into the action one iota.

Dominic took a deep breath, let it out slowly, then wandered away from the boys' department. He was shaken, unsettled, yet, inching in around the edges was a warmth, a strange peacefulness that was increasing with every beat of his racing heart.

"May I help you, sir?"

"What?" he said, jerking in surprise. Glancing around, he discovered he was now in the women's dresses section. "Oh, no, thanks. I'm just looking."

"That's fine, and do let me know if I may be of assistance."

Dominic nodded as his gaze fell on a dress the same color of blue that Tessa had worn when they had gone to dinner.

Tessa, his mind hummed.

Why had he asked her to go out with him on Saturday night? Because he'd wanted to be with her, pure and simple. He'd hollered that fact at her in front of his entire family in his mother's backyard and, by damn, he'd meant it. Responsibility had had nothing to do with it.

And why had he made love with Tessa Russell?

He dragged both hands down his face and felt beads of sweat on his forehead.

He'd *made* love with Tessa, because...because he was *in* love with Tessa.

He stood still, hardly breathing, allowing the truth to move through his mind, his heart, his very soul.

"Yes," he said, a smile breaking across his face. "I'll be damned...yes."

In the next instant, he frowned.

Tessa loved him and he loved her. The problem, however, was that if he showed up on her doorstep, she'd probably deck him. She was, with just cause, mad as hell at him.

And she was sad.

Lord, he'd hurt her so badly. He hadn't meant to, but that fact didn't erase the tears he'd caused to fill her beautiful brown eyes.

He had to regroup, think, plan. He had to win back his lady, the woman he loved.

Tessa was his now.

"Yes!" he said, punching one fist in the air.

"Sir?" a saleswoman said, eyeing him warily.

"What? Oh, it was nice talking to you." He spun on his heel and strode away.

"Weird," the woman muttered. "Gorgeous, but definitely weird."

Around midnight that night, Tessa awakened from a deep sleep; a small finger was steadily poking her on the arm.

"Jason?" she said foggily.

"Mommy, I don't feel good," he said in a whining voice. "My head hurts. I'm hot. My tummy is wiggling."

"Oh, dear," Tessa said, throwing back the blankets. She snapped on the lamp on the nightstand. "It sounds as though the chicken pox Jeremiah shared with you have finally decided to arrive." She got to her feet.

"My tummy is wiggling worse, Mommy."

"Come on, sweetheart, let's hurry to the bathroom." She paused. "Oh, darn, too late."

The next morning, Jason was covered in a generous display of chicken pox. He was running a slight fever, had no interest in breakfast and was not in a sunshine mood.

Despite Tessa's cheerful account of all the kids from Rainbow's End who had caught chicken pox from Jeremiah so far, Jason seemed to take his case of the polka dots as a personal affront.

"There you go, Mr. Grumpy," she said, tucking Jason in on the cot in her office. "Try to go back to sleep. I'll pop in and out as often as I can. Okay?"

"No. I want to play."

"Not today, my sweetie. You're not going to feel up to snuff until all the chicken pox have come from the inside to the outside. That's how it works."

"That's dumb."

"Your opinion is duly noted." She kissed him on the forehead. "Now then, I've put this little table right next to you here. Try to drink your orange juice, Jason. There are books, crayons, a coloring pad, all kinds of things for you to do. You look sleepy, though. I think you'll snooze if you close your eyes."

"Really, really dumb."

"Got it. I'm going to straighten up the kitchen before the kids start coming, then I'll check on you."

Jason sighed dramatically.

Tessa rolled her eyes heavenward, curbed a smile she decided Jason wouldn't appreciate and left the room. In the kitchen, she set about clearing away the remains of their breakfast.

Poor Jason, she mused. Chicken pox was a miserable thing to go through. She had a feeling he wasn't going to be one bit impressed by Joe's enthusiastic report that someone with the itchy disease looked like a birthday cake when covered with the necessary pink lotion.

She was going to be very busy for the next couple of

days until Jason began to feel perkier. She'd have to dash back and forth between her regular duties at Rainbow's End and the office where the grouchy patient was.

Well, she'd look at the bright side. Maybe all that busy, busy, busy would mean she wouldn't have time to think about Dominic.

Oh, dear heaven, she thought as she wiped off the table, she loved him. She'd fallen in love with Dominic. The remembrance of the lovemaking they'd shared caused heat to swirl within her, and a flush to stain her cheeks.

The dinner out, dancing, the Cinderella night, had been glorious, too, creating memories she intended to keep for all time.

But then the next morning had arrived, and the chilling argument with Dominic had erupted. She'd been so hurt when he'd shifted back into his responsibility mode, had begun barking orders and taking control of her life.

It would be a cold day in a hot place before she'd allow Dominic to buy her new furniture because hers was too shabby for Jason, a Bonelli, his son, to use. The nerve of that man.

His damnable "responsibility" had seemed to encompass everything they'd shared, *including* the exquisite lovemaking of the night before. She'd lashed out at him so cruelly with her awful remark about him producing his checkbook after spending the night in her bed.

She'd been wrong to say that because she knew in her heart that they *had* made love, not just engaged in casual sex. Dominic had been moved by their union, she was certain of that. Those hateful words she'd hurled at him should never have been spoken.

Tessa sighed and stared out the window over the sink.

Even if she went to Dominic and apologized for saying what she had, nothing would *really* be solved. Yes, they'd made love, but it wasn't enough. The cold, painful truth would remain the same—Dominic's sense of responsibility toward Jason *and* her was far greater than the caring she'd hoped was growing.

She loved Dominic, but he did *not* love her.

Quick tears filled Tessa's eyes and she blinked them away with an angry shake of her head.

Responsibility.

Oh, how she hated that word.

"Blak," she said, then headed for the front door as she heard the sound of children's voices.

Late the next morning, Carmen called Tessa.

"I won't keep you a second," Carmen said. "I know you're busy with the kids. Tomorrow is Saturday, though. That's play-day in my book. Could you and Jason come into town and have lunch with me?"

"Oh, Carmen, that sounds like fun," Tessa said, "but we can't. Jason has chicken pox."

"No joke? How grim. Does he feel awful?"

"He's not up to par yet. He's still running a slight fever and has no pep. I'm holding him prisoner on the cot in my office. He's not a happy camper." She laughed. "He's starting to feel well enough to be showing signs of being a B.I.T."

"A what?"

"Brat-in-training."

Carmen laughed. "I love it. Well, give him a smooch for me. We'll go to lunch another time."

"Thanks for the invitation, Carmen. Bye for now."

Carmen replaced the receiver, narrowed her eyes, then

snatched up the receiver again. Moments later, she was asking Gladys to put her through to Dominic.

"He's swamped today, Carmen," Gladys said. "And his mood is blacker than coal dust."

"I'll risk it."

"You Bonellis are a brave bunch. Hold on and I'll buzz him."

Carmen tapped her fingertips on the wall next to her telephone.

"What is it, Carmen?" Dominic said gruffly.

"Happy Friday to you, too," she said. "I'm in the mood to go out to lunch tomorrow. Want to join me? In all honesty, you're second choice. I invited Tessa and Jason, but they couldn't go. Poor little Jason is so sick. Anyway, I thought you might—"

Dominic stiffened in his chair. "Jason is sick? What's wrong with him? Why wasn't I told?"

"My stars, Dominic, don't get stressed out. He only has chicken pox. It's just that he's stuck in Tessa's office, he has a slight fever and he's generally not pleased with life. Tessa must be a wreck trying to tend to him as well as take care of things at Rainbow's End. Dominic, do you want to have lunch with me tomorrow, or not?"

"What? Oh, no, I can't. Thanks. Goodbye."

Carmen smiled at the dial tone, then replaced the receiver.

"Gotcha, big brother," she said, giving the telephone a friendly pat.

An hour and a half later, as Tessa was reading the after-lunch story to the children, she heard a car approaching the house. She continued to read, deciding she'd find out who was there when he or she got to the door. The attention of her audience was lost as the screen door was opened. She turned her head and her eyes widened.

"Hello, Tessa," Dominic said.

Chapter Twenty

Tessa forgot to breathe.

The sight of Dominic standing only a few feet away stole the very breath from her body. It wasn't until she attempted to return his greeting that she realized she was completely out of air. She filled her lungs and strove for a pleasant, casual tone of voice.

"Hello," she said.

She got to her feet, nearly cheering aloud when her trembling legs actually supported her.

Oh, Dominic, her mind hummed. He appeared so distinguished in his attorney uniform, so ruggedly handsome, and she loved him so very much. He was there, close, yet they were worlds apart.

Yes, Dominic was there but...why?

"We're in the middle of story hour," she said. "Was there something in particular that you wanted?"

You, Dominic mentally yelled. He was gazing at the woman he loved, the *only* woman he had ever loved and would love for all time. He wanted Tessa, needed her in his life to make him whole. He needed her, and Jason, his son, and the babies he and Tessa would create together in the future.

"Dominic?"

He cleared his throat. "Yes. I'm here to see Jason. I spoke with Carmen and she said he has chicken pox, so I drove out to spend some time with him."

Tessa frowned. "In the middle of your workday?"

"Gladys, my secretary, may never speak to me again because she had to reschedule a very full calendar for this afternoon but... May I see Jason?"

"Yes, of course. He's in my office."

"Fine. You just go on with what you were doing." He paused. "Oh, I hope you don't mind, but I gave Gladys your telephone number. I was waiting for some important information and if it reaches her, I'll have to tell her how to proceed, depending on what she learns."

Tessa nodded, then watched as Dominic crossed the room and disappeared into the kitchen.

Did this make sense? she asked herself, totally confused. Dominic had left his office in the middle of an extremely busy day to come to see Jason? No, that did *not* make sense. Where was his ever-famous sense of responsibility? He was an attorney with obligations and *responsibilities,* for heaven's sake.

"Are you gonna finish the story?" Jeremiah said, bringing Tessa back from her reverie.

"The what?" she said. "Oh! The story." She sat back down. "Okay, where were we?"

The story hour was finally completed, much to Tessa's

relief. Jeremiah had pointed out, none too happily, that Tessa had read the same page twice on three occasions before finishing the book.

Emma and Patty emerged from the kitchen to take the children to the play yard. Both women looked at Tessa questioningly.

"That's Dominic," Tessa said, picking an imaginary thread from her blouse. "He's one of the Bonellis. You know, the group that's been tromping in and out of here repairing the house."

Emma giggled. "Was Dominic the grand prize in the contest?"

"Contest?" Tessa said.

"The Fix-Up-Your-House contest that you won."

"Oh, *that* contest," Tessa said, nodding. "I remember that contest. That was really something, wasn't it?" She pressed one hand to her forehead. "Ignore me."

"Why do I get the feeling there's more going on here than meets the eye?" Emma said.

"Because there is," Patty said firmly. "Let's get these darlings outside and leave Tessa to do what she needs to do."

"Prepare the afternoon snack," Tessa said quickly.

"And whatever," Patty said, beaming. "Let's go, little ones. Put your story rugs in the pile where they belong, then we're off to play."

Much too soon to suit Tessa's frazzled nerves, she was alone, the sound of happy children reaching her from the play yard.

She took a steadying breath, squared her shoulders, then went, albeit rather slowly, to the doorway of the office. Tears burned at the back of her eyes as she drank in the sight before her.

Dominic had removed his jacket and tie, undone the two top buttons of his shirt and rolled the sleeves to midforearm. He was sitting on the side of the cot, an open storybook balanced on his knees. Jason had fallen asleep and Dominic was looking at him, simply looking at him, one of Jason's small hands cradled in Dominic's large one.

Dominic and Jason, Tessa thought, her heart racing. The two most important people in her world, the two she loved with all that she was.

The telephone rang and both Tessa and Dominic jerked at the sudden noise. Tessa turned to hurry to the wall telephone in the kitchen, hoping the shrill ring of the one on her desk wouldn't waken Jason.

"Rainbow's End," she said into the receiver.

"Tessa? This is Gladys, Dominic's secretary. May I speak with him, dear?"

"Yes, I'll get him."

"I'm here," he said from directly behind her.

He took the receiver from Tessa.

"Yep?…I see… That's good. Call Jamison and tell him we're a go, Gladys, that the report came in with what we wanted… Who?… Oh, hell, Baxter? He didn't have an appointment… Yes, I realize I squeeze him in if he comes to town unexpectedly, but not this time… No, he won't be happy, but those are the breaks. What I'm doing here is more important to me… Yes, you can have a raise as compensation for combat duty… Goodbye, Gladys."

He replaced the receiver and turned to see Tessa staring at him with a shocked expression on her face.

"Dominic," she said, wringing her hands, "I think perhaps you've misunderstood chicken pox. What I mean is, Jason isn't seriously ill. He's grumpy and a tad uncomfortable, that's all. There's no reason for you to disrupt your work schedule and upset an important client.''

He shrugged. "Don't worry about it."

"Don't worry about it?'' she repeated. "Good grief, Dominic, I don't want Jason to be the cause of your ignoring your responsibilities at your office.''

"My responsibilities,'' Dominic said slowly. "That word has played a major part in my life. In fact, it has been front-row center in the spotlight, hasn't it?'' He folded his arms across his chest. "As I recall, you're the one who was very vocal on the subject of my placing far too much emphasis on responsibility.''

"Oh. Well, yes, I was, but darn it, Dominic, you're confusing me.''

"Then by all means, Tessa, allow me to explain.''

He dropped his arms to his sides and started toward her. Tessa began to back up, frantically searching his face for some clue as to his mood, his frame of mind and failing to decipher a thing.

He came close. She moved farther back. She finally thudded against the refrigerator. Dominic braced one hand on either side of her head, trapping her in place. Her heart pounded as she stared up at him.

"Tessa,'' he said, his voice low, "I've spent many hours going over everything that transpired between us. Everything.''

A warm flush crept onto Tessa's cheeks as images of the lovemaking shared with Dominic flickered into her mind's eye. She willed the tantalizing pictures to *go away*.

"Responsibility,'' Dominic said, then shook his head. "It was all I'd known for so long that it was a way of life to me. I was *responsible* for a great many people who needed food and a roof over their heads. Later, the needs changed, and I saw to those too. It was up to me.''

''You did a wonderful job all those years for your family,'' she said, her voice hushed.

''To a point, only to a point. I've come to see, Tessa, because of you, and Jason, that there's more that should be given than just money, opportunities, material things. I left out a very important ingredient.''

''You did?''

''I did. I didn't reach deep enough within myself to find, then give, *love*. Until you. Until Jason.''

''What...what are you saying, Dominic?''

''Responsibility comes from the mind. Love comes from the heart.''

''Yes, Dominic, I know.''

''So do I...now. I'm here today because I *want* to be here. Responsibility has nothing to do with it. *It feels right.* I'm here to ask you to forgive me for hurting you. I didn't mean to cause you to cry, Tessa, but I know I did, and I'm so damn sorry.''

''I...''

''And I'm here,'' he went on, ''to tell you *from my heart,* that I love you. I am in love with you, Tessa, and I hope, pray, you'll agree to be my wife. We'll raise Jason, *our son,* together and, God willing, we'll add some more babies to the clan.''

Tears filled Tessa's eyes.

''Ah, hell, Tessa,'' Dominic said, his voice choked with emotion. ''I've been so wrong about this responsibility thing for so long. I'll need you to be patient with me until I really get a solid handle on how it's supposed to work.''

Two tears slid down Tessa's cheeks.

''Don't cry,'' he said. ''I don't know what to do when

you cry. Are you sad again? I love you, I want to spend the rest of my life with you. Am I too late? Are you beyond being able to forgive me? Is that why you're crying?''

"Oh, no, Dominic," she said, placing her hands on his cheeks. "These are tears of joy because I love you so much. I thought you were lost to me."

A sob caught in her throat.

"Yes, oh, yes, I'll marry you," she said, smiling through her tears. "The future looked so bleak, so lonely, without you. You were the treasure at the end of my rainbow that I believed I would never have. I love you, Dominic Bonelli."

Dominic closed his eyes for a moment and took a raspy breath.

"Thank God," he said, his voice thick with emotion. He looked directly into Tessa's eyes again. "And I love you, Tessa Russell."

He pulled her close, his mouth melting over hers as she moved her hands from his face to entwine them around his neck.

The kiss was searing, causing desire to consume them. The kiss was forgiveness and greater understanding. The kiss was happiness filling their hearts and sealing their commitment to forever.

"Mommy? Dominic?" Jason had left the office and was standing in the kitchen doorway yawning. "Dominic, when you're done doin' that kissing stuff with my mom, would you read more of the story to me?"

"Kissing stuff?" Dominic said with a burst of laughter. "Remind me to ask you how you feel about kissing stuff in about ten years, Jason." He looked at Tessa. "Should we talk to him now about our future?"

Tessa nodded. "Yes, but I don't think this is the time to explain everything. When he's older, we'll tell him about Janice. Is that all right?"

"It's fine, just fine."

They crossed the room and Dominic picked Jason up, giving him a hug. The trio went into the office and settled onto the cot, Jason nestled on Dominic's lap.

"Jason," Dominic said, "you and I are friends, right?"

"Right."

"Friends like each other, right?"

"Right."

"Well, my feelings for you grew bigger than just liking you as a friend. I love you, Jason, and I love your mother, very, very much. I've asked your mom to marry me, to be my wife."

"Oh," Jason said, frowning. "Does that mean my mom is the mom, and you're the dad, and I'm the little boy?" His face lit up with a smile. "Are we going to be a family, really for honest?"

"Really for honest," Dominic said. "Does that sound okay to you?"

Jason placed his small hands on Dominic's cheeks. "Are you gonna be my daddy?"

"Oh, yes, Jason," he said, tears filling his eyes. "I'm going to be the best daddy I can possibly be."

"Will you love me and my mom forever?"

"Forever and an extra day."

"*Buono!*" Jason yelled, then flung his arms around Dominic's neck.

"Oh-h-h," Tessa said, smiling even as tears spilled onto her cheeks.

"Jason," Dominic said, "this means that *all* the Bonellis will be part of your family for that forever and an extra day. How does *that* sound?''

''Neato!'' Jason wiggled off Dominic's lap. ''Wait, wait.''

He rummaged through a stack of papers, took one, grabbed a roll of tape from Tessa's desk and ran out of the room.

Tessa and Dominic looked at each other questioningly, then got quickly to their feet to follow Jason.

In the main room, Jason taped the paper he'd colored to the spot just above the empty pot at the base of the rainbow on the wall.

In the drawing were stick figures of a man, woman and child.

''That's me,'' Jason said, pointing to the smallest figure. ''That's you, Mommy, and that's you, Dominic. I drew that for my rainbow wish, and it came true. That's cool.''

Tessa and Dominic looked at each other, love shining in their eyes that glistened with tears.

''It's wonderful,'' Tessa whispered.

''It's forever,'' Dominic said.

Jason marched back into the office and busied himself looking at a book.

His mom and dad would read him a story later, he decided, but now they were doin' that kissing stuff again.

In the main room, a sudden burst of sunlight shone through the front window directly onto the glorious rainbow, making the vibrant colors glow even brighter.

Dominic lifted his head to speak close to Tessa's lips. ''*Io ti voglio bene.* I love you.''

''*Buono,* Dominic,'' Tessa said, smiling. ''*Buono.*''

Epilogue

One Year Later

Dominic crossed the large living room and settled onto the sofa facing a crackling fire in the hearth. He picked up one of Tessa's hands and kissed the palm.

"Is Jason asleep?" Tessa said.

"Out like a light. I read him the Buddy Bunny story again. I can just about recite that one by heart."

Tessa smiled. "It's his favorite, because Buddy Bunny found his family just as Jason feels *he* did. Oh, Dominic, Jason is such a happy little boy."

"And you, Mrs. Bonelli? How are you measuring on the happiness scale?"

"Up and over the top."

"Ditto." He gave her a quick kiss on the lips. "I'm

sorry I was late getting home. I hate not having dinner with you and Jason.''

"It doesn't happen very often, and you do have *responsibilities* at the office, Mr. Bonelli.''

Dominic rolled his eyes heavenward. "That word, that word. It will haunt me until I'm old and gray.''

"No, I just poke you with it once in a while so we never forget how close we came to not understanding each other, losing what was ours to share. I don't ever want to take our world for granted, Dominic.''

"Fair enough. So, sweet wife, what kind of day did you have?''

"Well, the drapes came for our bedroom, so I took the sheets off the windows. I gave Carmen my first official report as a free-lance accountant. The details are worked out for the barbecue here Sunday to celebrate our built-from-scratch new home, with all the Bonellis in attendance. And I signed the papers selling Rainbow's End to the single mother with the two little girls.''

Dominic chuckled. "Is that all? We need to talk about how lazy you've become.''

Tessa laughed in delight, then her smile faded.

"Dominic?''

"Yes, my love?''

"I did one other thing today.''

"Oh?'' He raised his eyebrows.

"Well, I... Oh, dear,'' she said, her eyes filling with tears.

"Hey, whoa,'' he said, encircling her with his arms. "What is it? What's wrong?''

"Nothing is wrong,'' she said quickly. "You get so upset at the sight of tears.''

"Yeah, well, they shake me up. Confess. What else did you do today?"

"I found out that we're going to have a baby."

Dominic opened his mouth, snapped it closed, then tried again.

"Are you sure?" he said. "Jeez, Bonelli, that was dumb. Of course you're sure. Oh, Tessa, that is fantastic. You're pleased, aren't you? I'd hate to be floating around on cloud nine all alone."

"I'm thrilled, Dominic. There aren't words to tell you how happy I am."

"Ah, Tessa, thank you. I love you, I love you, I love you."

He kissed her deeply, and their passion soared instantly, burning like the licking flames in the fireplace.

They stood only long enough to shed their clothes, then sank onto the plush carpeting, the fire's light casting a golden glow over their naked bodies.

It was all so familiar, yet, in the wondrous world of lovers who were truly in love, it was new and exciting.

Dominic splayed one hand across Tessa's stomach.

"Hello, little Bonelli," he said, his voice husky with emotion. "Hello, little miracle. You've got a dandy big brother, who's going to think you're the greatest thing since *gelato*."

"Do you hope it's a girl?" Tessa said.

"That would be nice. We'd have a son and a daughter. Or we'll have two sons, if it's a boy. It doesn't matter. We'll have two children. Ours. Ours, Tessa."

"Oh, Dominic, I love you so much."

He captured her mouth with his, and they gave way to their desire, hearts nearly bursting with love and the multitude of blessings they knew were theirs.

Hands and lips paid homage to a body soft and a body taut with muscles. They held back, anticipating what was yet to come, until they could wait no more.

Dominic moved over Tessa and entered her. They were one entity—hearts, minds, souls and bodies meshed.

They soared to their place, the private ecstasy that was theirs alone, reaching for it, higher and higher, bursting upon it moments apart as they whispered the name of the one they loved.

They lingered there, surrounded by the glorious colors of the rainbow.

* * * * *

Dear Reader,

Baby My Baby is one of my favorite books. I think the Heller clan is very special and Beth Heller— the only daughter of the family—sparks particular interest for me. Growing up with rough-and-tumble, protective brothers gives her unique qualities— some that serve her well and others that make her life more difficult. Especially when she finds herself pregnant by the husband she's divorced. The husband who still tugs on her heartstrings.

But then why wouldn't Ash Blackwolf tug on Beth's heartstrings? He sure tugs on mine! A proud, dignified, full-blooded Native American Sioux, Ash Blackwolf is accomplished, successful, true to his heritage, drop-dead gorgeous and so, so sexy.

I liked exploring the difference between his culture and hers, exploring how aspects of his culture colored his personality and character. I just plain liked Ash! And the story of a couple on a rocky road into love, out of it and back into it. I hope you enjoy it, too.

Happy reading!

Victoria Pade

BABY MY BABY
Victoria Pade

Prologue

Standing at her bedroom window in her family home, Beth Heller looked out over the swimming pool and the reunion that was going on below. Her brother Linc and her old friend Kansas Daye had clearly patched up the differences that had made their private rocky road to love a bumpy ride. Their feelings for each other were so apparent there was almost an aura surrounding them, and seeing it made Beth's heart ache like a bad tooth.

Only one thing could have them coming together so exuberantly—Kansas must have accepted Linc's proposal. No doubt there would be a wedding coming up.

Beth was glad for her brother. She knew how much he cared for Kansas and how worried he'd been that she might turn him down.

It was nice to see that some people did have happy endings.

Even if Beth wasn't one of them.

As she watched, Linc's three-year-old son, Danny, in-sinuated himself between his father and Kansas, wrapping a possessive arm around each of them.

The little boy's sweetness made Beth smile. It reminded her that her own ending hadn't been completely bad.

One good thing had come out of it.

One very good thing.

With that in mind, she pushed away from the window and went to sit on the bed, pulling the telephone into her lap.

But her hand stalled on the receiver as a terrible temptation washed through her.

What if she didn't tell him?

He might never know if she didn't.

They probably wouldn't see each other again. After all, there wasn't any reason for their paths to cross, since they hardly moved in similar circles. And without anyone in Elk Creek knowing him, chances were no rumors would reach him.

Of course, it was remotely possible Cele would tell him. But Beth doubted it. Technically, as her physician, Cele couldn't divulge confidential information unless Beth gave her permission to, and she didn't think the doctor would break that trust even though she was Ash's friend, too.

But as the temptation grew to keep the information to herself, so did the nudge of her conscience.

"It wouldn't be right," she told herself out loud. Then she added as firmly as if she were ordering someone else to perform a dreaded task, "You have to tell him, so do it and get it over with."

She took a deep breath and forced herself to pick up the phone, punching in the number she'd dialed far too many times lately.

GET 2

HOW TO GET YOUR
2 FREE BOOKS AND FREE GIFT!

1. Peel off the MIRA® sticker on the front cover. Place it in the space provided at right. This automatically entitles you to receive two free books and an exciting surprise gift.

2. Send back this card and you'll get 2 "The Best of the Best™" books. These books have a combined cover price of $11.98 or more in the U.S. and $13.98 or more in Canada, but they are yours to keep absolutely FREE!

3. There's <u>no</u> catch. You're under <u>no</u> obligation to buy anything. We charge nothing – ZERO – for your first shipment. And you don't have to make any minimum number of purchases – not even one!

4. We call this line "The Best of the Best" because each month you'll receive the best books by some of today's most popular authors. These authors show up time and time again on all the major bestseller lists and their books sell out as soon as they hit the stores. You'll like the convenience of getting them delivered to your home at our special discount prices . . . and you'll love your *Heart to Heart* subscriber newsletter featuring author news, horoscopes, recipes, book reviews and much more!

SPECIAL FREE GIFT
We'll send you a fabulous surprise gift, absolutely FREE, simply for accepting our no-risk offer!

5. We hope that after receiving your free books you'll want to remain a subscriber. But the choice is yours – to continue or cancel, anytime at all! So why not take us up on our invitation, with no risk of any kind. You'll be glad you did!

6. And remember...we'll send you a surprise gift ABSOLUTELY FREE just for giving THE BEST OF THE BEST a try.

Visit us online at
www.mirabooks.com

® and TM are registered trademark of Harlequin Enterprises Limited.

BOOKS FREE!

THE BEST OF THE BEST™ — Here's How it Works:

Accepting your 2 free books and gift places you under no obligation to buy anything. You may keep the books and gift and return the shipping statement marked "cancel." If you do not cancel, about a month later we will send you 4 additional books and bill you just $4.74 each in the U.S., or $5.24 each in Canada, plus 25¢ shipping & handling per book and applicable taxes if any.* That's the complete price and — compared to cover prices starting from $5.99 each in the U.S. and $6.99 each in Canada — it's quite a bargain! You may cancel at any time, but if you choose to continue, every month we'll send you 4 more books, which you may either purchase at the discount price or return to us and cancel your subscription.
*Terms and prices subject to change without notice. Sales tax applicable in N.Y. Canadian residents will be charged applicable provincial taxes and GST. Credit or Debit balances in a customer's account(s) may be offset by any other outstanding balance owed by or to the customer.

If offer card is missing write to: The Best of the Best, 3010 Walden Ave., P.O. Box 1867, Buffalo, NY 14240-1867

BUSINESS REPLY MAIL
FIRST-CLASS MAIL   PERMIT NO. 717-003   BUFFALO, NY

POSTAGE WILL BE PAID BY ADDRESSEE

THE BEST OF THE BEST
3010 WALDEN AVE
PO BOX 1867
BUFFALO NY 14240-9952

NO POSTAGE
NECESSARY
IF MAILED
IN THE
UNITED STATES

"Just this once, be there," she whispered as she listened to each interminable ring.

"Blackwolf Foundation," the secretary answered.

Beth swallowed hard. "Hi, Miss Lightfeather, this is Beth again," she managed, giving no indication that her insides were tied in knots.

"Hello, Mrs. Blackwolf," came the aloof response, announcing loudly the other woman's feelings that Beth was an interloper.

She considered reminding her former husband's secretary that she'd taken back her maiden name after the divorce, but she didn't. And she didn't bother with amenities, either. It would be a useless effort, she knew from long experience. Instead she plunged in. "I'm still trying to connect with Ash. Is he there now by any chance?"

"No, he isn't. And I'm afraid I haven't given him your messages. He's been even more busy than usual and has had a great deal on his mind."

"Nothing new there," Beth muttered to herself.

If the secretary heard her, she didn't acknowledge it. Instead she went on imperiously. "He's been called away to Alaska to see if the foundation can help in the defense of an Indian boy in trouble up there."

Beth doubted that any phone line in that great snowy north had more icicles forming along it than the one she was on at that moment. But she tried to ignore the arctic chill from the other end. "How long will he be there?"

"He's not coming straight home. He has to go to a seminar he agreed to do at Harvard on Native Americans, after which he's meeting with the head of Indian Affairs in Washington before he attends a joint tribal conference in South Dakota."

Old frustrations flooded Beth, leaving her weary and sad and even angry. But she didn't let any of it sound in her voice. "Maybe you should give me some phone numbers where I could try to reach him."

"Is it an emergency?" the formidable secretary asked.

"No. But it is very important that I talk to him."

"It would be best to wait until he gets back here to the reservation."

Was that a polite way to say she had orders not to give Beth the numbers, or did the protective Miss Lightfeather just not want her to have them? Beth didn't care to push it and discover the worst.

"Yes. I suppose it would be better to wait," she said on a sigh, dreading the idea of the delay. Ash might not be home for weeks.

"Was there anything else?" the secretary asked after a moment.

"No. Thanks anyway."

Beth hung up, wishing fervently—as she had each time this had happened—that she'd actually reached her ex-husband so she could have told him what she needed to and could finally put this behind her. For that was what she wanted more than anything—not to have to think about it anymore. Not to have to think about Ash anymore, or how he'd react.

Or how she'd bear hearing his voice again...

Then, as if in answer to that, her gaze settled on the desk in the corner of the room, and a new thought occurred to her.

She could write him a letter.

Why hadn't she considered that before? Certainly it seemed like the perfect solution. Getting hold of him was nearly impossible anyway, whether he was on the reservation or not. Writing would give her the relief of knowing she'd gotten it off her chest, and at the same time, she'd have the opportunity to choose her words, to make sure she conveyed just the right tone, just the right message.

Writing would let her keep her distance.

She went to the desk, sat down and took stationery and a pen from the drawer, wondering how exactly to begin.

"Dear Ash," she wrote in an unsteady hand.

Her mouth was dry and she considered going downstairs for something to drink. But she knew she was just procrastinating. And once more the terrible temptation not to tell him at all crossed her mind.

She set her teeth against it and put pen to paper with the determination of the damned.

I've been trying to reach you since before I left the reservation, but because I haven't had any luck, I thought I'd just drop you a note.

First, it's important for you to understand that I'm not writing because anything needs to change between us. I just thought you should know.

In a few months you're going to be a father...

Chapter One

"He's coming *here? Now?*" Beth said into the telephone to the woman who had been her friend and gynecologist on Wyoming's Wind River Indian Reservation.

"Apparently he arrived home around eleven last night and found your letter in his mail. He was waiting at my office door when I got there this morning," Cele explained. "I tried to convince him to just call you, to talk first, but he wasn't having any of that. He said there were a few things he had to take care of and then he was leaving for Elk Creek."

"You knew about this all day and didn't call me until now?" Beth asked, calculating how long the trip took from the western section of the state to the southeastern corner where Elk Creek was located.

"I'm sorry. I've been trying to find a minute to call you and this is the first one I've had. I don't know when he left, but I know he's gone, because I tried getting hold of him again before calling you and that nasty secretary of his said I was too late.''

Which meant that Asher Blackwolf, ex-husband, could be on the Heller doorstep anytime now.

Lord.

The phone Beth was using was on her nightstand, which was a good thing, because the starch suddenly went out of her knees and she had to sit on the bed. ''How did he seem?'' she asked, her tone ominous.

''Surprised—no, make that stunned. Confused—''

''Mad?''

''Maybe. Though it wasn't as if he blew off steam or anything overt. In fact, the way he acted sort of reminded me of you—all bottled up. I can just see the two of you together right now, *both* of you holding everything in, resolving nothing. It's not going to help the situation.''

Beth knew where her friend was headed with this. She'd been pulling for a reconciliation since the pregnancy test turned up positive. ''*The situation* will never get better, Cele. The marriage is over,'' she reminded, with an unquestioning finality and a determined straightening of her spine.

''The marriage may be over, but that baby you're carrying means your connection to Ash isn't.''

''Not necessarily.''

''Don't kid yourself, Beth.''

''He has enough other responsibilities already—*more* than enough. Too many. And—''

''Don't kid yourself, Beth,'' the doctor repeated. ''This is his child we're talking about—you know—flesh of his flesh, bone of his bone?''

''He didn't want us to have our own children.''

''But now you're going to. And mark my words, babies bring with them big changes.''

A click on the line warned that the doctor had another call and Beth was only too happy to end this one.

"Have you seen an obstetrician there yet?" the other woman asked hurriedly.

"Elk Creek only has one doctor and he's not a specialist. But I have an appointment with him in a few days."

"Good. Well, let me know what happens."

Beth assured her friend she would, said goodbye and hung up. But her eyes stayed glued to the phone as her mind spun.

She didn't want big changes in her life. Or at least no change beyond the one she'd just made, moving back to Elk Creek.

She'd come home to the ranch that she, her two brothers and someone named Ally Brooks had inherited to get back in touch with the familiar faces, familiar places of her childhood, to once again be where she belonged.

Because since leaving Elk Creek after high school, she hadn't been anywhere she really fit in.

She'd gone from the laid-back, small Wyoming town where she'd grown up, to six years of college in Boston, with its aloofness and formality. Then she'd joined the Peace Corps and spent four years in Tunisia—a place where men openly showed their affection for one another while women maintained a lower place in society, one far different from the show-'em-you're-as-tough-as-they-are way she'd been raised by her father, the irascible Shag Heller.

Then she'd met Ash. On the plane coming back to the States.

Asher Blackwolf. A full-blooded Native American Sioux.

Until the moment she'd seen him as she'd walked through first-class to coach on that plane, she'd have scoffed at anyone who believed in love at first sight. In eyes meeting and an instant sense of being drawn to a perfect stranger.

But that's what had happened.

And then she'd moved on, feeling absolutely ridiculous.

Until the plane had had to land unexpectedly in Albuquerque because of engine trouble. They'd been stranded there for the entire night.

He'd sought her out at the hotel the airline had put them all up in and asked her to dinner. But when dinner had ended, neither of them had been anxious to say good-night and so they'd drifted outside the restaurant into a balmy New Mexico evening.

Ash had shown her the sights of the old city as if he were a native, had entertained her with Indian folklore and tall tales. He'd talked just enough about himself to intrigue her, and listened to what she had to say about herself with such rapt interest that it had seemed as if they were the only two people in the world. Or at least in the city that slept through the night while Ash and Beth seemed exempt from that need themselves.

And though it seemed hopelessly cliché, there had been magic between them. Along with a sexual attraction so intense, it nearly took her breath away just to remember it....

Not that they'd acted on it until days later.

No, that night they'd merely indulged in the magic. Ash had enchanted her. Plain and simple. If enchantment could ever be plain and simple.

The sun had come up with them still talking and by then it was as if they'd known each other forever. Certainly as if they'd taken longer than that first glance and a dozen hours to fall in love.

But fall in love was what they'd done....

And now, for just a moment, that memory was unbearably sweet to Beth.

A whole lifetime together was what she'd been certain they'd have, for once she knew Ash, she couldn't imagine anything less. Couldn't imagine ever being with anyone else.

And the speed at which it had happened? It hadn't seemed crazy or impetuous or irrational, because being with him had felt so right, so perfect, so destined.... It was honestly as if he were her other half. That single person out there in the world who was meant for her and fate had just wreaked a little engine trouble to bring it to their attention.

She'd married him within the month, without a qualm or a doubt. She'd been so eager to begin her life with him, as if everything that had come before was only a rehearsal and the real thing wouldn't begin until they were wed.

The real thing had meant living on the reservation.

Memories of that were not so sweet.

She'd been accepted there. For the most part, Indian people were a warm, welcoming lot. But there was still a notable group who had resented her being white. Ash's secretary, Miss Lightfeather, among them. And there had been sacred places that were off-limits to her, rites and rituals she wasn't allowed to attend, customs and ceremonies that were very foreign to her.

Not that any of it had really contributed to the breakup of her marriage. Of the three places she'd lived since leaving Elk Creek, the reservation had been the most like home.

No, where she'd really felt the outsider there had been in her husband's life. And that was what had destroyed the marriage.

They'd been divorced for nearly two months now. After

wrapping up the details of her job and packing up her portion of the house, she'd driven away from the reservation and back to Elk Creek.

Back home. To her roots, her family, her friends.

"Just stay away," she whispered to the phone, as if the message might reach her former husband.

But he wasn't staying away. He was headed to Elk Creek.

Her brothers didn't know she was pregnant. She'd been putting off telling them, not sure what their reaction would be, and feeling that after herself and her gynecologist, Ash should be the next to know.

But obviously Ash knew now. She had to fill in Linc and Jackson before her ex-husband showed up on the doorstep.

Ignoring the nervousness that had her feeling wound tight as a clock spring, she stood with a new determination. But when she did, she caught sight of herself in the mirror above her dressing table and stalled.

After months of finding her face pale, her blue eyes dull, her usually full lips drawn tight, she saw something different now. And it surprised her.

"Maybe it's that glow of pregnancy finally settling in," she suggested, turning her head just a little, as if a slightly different angle would convince her.

Her dark brown hair *had* seemed fuller lately, she thought. It had been wavier, too, so that the wedgelike cut of it fluffed out at just the right bouncy angle and left the nicest tendrils against her temple. And certainly her sudden surge of energy and vitality had nothing to do with the possible reappearance of her ex-husband.

It was just a normal reaction to her pregnancy.

Her lack of appetite hadn't kept her stomach from beginning to pooch, but it had put a nice indentation in her cheeks that accentuated the high bones above them. And if there was suddenly a hint of pink there? The rosy blush of a healthy mother-to-be. No, the impending arrival of Ash Blackwolf served only to unnerve her.

"So get out of here and do something about it," she ordered.

Taking a deep, steeling breath, she left her room, meeting Linc in the hallway just outside her door as he said his last good-night to his son.

The middle Heller son was a tall, handsome man who'd just agreed to give up his wandering ways and settle down—or what he considered settling down—to open a honky-tonk on the edge of town. He was the less serious of her two brothers, the lighthearted, good-time-Charlie, and he met her with a grin to prove it.

"I need to talk to you and Jackson," Beth said in a hushed voice so as not to disturb her nephew.

"Sounds serious," Linc answered, his tone anything but.

"Downstairs," Beth instructed, leading the way to the wide-open, slate-tiled foyer of the sprawling house that was evidence of Shag Heller's success in both ranching and business. Jackson was standing in the sunken living room near the big-screen television, checking the listings for the evening's programs.

"Beth wants to talk to us," Linc informed their older brother.

Jackson resembled Linc, though he was a shade better looking, just the way he was a shade taller. Both men had the sparkling blue eyes, sharply planed faces, and the dent in their chins that had distinguished their late father.

But appearance was the only similarity between her brothers, for temperamentally, Jackson was more like Shag—serious, down-to-earth, no-nonsense. It wasn't surprising to have him set aside his program guide, turn off the TV, cross his arms over his chest and home in on her with an expression solemn enough for a war summit.

"It's about time," he commented to Linc's announcement. Little got past Jackson, and Beth knew that if either of her brothers had guessed her condition, it would be him.

"I have a problem I need you guys to help me with," she said. "I…" It was harder than she'd thought to say this. But Shag Heller would not tolerate pussyfooting around and she'd learned her lessons from him well. She cleared her throat and blurted, "I'm pregnant."

Linc took his wallet from his back pocket and handed a twenty-dollar bill to Jackson, who accepted it without taking his eyes off Beth for more than a moment.

"Are congratulations in order?" Linc asked, sounding partly as if he were teasing and partly as if he honestly weren't sure the sentiment was appropriate.

Jackson frowned at her. "What I want to know is, who's the father and where the hell is he?"

"That's what I need to talk about. Ash is the father." No money changed hands, this time. Beth was glad to know they hadn't been betting on that subject, at least.

"How'd that happen?" Jackson asked.

Linc threw him a look and shook his head. To Beth he said, "Black-and-white. Everything is black-and-white with him, just like with old Shag." To Jackson, he said, "When hearts and hormones are involved, anything can happen. Anytime. One of these days you're going to run into a filly who'll teach you that."

Jackson just stared darkly at him for a moment before pivoting his gaze to Beth again as if he was still waiting for an answer that made sense.

Beth had no intention of giving one. "The point is, I'm about five months along, but until the day before I left the reservation and finally saw a doctor, I thought stress was causing…my symptoms. So, of course, when I found this out, the divorce was final.''

"But the baby's still Ash's," Jackson reminded.

"Well, yes, but that doesn't really make any difference—"

"It sure as hell does." Again this from Jackson.

"Will you let her talk?" Linc asked.

Jackson remained stoic but silent and she went on.

"I couldn't reach Ash to tell him, so I finally sent him a note.'' Beth drew yet another deep breath, shoring up to hide the uncertainty she really felt about being a single mother. "I explained that this doesn't really have to mean anything to him, that I can afford to support the baby myself and want to raise it on my own, and he doesn't need to be bothered with anything—"

"Bothered?" Jackson raised his voice. "It's his baby, not a bother. Is that how he looks at it?''

"No. Well, I don't know. Jackson, will you calm down? Ash didn't want us to have kids of our own for perfectly good reasons I don't have the time to get into right now, and—"

"He doesn't want his own baby? I took him for better than that. I must have been mistaken.''

Beth closed her eyes for a moment and then opened them to Linc. "Would you throw some cold water on him so I can get this out?''

"Shut up, Jackson" was Linc's contribution. But it again stalled their brother.

"I don't know what Ash's reaction to the news was. He just got the letter last night and I haven't talked to him. But the thing is, he's on his way here. In fact, he could be here any minute, and I don't want to see him." Again she disguised her own doubts with a mask of strength she didn't honestly feel. "I don't need his help with the baby, and I don't want it. In fact, I don't need or want anyone to give it a second thought. I want you, Linc, to pay attention to your wedding plans and your honky-tonk, and you, Jackson, to just take care of the ranch, and Ash to go back to the reservation and go on about his business just the way he does normally."

"I don't know about that," Linc mused, and Beth knew she'd poured it on a little too thick.

But there was no admitting to anything less than complete independence. Not for her. Not for a Heller. So she forged on insistently.

"Ash and I are *divorced*. It was a clean break and I want it to stay a clean break. This baby doesn't fit in with his plans, anyway, so when he gets here, I want you guys to say I left Elk Creek and you don't know where I am," she finished like a boulder gaining momentum on a roll down a steep hill.

"By God, he owes his own child more than to just turn around and act as if it doesn't exist," Jackson nearly shouted.

"You know, Beth," Linc interjected reasonably. "Jackson isn't all wrong. No matter what Ash's plans were, or how he may or may not feel about it, he has a responsibility to this baby and to you now."

"You don't understand. I don't want—"

The doorbell rang right then to cut off her words.

Beth suddenly felt hot and cold at once, as if something were chasing her, and all she knew was that she had to get away.

"Please," she implored her brothers. "If that's Ash, just tell him I'm gone. Tell him I don't want anything from him but for him to leave me alone."

"Like hell I will!" Jackson headed for the door.

Beth turned a final plea to Linc. "Come on, trust that I know what I'm doing. It's really better if Ash and I don't see each other."

"I don't know about that, Beth," he repeated.

"Look, I'm going to slip out the back door, so telling Ash I'm not here won't even be a lie—for the moment at least. Just do it and get rid of him!" And with that she turned and hurried through the dining room in the direction of the kitchen.

She had every intention of doing just what she'd said, or getting out of the house, into her car and taking off—if not for parts unknown, then at least for the other side of town. For Kansas's house maybe.

But she only got as far as the swinging doors to the kitchen before she stopped.

Go on! she told herself.

And she meant it.

But somehow she was suddenly paralyzed. She turned toward the front door just as Jackson opened it.

And there Ash stood. Tall, proud, almost regal in his bearing and the pure power of his masculinity.

Her heart took a skip she didn't want it to, and then everything seemed to click into slow motion as she watched Jackson double his fist and land a punishing blow to her former husband's jaw.

Ash's head shot to the side, but that was all that was disturbed by the punch that would have knocked any man in Elk Creek across a room.

Then the big, powerful Indian again leveled his coal-colored eyes on her brother and, with a deadly calm, he said in his deep, rich bass voice, "I'm here to see Beth."

The instant the words were spoken, something made him look past her brothers into the dining room, where Beth had stalled. And just the way her gaze had been caught and held by his on that airplane the first time they'd met, so it was now.

Did she heard him whisper her name or only read it on his lips? She didn't know. But she knew he'd said it. And somehow she also knew it was filled with confusion. With pain. Maybe with longing....

No, that couldn't be.

But she suddenly realized those things were alive in her, even if they weren't in him. And she hated herself for it. For the fact that for just one split second it took away the anger she felt at him—for being there, for not having given her the life she'd been so sure they'd have together. Her anger at what would never be...

"Go away, Ash," she said in a voice that was barely audible.

In spite of her brothers blocking his path, he took a step forward, as if he wouldn't—or couldn't—stay away from her.

"Linc!" she called, sounding panicky, beseeching her brother for the help she'd requested moments before.

Then she saw Linc's hand go to Ash's broad, hard chest to hold him back.

And that was when she made her escape.

From the man who had fathered her child.

The man she'd divorced.

The man who had, once upon a time, enchanted her.

Chapter Two

Asher Blackwolf stood in front of the mirror in the bathroom of his rented log cabin in Elk Creek's only tourist
accommodation—the ten-cabin hunting lodge. With a hand
on either side of the old-fashioned pedestal sink, he leaned
close and turned his stiff jaw carefully from one side to
the other, angling his head slightly to give himself the full
view of his jawbone.

There was soreness to go with the slight discoloration
where Jackson Heller's fist had landed the night before,
but he'd live, he thought wryly.

And a punch in the face was the only thing he'd gotten
for his trouble.

"Damn you, Beth," he muttered under his breath, not
really blaming Jackson—or Linc, either—for being upset
and feeling protective of their sister. In spite of the fact
that she wasn't in need of protection.

Even Linc, who he knew to be the more mild mannered

of the two, had looked as if he wanted to bruise the other side of Ash's jaw. But then, if he had a sister who was pregnant by her ex-husband and ran out of the house as if she were afraid of him, he doubted that he'd be well-disposed toward that ex-husband himself.

Of course, she didn't have any damn reason to be afraid of him. Or to run from him, for God's sake. And he didn't really understand why she had. Did she hate him that much?

That thought twisted his gut, though he told himself the response was uncalled-for. Whether she loved him or hated him shouldn't matter. Their marriage was over.

But what he had every right to resent was her leaving him alone with his two former brothers-in-law glaring at him as if he were a mass murderer.

For three hours he'd sat there facing them, none of them knowing what to say, none of them happy. Jackson downright mad, and Linc only repeating again and again that Beth had begged him to tell Ash to go back to the reservation and leave her alone, and suggesting that maybe that was what he should do.

Ash had certainly spent more pleasant evenings.

It hadn't even been informative. Beyond the fact that their sister was pregnant, neither Linc nor Jackson knew any more than Ash did.

And he had plenty of questions. Like why the hell she hadn't come to him personally with news like this. Why she'd waited so long. Why she hadn't told him before the divorce was final. What they were going to do now...

Ash let his head hang down between his shoulders as the impact of the news washed over him the way it had been every few minutes since he'd found out.

She was *pregnant*...

Was she happy about it? Unhappy about it? Did she

resent that the baby was his? Was that why she wanted to exclude him—so she could try forgetting it was his child at all?

No doubt about it, there were questions he needed answered.

Linc had assured him he'd try to reason with her about seeing him. But whether or not his former brother-in-law convinced her to agree to it, Beth Heller was going to see him today. She could do it willingly, or she could do it unwillingly, but she was going to see him.

Because the one thing he wouldn't do was accept her orders to ignore the bombshell she'd dropped on him.

He pushed off the sink and went back into the room where one double bed, a small table with two chairs and a bureau with a TV on top of it filled the space. His suitcase was open on the rack at the foot of the bed and as he bent over it to get a clean shirt, he caught sight of Beth's letter out of the corner of his eye.

His teeth clenched at just the thought of it, but rather than taking his shirt out the way he'd meant to, his hand reached to the letter.

He'd read it a dozen times since finding it in the mail that had accumulated while he was gone, but for some reason he was compelled to open it and read it yet again.

It was just like her, he thought, feeling a dull ache in his jaw from muscles that tightened in anger.

She didn't want his help.

She didn't need it.

She had everything planned out. Everything under control. Everything taken care of.

He was superfluous.

Excess baggage.

No, she hadn't said he was superfluous or excess baggage. Not in so many words, anyway. But he knew it was what she was telling him.

But, damn it, this baby was his, too. And he wasn't going to be written out of its life before it was even born. Or after, either, for that matter.

He sat on the edge of the bed and stared at the words on the white paper.

In a few months you're going to be a father... Once more that wave of shock and awe and disbelief washed through him.

They were going to have a *baby*.

He and his beautiful Beth...

Ash's eyes pinched closed in rejection of that thought that had come on its own and he shook his head the way a dog shakes off water.

She wasn't *his* Beth anymore.

They were divorced and he had no claim on her.

Or did he? The baby changed things, that was for sure. It tied them together despite the legal severing of their marriage.

But did it give him claim to Beth again?

Probably not.

Not that he wanted claim to her again.

They'd been right to get divorced. Somehow they'd lost that precious spark that had brought them together. She went her way. He went his. And every now and then they met up. Usually accidentally. Or coincidentally.

Or in bed...

But he was better off not thinking about that.

He still held the letter, and once more he focused on the impeccable handwriting on the crisp white stationery, hating the words that were there. Not for their message of the baby, but for what they conveyed about Beth not needing him.

It didn't surprise him. Why should this be any different?

But he couldn't help wishing that just this once it had been.

Deep down, in a secret place he didn't want to acknowledge even to himself, he envisioned the letter he wished he'd received. *We're going to have a baby and I need you by my side. I want you...*

He blew out a wry, mirthless sigh at the very thought.

Not Beth Heller. The earth could open up under her feet and she wouldn't holler for help.

She was the damned most self-sufficient person he knew. And the stubbornest.

Not that anyone would think it to look at her. She was so thin, so fragile looking, with that alabaster skin and those wide blue eyes the color of Colorado columbines. Delicate—that was the word for how she appeared, her high-cheekboned face haloed in that thick, coffee-bean-hued hair, those soft pale lips, that thin nose that could have belonged to a porcelain doll...

Ha! She was no porcelain doll. Beneath it all beat a will and determination stronger than any man's. Furniture to move? Beth Heller would do it herself. Or die trying. A tight lid to open? She'd beat on it, run it under hot water, use pliers, nearly break the jar rather than admit she couldn't do it herself. Heavy boxes? If she couldn't drag them, she'd devise something else—once she'd used roller skates—but she sure as hell wouldn't ask for help.

Funny—when they'd first met, her independence had been one of the things that had attracted him to her. But her determination had somehow lost its charm. Ash wished that, just once, she would break down and admit she needed him.

But maybe what she'd told him was the truth. That even pregnant with his child, she didn't want him or need him.

It had been such a long time since Ash had been able to read her feelings. She'd never been the type to say "I love you." In the early months of their marriage, though, he'd always seemed to sense what she was feeling.

Somewhere, they'd lost their connection. She hadn't so much as let him comfort her in her grief when her father had died. All she'd shown him was a stiff upper lip. Stoicism. Resolution. Death, she'd said to dismiss his concern for how she might be taking the news, was a fact of life.

Then, in the middle of the night when she'd thought he was asleep, she'd locked herself in the bathroom to cry for the old cuss. And when Ash went looking for her, would she unlock the door and let him hold her? Let him console her? Not Beth Heller. She'd gotten angry that he'd discovered her and she refused to open the door. She'd spent the whole damn night in that bathroom. And when she'd come out the next morning? Not a word about it. Not a tear or a sign that she'd ever shed one.

And he'd been left with empty arms aching to hold a woman who didn't want him to.

No, the way she looked was no indication of the way she was. It didn't reflect the core of steel that she wanted everyone to believe ran right through the center of her.

Whether it really did or not.

Ash threw the letter back into his suitcase and snatched his shirt with a vengeance.

That was all old business. Finished. Now there was something else to deal with, something else to concentrate on.

They were going to have a baby.

In spite of it all.

Late June sunshine flooded the cheery guest bedroom in which Beth woke up that morning. All of Kansas Daye's house was like that particular room—bright, warm, homey, comforting. But it didn't help the knots that formed in Beth's stomach the minute her eyes opened and she recalled the reason she'd appeared on her old friend's doorstep the night before, asking to sleep over.

She'd driven around for a long time after leaving the ranch, hoping to give her brothers enough of a chance to get rid of Ash for her.

But when she'd gone back, his car was still there.

She'd been afraid he was stonewalling, refusing to leave until he spoke to her, and so she'd sought refuge with Kansas.

Lord, but she didn't want to confront him!

It had probably been unrealistic, but she really had hoped he would take her letter seriously and leave her alone. That he'd just go on with his life the way it was and let her go on with hers.

But no, he had to come to Elk Creek.

Why, exactly? she wondered, staring up at the ceiling.

There wasn't anything he could do. It wasn't as if he could take a turn carrying this baby. Any involvement on his part couldn't happen until the child was born, and that wouldn't be for months yet. So what was the point?

Maybe he'd come just to let her know how unhappy about it he was.

After all, she knew he'd been against their having kids of their own. On the few occasions when the subject had come up, he'd talked about adopting hard-to-place Indian babies at risk of being given to people outside of their culture when homes with Native American parents couldn't be found.

But he'd only spoken of it as something far down the road, when he wasn't so busy with work, and Beth hadn't believed that it would ever happen, that Ash would ever have time to be a father to any child.

Any more than he'd had the time to be a husband.

The trouble she'd had reaching him to tell him she was pregnant wasn't out of the ordinary. Sometimes she thought he must believe there wasn't another person in the world who could deal with the problems and causes of Native Americans. Maybe it was a cliché, but it was true that the man had been more married to his work than to her.

The Blackwolf Foundation. Demanding wife, exacting mistress and needy child, all rolled into one package.

Ash was head of an organization he'd established with a portion of the substantial estate he'd inherited from his paternal grandfather.

Beth had never met her former husband's namesake. The man had been dead several years when she and Ash first encountered each other, but she knew he'd been a renowned and very successful metal sculptor who had amassed a fortune late in life, a fortune large enough to make Ash a wealthy man and still help fund the foundation.

And the foundation did good work. Valid work. Necessary work in areas of drug and alcohol rehabilitation, in programs that trained Native Americans for better jobs, in family counseling, in aid for the needy, in college grants and scholarships, as well as keeping an eye on legislation that might help or hinder the rights of Indians, and helping to find legal representation for Native American individuals or businesses that ran into problems.

And Ash did it all.

He was a hands-on kind of person. When there was a problem—and there was *always* a problem somewhere— he was right there to see what could be done.

She admired that about him. She respected his devotion to the plights of his people. She was impressed that a person who could easily have used his inheritance to become a man of leisure was instead the first person to roll up his sleeves and dig in.

But it made for a lousy husband.

As the years had passed she'd come to feel almost like an incidental speck in the corner of the much bigger picture of his life.

His secretary had been more involved with him than Beth had. At least the daunting Miss Lightfeather always knew where he was at any given moment and how to reach him. Beth had rarely known even that.

There had been many times in the past when one crisis ran into another commitment that overlapped yet another engagement or responsibility and kept Ash away for so long that she'd begin to wonder if he even remembered he had a wife.

She'd tried hard to keep busy with her own work, but accounting was a nine-to-five job for the most part, and it still left her with long evenings and weekends alone.

She'd volunteered for his pet projects and programs, hoping that immersing herself in his causes, his interests, might bring them together.

He'd appreciated that, welcomed her help and her contribution, but before long he'd start to act as if she were his delegate, leaving her to represent him while he went on to other pressing obligations.

She'd made friends and built a social life, but somehow it wasn't enough. Something was missing from her life.

And then, late one night, she'd realized she was just plain lonely. Deep down, depressingly lonely.

The oddest thing about it was that it had happened after a terrific round of lovemaking.

Not that their lovemaking wasn't always terrific. It was. It was the one thing in their marriage that was an unqualified success. But each encounter in bed only made her hungry for more of him. More time with him. The chance to really get to know him. To talk to him. To have a life together.

But that never happened and for some reason, that night, she'd finally accepted that it never would. That she'd never be first on his list of priorities. And she'd finally admitted to herself that she couldn't accept it any longer.

She'd sat up the rest of the night and when his alarm went off at five the next morning, she'd told him she was divorcing him.

And he hadn't really argued.

Beth swallowed back the lump that memory could still put in her throat.

He'd moved in with his maternal grandfather while Beth filed the necessary papers and finished tax season, wrapping up her job and her life on the reservation at about the same time the final decree was handed down.

Then she'd packed her things. And, for the first time, she'd begun to wonder about some of what was happening to her physically. And what wasn't happening, and hadn't for a long while.

So, just before she was set to leave, she'd gone in to see Cele.

That was when her friend and doctor had told her that missed periods and fatigue were not because of the stress of divorcing a man she would have rather had a future with.

So this is what has to happen to get him to take notice, she thought.

Unfortunately, it was too late.

Too late for anything more than wondering if things

would be different had she known on that last night they'd made love that she was already carrying his child.

Beth got out of bed and pulled on the clothes she'd been wearing when she'd arrived. How much easier it would be if she'd divorced Ash because she didn't have any feelings for him anymore. Because she wasn't attracted to him anymore. Because sparks couldn't be ignited between them.

But the fact that she still cared didn't change anything.

She'd learned very well what being married to him was like and there was no going back to it.

Not that Ash would even want her back.

The sound of her brother's voice drifted to Beth even before she reached her friend's kitchen. Linc was teasing Kansas about how deprived he'd felt not seeing her the night before.

When Beth joined them she found Linc sitting on a kitchen chair with Kansas on his lap. The evidence of their playful affection gave her an instant twinge of jealousy that she fought back.

"Morning," she said to announce herself.

"Hi," Kansas responded with a laugh in her voice as Linc nibbled her earlobe. Then she pushed out of his arms and stood.

Beth was grateful for that.

"How about some breakfast?" Kansas offered. "I'll make you pancakes and top them with powdered sugar and a few sprinkles of fresh squeezed orange juice like we used to have after our sleepovers when we were kids."

Beth smiled at the memory. She and Kansas had grown up together, but their friendship had really blossomed when they were teenagers. They'd spent a lot of time together through junior high and high school, then drifted apart when they'd gone off to different colleges and over the years that followed. But it was good to rekindle that friendship now. Especially when Beth really needed a friend.

What she didn't need was food. Her stomach was still in knots. "Let's do our special pancakes another time. I'm not hungry right now."

"Coffee? Tea? Milk?"

"Nothing. Thanks."

Kansas refilled Linc's cup and then sat on a separate chair. Beth took a third, all the while feeling strongly her brother's unwavering stare.

"I think you got things confused last night, Liz-a-Beth," he finally said, using the name he'd teased her with when they were kids, clearly meaning to soften the chastising tone in his voice. "I was supposed to come here to be with Kansas and you should have been the one with Ash."

Beth grimaced. "How did it go?"

"It was no party, I'll tell you that. We didn't know what the hell to say to him and he sat there waiting for you damn near till midnight. I couldn't leave him alone with Jackson and the only way I could get him out of there was to give him my word I'd try convincing you to see him today."

"What about convincing him to go back to the reservation?"

"I let him know that's what you wanted him to do. But he's not budging." Linc frowned at her. "And I can't say as I blame him. In his shoes there's no way I would."

"I thought you were on my side."

"I am, I am," he assured her halfheartedly. "I just don't understand what your side is, exactly."

"What's Ash's side?" she asked rather than explaining herself.

"Well, I don't know that, either. I only know that if my wife were pregnant with my baby and ran out the back door rather than talking to me about it, I'd want to turn her over my knee."

Was he telling her that was what Ash wanted to do? That he was that angry? "I'm not his wife. Not anymore," she said defensively, as if that were an answer that made sense.

"That's just splittin' hairs," Linc said.

"Don't you think you should talk to him, Beth?" Kansas put in quietly, breaking the silence she'd held until then.

"Yes, I know I should," Beth grumbled, more to herself than to either of them.

"*Should* nothing, he isn't going to let you get away with not talking to him," Linc warned her.

Beth rolled her eyes. "I said everything I needed to in the letter I wrote him. I don't know what else he wants to hear."

"Maybe he has something to say to you."

That tightened the knots in her stomach.

Linc went on, "He was going from our place to the hunting lodge to take a cabin there. We could have put him up but—"

"Oh, I'm glad you didn't." Beth breathed out a gust of panicky air at just the thought. Wouldn't *that* have been grand? She could have had Ash in the bedroom right next to hers. She'd have met him coming and going at all hours of the day and night; she'd have had to see him the way he was at home—relaxed, casual, sexy, appealing...

"It was definitely better that you didn't invite him to stay at the ranch," she reiterated firmly, as if it still might be a possibility.

"I felt rude and inhospitable not asking him to, but between you running out and Jackson all het up over this thing, I didn't think I'd better.''

"Jackson didn't hit him again, did he?'' Beth asked, her concern sounding.

"No. Just the one punch. In fact, he calmed down considerably when he realized it wasn't as if Ash was denying his responsibilities. But still, I didn't think it was a good idea to have Ash close at hand in case he did something else Jackson might take offense to. You know how he is. He always thought he needed to fight your battles for you.''

"I hope this won't be a battle.''

Linc's expression said he didn't see it being anything but.

It made Beth wonder yet again just how unhappy Ash was about her pregnancy.

But there was no sense sitting around worrying about it. Even if she was susceptible to just the sight of her former husband, Shag had taught her to ignore weaknesses like that. And certainly not to let anyone else see them. Running out the night before had been a show of weakness. It wasn't something she was proud of.

She had to tough this out, she told herself. And that was what she was going to do.

Besides, apparently Ash wasn't leaving, and if she had to deal with him sooner or later, it might as well be sooner.

She laid both of her palms on the tabletop and pushed herself to her feet. "Do me a favor and call him at the lodge, would you? Tell him to come back out to the ranch in an hour. That'll give me a chance to shower and put on clean clothes.'' And having her brother make the call would buy her that much more time before she had to actually talk to Ash herself.

Linc eyed her suspiciously. "You aren't just stalling so you can go home, pack a bag and leave town, are you?"

Tempting thought. But it would only postpone the inevitable and she knew it. At that moment she was wishing she'd have stayed to confront her former husband the night before. Maybe he'd be on his way back to the reservation by now if she had. "I'll be at the ranch when he gets there," she assured.

Then she thanked Kansas for the refuge and left, trying not to notice that the knots in her stomach had turned to all-out jitters.

An hour didn't give her much time, and once she was back at the ranch, Beth rushed through her shower.

Choosing what to wear took longer. She had a bit of a stomach but not so much that she couldn't still wear some of her regular clothes as long as they were fairly loose fitting.

She didn't want to appear dressed up, but she didn't want to look sloppy, either, so in the end she opted for a tunic T-shirt and a pair of stirrup pants that she thought looked casually chic.

Her hair air-dried and required only some scrunching with her hand to give it bounce. But she was careful about the makeup she applied. A touch of pale eye shadow, just enough mascara to darken her lashes, and a hint of lipstick. She'd have used blush, too, but again this morning her color was naturally high and she didn't need it.

All in all, she was pleased with the results, and though she told herself it shouldn't matter, it did. Regardless of how she felt about this meeting, it was important to her that she seem cool, calm, collected. And if one look at her made Ash think he'd been a fool to take her for granted?

Well, great! It wouldn't change anything, but she wouldn't mind at all if he suffered a pang or two of regret.

Feeling more or less on top of things, she headed downstairs.

She'd be fine, she thought, running through a scenario of the meeting in her mind. They'd have a simple conversation. She'd confirm that she'd meant what she'd written in her letter. He'd want to know when the baby was due and make sure she had a plan, that she really was willing to have and raise it on her own. He'd tell her to notify him when it was born. Maybe he'd want to arrange some sort of visitation. Then he'd leave. He'd go back to the reservation. She'd go on the way she'd intended all along, and everything would be fine. Just fine.

So how come at the bottom of the steps she wilted like an unwatered rose?

In the three weeks since she'd realized she was pregnant, she'd thought mostly of Ash. Of trying to get the news to him. Of wondering what his reaction would be. Of convincing him she didn't need or want his help or anything from him.

But now that she was actually faced with sending him away, she suddenly felt herself confronting the fact that she wasn't convinced herself.

Oh, sure, doubts had been creeping across her mind all along and she'd been fighting them. But now they weren't only creeping. They'd walked right in and taken over.

Could she really do it all alone?

Having a child was a daunting prospect. Raising it by herself was an even more daunting one.

She'd be a single mother. On her own no matter what the child needed, no matter when or where.

There wouldn't be anybody else to turn to for relief when she was too tired to move. No one at all to share the load. Or the joy. No one to help make decisions. To worry with. No one but her.

There wouldn't be anyone to let her know if she was doing a good job or a bad one. Or anyone to be a sounding board when she was unsure of herself.

There wouldn't be anyone but her...

"Oh, my God," she whispered. "What am I doing?"

But what was her alternative to being alone in this? she asked herself.

There wasn't one. Because even if she and Ash were still married, she'd be almost as alone with a baby as without one.

Ash didn't love her anymore. His thoughts were elsewhere. If he were to take her back out of a sense of obligation, their second marriage would be as doomed as the first. And their baby would never know a full-time father.

When Beth needed relief from night after night of interrupted sleep, he'd be in Washington lobbying for the return of more Native American lands.

When the baby had colic, he'd be making sure a plumber was doing what needed to be done at the rehab center.

When the baby took its first step, he wouldn't be there to share the moment with her, he'd be off doing paperwork at the office.

When she was up worrying about bad behavior in school, he'd be making plans for fund-raising for new scholarship programs.

No, she was alone in this no matter how she looked at it. At least now, living in Elk Creek, she had her family and friends. She could count on them. She could turn to Linc or Jackson or Kansas when she needed help or moral support or bolstering.

And she wouldn't have to go through Miss Lightfeather to do it.

Not that she expected to need a lot of help, anyway, she thought as she began to make some headway at shoving her doubts back into the corner of her mind.

Her father had taught her to be independent, not to need anything from anyone. In fact, there would have been hell to pay if old Shag were around and knew she'd even had this lapse in confidence. Weak, sniveling, whining—that's what he'd have called it. And he wouldn't have tolerated it. He'd have sent her out to work twice as hard, made her do something so bad that no matter what she was fretting over, it would end up seeming like nothing next to what he'd have her doing.

She was tough.

She was a Heller.

She could handle anything.

She hoped....

Certainly taking care of one little baby couldn't be as hard as driving a herd of cattle through a torrential downpour, or smoking nests of snakes out of the barns, or slaughtering cows, or any of the gazillion other backbreaking, bone-wrenching work she'd done on this ranch.

Could it?

Of course it couldn't. And even if it was, she'd done all that. She could do this.

She hoped....

She straightened her shoulders and took a deep breath.

Now wasn't the time to doubt herself. She had to concentrate on dealing with Ash.

She headed for the living room, meaning to sit quietly, maybe read a magazine until he got there. But somehow her feet took a detour and she ended up across the entranceway at the window beside the door, with one hand nudging the drapery panel aside just enough to peek through.

The house was built in an H-shape and she looked out over a bricked courtyard between the two front arms of the H. Beyond that was the circular driveway that made a horseshoe out of the road that connected them to the highway into town.

Her car was parked at the edge of the courtyard because she'd been in too much of a hurry to pull around to the garages, which were in a separate building just off the south corner of the house.

She considered going out now and moving her car, but just as she was about to, she spotted Ash's black sedan turning onto the road.

Lord, how she hated the fact that that was all it took to kick her heart into double time. Much as she wanted to let go of that curtain rather than watch him coming, she was frozen to the spot.

His windows were tinted, so she couldn't see him until he got out of his car.

And then all she could think was that she wished he'd have stayed away.

The man was striking. All the dignity of his proudest ancestors was there in his straight, broad shoulders. And though he was wearing a pale yellow shirt with the sleeves rolled to his elbows, and a pair of khaki slacks, she knew well what was inside of his clothing—a hard, muscular body that could easily have gone into battle covered with not much more than war paint.

But at that moment there was nothing about him that wasn't the modern man. Even his long black hair tied at his nape could have served a rock singer. He always wore it that way, freeing it only for ceremonial rituals, and he was easily man enough not to be feminized by it even slightly. The faint dusting of premature gray at his temples didn't hurt anything, either. In fact it contributed a dash of maturity that was all the more enticing.

As Beth watched, he went around to the trunk of his car and opened it. But she didn't pay much attention to the small orange crate he took from it. She was more intent in relearning his profile. She'd never seen a man with bones as beautiful—the broad, flat forehead that formed a sharp ridge for bushy eyebrows; the high cheekbones and the thin, almost hawkish nose; the razor-edged jawline. All encased in that tawny skin that made him look healthy and robust even on the rare occasions when he wasn't.

Holding the orange crate against his hip, he slammed the trunk lid closed and took long, purposeful strides toward the house.

That managed to unfreeze Beth in a hurry. She let go of the curtain and nearly jumped back from the window so as not to be caught spying.

But she could hear his every step on the courtyard tiles and each one seemed to fall on a separate beat of her heart.

Remember you're divorced. And for good reasons. That's how you wanted it. That's how he wanted it....

When he rang the doorbell, it seemed to echo all around her. Fleetingly she considered not opening it, sparing herself the effect of having him at close range. Why couldn't he have just left well enough alone?

But Shag Heller's daughter couldn't be a coward, at least not more than she'd already been, and when the bell rang a second time she finally opened the right half of the door.

That was when he took off his sunglasses and she had to look up into the face that his grandfather couldn't have sculpted to more rawboned perfection. Eyes the color of coal homed in on her and she saw a muscle along the side of his powerful neck flex and unflex, warning her that he was not happy. To say the least.

"Hello, Ash," she greeted, as if letting him know from the get-go that she would give no quarter, even though just the initial sight of him was already awakening things inside of her that she didn't want awakened.

He didn't respond. He merely stood there, glaring at her.

She pretended not to notice, stepped aside and said, "Come on in."

He folded the temples of his sunglasses by pushing them against his chest. Then he slipped them into the breast pocket of his shirt. She had a little trouble removing her gaze from that wide expanse when he'd finished.

He swung the orange crate around in front of him, and that distracted her. But appreciating the hard muscles in his forearms, and his thick wrists and big, capable hands, didn't improve what was already thrumming in the pit of her stomach.

She forced her focus in the direction of the orange crate. "What's all that?"

"Things you left behind," he said, breaking the silence with a cutting tone in his deep voice. "You forgot some clothes at the cleaners and a few things that were in the extra closet."

But some of what she could see didn't qualify for either of those categories. They were things she'd purposely omitted from her suitcase.

She waggled a finger in that direction. "Those on top are yours. Even though I wore them, I sort of thought divorce reverted them back to you."

"I considered them yours."

Did that mean that once she'd used them, they were contaminated and he didn't want them back? Or that he still wanted her to have them?

She didn't know. And was afraid to find out. So she just said, "You can set the crate in the corner."

While he did, she closed the door and headed for the living room, sitting on one of three couches that formed a U around the big-screen TV, hoping she looked nonchalant.

Her former husband followed her, but he stayed standing, facing her from behind the opposite sofa, watching her as if it were dangerous to take those dark, penetrating eyes off her.

He folded his arms over his chest. "Talk to me," he ordered.

"I said everything in the letter."

"Not everything. You failed to tell me how it is that it took five months for you to let me know you're pregnant."

"Oh, don't get on your high horse about that. I didn't know it myself until a few weeks ago."

"How is that possible?" he challenged. "If you're five months gone, you were pregnant even before you filed for divorce."

"What are you thinking? That I knew and kept it to myself until after the divorce was final?"

His silence and one raised eyebrow answered her.

"Well, that's not how it was. I was so harried with tax season, and there was all the tension of the divorce, and you know I was never...regular...that I could skip a month or two and not have it mean anything..."

Somehow discussing the very personal issues of this subject suddenly seemed terribly awkward. She knew it was crazy. This was a man she'd shared the most intimate details of her body and its functions with for five years. But she was acutely aware of the fact that he wasn't her husband anymore. They were just two separate people now.

Still, there was no way around it.

She cleared her throat and forged on. "You also know we were using birth control. The fact that it might have failed just didn't occur to me until I really sat down and figured out exactly how long it had been since...I'd had a cycle. I finally went to see Cele and she ran a pregnancy test."

"Which was when?"

"Three weeks ago. I tried to see you. I went to your office, but Miss Lightfeather couldn't work me into your schedule." She bit off the cutting edge in her own voice. "Then I tried calling, but she said you'd been busier than usual and had a lot on your mind, so she hadn't relayed my messages. Your grandfather was out of town, I never seemed to be able to catch you at his house, and then Miss Lightfeather said you'd been called away, too. I was all packed by then, so—" Her voice had risen and the words tumbled out faster and faster, and Beth took a breath to slow it all down and retrieve the dignity she felt was slipping. "So I came home. I called a few more times and then just wrote," she finished flatly.

"Miss Lightfeather and I are going to have a serious chat."

"She's just keeping your priorities in order."

He ignored that comment. "Are you all right? Is the pregnancy normal? Healthy?"

"Everything is just fine. There was honestly no need for you to come here. I think I have the whole thing under control."

But even she heard the hedging in that. To hide it, she expounded. "You know that financially I'm in good shape. Even though Shag's will gave a quarter share to his lady friend—or whoever Ally Brooks is—what's left for Linc, Jackson and me to split is substantial. I'll be doing the accounting and investments for the three of us now, but that'll be my only job, so I can work right here and be a full-time mother. I know how you felt about us having kids of our own and this doesn't have to change anything for you. I'm willing to have and raise the baby on my own, and you don't even have to acknowledge it."

"As if I'd be happy to hear that!" he shouted.

It made her sit up a little straighter, a little stiffer.

"You know, sometimes you take being self-sufficient too damn far," he said through clenched teeth.

"It isn't a matter of being self-sufficient. It's just that I know this isn't what you'd planned, and I want to make it clear that it doesn't have to interfere—"

"No matter what I wanted or planned, it doesn't mean I don't want this baby now that it's on the way. Or that I'll let you treat me like a nameless, faceless sperm donor whose part in this is finished."

"I thought you'd be happy to be absolved of—"

"Well, you were wrong!"

She didn't like being yelled at and she suddenly found herself out of her seat, around the back of her own sofa, faced off against him. "Don't scream at me."

"Screaming at you is the least of what I'd like to do," he shouted. "You think I don't know that you want me to just disappear? That you'd like to believe you don't need me and you sure as hell don't want me? But this is one thing you're not doing on your own, damn it. This is my baby as much as it's yours."

"I never said it wasn't. I'm the one who repeatedly ran up against the brick wall of your schedule trying to let you know it *is* your baby, remember?"

"And that's as far as you figured to let it go? Tell me and then write me off while you do everything yourself— Superwoman?"

"What exactly is it that you think you can do? Carry this baby for the next four months? Give birth to it?"

That stopped him cold. For a time he merely stood there, his dark eyes boring into her, and Beth suffered a terrible warring between recognizing the pure magnificence of him and wanting him out of her life before that recognition could have too much effect on her.

"I don't know what we're going to do," he admitted. "What I do know is that for the first time this isn't just your business or responsibility, or just my business or responsibility. It's ours. And we're going to work it out together."

"There's nothing to work out. I'm going to have the baby, and after it's born if you want visitation—"

"You are not going to do that to me," he said, once more through clenched teeth, stabbing one long index finger her way. "You are not going to exclude me from this."

"What do you propose, then?" she rephrased her earlier question, feeling her own temper rise at the increasing possibility that he wouldn't just go away and leave her alone, that he wouldn't be satisfied with what she had in mind to keep her distance from him.

"All I know is that I'm going to be a part of this. From this minute on, any way I can. We made this baby together, we're going to have it together, and one way or another, we're going to at least collaborate to raise it together."

"Collaborate," she repeated. "Let me guess, you're going to have Miss Lightfeather fax me instructions on breast feeding."

His eyes narrowed at her and though it didn't seem possible, they grew even darker. "For now I'm not leaving Elk Creek. I'll take today to do what I need to to free up some time and then I'm dogging your every step until you and I have hashed through this and I'm satisfied with what my place in this baby's life will be.''

Beth's initial reaction was to argue. She didn't want him within a hundred miles of her, let alone *dogging* her every step. It was too easy for old feelings to be rekindled, for her to lose sight of why they'd divorced, and fall under the spell of the attraction that had put them together to begin with.

But then she realized she was being foolish.

He wouldn't stick around long, no matter what he said. For the entire time she'd known him, something had been coming up to take him away. She had only to wait him out. Before she knew it, there would be a meeting he couldn't reschedule or a problem he couldn't ignore, and he'd be gone.

"Suit yourself," she said with complete confidence.

He continued to study her, as if he were suspicious of her agreement. But after a moment he merely said, "I'll be back. And don't even think about running out like you did last night, because I'll find you if it takes every dime I have."

"It won't be me who leaves," she said caustically and somewhat under her breath.

If he heard it, he chose not to address it. Instead, after another moment of piercing her with his heated glare, he turned and walked out the way he'd come in.

Beth hated that her gaze followed along, slipping down the expanse of his shoulders to the sharp narrowing of his waist, feasting on the sight of a derriere to die for. But follow along it did.

Only when he went through the front door and shut it behind him did she close her eyes and set her teeth together in determination.

He had a right to the baby and she wouldn't deny him that right.

But she'd be damned if she'd let him get to her. She'd ignore him. She'd go on about her business as if he weren't around. She'd find a way to keep herself removed from him, emotionally if not logistically.

And if, deep down, there was a tiny flicker of relief, that she might not be as alone in this as she'd thought?

She didn't want to admit it.

Not even to herself.

Chapter Three

As Ash showered and dressed early the next morning, he told himself to get a grip. Being mad at Beth didn't serve any purpose, and arguing with her, shouting at her, upsetting her, couldn't be good for the baby.

It was just that he was so damn frustrated!

He knew her, knew she'd go to any lengths to do this alone. Hadn't she sat there smugly and challenged him to tell her just what he thought he could do to be a part of things right now?

Of course he hadn't an answer. Pregnancy was a woman's domain. But he knew for certain that if he didn't make a stand now, if he didn't get involved in whatever way he could, then he'd never be a part of the baby's life once it was born, either.

But how long would it take to make his stand, to be truly involved? he asked himself. The baby wouldn't be born for four months. And there was no way he could put everything on hold with the foundation for that long.

Still, he could manage it for a little while. At least until he felt he'd established with Beth that he'd accept nothing short of his full role as father to this child.

And even then, when he went back to the reservation, he'd still have to find some way to keep in close contact with her, because he wanted to be in on this whole thing. It aggravated him that he'd already missed five months.

Although that aggravation couldn't have surprised him more.

Beth was right. He hadn't wanted them to have kids of their own. The days when there were a surplus of babies in the world to adopt might be all in the past, but there were still those who were hard to find homes for—babies born with handicaps, with fetal alcohol syndrome or drug addictions. The Native American community had many such children, who often had to be placed with families outside the culture.

Ash was among those who didn't like to see that happen, both because he believed Indian children should be raised knowing their heritage, and because recent programs attempting to reclaim children already outside that circle struck him as painful business for everyone involved. So he'd decided that when the time came for him to become a parent he wanted to do what he could to keep at least a few of those kids from being adopted out to non-Indian parents in the first place.

But that didn't mean he was going to turn his back on his own child. Beth was out of her mind to think he might. It was more than just doing the right thing.

This was *his child.*

There was something incredible about that. About the fact that he'd created a human being. Before, when he'd made his decision to build his family through adoption, he hadn't considered it any big deal to have a child of his own.

But he'd been wrong. It was a very big deal.

He was bowled over by the pure wonder of it. This child was *his*....

Would it look like him? Would it look like Beth? Would it have his paternal grandfather's artistic talent and give the world more that was beautiful and meaningful? Would it have his maternal grandfather's wisdom and kindness and irrepressible sense of humor?

It was just so damned amazing.

And he hated this feeling he had of being on the outside looking in.

There was no doubt about it, he was determined to be a force in this child's life. A presence as strong as Beth's. Even though he wasn't exactly sure how he was going to do that when he was divorced from the baby's mother and living on the other side of the state.

But he'd find a way, he vowed to himself. He would definitely find a way.

"Not through anger and confrontations like yesterday's, you won't," he told himself.

He knew he needed to forget that he'd already lost five months of this pregnancy. He needed to forget that Beth was doing her usual best to make him incidental. He needed to stop thinking that maybe if she had paid enough attention to what was happening in her own body and realized before the divorce was final that they were going to have a child, they might not have gone through with it in the first place....

But regrets about the divorce were useless. Hadn't he been telling himself that since the day it was final?

He'd be, more or less, a single father. And he'd just have to make every precious moment with his child count.

And yet, there was something very lonely about that idea. So lonely it was like a fist in his gut.

The picture his mind should have been conjuring up was of Beth and him standing together over the crib. Or of both of them watching the baby splashing in the tub. Or of their taking turns rocking it or walking the floors with it through the night…

"Well, that's not how it is. Or how it's going to be, so get over it," he ordered himself, trying to shake off the anger and those regrets he'd been fighting.

It wasn't easy, though. Nobody could get to him the way Beth could.

Good and bad.

And it didn't help that some of the good was still there.

Even in the midst of his rage at her yesterday, he'd still been drawn to her.

He'd watched her walk into the living room ahead of him and his hand had itched to reach out and touch her.

He'd remained standing behind the couch, hoping that distance and the barrier would keep things in perspective for him, when his damn brain had suddenly kicked in with images of what she looked like after they'd made love— all soft and warm and heavy lidded; of what she tasted like when he kissed her naked shoulder and found her slightly salty from the mingling of his sweat and hers from the heat of the moments just before; of what it felt like to be inside of her, to have her hold on tight to him, wrap her legs around him, cry out his name…

How the hell could he be so mad at her and hungry for her at the same time?

But he had been.

He was.

Wanting her didn't change anything, though, and he knew he had to keep himself focused on the future, not on the past.

The baby was all he needed to think about. And carving out his place with it.

He had no business at all thinking about his wife.

His ex-wife.

And that distinction was something he'd better not forget.

Beth had a lot planned for that day, but she was having a hard time getting herself going. She'd made it as far as into her bathrobe and downstairs to fix herself a cup of tea, but that was it. Here it was, late in the morning, and she was back in bed, still sitting propped on her pillows, staring into space.

Well, not exactly into space.

She was staring at that orange crate Ash had left the day before. She'd carted it upstairs after he'd gone and set it on the floor in the corner.

She might have just put the whole crate in the trash except that she knew the things she'd forgotten at the dry cleaners were some of her best. The trouble was, to get to them, she had to go through those items that really belonged to Ash.

Why hadn't he just kept them? Or thrown them out, if he hadn't wanted them back? Surely leaving them behind had made it clear she didn't want them.

Except that she sort of did.

It was just the memories that went with them that she didn't want.

But neither the crate nor the memories were going away, and she'd been sitting there much too long willing them to. She knew she was being silly. And silliness was another of those things that Shag would never have allowed in this house.

"Just pull out the stuff that's yours and then put the crate and the rest of it in the trash out back," she told herself as if there were nothing to it.

Pretending that that was the truth, she got out of bed, crossed the room, knelt down beside the offending box in the corner and quickly took the four top items off, setting them aside without more than a cursory glance at them.

"See? You were making a mountain out of a molehill."

What was left in the crate was a silk suit and a blazer still in the cleaner's plastic. She took them out and hung them in her closet. Then there were several items of winter clothing she'd kept in the bedroom of the house on the reservation that would have been the nursery. Those she stuffed into the bottom drawers of the bureau that faced the bed.

And that was that. She had only to toss those first few articles back into the crate, get rid of it, and she could be done with this whole business.

But was she sure she really wanted to just throw those things away? her traitorous mind asked her as she bent over to pick them up.

There was a great big, plaid cashmere bathrobe that was so old and worn around the edges that it wasn't even fit to give to charity. And yet when her hands clasped the downy softness, she couldn't resist fingering it, rubbing her palms against it, finally slipping it on, smoothing the ragged lapels over her chest.

She'd replaced it for Ash their first Christmas together, but when she'd been about to throw it out the next day she hadn't been able to. It had occurred to her that if she got rid of it she wouldn't have it to wear on cold Sunday mornings when she was padding around in her pajamas and stocking feet, or to pull over her when she was sick and lying on the couch.

There was something comforting about it in a way her own robe didn't match. It wasn't just that it was warm or soft or broken in; it always made her feel as if Ash himself were wrapped around her.

Just like now...

"This has to go," she said firmly, shrugging out of it as if it made her itch and tossing it into the crate.

Then there was his college sweatshirt.

She thought he would have wanted that back for sure. After all, it was a memento of his fraternity.

For Beth, on the other hand, it was a memento of something else.

The first time she'd worn it had been during a game of Boat.

Boat was something she'd heard a therapist on the radio suggest to a caller with marital problems. Beth hadn't considered what was happening in her own marriage a problem at that point—after all, it had only been a month since their wedding. But the game had seemed like a way to lure Ash home from doing paperwork at his office on a Sunday afternoon.

The instructions were to gather special foods and wine and maybe some body oils or lotions in a basket. Thus equipped, the basket was then to be taken to the bed, which was designated as a boat in the middle of the ocean, and, for a time, they couldn't leave it for any reason.

Ash had been only too happy to go along with the idea. He'd undressed her and flung her clothes far out into their imaginary sea. After they'd put the lotions and oils to good use, the only article of clothing she could reach when she'd wanted to dress again before their picnic had been his college sweatshirt.

That sweatshirt had become a part of the Boat basket from then on.

Unfortunately Boat had lost more and more of its power to bring Ash home as the years had gone on, until Beth had given up trying. Still, the memory of that first time was so sweet it hurt.

She folded the sweatshirt and set it in the crate with the robe.

A white dress shirt was the third item lying on her bedroom floor at that moment. It had become hers during a long business trip Ash had taken early in their marriage. He'd left it for her to launder. But when she'd tried to do that, the scent of it had reached out to her. Ash's scent. That mingling of his clean, spicy after-shave and the masculine smell of his skin.

She'd ended up not washing it at all, but wearing it around the house to stave off the loneliness.

It surprised her a little that he'd known to bring it to her. It was a plain white shirt, like so many of his others, except that it had a tiny flaw in the weave of the cuff. From that trip on, she'd kept the shirt, laundering it only when she knew he was about to leave again and slipping it in with his other shirts so that he'd wear it just before, infuse it with his scent, and then she'd have it after he'd gone.

"He knew all along," she whispered, embarrassed that he had realized what she was doing.

He'd never let on that he was aware the shirt appeared in his drawer only periodically before disappearing again. But obviously he'd known that she'd considered it *her* shirt.

On their own, her hands brought it up to her nose and she breathed in the faint lingering of what had comforted her before. But there was no comfort in it now. There was only a terrible pang for what was lost.

She folded it with the care of a soldier folding a burial flag and set it in the crate.

That left the pajama top. Ash's pajama top.

From the beginning of their marriage he'd worn the bottoms and she'd worn the tops of every pair he'd owned during their years together.

Technically, she thought, they were as much her pajamas as his. He'd never worn this half.

Yet somehow, the day the divorce was final, she'd decided to put away that portion of the pajamas they'd shared along with the life they'd shared. So when she'd taken off her wedding ring, she'd also removed these pajama tops from her drawer and set them in one of his.

Unfortunately, since then she'd been trying to find something else she liked as well to wear to bed.

Women's pajamas, T-shirts, nightgowns, nightshirts. She'd even tried sleeping in the nude. But nothing was as comfortable as the silk pajama top she held in her hands at that moment.

"I bought them," she said. "Think of it as him wearing the bottoms of *my* pajamas."

But she wasn't sure she could.

And yet she also couldn't seem to make herself put them into the orange crate.

Lord, what was wrong with her? She'd never been so indecisive, so sentimental, so emotional.

And then it occurred to her that maybe more than her appearance could be under the influence of pregnancy hormones.

Of course, that was all it was, she told herself. The roller coaster emotions were caused by the increased hormones in her body. She even remembered reading something about that very thing.

But could they turn her into a different person? For here she was, Shag Heller's daughter, crying over a pair of pajamas, of all things.

Well, regardless of the cause, she could fight it, she decided. She *had* to fight it. She wasn't so weak willed that it could get the best of her.

She snapped the pajamas through the air with one hard flick as if that would rid them of the baggage they came with, spun away from the orange crate and stuffed them into her drawer, slamming it shut so firmly that it set the clock on top of the bureau rocking back and forth.

Twenty minutes to twelve? She couldn't believe it. And there she was, not even showered yet.

Enough mooning, she told herself, turning toward the bathroom that connected to her room.

She'd throw the clothes out later.

But somewhere in the back of her mind a little voice called her a liar.

And she knew it was right.

Especially when she took a detour and slid the crate into the back of her closet.

An hour later, Beth finally went downstairs, showered and dressed in a sleeveless, oversize chambray shirt with tails that reached nearly to her jean-clad knees, her hair freshly washed and fluffed. She intended to go straight out the front door and make her first stop Kansas's country store to see if by some chance her old friend might not have had lunch yet and could be persuaded to join her. But she only made it as far as the bottom step before spotting Ash sitting in the living room watching for her.

She couldn't believe it.

She'd never known him to actually free up time before, so she hadn't really taken his threat to do it now too seriously. At the most, she'd expected that he might do business from his cabin at the lodge for a few days, popping up once or twice in the evenings before being called away again.

But there he was, in the middle of the day, with a cup of coffee in one hand, an open briefcase on the table in front of him, a file folder in his lap and papers scattered around as if he'd been there for a while already.

"Morning. Not that it still is. Have you been upstairs asleep all this time?" he greeted amiably.

But Beth was not feeling amiable about his being there. Nor was she going to admit that she'd been awake but crying over his old things. "What are you doing here?" she demanded ungraciously as she crossed to the living room.

"Exactly what I said I was going to do. My calendar is clear and I'm all yours."

Her heart took a wild skip at that but she tamed it in a hurry. He hadn't been all hers when they were married, he certainly wasn't now. "This is crazy. You're a busy man, I don't need or want a shadow, so why don't you just get in your car and—"

"I'm not going anywhere," he told her with enough finality to end her rebuttal. He scooped all the papers into the file, deposited it in the briefcase and closed it with a loud snap that seemed to seal the end to the argument. Then he stood.

And she wished he hadn't.

He had on a black T-shirt that smoothed across his broad shoulders and stretched so far around his biceps that the seams were strained. Gleaming against the mock turtleneck just below his throat he wore a talisman he was never without—a burnished copper eagle arrowhead hanging from a thin black cord. His stomach was perfectly flat beneath the taut knit, and when her gaze drifted down that washboard hardness she found a pair of tight, faded blue jeans.

No one could do for a pair of jeans what Asher Blackwolf could.

They rode low on his narrow hips and cupped his every bulging muscle like a second skin. Beth had always loved the way jeans looked on him, though she didn't get to see the look often because he didn't spend a lot of time dressed that casually. Maybe part of the reason she liked it so much was that those rare occasions meant she really did have him all to herself.

But she didn't *want* him all to herself anymore, she reminded herself. She couldn't.

"What's on your agenda today? You looked as if you were headed out," he said, drawing her attention away from his appearance.

"I have errands to run," she answered, her words clipped and her irritation sounding.

"Great. I'll drive."

"*Shopping* errands," she said, upping the ante. "You know, the kind of thing Miss Lightfeather does instead of you?"

He ignored the barb and repeated, "I'll drive."

"This is ridiculous. The things I have to do today will bore you to tears and they don't have anything to do with the baby." Well, that wasn't exactly true, but the errand she needed to run that *did* have a connection to the baby was not one she wanted Ash's company on—she needed maternity bras.

"You're not getting rid of me, Beth."

"There just isn't a point to this," she insisted, exasperated by his stubbornness. "How about if I agree to start sending you a newsletter? I'll write once a week, tell you about every ache or pain or twinge I have, keep you completely updated. You'll know as much about my heartburn as I do. It'll be the same as being here, only you can go on about your business and so can I."

His expression said he was annoyed with her, but he merely tilted his head and stared at her out of the corner of his eye. "I'll drive," he repeated yet again.

The way he'd angled his chin had given her a view of the fading bruise left by Jackson's punch, and the sight of it made her feel slightly guilty. It cut short the argument that was bubbling inside of her. He wouldn't be around long anyway before something called him away, she reminded herself. "Oh, fine. But don't say you weren't warned."

For the second time that day she spun on her heels, heading for the door ahead of him. But his legs were much longer than hers and they reached the door at the same time, with Ash bending over her to open it before she could.

Did he think being pregnant made her incapable of opening a door for herself, for crying out loud? But more than the courtesy, what irked her was that when he got that near to her she could smell his after-shave and it went right to her silly head.

"How about some lunch?" he asked as they walked to his car.

"I'm not hungry," she snapped, because it was true. The man irritated her so much she'd lost her appetite.

"Hungry or not, you need to eat. You're skin and bones," he decreed as he held the car door for her, too. "It looks like somebody better pay some attention to what you're doing to yourself and my baby."

Beth merely glared at him as he ordered her to buckle her seat belt and closed the door.

Their first stop was at Margie Wilson's café, where Ash canceled Beth's order of a sweet roll and coffee and instead insisted she be brought a turkey club sandwich, a salad and a glass of milk.

Beth seriously considered letting the food sit there and rot, but by the time it arrived, her appetite had returned, too, and she ate.

Besides, it was served by Margie Wilson herself, who always fussed over her, and Beth wouldn't have hurt the other woman's feelings for the world.

"I see she carries more weight with you than I do," Ash observed when the café owner left them alone after actually persuading Beth to drink some of the milk he'd ordered.

"Margie is a nice lady. And I've always felt bad that my father didn't do right by her."

Ash's eyebrows rose in curiosity as he chewed a bite of his hamburger.

Beth wasn't fond of sitting in silence, so she elaborated. "Shag kept company with her for years. Not openly. He believed that it was wrong for Linc, Jackson or me to ever see him with a woman other than our mother—"

She stalled a moment, thinking that she understood that notion now, because she didn't at all like the idea of her child seeing Ash with another woman.

Or of her seeing him with one, either, for that matter...

She pushed the thought and the feelings that came with it away and went on. "But everyone in town—including me and my brothers—knew that Margie had back-door visits from Shag for years. We all thought that eventually—probably when we were grown—he'd marry her."

"But instead he took up with the mysterious lady friend in Denver," Ash surmised, fitting a piece of the puzzle.

"Ally Brooks," Beth confirmed. "At least that's who we think she is. He never referred to the woman he spent time with there as anything but his 'lady friend,' so we don't really know for sure. It's just a good bet since he left her an equal share of the house, the ranch, the oil rights, all the stocks and bonds and other assets. We all figured we'd finally get to meet her at the funeral, but you know about that."

"Mmm," Ash said as he swallowed. "I know it hurt you that the orders in his will were for you and your brothers not to be notified of his death until after he was already buried in Denver."

"It didn't *hurt* me," she denied, raising her chin in the air, because a Heller never admitted to such a thing. Even if it was true.

Ash just shook his head as if he knew better and something about it saddened and aggravated him at the same time.

But rather than go into it, Beth launched into small talk about this Ally Brooks person not answering any of Jackson's attempts to contact her to buy her out of the ranch.

That managed to fill the time until they finished eating and she could finally put her attention into her errands.

Saying goodbye to Margie Wilson, Beth headed up Center Street at an energetic clip. She greeted Elk Creek's citizens, gazed in windows and basically did her shopping. And as she did, she tried hard to ignore Ash.

But having him along was a pain in the neck.

It was as if he didn't know what to do with himself and this leisure time. He merely followed her like a shadow, not even looking around, and driving her absolutely to distraction with his overbearing coddling.

He didn't want her bending over to try on the shoes she was shopping for to wear to Linc and Kansas's wedding. He didn't want her carrying a single bolt of cloth in the fabric shop where she needed material to make a dress for herself. In the drugstore he didn't want her reaching to the top shelf for the shampoo she needed. He didn't even like her walking as fast as she walked and he wanted her to stop and rest every hour on the hour.

And opinions! The man had an opinion on everything.

The heels on the shoes she wanted were too high. She shouldn't have the clasp on her watch fixed, she should just buy a new one. The flowered pattern on one fabric was too big, while the dots on another were too bright.

Even the lace she wanted for Kansas's gown was deemed not elegant enough and he'd picked out another, more expensive one and paid for it himself to make sure he got his own way in that, too.

By the time they reached the maternity shop at five, Beth was ready to punch him herself and it occurred to her that their marriage might have ended a lot sooner if he *had* spent more time with her.

"I need to go in here alone," she told him in no uncertain terms, not happy to find his interest apparently piqued for the first time as he peered in the window that displayed not only maternity clothes but also Elk Creek's only selection of baby furniture.

"I don't know why," he said, dismissing her claim.

"Just please wait out here."

"Give me one good reason?"

"What I need in here is none of your business."

"Seems to me this is the only place we've been today that *is* my business."

"Look," she said, anger ringing in her voice, "I've put up with you and your ideas on everything today, but this is where I draw the line. What I need in here is *underwear* and I don't want an audience when I buy it.''

The corners of his mouth crept up into a maddening smile. "I've been with you when you bought *underwear* before, Beth,'' he said, mimicking her. Then he bent so close to her ear that she could feel the warmth of his breath against her skin and added, "I've even seen you in it, remember?''

Oh, she remembered all right. Things she didn't want to remember. Like plunging, lacy red teddies and sheer black sets that left nothing to the imagination. Unfortunately, she also remembered where wearing them led....

But those days were long gone. She ignored the heat she could feel in her face. "I have a right to some privacy.''

He chuckled at that and she wondered why it was that she'd never noticed before how annoying he could be. He might be glorious to look at, standing there with that snow-dusted black hair, his gorgeous face relaxed with amusement and his arms crossed over his broad chest, but he was still insufferably smug. If he were one of her brothers and this was fifteen years ago, she'd have doubled her fist and landed a right cross to that washboard stomach of his.

But he wasn't one of her brothers and it wasn't fifteen years ago and she'd never let him know he was getting to her. In any way.

"Never mind. I'll do this when I get rid of you." She took a step away from the shop door, but that was as far as she went before his hand caught her arm and stopped her.

"You'll go a long time needing underwear that way,'' he warned, still apparently amused by her.

Then he did the most horrible thing. His thumb rubbed

slow, sensuous circles against her bare skin and red-hot sparks skittered all the way to her stomach.

It was the first time he'd touched her since the night she'd decided to get a divorce. And it was not heartening to discover there was still power in even such simple contact.

She meant to tear her arm away indignantly. But somehow the best she could do was shrug out of his grip.

"Come on," he said, as if he'd been left completely unaffected. "I'll look at baby furniture and you won't even know I'm in the same store."

Oh, she'd know all right. But for some reason she didn't even want to think about, she was suddenly, uncomfortably aware of just how tight her regular bras had become. In fact she felt as if her breasts might burst right out of the cups. She definitely needed new bras. Right now. Whether he was there or not.

"Fine," she muttered. "But you'd better steer clear of me."

"Absolutely," he assured with so much laughter in his tone she really did want to hit him.

But instead she yanked open the store's door and marched in ahead of him.

The shop took up two storefronts—one for the maternity clothes and the other for baby furniture and accessories like car seats, booster chairs, mobiles and just about anything else mother or child could need. Three-quarters of the wall between the two sections had been cut away at the center so though there was a separation, most of each store was visible to the other.

Beth weaved her way slowly through the racks of clothes, keeping an eye on her former husband to make sure he was doing as he'd said he would and staying on the furniture side.

He was. In fact he was so interested in reading a potty-chair box that he seemed unaware she was around at all. Reassured by that, she nabbed a saleslady and asked for assistance with bras.

Unfortunately, the saleswoman, one of the few people in Elk Creek she didn't know, happened to have a very loud voice. Beth had asked if bras existed that could expand along with her body so she wouldn't have to replace them again from now until the end of her pregnancy, and the woman's answering lecture might as well have been given over a loudspeaker.

Standing near the rack the woman had led her to, Beth shot a glance at Ash. This time his interest was not in potty chairs. It was on Beth. Specifically, on her breasts, as he apparently checked for evidence of the need for this particular new underwear. And to make matters worse, she felt the heat of his gaze like a blast furnace.

Damn him!

Damn the saleswoman!

Damn herself for responding to the appreciation in his expression and the awful memories of having more than his gaze on her and how good it had felt once upon a time!

"Thanks for your help but I'll just browse myself now if you don't mind," she said in a hurry, taking a step behind a turnstile as she spoke. And if her tone was abrupt and offended the woman, at that moment she didn't care. Her only concern was for stopping the loud talk of engorged breasts and ultrasensitive nipples, and escaping from Ash's view of exactly those two things.

Hidden behind the rack, Beth looked for a back door to slip out of so she could escape. There wasn't one and she had no choice but to tough this one out, too. But, Lord, how she wished she'd never come into this store! The fact that this errand had turned into one of the most embarrassing of her life seemed a direct result of Asher Black-wolf and his stubbornness.

Damn him anyway.

He was making her sorry she'd ever told him about the baby. He didn't have any business here. Not in Elk Creek. Not in this store. Not in her life. And she was going to tell him so, she decided as she searched for her size and snatched three bras off their hangers. She was going to tell him in no uncertain terms to get out of town, that she'd keep him informed about the baby, but that was as far as she would go with him and he'd better just accept it.

And if he didn't?

Then she'd leave. She'd pack up in the middle of the night and she'd disappear. She wouldn't even let her brothers know where she was so there was no risk of one of them telling Asher Blackwolf.

Damn him anyway!

But then she stepped from behind the turnstile and caught sight of him again.

And some of the steam fizzled out of her.

He wasn't watching her anymore. He was studying a crib. Very intently. Very seriously. Checking its sturdiness. Checking the movement of the side and how secure it was when it was up. Checking the width of the gaps between the spindled bars.

And there was something very touching about the big man so intent in thoughts of his child's safety that it gave her heart quite a lurch.

Damn him anyway...

It struck her then that he was going to love this baby, just the way she was. Just the way she already did. That no matter what he'd thought or said before, now that it was on the way, he really did want it.

He really did want to be included in it all. And she knew

she had to accept that, in spite of her own feelings about him. Feelings she was just going to have to control. No matter how difficult that might be.

Because regardless of what was between them, she couldn't deny him the pleasure of planning for this baby any more than she could deny him the baby itself after it was born.

But she could keep hoping something would distract him or call him away, to ease the burden of those feelings for a man who no longer wanted her.

The saleswoman recovered from her pique at Beth's curt dismissal and returned to take the bras to the register. She was still in a bit of a huff, which subdued her enthusiasm and, thankfully, her voice, so that Beth managed to pay for her underwear without more embarrassment.

When the transaction was complete, the baby furniture seemed to call to her, too, and she joined Ash.

"I think we should buy this set, tie it to the roof of the car and take it with us," he informed her decisively over an oak dresser, crib and matching changing table.

"It's too soon for that. And even if it wasn't, until Linc and Danny move in with Kansas, there's no room for it all."

That wasn't exactly true, but it seemed viable. The truth was that something about the purchase made Beth feel uncomfortable.

It wasn't that she had any more than the usual concerns about carrying the baby to full term or delivering a healthy infant; this had more to do with Ash. With the awkwardness of their situation. With her unwanted and unrealistic wish that they were choosing furniture to put in the nursery of the home they'd share with their child instead of the house she shared with her brothers.

"I don't think it's too soon," Ash persisted, oblivious

to her thoughts and lost in his own. "But if you don't like it, maybe I'll have it sent to my place."

Everything seemed to stand still for Beth. "Your place?"

"Sure. I'll need the whole setup, too. For when the baby is with me on the reservation."

Beth felt as if he'd hit her. Hard.

She could barely breathe, let alone respond to that. All she could do was turn and leave behind the store, Ash and the beautiful furniture while she dealt with the sudden harsh realization that he was right, that there would actually be times when she would have to hand over her baby to him.

Somehow, in all of her previous thinking, that hadn't occurred to her. She'd pictured the baby with her. She pictured Ash spending—at most—a few hours or an afternoon with it. Not actually taking it across the state for days or weeks or *months*...

Outside she took long gulps of air to fight off the tears and anger that were tearing at her insides like claws.

"Beth?" Ash came out of the store behind her, his voice and expression rife with concern.

She wanted to shout at him, to scream that this baby was hers, that he could visit with it but that he couldn't buy furniture and set up a nursery and take her baby away!

But of course the rational part of her knew he could. That he would. That being the father would not be limited to visits.

"Are you all right?" he asked with an edge of panic to his voice.

"I'm going home" was all she could say, heading off around him with no idea of how she was going to get there.

But for the second time Ash stopped her, taking both

her shoulders in his big hands and bringing her face-to-face with him. "Are you sick? Do you need a doctor?"

"No!" she yelled, trying to yank free of his grip, but he was holding her too tight to manage it. "I just want to go home."

The concern in his features edged toward confusion, but she had no intention of enlightening him. What could she say, after all? That she was feeling selfish and possessive and couldn't bear the fact that this baby she was carrying might say its first word or take its first step during his time with it instead of hers? That the reality of sharing this child had just struck her like a ton of bricks?

"I just want to go home," she repeated.

"Then let's go," Ash answered, turning her in the direction of his car.

Neither of them said any more as they drove back to the ranch. Beth was lost in her own thoughts, her own regrets that this baby would be brought into such a complicated situation. By the time Ash pulled up in front of the house she wanted only to go in and be alone.

But he wasn't having any of that. He insisted that he wasn't leaving until he'd made sure she had a well-balanced meal and really was okay.

And so they fixed dinner together. Ash barbecued two steaks while Beth prepared a salad, a fruit cup and sliced bread, all in silence, punctuated with loud closings of cupboard doors and the clattering of dishes, glasses and silverware placed heavily on the kitchen table.

She could feel Ash watching her as if he thought she'd lost her mind and might run screaming into the night at any moment, but it didn't matter. She almost felt as if she *could* run screaming into the night at any moment.

"Are you going to let me know what I did wrong?" he finally asked as they began to eat.

"You didn't do anything wrong," she said, her tone belying the words.

"You always have a violent reaction to the suggestion of buying baby furniture, is that it? Is something wrong that you aren't telling me?"

"Everything is fine. Just drop it."

Still, his black eyes bored into her while he chewed a bite of steak. "Do you want this baby, Beth?"

Her own fork stopped halfway to her mouth as she stared back at him. "Of course I want this baby. Not having one of our own was your plan, not mine."

Both his bushy eyebrows rose at that. "You never disagreed with it. If you wanted to have a baby, why didn't you say so?"

"I didn't really think you'd ever find a big enough break in your schedule to work it in either way."

"But what if I had? Would you have just gone along with the adoption idea and resented it rather than speak up and tell me how you felt?"

"I didn't say I resented anything."

"You didn't *say* a damn thing."

She merely went on eating without saying anything now, either.

He frowned at her. "Did you get pregnant on purpose?"

"No, I didn't. I wouldn't do something like that, in the first place. And in the second place, why on earth would I have willingly gotten myself into what's a long, long way from being ideal circumstances to bring a child into?"

"But you do want it now that it's on the way?"

"I said I did."

"You just don't want to buy a crib for it."

He wasn't going to get her to admit to what had hurt her in that maternity shop. To let him know that the idea of his taking the baby to the reservation was a weakness she had, a vulnerable spot. No way. Never. Shag Heller's daughter knew better than that.

"It's just too soon," she repeated.

He went on watching her as if he knew she was lying but didn't understand why.

Beth wished he'd leave. That he'd take his finely chiseled bones and his penetrating eyes and his broad shoulders hugged by that tight T-shirt and get out of her kitchen, her town and her life once and for all.

He finished eating and pushed his plate away, resting his hands on the table where his fingers drummed against the top in a slow rhythm.

She stared at those hands with their long, blunt fingers and she had a flash of what they felt like against her bare skin. Against her breasts. Against her nipples that were erect and straining within the too-small confines of her bra.

And then she noticed something else.

She noticed that there was a very faint tan line on the third finger of his left hand where his wedding ring used to be. And two things struck her. One—that he must not have taken it off until recently, even though the divorce had been final for a long time.

And, two—that even though it might have been belated—or even reluctant—he *had* taken it off.

And that fact was yet another jab at her heart.

Of course it was unreasonable. They were divorced. She'd taken off her rings, certainly he had to take off his.

But somehow, looking at that bare finger, where she'd once placed his ring, where it had stayed throughout their marriage, was painful, and she felt tears well up behind her eyes.

As she fought them, he spoke again and she had the sense that he could see some of what was going on inside her, because his deep voice was very quiet, very solemn, raising the lid on more unwanted feelings. "I wish that, just once, you'd let me know what's going on with you. Did you ever think that I might be able to make even one thing easier if you did?"

She snatched up her plate and took it to the sink. "You could make things easier for me if you'd go back to the reservation and leave me alone," she said, meaning for it to be curt and cold, yet it came out softly, almost a plea.

She set her plate on the counter, but she didn't turn back to him. She stared down into the sink as pure weariness washed through her and splashed against the tension in her neck like tidal waves against rocky cliffs.

"Why can't you just go away?" she nearly whispered, digging her own fingers into her nape.

She heard his chair scrape back and the sound of his heels on the tile floor as he came up behind her.

He stopped very near and took her hands away to replace them with his, kneading the tension with strong, capable fingers that seemed to know the exact spot and the perfect pressure to ease the taut muscles and tendons.

Her gazillionth wish for that day was that it didn't feel so wonderful or work so well.

But it did, and little by little she felt herself relax beneath his expert ministrations, even leaning toward him until she was almost resting against the hard expanse of his torso.

"I only want to help," he said in a husky voice, just before he pressed a kiss to the side of her neck with warm lips.

And then, somehow, she was facing him, gazing up into his inscrutable eyes as his mouth lowered to hers, capturing hers in a kiss that had nothing to do with stress relief.

She knew this kiss well. The tenderness in it. The anticipation. The sweetness before the storm of passion. And more than being familiar, it awakened things inside her that had no business being awake. Desires. Yearnings. Cravings for what she knew could be so good between them.

But it was the only thing that was any good between them, and she also knew that indulging in it would only further complicate an already too-complicated situation.

Besides, deep inside she carried with her the vivid memory of the loneliness that had followed that last time they'd made love, the loneliness of her entire marriage to him. Nothing was worth revisiting that.

She pushed from his kiss, from his arms, sidestepped away from him and, without looking at him, said, "You'd better go."

He didn't move, but she could feel him staring at her again; she could feel his confusion, his anger. After a moment he said, "I'll clean up here first. You've had a long day. Put your feet up and watch some TV or go to bed."

It was a direct order, given in a voice tight with control. But Beth decided to obey it just to finally put the needed distance between them.

She didn't say good-night or thank him for lunch or dinner or clearing the mess. She simply straightened her shoulders and walked out.

Because to say anything else, to do anything else, to even raise her eyes to his one more time, could all too easily have put her back in his arms.

Where a part of her wanted much too badly to be.

Chapter Four

"Robert Yazzie here."

"That sounded very official, old man," Ash answered his grandfather's telephone greeting affectionately, when he reached the elderly Indian at the offices of the Blackwolf Foundation early the next morning.

Robert laughed as if he'd just pulled off a good joke. "It's this big chair of yours. Makes me feel like the president."

Ash had asked his maternal grandfather to oversee the foundation during his absence. Robert Yazzie was not a businessman, but he had common sense and an easygoing nature that let him handle things without panicking. Plus, Ash knew he wouldn't try tackling anything beyond figurehead status. And the elderly man enjoyed brief interruptions to his retirement.

"How's that bum knee of yours?" Ash asked, settling down on his unmade bed to talk.

"It's keeping me off the golf course or I wouldn't be making your apologies for you to all those people you're standing up," Robert answered with yet another laugh that made him sound as jolly as Saint Nick.

Ash had been raised by both his grandfathers, but his relationship with Robert was the closer of the two. He'd stayed with Robert the majority of the time, going to work with him on weekends and during vacations from school. As the less temperamental of the two grandfathers, Robert had seemed to enjoy having his grandson's company, and Ash had preferred to be with him, too.

It was Robert who had instilled in Ash the importance of family and Indian ways and community. But most of all, the old man was just plain fun to be around. His love of life was infectious. Ash counted him not only as grandfather, mentor and teacher, but also as his best friend.

"You aren't driving Miss Lightfeather too crazy, are you?" Ash teased him back, sitting against the headboard and swinging his feet onto the mattress to cross them at the ankle.

"I don't think that woman likes me," Robert confided in a lowered voice as if the secretary might overhear.

That made Ash laugh. "Miss Lightfeather doesn't like anybody."

"Except you. I think she had a crush on you. But I told her about the baby the way you wanted me to and it didn't sit well with her. She even asked me if I was sure it was yours, like she was hoping it wasn't."

"It's mine."

"That's what I told her and I got cold coffee the rest of the afternoon yesterday because of it."

"Don't let her get away with that. Be firm with her."

"Ha! She might hurt me."

Again Ash laughed. His grandfather was over six feet

tall and weighed upward of two hundred pounds. Compared to that, even the pudgy Miss Lightfeather was a bantamweight. "How's everything else going?"

"Fine, but where is everybody? Don't you have a staff of some kind?"

"Not really, you know that."

"I knew you didn't have any full-time help, but I thought you at least had some part-time people. Nobody's been around but Miss Lightfeather and me."

"I don't schedule my part-timers regularly, only as I need them. I do as much as I can myself—or should I say, Miss Lightfeather and I do as much as we can. It cuts costs, and that way, rather than putting a lot of money in salaries, I can spread it around where it can do more good."

"Ahh. I've been hearing a lot about cost effectiveness and money, that's for sure," Robert said. From there the elderly Indian brought him up-to-date on the proceeds from a benefit dinner the night before to raise money for the homeless. He told him about a bequest that had been left to the foundation by a Native American woman who had just died, and related several other, smaller events, as well as news of the trial of the boy in Alaska whom Ash had hired legal counsel for.

"So how's our little Beth?" Robert asked when he'd finished.

Ash knew his grandfather and Beth were close. They'd shared interests in several things and Robert had taken her under his wing. "She's too skinny."

"That's not good. We're a family of big babies. She's going to need her strength and some meat on her bones when it comes time to deliver your son."

Ash smiled. "You're sure it's a boy, are you?"

"Just hoping. It's good to have a boy to carry on the

name.'' Robert paused and then ventured cautiously. ''Now that the shock has worn off, how do you feel about this?''

''A little giddy,'' he admitted what he wouldn't admit to anyone but his grandfather.

Robert chuckled. ''Then you're not unhappy about it?''

''I've surprised myself by how excited I am.''

''Babies will do that. There's something magical about them.'' This time Robert cleared his throat. ''So, uh, what're you going to do about it?''

''What am I going to do about what?''

''Well, you know, babies have a right to be born into a loving house complete with a mother and a father.''

''This one will be born into two loving homes, one with a mother and one with a father. It gets a bonus,'' Ash said, trying to make light of what he really didn't see that way.

''Is that how you want it?''

''We're divorced, Pap, that's just how it is.'' Ash didn't have to be in the same room with his grandfather to see him nodding his head in that sage way that accepted what he said and still managed to disagree with it.

''I surely do miss that girl,'' Robert said. ''She plays a mean gin rummy. Haven't had as good a game as she gives me since she left.''

''Are you telling me you're sorry she didn't get custody of you in the settlement?'' Ash joked.

''Just saying I miss her. Thought you did, too, the way you were grumbling around here when you moved in. You sleepin' nights yet?''

''I sleep fine,'' Ash lied.

''And here I was thinking all those times I heard you up walkin' around were because your bed was too lonely without her.''

''I've slept in plenty of beds without her.''

"Humph. Maybe too many. Sometimes it seemed like she spent more time with me than she did with you."

"She never complained about it. But if you have something to say to me, old man, spit it out."

"Only thinking that with a baby coming now, maybe she'd take you back."

"She acts like she can't stand the sight of me."

"Must have kept her eyes closed to get that baby in her belly, is that what you're tellin' me?"

"She must have."

"So what're you doing there?"

"Claiming what's mine."

"The baby, you mean."

"The baby."

"Are you sure that's all that's yours? Maybe Beth could be, too, if you handled things right."

"Maybe you ought to come here and *handle* things and I should just stay on the reservation and run the foundation. I think she likes you better anyway."

"Maybe. We had some good times together, me and that little girl."

Ash said, "Look, Pap, I have to go. You have the number here at the lodge and the one at the ranch, in case you need me, right?"

"We'll be fine. Between Miss Lightfeather and me, we could run the world. It's Beth who needs you now."

"That'll be the day."

"Don't be too sure of it."

Ash exchanged goodbyes with his grandfather rather than comment on that and hung up, thinking as he did that if there was one thing he *was* sure of, it was that Beth Heller didn't think she needed him. For anything.

Except maybe making this baby. She hadn't been able to do that alone. And there was one other thing he was sure of, though he wouldn't have admitted it even to his grandfather. He was still more attracted to her than to any woman he'd ever met.

He leaned his head back and stared up at the ceiling, thinking about the night before.

He couldn't believe he'd actually kissed her.

After the day they'd had together, with her letting him know his very presence irked her, he'd kissed her, of all things.

And worse than that, he'd wanted to do a whole lot more than kiss her.

Old habits die hard, he told himself. That was all it was.

Sex had always been good. Toward the end of their marriage, it was the only time he ever felt close to her. The only time it seemed that he could reach her, understand her and what she wanted and needed and would accept from him. The only time he wasn't so damn frustrated by her.

In fact, making love to her had often been a way to overcome those other, less than pleasant feelings she'd raised in him. So last night, at the height of her confusing and frustrating him and making him feel helpless and useless and all the things he hated, he'd just naturally turned to what he'd always done before.

"Right. As if you weren't so hot for her you could have sizzled those steaks on your skin," he said out loud.

All right, it hadn't just been a response to other things. He'd wanted her.

She'd turned to face him and raised those big blue eyes to him, parted her lips in what had looked like an invitation, and at that moment—just as when they were married—nothing else had mattered.

And when he'd kissed her, she'd kissed him back. One hundred percent.

For a few moments, anyway. Before she'd ended it and acted as if she couldn't even stand to look at him.

The woman drove him crazy. She really did. He didn't know what the hell she wanted.

But he knew what he'd wanted.

He'd wanted to take her upstairs to the nearest bed and make love to her until neither of them could walk.

Ash swung his feet to the floor and jammed his hands through his hair in self-disgust at the fact that just thinking about kissing her flooded him with a fresh wave of desire.

But he knew he had to control it. She didn't want him. She didn't want anything to do with him. That was obvious. Hell, she hadn't even been able to pick out baby furniture with him.

It was just too bad her total contempt of him didn't cool things off inside of him.

Because it was pure hell to be burning up with wanting a woman who couldn't even tolerate him.

Beth was a little surprised not to find Ash there when she went downstairs around noon that day. She'd been down much earlier, having gotten up at the crack of dawn, fixed herself a light breakfast and then gone back to her room to work on Kansas's wedding dress. Of course he hadn't been around then. But she'd thought that on her second trip she'd probably find him waiting, the way he had been the day before.

Not that she wanted him to be.

But she'd thought his claim that he was sticking around would last more than one day before he answered some summons from somewhere.

Or maybe he'd been as shaken as she was by that kiss and it had convinced him that their being together was not a good idea. Maybe it had driven him back to the reservation all on its own.

And if she knew just a pang of disappointment at the thought that his time here had been so short-lived?

She beat it down like a spark in a hayloft.

If he had left Elk Creek, it was for the best, she told herself as she headed for the kitchen. It was just what she'd wanted. What she'd hoped for. Now she could concentrate on the baby and carving out a new life for herself back in her old hometown without giving Asher Blackwolf another thought.

In the kitchen she went straight to the refrigerator. But as she stood in the open door and looked at her choices for lunch, she realized that somewhere between her bedroom and here she'd lost her appetite again.

Maybe if she waited awhile, it would come back. Kansas was due for a fitting anytime now, and, once her friend got here and she had some company, she might be able to eat then.

As she closed the refrigerator door a loud clanging of metal hammering metal sounded from outside.

She hadn't realized Jackson was working nearby today and, grateful for the distraction, she went to the window above the sink to see what he was doing.

But out at the barn off the southwest corner of the house, her brother wasn't alone. And, to Beth's immense surprise, he wasn't the one working the forge and bellows to form a horseshoe. Ash was.

Beth couldn't have been more stunned if she were looking at the pope on a bucking bronco, for never had she seen her former husband do any sort of manual labor. Ash was a businessman through and through.

Or so she'd thought.

He'd hired Indian boys on the reservation to mow the

lawn in the summers and shovel the snow in the winter-
time, and men to paint the house and fix anything that
needed it around the place.

And yet there he was, stripped to the waistband of another pair of hip-hugging blue jeans, doing the work of a
burly blacksmith.

"Amazing," she whispered to herself as she absorbed
the idea.

But the sight was pretty amazing, too.

Hot weather had definitely arrived on this last day of
June. The temperature was easily in the nineties. The heat
emanating from the forge was so intense she could see the
wavy distortion in the air, and she marveled over the physical exertion that went with melding iron into shape. Sweat
glistened over Ash's naturally bronzed flesh.

And it was something to behold.

There was a very primitive and purely masculine beauty
in what her eyes feasted on. Hard, honed muscles in his
shoulders, back and biceps rose and rippled and proved
their power. Even the planes of his handsome face seemed
sharper, the skin more taut over the chiseled bones.

For a few moments she watched in wonder as his big,
black-gloved hands worked the forge bellows and then
took the shoe to the anvil, where he wielded the hammer
with a skill she hadn't known he possessed. But appreciation for his workmanship couldn't keep her gaze from
sliding up the tensed tendons of his forearms, all the way
to his back again.

As always, he wore his coarse, straight hair in a queue
that reached to the middle of his spine, clinging to it and
pointing downwards like a shaft and arrow to where two
slight dimples winked at her from just above his jean pockets.

Holding the finished shoe in long pincers, he plunged

the hot metal into a bucket of water, sending a loud sizzle through the air. Beth thought cold water thrown against her own skin at that moment might have made the same sound.

And something in the pit of her stomach knotted and twisted with yearning.

Her hands itched to glide along his ribs, to feel the power in his arms beneath her palms, to absorb the heat and the potency of him. She wanted to bury her face in the slight valley of his pectorals, to taste the saltiness of his flesh, to feel the hardness of those muscles against her softer parts, to kiss a path down the center line of his torso to his navel, and maybe lower...

And then, suddenly, there was a knock on the front door just before it opened and Kansas called, "It's me."

Beth was jolted out of her study of her former husband, and she struggled to find her voice through the tightness in her throat. "Come on in," she answered, hoping her old friend didn't hear the breathy undertone.

Her heart was racing; perspiration dotted her palms, and even knowing she was about to be caught in the act, she had trouble tearing her gaze from Ash. Instead, still staring, she turned on the cold water, dampened her hands and pressed cool, moist fingertips to her cheeks in an attempt to calm the color she knew flushed them.

"Where are you?" Kansas asked from what sounded like somewhere in the living room.

"The kitchen," Beth answered, snatching one last glance of masculine magnificence before she turned away from the sink and tried to look nonchalant.

Kansas came through the swinging door with a jaunty stride. A serene smile brightened her face. "Hi," she said, setting her purse on the countertop just inside the door.

Beth returned the greeting and took the few steps to the

butcher block in the center of the room. She knew it was absurd, but she had the sense that her back was being scorched by the heat of the scene she'd been observing. "Have you had lunch?" she asked too eagerly.

"Just before I came. Linc and Danny brought burgers to the store so we could eat together. I'll sit with you while you have something, though."

But what Beth was really hungry for was not food and so she shook her head. "No, that's okay. I'm sure you want to get back to work. Why don't we just pin up that hem so you can?"

Apparently there wasn't evidence of what had been going on in Beth's mind moments before, because Kansas didn't seem to notice anything amiss. "If you aren't starving, that would work better for me. My sister is holding down the fort while I'm gone, but she has some other things she needs to do today, so I hate to keep her any longer than I have to."

"Let's go up and get to work, then."

Kansas talked about the weather and her general store's air-conditioning being on the fritz as they went upstairs, but Beth was concentrating on getting some control over herself.

In her room she tried to avoid the window as Kansas slipped out of her clothes and put on the dress, but somehow the sill was where she ended up perching, and more than once she stole glances down as Ash formed and fitted another shoe and Jackson looked on.

And though she hated herself for it, she had to fight a strong reluctance to leave that window and the sight of Ash.

But of course she forced herself.

While Beth pinned the hem, Kansas chatted about Danny and something funny the three-year-old had said.

Beth barely heard her as her attention kept straying toward the window. Even though she couldn't see out of it from where she knelt at the base of the chair her friend stood on, she was acutely tuned in to every sound. So much so that she even knew the moment the last nail was hammered into the last shoe and the horse was led through the squeaky paddock gate.

"I must be boring you to death," Kansas said at about the same moment.

"No, no, I'm just a little drifty today," Beth assured her, not really knowing whether she'd missed something important or not.

"Are you feeling okay? Do you have morning sickness or anything like that?"

"I feel great," she answered, thinking that feeling hot and bothered and inappropriately aroused by the wrong man didn't count. Then she added, "I never had any morning sickness, even early on, or I might have realized I was pregnant sooner." But she didn't want to say much more about her pregnancy, knowing it was insensitive in view of the fact that her friend couldn't have kids.

Luckily she'd finished pinning the hem by then and so could change the subject naturally. "That's it. We're all set. You can take the dress off and get back to the store. I'll have it finished by tonight."

Kansas seemed in no hurry to get out of the gown and instead went to the cheval mirror in the corner to admire Beth's handiwork for a few more minutes before actually changing out of it again.

To make amends for her inattentiveness, Beth asked a number of questions about how the preparations for the wedding were coming. The effort helped to finally get her own mind off Ash, so that by the time they headed back to the kitchen to get Kansas's purse, she felt like herself again.

But it lasted only until they went through the swinging door and came upon Jackson and Ash.

The scent of clean, honest sweat was in the air and though Beth knew it was crazy, the fact that part of it came from Ash acted like an aphrodisiac on her, rekindling much of what she'd thought she'd conquered.

But there he was, standing in the same spot she'd been at the sink, washing his hands, and she had the awful urge to walk up behind him, wrap her arms around his narrow waist and do silky, sexy things to his bare back.

Greetings and small talk between Kansas, Jackson and Ash made her lack of participation unobtrusive as she struggled with the urge, but struggle she did.

Until Kansas invited them all to dinner that night.

"Sounds great," she heard Ash answer before she could refuse.

"I have a Cattleman's Association meeting," Jackson declined as he unburdened the refrigerator of ice tea and the fixings for sandwiches. "But you all go ahead without me."

"And that way you can bring the dress," Kansas added, sealing the date before Beth could manage to utter a word.

"I can bring the dress by without your having to cook," she said, belatedly trying to get out of what would be a social evening that coupled her with her ex-husband.

But by that point, Kansas wouldn't hear of their not going to dinner, and she was locked in.

"About seven," her soon-to-be-sister-in-law said as she slipped her purse strap over her shoulder.

Beth only smiled in answer, hoping it didn't look as wan as it felt.

Goodbyes were said all around. When Kansas left, Beth felt as if she'd been abandoned to the wolves.

Silly thought.

"Have you had lunch?" Jackson asked her then.

Just the idea of sitting a few feet away from Ash and his naked torso while she ate a sandwich was an exercise in agony. "I ate before Kansas got here," she lied to get herself out of it. She'd eat something after Ash was gone.

Ash was leaning his hips against the edge of the counter as he dried his hands and watched her. "What do you have planned for this afternoon?" he inquired, the first words he'd said directly to her.

"I'll be up in my room hemming the wedding dress," she answered in a hurry, hoping it would convince him to leave.

He nodded, pushed off the counter and went to the butcher block, where Jackson was building four enormous sandwiches. Ash swung a long leg over one of the bar stools there and the flash of his zipper as he did made Beth catch her breath.

"I guess we can shoe those other two horses, then," he told her brother.

"Great," Jackson said enthusiastically, clearly over his anger at his former brother-in-law.

Beth's gaze had taken a rocket leap and landed in the hollow of Ash's throat, where the arrowhead nestled against his skin. Hearing their plans, she wondered how she was going to get through the afternoon without gawking at him.

"I thought you were using preformed shoes," she said peevishly to her brother.

Jackson's expression told her he found her curt tone curious. "I have been. But the red mare has a bad foot and needs a special fit, and since we're all set up and Ash is willing, we might as well do it for the other two, too.''

Dandy.

"Did you need me for something else this afternoon?" Ash asked her.

What flashed through her mind was not something she was about to share with him. "I'm hemming a dress," she repeated.

"Then it shouldn't matter if I work with the horses."

Both men apparently knew something was going on with her and, hating that she was so transparent, Beth drew herself up into a ramrod-straight posture and shrugged as if they were imagining things.

"It doesn't matter to me at all," she lied again, turning to leave.

About the time her hand reached the door to push it open, Ash said, "I'll go back to the lodge when I'm finished, shower and pick you up a little before seven."

Beth bristled, ignoring the faint tingle of excitement that ignited deep inside her at the same time. "No, thanks. I'll just see you there," she said firmly.

"I don't want you going out alone, late at night. I'll pick you up," he insisted.

"What could possibly happen to me? I'm only fifteen minutes outside of town."

Ash looked at Jackson and said, "You know, she's the most stubborn person I've ever met."

"Ha! You didn't know Shag very well then."

The exchange that excluded her only got her back up more. "Let's not be ridiculous about this. I'll drive myself to Kansas's house."

"I'll pick you up a little before seven."

She rolled her eyes and took a breath, shoring up to really let him have it.

But then she realized that arguing with him left her in that kitchen all the longer.

Besides, for some reason, this new quest of his to be a conscientious father made him far more stubborn than she was, and she knew he would take this to the wall rather than give in. It was better for her to concede, she decided, and escape.

"Oh, fine. Have it your way," she finally said ungraciously. Then she turned on her heels to leave.

But as she did, she knew that having Ash out by the barn, shoeing horses, was going to make for a long afternoon.

And she wasn't looking forward to the evening, either.

By a quarter to seven that night Beth felt more in control of herself again. It helped that Ash had been gone more than two hours and that she'd taken a cool shower.

It also helped that she'd found a logical explanation for the even more intense attraction she'd been feeling toward him since his arrival in Elk Creek. Pregnancy hormones might well be causing these strange physical reactions, as well as her overly emotional state.

It was possible, she'd decided, that some biological quirk drew a woman to the father of the child she was carrying as Mother Nature's way of uniting them in spite of whatever other circumstances might exist. And somehow, the thought that it was just one more thing to endure—like the weakening of her bladder—put a new perspective on it for her.

She'd just ride it out, she told herself. She'd use better judgment and common sense to keep a lid on it. And it wouldn't be long, she was still convinced, before Ash left anyway.

With this new outlook, she felt sure that even the evening she faced could be passed with no more involvement than if she and Ash were any two acquaintances having dinner with another couple.

And the fact that she'd dressed up for the occasion had nothing whatsoever to do with her former husband. She'd merely felt inclined to celebrate this new lease on things with an airy halter sundress that fit loose enough to conceal her stomach, lacy espadrilles, and her hair gathered into a small cascade of curls at her crown. Everything worked together to make her feel cool and confident, and that was her goal, she told herself. Not to be attractive to Ash.

She was watching for him when he drove up, so she could forestall his coming to the door. This wasn't a date, after all.

He was out of the car by the time she left the house and so he went around to the passenger side to open that door for her.

She said a cursory hello and let him take the wedding dress and lay it across the back seat while she got in the front.

Beth tried not to notice how good he looked as he rounded the car on his way to the driver's side. He was freshly showered and wearing a pair of gray slacks and a crisp white shirt with the sleeves rolled to his elbows.

This was the Ash she was familiar with—casually chic, the businessman out for an evening with friends. It was less heady than the sight of him earlier today had been, though one whiff of his cologne as he joined her in the car did make her stomach flutter.

Hormones, she reminded herself. Nothing more than hormones.

He didn't start the engine right away. Instead he turned in her direction, propped one elbow on his headrest and the other on the steering wheel, and took a slow appraisal of her from topknot to toe.

"You look wonderful tonight," he said when he was finished.

"Thanks," she responded as if the compliment didn't matter, when in fact it secretly pleased her no end.

"There really must be a glow that comes with pregnancy because you seem all pink and healthy and—"

"Maybe you just never took the time to notice before." The words were out before she had a chance to think about them, and before he could say anything she poked her chin in the direction of the key in the ignition. "Don't you think we ought to get going?"

"Sure," he said as if he didn't quite understand her attitude in response to courtesy and compliments. He faced forward and started the car. "I spoke to my grandfather this morning," he went on then, showing better manners than she had, she knew. "He's missing you as his gin rummy opponent."

Just the thought of Robert Yazzie softened her mood and made her smile. The old man was truly a gem. He'd kept her company, explained Indian customs, helped her to know where she could and couldn't go on the reservation so she didn't embarrass herself. He'd been more friend to her than in-law.

"I miss him, too. How is he?" she asked, hearing the distinct change in her own tone of voice.

"He's the same—full of life." Ash took his eyes off the road to glance at her. "You know, I was always a little jealous of what the two of you had between you."

The last thing she needed was for Ash to flirt with her, and she refused to encourage it, so she merely confirmed what he'd said. "We did have fun together. You must be more like your other grandfather." She hadn't meant that to be an insult, merely an observation, but it had sounded pretty bad. She tried for a quick recovery. "I mean—"

"I know what you meant," he said grimly.

It was clear she'd insulted him and it left her feeling very small and petty as the third strike seemed to end his attempt to make this evening pleasant.

But it wasn't only *this* evening, she thought as his attention turned to his driving and left her to consider her recent behavior toward him.

With the exception of that first day they'd seen each other and argued, he'd been working to keep things between them calm and easy for her. Even when she knew she'd annoyed him, he hadn't vented it; he'd merely turned his anger inward, like now. But she'd been acting like a spoiled child or some sort of prima donna.

Of course she had a good reason—anything was better than succumbing to her softer, warmer, sexier feelings for a man who didn't want her. But still, she wasn't proud of herself. Hormones or no hormones, roller coaster emotions or not, she wasn't handling things well and she vowed to curb the hostility she used like a shield. Fighting the attraction she felt to him was no excuse for flinging all his efforts in his face or offending him. In the future she had to find a way to control her own feelings without being so prickly, or she wouldn't be able to live with herself.

Besides, she honestly didn't believe he'd be here for long and it seemed silly now to make it so miserable for them both. And she also realized that trying to establish a more amiable relationship would serve the two of them and the baby in the long run.

But they'd reached Kansas's house by the time she'd come to that conclusion, and Ash was out of the car before she'd thought of a way to make amends. She did, however, thank him for opening her door, venturing the first smile she'd allowed him since he'd been in Elk Creek.

Unfortunately, he didn't see it; his gaze seemed to go over the top of her head, as if that were the only way he could refrain from letting her know what he thought of her and her contrariness.

He took the wedding dress out of the back, and as Beth accepted it from him, she reconsidered an attempt to rectify things before they went inside.

"Look, I'm sorry," she tried on the way up the porch steps, but apologies were no easier for her than sharing any other feelings, and it came out sounding impatient and uncontrite.

"Forget it," he said as he rang the doorbell, still not looking at her, his own tone clipped as he stood there as straight and stiff as any cigar-store Indian.

And Beth couldn't help wondering if ever there were two people worse together than they were.

Before she could say any more, her nephew answered the door.

All two and a half feet of Jackson's same brand of solemn stoicism, Danny regarded them seriously, his big green eyes taking in Beth and then rolling slowly up the full length of Ash.

Linc kept Danny with him most of the time, either at the honky-tonk he was building or here at Kansas's house. When Ash had been at the ranch, Danny had either not been there, or been in bed asleep. This was his first sight of the big man.

Beth opened the screen. "Hi, sweetheart," he said to the little boy. "I'll bet you don't remember Ash, do you? You were barely more than a baby the last time your dad brought you to see us."

Danny stepped out of the way so they could go in; he

stared at Ash the whole time. "He gots lo-ong hair," the three-year-old marveled.

"Hi, Danny. It's good to see you." Ash held out his hand to shake Danny's much, much smaller one, but Danny snatched his behind his back rather than let Ash touch him, and dived for Beth's side, where he wrapped his other arm around her legs as if he needed protection.

Ash only smiled, took something from his pocket and hunkered down on his heels so he was nearer to eye level with the little boy. "I brought you something," he said, upturning his closed fist and opening it. "An Indian arrowhead."

Danny merely frowned at Ash and then at the arrowhead lying in his palm.

Ash picked it up between two fingers and held it out to him in a way that it could be taken without there being any contact between them. "Just carrying it around with you makes you strong. See, I wear one all the time," he added, pulling his from inside his shirt.

That seemed to interest the little boy, who carefully reached for the arrowhead, comparing the polished stone to Ash's burnished copper.

"What do you say?" Beth urged gently.

"Thanks," Danny muttered. Then he let go of Beth's leg and made a beeline down the hallway that led to the kitchen, shouting for his father.

Kansas appeared at the doorway through which Danny had gone, wiping her hands on a dish towel. "Come on in," she said, before noticing the wedding gown Beth carried. When she did, she hurried to them instead. "Oh, I don't want Linc to see the dress. Let me take it upstairs."

She did just that, sending Beth and Ash into the kitchen, where they found Linc studying the arrowhead Danny seemed very impressed with in spite of his leeriness of the man who had given it to him.

Linc sent him out to play then and turned his attentions to Beth and Ash, and the evening got under way.

Danny's wariness didn't lessen through most of the dinner they ate on the picnic table in the backyard to escape the heat of the house. The little boy kept a close eye on Ash, warming up to him only at a snail's pace.

But by the time Linc rounded his son up to be put to bed in Kansas's guest room, the three-year-old had overcome his trepidation enough to make a muscle to show Ash the arrowhead was already working its magic.

While Linc was gone, Kansas, Beth and even Ash did the dishes. Then Linc came back and the four of them had dessert outside, too, settling into more of the easy conversation that was making it a pleasant visit.

It was after eleven before Beth knew it, and though she hadn't had much of a chance to prove to Ash directly that she intended to be nicer, things between them had eased her in that direction.

Linc and Kansas walked them out, their arms wrapped around the small of each other's backs, and Beth knew a sharp tug of regret that she and Ash didn't share that kind of closeness and affection. But she reminded herself that it was only the hormones causing her to envy them, probably coupled with the weariness that came with the late hour, and she forced the feelings away as they all went out onto the front porch.

"Jackson tells me you're having trouble finding a roofer," Ash said to Linc just as they were winding up for good-nights.

"The guy who was going to do it for me broke his leg," Linc confirmed.

"I've done some roofing. Between you and Jackson and me I think we could handle it."

"No kidding? That'd be great. It would save me losing two months or having to get somebody in from Cheyenne at double the expense."

While they went on to arrange a time to do the work, Kansas was thanking Beth for making her wedding dress, but Beth heard only a portion of either conversation as she stared at Ash in her second surprise of the day.

He was a roofer, too?

She was still having trouble believing it when they finally got around to saying good-night and went out to his car.

This time it was Beth who studied Ash as they headed for the ranch.

"Okay, who are you, and what have you done with Asher Blackwolf?"

He frowned at her as if she'd lost her mind. "What?"

"I was married to you for five years, remember? You didn't polish your own shoes, let alone make them for a horse. And I didn't think you knew which end of a hammer hit the nail. But here you are claiming you can roof the honky-tonk."

His frown turned into a slow, satisfied smile. "Did you think I was born in a three-piece suit?"

"Something like that."

"Well, I wasn't."

"So how come you always hired other people to do everything?"

"Because I was also fortunate enough to find myself in a position that afforded it, and hiring other people helped spread some of that around."

Of course that sounded like him. He'd put a number of Native American men and kids to work. And here she'd always just thought of him as too much of a desk jockey to dirty his hands.

Once again she was ashamed of herself.

"Where did these hidden skills come from?" she asked in a quiet voice that was the best she could do to convey her admiration of what he'd done while she'd been giving him less credit than he was due.

"Where else? My grandfathers."

"Your Grandfather Blackwolf was a sculptor," she reminded.

"He didn't start out there, though. He was a blacksmith and welder by trade before that."

"And he taught you?"

Ash nodded. "The Indian way is to pass things down. Stories, customs, skills. I knew my way around a forge and an acetylene torch by the time I was nine. But I preferred the construction work Pap did. Or maybe it was just that being around Pap was a better time," he added pointedly, tossing her a sidelong glance.

Since she'd already blown an apology for that earlier comment, she didn't think she ought to try a second. Instead she said, "I knew Robert worked in construction before he retired, but I didn't know you did, too."

"It paid my way through college."

For a moment Beth was lost in the image of Ash in completely different scenarios than she had ever pictured before. She was aware that his two grandfathers had shared in raising him after both his parents were killed in a drunk-driving accident when he was seven—his father having been the drunk driver, his mother the drunk passenger. Each of them had had serious alcohol problems. But he'd never said much else about his growing-up years.

"Amazing," she muttered to herself for the second time that day.

"What? That I can actually work with my hands and back, along with my brain?" he asked as if he expected another insult from her.

"No. That I could be married to you for five years and actually know so little about you."

He pulled up in front of the ranch house just then, but he left the motor running. Even so, Beth didn't move to get out and neither did he. Instead he turned toward her much the way he had when they'd begun the evening; this time, though, he stretched his arm across the back of the seat, close enough to her neck for her to feel the heat of him.

She looked up into the dark shadows of his eyes. "What else don't I know?"

He shrugged as if he weren't sure what to tell her.

"Were you a bed wetter? Did you suck your thumb until you were twelve? Were you an unruly teenager who got arrested a dozen times before you settled down? Did you lead a madcap college life? Do you knit?"

He laughed at her suggestions, and the deep, rich sound seeped in through her pores to sluice along her nerve endings like warm honey.

"I was not a bed wetter or a thumb sucker, but yes, I was a pretty bad teenager. I smoked and drank and gave my grandfathers fits. I never got arrested, but there were a few times that the cops brought me home or showed up on the doorstep. Either they were warning me to stop drag racing or they had a pretty good hunch I'd been a part of a bunch of kids who'd vandalized mailboxes in a drunken spree. And college—well, that started out as one big party, but by my senior year I cleaned up my act."

Beth blew a wry sigh and shook her head. "I can't even imagine you like that. Especially the drinking part. You rarely even have wine or a beer, and I've always thought that because of your parents' problem you had an aversion to it.''

''More like because of my parents' weakness to booze, I was drawn to try it, too. I don't know. As a kid maybe drinking and being as wild as I'd heard they were was my way of feeling connected to them. It proved I was their son.''

''What straightened you out?''

''Not what. Who. Pap. My other grandfather died just before the end of my junior year in college and I was about to inherit everything he had. I thought it meant life from then on was going to be one big party. Or one big drunken brawl, which was what the parties always turned into.''

''So why didn't it mean that for you?''

''Pap kicked my butt, to be blunt. And then he met with the elders of the tribe—a number of men in key positions in the community who Pap happens to be close to—and they devised a plan for how I was going to spend my summer vacation that year.''

''Not as a kids' camp counselor, I take it.''

''Hardly. They managed to temporarily delay my getting my hands on any of the inheritance. I couldn't get a soul on the reservation to hire me, and Pap refused to let me live with him, turned his back on me completely. All of a sudden I was on the streets, literally, forced to sleep with the derelicts, eat at the soup kitchen, clean toilets at the bathhouse in exchange for an occasional shower. And more than once I was picked up by a cop friend of my grandfather's so I could get a firsthand look at a drunk driving accident or the corpse who came out of it.''

Having lived on the reservation herself, Beth understood enough about the Native American community to believe this closing-of-ranks to scare one of their own and save him if they could.

"Sounds awful," she said. "But it turned you around?"

Ash nodded. "I really saw how tough life could be. And how easy I'd had it. It lit a fire under my conscience. Plus, having Pap turn his back on me was terrible. I knew it was only a matter of time before the inheritance had to be released to me, but I also knew that if I didn't stop drinking, he'd disown me for good."

"So you stopped."

"I did. Luckily I wasn't to the point yet where it was an addiction. And then I decided to do what I could with my other grandfather's money, to help out where I'd witnessed the need for that help. And that's how I turned into this boring guy you see before you."

Beth knew it was another reference to her earlier comment and this time she thought she'd better address it. "I didn't say you were boring—"

"Just no fun. And maybe you're right. You know what they say about all work and no play..."

But at that moment his overworking wasn't what was on her mind. It was still difficult for her to believe that she was hearing so much about him that she'd never known before. It was as if they'd just met.

"Amazing," she repeated.

"That I was once a wild man?"

"That you didn't tell me about it when we were married."

"Talking was not what we did best together," he reminded her, in a voice with a husky, sensuous intonation that alluded to what they *had* been good at.

But that Beth knew all too well. Their sexual attraction to each other had been so intense right from the start that apparently they'd skipped a lot of important aspects that normally happened early in a relationship—such as just plain getting to know each other.

"This earthier side of you—it's nice—for a change," she ventured.

Only one corner of his mouth tilted upward. "Is this Beth Heller trying to say there's something she might actually *like* about me?"

"It's just good to know what went into making you the man you are."

"Is it?" he asked, but in a way that made it seem more than an offhand comment. A way that seemed to wonder, just as she did, if there were more good things happening between them at that moment, for the air seemed charged with a new closeness that hadn't been there before.

A closeness that weakened her resistance to him.

His eyes were holding hers, searching them in the dimness of dashboard light, maybe for signs of what was going on here.

But he couldn't have found an answer, because Beth didn't know herself.

She knew only that she wanted more than anything for this man, who had just revealed such personal things to her, to close the gap between his arm and her shoulders, to pull her to him, to—

And then he did.

He leaned forward, wrapping his arm around her and bringing her to him so that he could cover her mouth with his in a kiss that held considerably more heat than the one they'd shared the previous night.

His lips parted over hers and his tongue traced the uneven edge of her teeth just before coming inside to play, to assert himself.

And Beth welcomed him. Welcomed the mingling of his breath with hers, the circling of their tongues, the thrust and parry.

His arm tightened around her, bringing her up against

his chest, forcing her to circle the breadth of his shoulders with her own arms and giving her the opportunity to splay her hands against that hard back. Visions of those muscles working just beneath the taut, sweat-dampened skin she'd watched most of the afternoon danced through her mind and lit new sparks inside of her.

She had feelings for this man that she shouldn't have. That she didn't want to have.

And the longer that kiss went on, the more they sprang to life, until they scared her nearly to death and shoved her out of his embrace.

"I don't want this to happen!" she told him in a near panic.

And if she'd struck a blow earlier in the evening with her comment about his not being like Robert, she saw that she'd struck a much greater one with this.

Ash drew away as far as he could go, leaning his back against the door, taking his glorious arms with him.

"Then it won't," he said, in a tone she hated, for it told her he'd given his word and once he'd given his word, he didn't break it.

She closed her eyes and let her head fall against the window on her side as she fought the urge to make him take it back right then, to fling herself into his arms again and show him she didn't mean it.

But she did mean it.

She had to mean it.

She dropped her chin and opened her eyes to look at his again. "This is what we did when we met. We let ourselves get carried away and we never really got to know each other. So of course the marriage failed. But we're not married anymore. And the relationship we need to form now certainly can't be like this. If you're going to stick around—even for just a little while—we have to try to be friends, or at least courteous acquaintances, for the baby's sake. But we can't do this.''

For a moment he just stared at her, and she thought that he really must have wanted to strangle her, because his eyes were so cold, so hard.

But then he nodded. ''You're right.''

''Good,'' she said, though she hadn't intended it to sound as halfhearted or as disappointed as it did, any more than she had intended to *feel* as disappointed as she did.

But once again she tamped down on it. ''I have to go in.''

He repeated his slow, solemn nod.

''Good night,'' she said, opening the door.

Once more his only response was the nod.

But she couldn't wonder about it, wonder what was going through his mind, wonder if he was mad at her because she'd stopped the kiss or mad at himself for starting it. She had to just get away from him before she began it all over again.

She closed the car door after herself and went up to the house, feeling his eyes boring into her as if they were laser beams. But she let herself in without so much as glancing back at him.

And once she was inside and the door closed her off from him, she fell against it as if the starch had gone out of her.

Hormones, she told herself. Crazy, intense hormones— that was the reason tears were flooding her eyes.

It didn't have anything to do with Ash.

Or wishes that, somewhere along the way, things could have been different between them.

Chapter Five

Elk Creek's medical facility was across the street from the park square at the north end of town. Originally it had been the old Molner mansion—a three-level, red brick, Georgian-style building, its flat front interrupted by a big whitewashed porch.

The first floor was divided into a reception and waiting area, offices and examining rooms. The second floor was a small hospital, complete with two surgical suites for minor procedures and three rooms for inpatients, though it was rare that anyone stayed over. And the third floor held a lab, X-ray equipment and a rudimentary physical therapy section.

The entire staff was comprised of a doctor, a dentist—a coup for the small town—one nurse, one dental assistant, and Janet Gaultbien, who was receptionist, bookkeeper and administrator and just generally ran the whole shebang.

Beth's appointment with the doctor was at nine o'clock.

She'd changed it since Ash had arrived and begun following her around, thinking that if she chose the earliest one, it would allow her to go before he showed up to tag along.

But Ash, Jackson and Linc were roofing the honky-tonk today and had begun at dawn, so she needn't have worried.

And as she climbed the porch steps, she wished she'd kept her afternoon appointment so she could be in bed still, catching up on the sleep she'd missed during the night. She promised herself that when she'd finished here she'd go home to her nice, air-conditioned house and take a nap.

That was what she was thinking about as she went in the front door, expecting to find the receptionist alone in the waiting room.

But the tall, boxy woman was not the only one there. Ash was, too, intent on a book Janet was showing him while she explained the development of the fetus at five months. Neither of them looked up.

"What are you doing here?" Beth blurted out, forgetting her vow to be nicer to her former husband.

He was leaning on the counter, his rear end jutting out at her from inside a pair of Jackson's oldest, rattiest jeans. His biceps bulged from the ragged armholes of a work shirt that had had sleeves once upon a time, before her brother had ripped them out, and he bore absolutely no resemblance to a businessman.

Her question drew Janet's attention, but it was a moment before Ash slowly straightened up and turned to look at her.

"I saw the note for your appointment on the calendar next to the phone in the kitchen yesterday. I didn't want to miss it."

"I think it's just wonderful to see a father-to-be so interested and supportive," Janet defended him.

And once again Beth felt like the bad guy. She tried to

curb her tone of voice. "I thought you were busy roofing the honky-tonk today."

"We hoisted everything up and I showed Linc and Jackson how to get started. I'll go back as soon as we're finished here."

We? Well, terrific. Get this man into a set of stirrups on the double.

"When I wanted him around, he was too busy. Now I can't get away from him," she muttered to herself. Then, to him, she said, "I think we better talk about this."

"I'll tell Ramona you're here," Janet suggested tactfully.

When they were alone, Ash's eyes bored into her with the coldness that said he was angry with her. Already. "You know, it wouldn't hurt for you to be a hair less independent and let me help you with just one thing. For a change."

Beth reminded herself to be civil. "I know you're going to say something about our already having been intimate enough to get me here, but this is the first time I've seen this doctor and he'll want to do a full exam. And a pelvic is bad enough without an ex-husband as an audience. You can't come in. You've wasted your time being here."

His bushy brows drew together in a frown. "Actually, I hadn't planned to go in with you during the exam. I just wanted to be here with you. To be here *for* you," he answered through clenched teeth.

"Oh." Beth cleared her throat, again feeling chagrined.

He pointed his chin in the direction Janet had gone. "The receptionist said I could come in before and hear the heartbeat, but I won't even do that if it bothers you."

Great. He'd already discussed it with Janet. Janet, who thought his interest was wonderful. And who would turn around and repeat to the entire population of Elk Creek—

by way of the small-town grapevine—either that, in spite of being divorced, they were acting like civilized adults and sharing this experience; or that Beth had turned her nose up at Ash's wanting to hear his baby's heartbeat.

Maybe coming back to Elk Creek hadn't been a good idea after all, Beth thought.

"Forget it," he said suddenly into the silence that she'd left while she thought about this. "I'll go back to work."

"No," she grumbled as he headed for the door. "I suppose I can stand for you to see my fat belly. But that's all."

He turned to her again, his gaze dropping to her middle as if he'd overlooked something before. But the bulge of her stomach was well concealed behind the oversize shirt she wore. "If it makes you uncomfortable—"

"It's all right." She didn't know if Janet had been secretly listening, but at that moment the receptionist reappeared to usher them both into one of the examining rooms without so much as questioning whether or not Ash would be allowed to go.

There was a bathroom connected to it and Beth was handed a gown and told to undress there while Ash was awarded a chair in which to wait for her.

She wasn't thrilled about going back into that room after she'd changed. A thin hospital gown with a single tie at the back of the neck was hardly a confidence booster. But she didn't have much choice.

Holding the gown closed behind her, she took a deep breath and tried to hide her real feelings about this, all the while wondering how she'd ever gotten herself into it.

The nurse was there by then and Beth was glad to see her, if only as a buffer between her and Ash.

Having Beth sit on the doctor's stool, Ramona took her blood pressure and pulse, finding both slightly elevated but accepting Beth's explanation of doctor's-visit nerves. Then she asked her to get on the table and lie down.

No mean feat, that. At least not while retaining her dignity and trying not to flash bare buns. But once Beth was there, Ramona helped out by covering her lower half with a paper sheet before pulling up the gown to reveal her stomach.

"Come on, Dad. You won't be able to hear from over there," the nurse urged.

Beth could feel her cheeks heat as Ash stepped to her side, standing just off her shoulder while Ramona squeezed a mound of jellylike ointment onto the small mesa of her naked middle. Then the nurse put an odd-looking stethoscope she called a Doptone into her own ears and slid the other end through the gel like a spatula spreading frosting until she found what she was searching for.

Beth and Ash both looked on as Ramona checked her watch, counting the beats before she held the business end of the stethoscope in place and handed Beth the binaurals. "Mom first."

Beth had heard the baby's heartbeat once before, at Cele's office, but it still gave her goose bumps as she listened while the nurse explained to Ash what it would sound like.

When Beth finally relinquished the device to him, he wasted no time bending low enough to fit the tips into his ears.

She could tell by his immediate frown that he wasn't sure he was hearing what he was supposed to. But as she watched, his eyes lit up and widened, his brows took flight nearly to his hairline and his lips parted.

And then, as she studied the pure wonder in his expression, Beth saw his eyes fill.

He caught up her left hand in his right, holding it tight

and pulling it to press the back to his chest, just over his heart, in a gesture that joined their tiny family, that cherished her and their baby and brought hot tears to her own eyes.

And then she felt the baby skitter away, as if it had had enough of being eavesdropped on, and the moment passed.

Ash blinked the moisture out of his eyes, squeezed her hand one last time and let it go so he could pull the stethoscope out of his ears and give it back to the nurse.

But it was to Beth he said a quiet, sincere thank-you that made her rue ever thinking to refuse him this.

"I won't hang around," he told her then, as if giving a compromise of his own in appreciation. "Unless you want me to..."

She did want him to. She wanted him there with her—not through the pelvic exam—but to wait for the doctor, to talk about the baby, about hearing the heartbeat, about the nurse's guess that it was a boy.

But she couldn't bring herself to say it.

"You have a lot of work to do today. You'd better get back."

He nodded, just once, and if his smile seemed a little tight-lipped, she didn't understand why.

Then he left, along with the nurse, and she was alone in that room. Alone with the baby.

And wishing she wasn't.

Linc and Jackson were busy with the roofing when Ash got back to the honky-tonk. He climbed the ladder and pitched in without any of them saying much, and for the remainder of the morning that's how the time passed, leaving Ash free to think.

Hearing the baby's heartbeat had given him a new sense of connection to it. He could have stood there all day long listening to that tiny pulse beating its rapid rhythm through the rush of amniotic fluid.

And as he worked, it occurred to him that if he'd been loath to end that, how was he ever going to leave the baby behind once it was born? For even if he had custody half the time, that would still leave the other half the time that he'd be away from it.

But what was his alternative?

His mind wandered to one—if he and Beth got married again, he could take her and the baby back home....

But that idea was too farfetched to even consider. Beth could barely be civil to him. Even in front of the receptionist this morning, she'd nearly bitten his head off just for being there.

She'd mellowed, though...

Lying on that examining table, she'd let him take her hand. More than that, she'd held his in return, squeezed it back, hung on as if—for only a moment—she'd liked having him there.

He was probably just imagining it. Hadn't she basically shooed him away after that? Even when he'd offered to wait?

But there had been that moment, that one, brief moment, when they'd shared something very special. When they'd shared their baby. And that had been good.

Maybe good enough to build on...

Beth had a soft spot where the baby was concerned. No matter how tough she wanted him to think she was, how strong and resilient and capable of doing this on her own, the baby itself was her Achilles' heel....

But her feelings for Ash didn't seem even lukewarm.

And there was no denying the problems they'd had in their marriage. Could they be overcome? Could he and Beth fix them and try again so they could be together in parenting this child? He honestly didn't know. But he had to explore the possibility.

For the baby's sake.

For his sake.

As a father.

And as a man who still had feelings for his ex-wife...

Did he have feelings for Beth? Maybe. But he didn't know what they were. One minute he wanted to wring her neck. The next he wanted to take her to bed.

How could remarrying her possibly be a good idea under those circumstances? Assuming he could even get Beth to consider the idea?

"Shall we break for lunch?" Linc suggested into his preoccupation.

Ash hadn't realized how late it was. Or how hot. "Sounds good to me," he agreed, all too willing to put aside what suddenly seemed like crazy ramblings.

He and Beth getting remarried? Maybe he was on the verge of sunstroke or heat prostration, because surely he was out of his mind to even consider such a thing.

Jackson put down his hammer, too, and they all headed for the ladder. Once on the ground, they went inside the honky-tonk long enough to douse themselves liberally with cool water, then met under the shade of a huge oak tree alongside the building to share the sandwiches Linc and Jackson had packed for the three of them.

"How'd the doctor's appointment go?" Linc asked.

"Fine. At least it went fine for as long as I was there. Beth didn't want me hanging around," Ash answered, watching a train come in at the station across the street.

"What's going on between the two of you, anyway?" Jackson demanded unceremoniously.

Ash glanced at him and then at Linc. "Should I be guarding my jaw?" he only half joked.

"I'm not sure," Linc answered, swiveling his gaze to his brother. "Are you askin' what his intentions are?"

"I guess I am. I caught Beth cryin' last night."

That took the humor out of Ash. "You must have needed to use the bathroom," he muttered, more to himself than to his former brother-in-law.

"I was just headed to bed after havin' a midnight snack. She had her back against the front door and big tears running down her face. I guess she didn't expect anyone else to be up, because she got plenty mad at me for catching her at it."

"That's Beth," Ash confirmed.

"Did you two fight after you left Kansas's place?" This from Linc.

"No, in fact, things went pretty well. For the most part. At least until the end."

"What'd you do then?" Jackson asked as if he were interrogating a criminal.

"Maybe you ought to mind your own business," Linc suggested.

Ash decided that confiding in her brothers might allow him some insight and answered Jackson anyway. "I kissed her."

Linc gave a hoot and a holler of a laugh. Jackson stayed as sober as Ash did.

"Guess she didn't want you to, huh?" Jackson said.

"Seemed like she did. Then all of a sudden she pushed me away and said she didn't. But she was dry-eyed when she got out of the car."

Linc chuckled. "When Virgie was pregnant with Danny she was like that. Crazy. One minute she'd be happy as a lark, the next I'd find her bawling her eyes out. It's hormones."

"You sure about that?" Jackson asked dubiously. "That

doesn't sound like Beth. Beth's not a cryer. Shag fixed that when she was a just a little girl.''

Linc looked at his older brother as if he were out of his mind. "Not even Shag could have kept a pregnant woman from crying.''

Jackson stared at Ash directly again. "So what are you going to do about it?''

"Ha! I wish I knew'' was Ash's only answer.

"Stay out of it,'' Linc told Jackson then, firmly this time.

"Just seems to me two people should be married when they're havin' a baby,'' Jackson said, as if he felt it his duty to get the words out.

But Ash didn't agree or disagree.

He was too lost in thought again.

Wondering what the hell it meant that his kiss had made Beth cry.

It was after dark by the time Beth heard Jackson, Linc and Ash come in the ranch house's back door. She was in her room working on the bridesmaid dress for Kansas's sister Della, and her first inclination was to rush downstairs.

She curbed it and just sat listening.

The house had been so deadly quiet all day and evening, and suddenly it was alive with the hum of deep masculine voices as her brothers and former husband apparently raided the refrigerator.

Then she heard them go outside again. She moved to the window where she saw Jackson slap steaks on the grill before he, Ash and Linc—now in swimming trunks—dived into the pool like three boys.

It felt good not to be alone anymore, even though she wasn't really with them. But when she analyzed the feeling, she knew it wasn't really her brothers' return she was glad for. It was Ash's. In spite of all her arguing against his hanging around, she'd missed him.

That was a terrible sign.

Since the air-conditioning was on in the house, her window was closed. She eased it open and propped a hip on the sill.

Tall, wrought-iron Victorian-style streetlamps surrounded the bricked patio but didn't cast much illumination on the pool, so she couldn't actually see them in the water. Rather than try, she closed her eyes, leaned against the window frame and merely listened, eager for the sound of Ash's voice joking and teasing her brothers as if he were a member of their close-knit club.

They weren't saying anything important. In fact they sounded slaphappy, no doubt from putting in a fifteen-hour day of backbreaking work in ninety-six-degree heat. But it was still good to hear. In fact, it made her smile.

Twice the ringing of a timer sounded to remind them to turn their steaks. They argued about who would get out of the water to do it, but both times Jackson did, grumbling about ruining good beefsteak. When the timer went off a third time, Beth opened her eyes and watched as they all got out, not bothering with towels, and disappeared from her view, no doubt to sit at one of several tables closer to the house to eat.

That they did in silence, making Beth smile again at the seriousness with which men attacked a steak. Or maybe they were all too tired to say anything, because their meal was over quickly, and once again Beth heard chairs scraping the brick. Both Linc and Jackson announced they had to get some sleep, inviting Ash to stay in the guest room.

Beth's pulse doubled, but she wasn't sure if it was from the thought that he might accept or that he might decline.

He declined. "Beth wouldn't be happy about that," she heard him say. "I'll just lie here and rest a minute and then I'll go back to the lodge."

She couldn't see him but assumed he'd moved to one of the loungers. And with the thickness in his voice as they all said good-night, she knew he was halfway asleep by the time her brothers came inside.

There'd be dishes to clear in the morning, because she didn't hear so much as a single plate hit the sink before her brothers climbed the steps, mumbled more good-nights and closed their bedroom doors behind them.

She could tell that Linc immediately threw himself on his bed and that was that. From Jackson's room there were sounds of him puttering around a little before his bedsprings squeaked and all grew quiet.

Then there was only silence in the house again.

And outside of it, too.

She didn't have to see Ash to know he was sound asleep down there, and for a moment she considered just letting him be. But she hated to see him spend the night in a lawn chair after the work he'd done to help her brother. She decided to go down and offer to drive him to the lodge so he could get some decent rest.

There was also the fact that she had an irresistible urge to see him, but she didn't want to think about that.

She was still dressed, wearing a pair of cutoff jeans that barely peeked out from beneath her sleeveless chambray shirt. Her feet were bare, but she didn't bother to put shoes on.

She padded noiselessly through the house as far as the sliding door in the kitchen that led to the patio. But instead of going out, she stood at the screen, studying Ash.

Just as she'd imagined, he was on one of the redwood loungers. But he wasn't exactly lying on it. It appeared that he'd sat on the end of it and just lain back, because his head was midway up the seat and his feet were still planted on the bricks of the patio.

It couldn't have been too comfortable, yet apparently he was so tired it didn't matter. He was out like a light, his arms crossed over his flat stomach and one big thigh drifting like a yardarm in a breeze.

And for some reason she couldn't have explained if her life depended on it, the sight touched her.

He really was putting a lot of effort into smoothing the waters here. With her. With her brothers. And what he was getting for it was hard work, her bad attitude, and a feeling that he should be grateful just to be allowed to hear his baby's heartbeat for a few moments.

Maybe he did deserve a night in the guest room. Even if it would be difficult for her to know he was right next door.

She finally went out to him, standing at the foot of the lounger, between his knees. Although this man had been her husband for five years, she suddenly felt it an invasion of his privacy to be watching him as he slept. She was also trying not to pay attention to his bulging biceps or his thick, muscular thighs and well-defined calves.

"Ash?" she said softly so as not to startle him. "Ash, wake up."

His forehead knitted in a frown, but he didn't open his eyes.

"Come on, you don't want to sleep out here. Come inside."

Still, his eyes remained closed, but the corners of his mouth quirked up in what could have been called a drunken grin, except that she doubted he'd been drinking. Then his long, thick lashes finally made a leisurely sweep to half-mast. "Is this an invitation?"

"To the guest room," she said, still quietly, as if she might wake someone else.

"Nah, that's all right. I know you don't want me here."

"It's okay."

"I'm gonna get going to the lodge. Soon as I can move."

"Maybe you are drunk," she muttered, referring to the slow motion of his words and the ridiculous smile on his face.

"Did somebody say I was?"

"You just seem so silly."

"Do you like it?"

She did. A little. For once Mr. Take-Care-of-Every-thing-and-Everyone couldn't even seem to take care of himself. But she wouldn't admit it. "Have you been drinking?"

"Water. Lots of it."

"So you're just tired."

"Haven't done this kind of work since I was a pup."

"Well, come on and put your old bones to bed up-stairs."

He sighed. "I don't think I can move just yet."

Beth didn't want to touch him. Any physical contact between them would be like holding a match head to a hot burner. But she didn't think he could move on his own, either, so she held out her hands to him. "Come on, I'll help you up."

A loopy, one-sided smile curled his mouth and he raised his arms, clasping her hands in his. But the moment he did, his weakness disappeared, and he pulled her down gently on top of him—chest to chest, stomach to stomach. With his thighs still spread wide, she had no choice but to bend her knees and let her feet fly like flags in the air, making her contact with his lower regions all the more complete.

"Very funny," she said.

"I thought so."

She tried pushing herself away but his arms were crossed over her back, a hand on each hip, locking her to him. The best she could do was raise her head and shoulders slightly above his.

"So much for being weak and tired," she said, trying not to be too aware of the feel of him beneath her.

"I missed you today," he told her in a way that left her wondering if he was joking.

"You saw me this morning."

His smile stretched into a grin. "That was something, wasn't it?"

She had the urge to rest her cheek on his chest, to relax atop him, let herself ride the hard hills and valleys of his big body like water over rock, and talk about the wonders of what they'd created together.

But of course she couldn't do that.

The best she could do was agree. "Hearing the heartbeat is incredible."

"I think I did pretty well at this baby making. Gave him a strong heart."

Beth laughed. "What should I take issue with first? That you're so cocksure the baby is a boy? Or that you're taking all the credit?"

"Doesn't matter. They're both true," he goaded.

"Seems to me that you only contributed one ingredient. I'm doing the rest."

The sun had darkened his skin to a ruddiness that she could see even in the golden glow of lamplight, and it gave a sharper edge to his facial structure, which made her think suddenly of a warrior, especially when his features contorted into a mock menacing expression.

He covered the sides of her rib cage with his splayed fingers. "Don't make me tickle you into taking that back, woman," he threatened.

"Tickle me and you'll never see daylight again," she countered, squirming a little to try to escape.

Not a good idea. She felt the bulge inside his swimming suit rise against her.

"Come on, let's just get you set up in the guest room," she said, in a hurry to end this play before it led to anything more.

But Ash wasn't so inclined. He did a slight, speculative tickling of her sides. "Admit what a good job I did making this baby."

"It's me who's making this baby."

"You're asking for it," he warned, giving her another taste of what was to come.

She tried again to push herself out of his grasp but it was useless. He held tight.

"Last chance," he said. "Tell me what a good job I did."

"I might holler for help and get my brothers down here after you, but that's all you're hearing from me."

"Okay. You asked for it."

Beth hated to be tickled and he knew it. A devilish smile played on his lips again and those fingers began to torture her sides.

She couldn't help writhing and wriggling even as she tried to get free. But all she accomplished was to bring herself closer in contact with him. Her traitorous nipples kerneled and strained inside even the bigger sized bra she wore, until finally she shouted amidst her own miserable laughter, "Okay, okay, I give up."

He stopped tickling her, letting his hands follow the curve of her ribs instead, the tips of his fingers just barely brushing the sides of her breasts. "Tell me what a good job I did," he demanded in a voice grown husky since it had last been used.

Her arms were tiring and if he didn't let her go soon, she wasn't going to have any choice but to collapse completely on him. "You did a wonderful job," she deadpanned insincerely.

"Not heartfelt enough," he claimed, curling his fingers for a second assault.

But just as he did, the baby gave the biggest kick Beth had felt yet. A kick big enough and close enough to the outside of her stomach for even Ash to feel it.

He stopped short, staring up into her eyes with a sudden look of shock and alarm. "What was that?"

Beth laughed at him. "What do you think it was?"

"The baby?"

Then it happened again.

"Is it all right?" Ash demanded.

Beth laughed again. "You did know they kick, didn't you?"

"This soon?"

"Sooner. I was feeling it by the time I went to see Cele, but then it was only a fluttering and I just thought I had butterflies in my stomach or was hungry or something. It's only been what I'd call kicks for the past couple of weeks, but this is the first time it's been this hard. It must not like to be tickled, either."

But everything that had come before seemed lost on Ash. His bushy brows were beetled and he sat up, swinging Beth to his lap at the same time and beginning to place a hand on her stomach.

He didn't quite make it before apparently remembering that he didn't have the freedom.

"Can I feel it this way?"

"You can try, but there's no guarantee it'll happen again right now."

He placed his hand over the bulge of her middle as carefully as if she might break, staring down at it as he did.

There were all sorts of shoulds and shouldn'ts that went through Beth's mind, but she quieted them and let herself enjoy the moment.

It felt good to be there, perched across Ash's thighs, the heat of his body all around her, one of his long arms bracing her back, his big hand palming the mound his baby made as if it were a small basketball.

He was so intent, so serious, so awestruck. All the playfulness had gone out of him, and he waited motionlessly, soundlessly, as if he meant to hold that pose no matter how long it took for him to feel the baby kick again.

Then it did, but much farther to the side.

"It moved," she told him, redirecting his hand just in time for yet another kick, though this one was more like what she'd been feeling before, just a gentle thump.

"Does it hurt?" he asked, sounding concerned.

"No," she answered with yet another laugh, hearing the sensual timbre of her own voice.

Being so close to Ash, having him touch her with a certain amount of intimacy, was getting to her.

Her own hand still covered his where it rested over her stomach, and she was suddenly very aware of the texture of his skin, of the sharp bones of his knuckles beneath her palm, of what it felt like to be caressed by that hand—for he was caressing her.

Somewhere along the way he'd stopped just waiting for

the baby to move again and begun to knead her middle
much the way she'd known him to knead her breasts in
times past.

He also wasn't watching his hand anymore. When she
glanced up, she found him studying her face. His eyes
were coal black and shaded by the shelf of his brows and
she knew he wanted to kiss her again. That he wanted to
do more than kiss her.

And she wanted him to. Lord help her. She wanted him
to.

All on its own her chin tilted, her lips parted.

His gaze dropped to them. He moved slightly nearer.

But then he stopped.

He'd given his word the night before that this wouldn't
happen again. Beth knew he remembered it. And that he
wouldn't break it.

But never in her life had she craved anything as much
as she did the feel of his lips on hers at that moment. And
she *hadn't* given her word.

Still holding his hand to her stomach, she reached with
her free hand to the side of his face and raised herself
enough to press her mouth to his as tentatively as if she'd
never kissed anyone before. It flashed through her mind
that if he rejected it, she had it coming for the two times
she'd rejected him.

But he didn't.

His lips parted and he accepted the kiss, answered it
with a patience that somehow seemed strained, as if he
had to force himself not take over.

His arm around her back tightened. His hand at her middle kept up the caress her breasts yearned for, and his
tongue followed her lead, but he initiated nothing, driving
her all the wilder inside with wanting him.

Then he ended the kiss, slowly, gently, regretfully

enough that it wasn't a rejection but more like a first-date kiss that had gone far enough.

"Your idea of getting to know each other without sex clouding it—the way we should have the first time around—was a good one. Let's work on it."

At that moment, with every nerve in her body awake and alive and desire already turning her skin sensitive, that seemed like the worst idea she'd ever had.

But she wasn't about to let Ash know that, so she merely nodded her agreement. And this time when she tried to get up, he let her go.

She glanced in the direction of the house. "It really is okay if you stay in the guest room," she lied, because wanting him the way she did at that moment made it less okay than it had been before.

He shook his head. "I wouldn't stay in the guest room. I'd last about ten minutes and then I'd be in your room."

Sounded good to her. Not that she'd say that, either. "Then let me drive you to the lodge."

"I wouldn't let you drive back out here alone last night, and I'm not going to tonight." He stood and her eyes rode his chest all the way.

"What if you fall asleep behind the wheel?"

"I won't. I'm wide-awake now."

She understood the feeling. Desire pumped adrenaline through her, too.

He cupped her chin between two fingers and tilted it as he bent low enough to kiss her once more, chastely, gently. "We have to finish the roof tomorrow, and Linc's bachelor party is in the evening, so I may not see you until the day after."

She laughed at that, though wryly. Hearing it sparked vivid memories. It seemed their entire marriage had been a series of similar statements—one job or engagement or expectation on top of another, all strung together to keep him busy elsewhere. And even though his absence was what she'd been telling herself she wanted, even though it was her brother he was helping, her brother's party he was going to, it felt bad.

Bad enough to remind her that there were things she needed not to forget.

"Sure," she said.

Her tone made him frown again, more seriously this time, but she didn't give him the chance to ask.

"Be careful driving back to town," she said, turning from him.

"Beth?"

She didn't pause. "Good night," she called as if he hadn't said anything, going into the house and locking the sliding door behind her.

Ash was still standing where she'd left him, watching her, his hands on his hips, his confusion obvious even from a distance.

But rather than let him know what was going on inside her, she gave him a small smile and a parade-pretty wave.

Then she went through the kitchen and up to her room, wishing all the way that the reminder had the power to keep her from wanting him with her so much she could cry.

Again.

Chapter Six

Beth spent the following day doing the final handwork on Della's bridesmaid dress for the wedding and listening intently for sounds of her brothers returning from roofing the honky-tonk. Try as she might, she couldn't help waiting anxiously, hoping they'd be done early and Ash would come home with them.

It didn't happen.

She delayed leaving for Kansas's house until Linc and Jackson returned, but Ash wasn't with them. He'd gone to the lodge to shower and change for the bachelor party.

It was good, she told herself as she drove to Kansas's place. Good that she'd had all day to feel the old loneliness, the old longing to see him. It was good that now she felt the old disappointment, the old sense of taking a back seat to other things he was doing; of being out of sight, out of mind.

It was all good, because it put things into perspective

for her. Things it was easier for her to lose sight of when her view was filled with Ash.

Kansas's sister Della and her four kids were already there when Beth arrived. As was Danny, who had been staying with Kansas while Linc worked on the roof.

They ordered pizza and broke out a bottle of wine for their own small wedding-eve celebration, taking care of last-minute details while the kids all played outside.

Of course Beth didn't touch the wine, but she did enjoy the companionship and camaraderie of the two Daye sisters as the liquor loosened them up.

Della drank by far the most, and by the time she gathered her kids to walk home, she'd gone from being giddy to being sentimental.

"I'm glad you're marrying Linc," she told Kansas, as Beth stood by while the sisters hugged.

Kansas thanked Della and told her she loved her, then made a joke to lighten the moment before Della finally left.

"Let's get Danny to bed and then we can relax," Kansas suggested as they herded the little boy back inside.

Beth didn't do much in the way of putting her nephew down for the night. Kansas was already mothering the three-year-old and Danny seemed to have accepted her as just that—his mom.

Things would be good for Linc and Kansas and Danny, Beth realized, feeling a wave of sentimentality of her own. They might be a ready-made family, but they seemed to fit together as if it were meant to be. And, as she so often did, she envied them what they had together.

When Danny was in bed, Beth and Kansas took two glasses of ice tea and sat on the white wicker chairs on the front porch.

"So, how are things?" Kansas asked then, making it sound very much like a leading question.

"Good. Everything's good," Beth answered as if she hadn't understood her friend's intention.

"You know, Linc and Jackson are worried about you."

"I don't know why. There's no reason to be." Beth could feel Kansas watching her in the dim glow of the porch light, but she merely pretended a great interest in the railing.

"Is everything all right between you and Ash?"

How did a person answer a question like that under the circumstances? Beth shrugged. "He's still here" was all she could think to say.

"Is that good or bad?"

"It would be good if he left."

"Then it's bad that he's here," Kansas concluded.

"Well, not really bad, no," Beth hedged, for her conscience wouldn't allow her to make Ash the villain. The only thing bad about his being here had been her own difficulties controlling her feelings for him.

"Is it just that I had wine and you didn't, or is there another reason I'm confused?"

"Maybe because I am."

"Ah," Kansas said as if they'd hit on something. "Let me guess—you're still attracted to him, even though you're divorced."

Beth couldn't openly admit to that. Instead she said, "Ash is a good man. He really is. I admire and respect him."

"Umm-hmm," Kansas agreed with suppressed laughter just below the utterance.

"I always did enjoy his company—what I had of it," Beth conceded, feeling as if she were going a little further out on a limb and yet unable to stop herself. "He has a

great sense of humor and he can be very attentive. He's
generous and caring and sensitive…'' Just remembering
the sight of tears in his eyes as he'd listened to the baby's
heartbeat the day before made her own eyes sting. ''And
I'm sure he'll be a good father,'' she added quietly.

''None of that makes him sound like someone you
wouldn't want to have around. Does he repulse you physically or something?''

Beth laughed spontaneously and wryly at that, giving
herself away. ''Lord, I wish he did,'' she muttered.

''Then you *are* attracted to him.''

Turned on by him. So hot for him she could melt—and
very well might have the night before if he hadn't stopped
things before they even got started. But she avoided responding to her friend's statement. ''His being here is only
an interlude. A brief interlude, I'm sure.''

''And then what?''

''And then he'll leave. Like the last two days with the
roofing, for example. Someone or something somewhere
will need him—for a good reason, a good cause, in a way
that I totally agree he should accommodate—and he'll be
off again. His being here now, spending time together,
isn't the reality of what life with him is like.''

Kansas murmured knowingly. ''Linc said that whenever
he visited the reservation he barely saw Ash, that he never
knew if it was because Ash was leaving the two of you
alone to catch up or if it was always that way.''

''It was always that way. Ash and I never saw much of
each other. He was—is—a busy man. He's diligent and
selfless when it comes to his foundation. And it's important work. That's part of what I respect and admire him
for.''

''Still, if the two of you were separated a lot—well, you
know what I think about that. That was why I refused to

marry Linc the first time he asked. It must have been awful for you, being married to someone you hardly ever saw."

"It wasn't good for either of us," Beth said, her voice sounding far away even to herself. In the back of her mind she was revisiting that awful moment when she'd announced she no longer wanted to be married to him and he'd so calmly, so matter-of-factly, agreed. "Although I have to admit I didn't know he was unhappy, too, until I told him I wanted a divorce." She was surprised to hear herself admit that out loud. "Up until then I thought he was okay with the way things were, that it was just me who the marriage wasn't working for."

"And it wasn't?"

"I guess not," Beth answered, hating that her voice cracked and she was unable to elaborate, even though it was obvious Kansas was waiting for her to. How could she explain something she didn't understand herself?

Instead she cleared her throat and went on as if she hadn't been bothered in the slightest. "So he moved into his grandfather's house by noon the same day we talked about it and that was that. Quick, clean and easy." Except that their divorce hadn't been any of those things, no matter how she'd been able to make it look then or sound now.

"Does that mean that even having the baby doesn't make you want to go back to him?"

"I wouldn't ever want to go back to the way things were before, no," she said sadly. Then, as Kansas had done with Della's parting emotionalism, she tried to lighten the tone. "If someone promised I could have what you and Linc have together, though, who knows?"

"Babies should have fathers in the home." Kansas seemed to think she was agreeing with something.

"Like I said, I'm sure Ash will be a good father anyway,'' Beth insisted, trying to keep up a positive attitude, although the image of her and Ash and the baby as a small family was achingly appealing. But what kind of lessons would her child learn if it was raised in a loveless marriage? ''We were just lousy at being married,'' she added firmly, hearing the note in her own voice that said she needed to remember that.

Ash had arrived at the ranch long before Linc's bachelor party was set to start, in hopes of having a few minutes with Beth. But he hadn't known she was going to Kansas's house for the evening, and by the time he got there she was gone.

As the night wore on, it seemed more and more likely that he wouldn't see her at all today, and while he nursed a glass of soda water, sitting back from the rest of the guests, he wondered at his own feelings about being away from his former wife these past two days.

It was like old times—his being busy, their both going in different directions so that their paths barely crossed.

But unlike before, now it was bothering him.

And he wasn't sure why.

Probably, he decided, it had to do with the baby. With this sense he had of wanting to catch up on the five months he'd already lost.

And yet, as much as he didn't want to admit it, his mind wasn't really on the baby. It was on Beth.

And that made him begin to analyze his feelings for her.

Because he did still have feelings for her and he was kidding himself to deny it. He cared about her. And not just about her health and well-being because she was carrying his child. He cared about the woman herself.

Maybe more than he had in a long time.

And that realization shocked him.

The only explanation he could come up with, when he thought about it, was that for some reason marriage had buried those feelings.

Was it possible that after three years of being with a woman who kept every emotion under tight wraps, he'd closed himself off, too? That he'd hidden his own feelings even from himself?

Maybe it had been a protective mechanism, he thought as a cheer roared up in the room from a raunchy videotape someone had started in the VCR. Maybe after a long time of never hearing her tell him she loved him, of her never letting him know she felt anything for him at all, he'd locked up his feelings for her, too. Because even though he'd tried to convince himself she must care for him at least a little, the longer he'd gone without a sign, the more he'd begun to wonder. And the more he'd buried his own feelings just in case they really weren't reciprocated.

But he was seeing different things in her now, in spite of all her attempts to maintain her usual show of imperviousness. He'd actually seen tears in her eyes at the sound of the baby's heartbeat, and she'd held his hand—hard—and shared that moment with him as much as any loving wife might have. He'd seen regret that she'd insulted him by saying he wasn't like Robert. And there was a general softening to her, a new warmth that seemed to sneak out when she wasn't hiding it.

Could it just be related to the onslaught of those pregnancy hormones Linc had talked about? Or was it possible that she might still have feelings for him? In spite of all she'd done to push him away?

He hoped it wasn't only pregnancy hormones.

Because if he had to face that his own feelings for her might be lurking beneath the surface, close enough to find new life, he wanted to believe her feelings for him were in that same position.

A loud hoot called his attention to the big-screen TV, and he was glad to be drawn from these thoughts he couldn't be completely comfortable with.

But he didn't have a taste for the movie, and rather than join the group, he headed for the kitchen. He hadn't noticed that both Linc and Jackson had slipped away from the festivities, but there they both were, too.

"Need a fresh drink?" Jackson asked.

Ash handed over his glass and popped a few peanuts into his mouth. While he ate them, he craned around the two brothers for a look through the window at the garage. "Is Beth spending the night with Kansas?" he asked Linc, who was clearly feeling no pain as he leaned against a counter with a ridiculous grin on his face at nothing in particular.

But it was Jackson who answered. "Nah, she got home a few minutes ago. She was sneaking up the stairs when I came in here."

Ash had been trying to keep a pretty close eye on the front door so he'd know if she arrived, but clearly he'd been so lost in his own thoughts that she'd managed to slip past him.

"Hold off on refilling my glass," he said in a hurry just as Jackson was about to. "I think I'll go up and say good-night."

Linc began to chuckle at that but Jackson only shrugged and set the bottle of soda water back in the refrigerator.

"Hers is the second door on the left," Linc offered.

"Thanks." Ash went back into the living room, heading for the stairs. Leaving the cleaner air of the kitchen, he noticed for the first time that the celebratory cigars had left the rest of the house thick with smoke that drifted to the second level.

If he had his way, he thought as he took the steps two at a time, he'd pack up Beth right then and take her to the lodge with him, away from the smoke and noise and bawdy movies playing in her living room.

And alone with him for the night...

But of course, he wouldn't have his way, so he curbed the idea as he knocked on her bedroom door.

She must have seen enough of what was going on downstairs to be wary, because she called a cautious, "Who's there?"

"Just me," he answered, half wondering if she'd let him in or tell him to go away.

But then he heard the sound of her lock clicking back and she opened the door.

She wore a loose-fitting sundress that left her shoulders bare, and it shot through Ash's mind to press hot kisses to one and work his way across to the other.

He fought the urge just as he'd curbed his thoughts.

What he did do, though, was surprise her, by moving her out of the way so he could step inside and close the door behind him.

"The place is full of smoke. Don't let any more of it in here than there has to be," he said by way of explanation as he looked down into her wide blue eyes. Then he released her and crossed the room to the two large windows on the facing wall, opening them both. "I don't want you sleeping in it, either, so leave these open all night, even if it does waste the air-conditioning."

He waited for her to argue, to get mad at him for giving her orders, but it didn't happen.

Instead, in a congenial voice, she said, "The party

seems like a success. Are you having a good time even though you don't know anyone but Linc and Jackson?''

"Sure. Elk Creek is a lot like the reservation—everybody's friendly,'' he answered as he turned from the windows, thinking that no matter how friendly the partiers downstairs, he'd rather be up here in this room with Beth. But he didn't say that.

She was standing in the middle of the room, her hands in the two front pockets of her dress, her feet bare, one perched atop the instep of the other. She looked fresh and beautiful, and something hard clamped his heart at the thought that she wasn't his anymore.

He told himself to leave the room and escape the feelings, but his desire to spend a little time with her was stronger. He crossed his arms over his chest to keep them from reaching for her, shifted his weight to one leg and searched for something to talk about.

The party—she'd asked about the party and his feeling like an outsider...

"Actually, I've been downstairs watching Linc get toasted into a stupor, and thinking that it isn't too far from some Indian purification rituals that prepare a man for marriage. So I don't feel too far from home.''

She laughed lightly and he let the sound wash over him like cool spring water over sun-warmed skin.

"He's getting polluted, not purified,'' she amended.

"Before a wedding ceremony, some tribes give the groom a drink that makes him violently ill to purge and purify him. I don't know how Linc handles his liquor, but at the rate this is going, I'll be surprised if he doesn't get sick. Other tribes take the man into the sacred underground kiva, turn it into a sort of sauna and sweat the impurities out of him. With all the bodies, and the cigars burning, the living room is about twenty degrees hotter than it is up here—not quite a sauna but close.''

''I see your point.''

Ash glanced around the room, taking in the single bed without so much as a headboard, the tall bureau on which several pictures rested, the desk that was stark enough to have come from a military school, the small television he'd bought her the Christmas before. The single item that could be considered either feminine or pretty or anything more than purely functional was a cheval mirror in one corner.

''Was this your room as a kid?'' he asked.

''This was it,'' she confirmed.

Glancing around again, he assumed she'd stripped the place now that she'd taken up residence in it again, and hadn't begun to redecorate yet. Not that he had anything on which to base that. He'd never seen the room before. When they'd come back here for the few visits they'd made during their marriage, Beth had always insisted they stay at the lodge, in spite of the fact that this house had plenty of room for guests. But her father had been alive then and this had been his house....

Samuel Heller. Shag.

Not a nice man.

He hadn't liked the fact that his daughter had married an Indian.

''Have you cleared your little-girl things out since you moved back or were they gone already?'' Ash asked now.

She laughed again. ''Little-girl things?''

''Ruffled bedspreads and curtains, a dollhouse, dolls, stuffed animals, a dressing table—those kinds of little-girl things.''

She pointed to the mirror in the corner. ''I bought that last week. With the exception of it and the TV you gave me, this is exactly the way my room was the whole time I lived here.''

Ash could feel his eyes widening at the thought. ''I know you were a tomboy, but—''

''I did have a rag doll my mother bought for me before she died, but you've seen that.''

''And that's it?'' He couldn't keep his surprise out of his voice.

''Shag wasn't big on toys, and especially not dolls or stuffed animals. He said he might have gotten stuck with a daughter, but he sure as hell wasn't having a prissy little miss in his house.''

No, his late father-in-law had not been Ash's favorite person. He'd always resented the older man's intolerance toward him as a Native American. But Beth had never said much about what kind of a father he'd been, just that after her mother had died, she and her brothers had lost what ''rounded his sharp edges.'' And though Ash had assumed Shag Heller hadn't been overly kind or loving, he hadn't known the details. Hearing some of them now did not endear the man to him.

''What did you get for gifts?'' he asked, his curiosity roused.

Beth shrugged. ''The same things Linc and Jackson got—a hunting rifle, a new saddle, new boots, fancy belt buckles, expensive cowboy hats, things like that. He was generous—he just wouldn't allow anything froufrou, as he called it, anything that would make me a sissy.''

''But you were a little girl. Little girls are supposed to be sissies and have things that are froufrou.''

''Not with Shag as their father. I had to be as tough as my brothers. Sometimes tougher, and if I let him see anything less—'' she rolled her eyes ''—I'd pay dearly for it.''

"How?"

She laughed as if she found the reminiscence funny even though the reality hadn't been. "How? Let's see, double chores, worse chores or maybe I'd find myself sleeping in the barn for a month. One time he caught me crying over something—I was about ten and I don't even remember what I was bawling about. He sent me out in a torrential downpour to herd cows from one pasture to another, in the dark, late that night, by myself, knee-deep in mud and muck."

"Just for crying?"

"Especially for crying. Or letting him know how I felt about anything—he read that as a weakness. That time he said I was flooding his house and he didn't want to look at such a sorry, soggy sight, that I might as well be out where everything was already wet so I'd fit right in."

She was still smiling wryly, but Ash found nothing in what she'd said funny. "I can't imagine that."

"No, I can't imagine your grandfather doing something like that to a little kid, either. But Shag? Well, he was nothing like Robert." She shook her head. "He had an answer for everything. If we complained we were tired, he'd show us what tired was—he'd have us baling hay until our backs broke. Gripe that none of our friends had to milk cows by hand just to keep in practice, and instead of not using the machines for a day, we wouldn't get to use them for six months. Whine that just once we'd like to sleep in on a Saturday morning, and he'd have us up at four instead of five every day. Complain about anything, and he taught us a lesson for it. We learned to keep our mouths shut about whatever was going through our heads."

Or their hearts. "Maybe it's a good thing I didn't get to know your father any better than I did," Ash muttered through a tightness in his jaw muscles at the thought of someone treating *his* kids like that.

"He was a hard man," Beth agreed. "That's why I told you it wouldn't do any good for you to try overcoming his prejudice. But he was still my father, and there were good things that came from his being a taskmaster. Just think of what a sniveling woman I might be if it weren't for Shag."

Or maybe she wouldn't have to hide when she needed to cry, or get fighting mad at anyone who caught her at it, Ash thought.

But he didn't say it. He just wondered why he hadn't known these things about her before. Might understanding what made her do the things she did have helped him to be more accepting of them? Of her? Could it even have given him the chance to break down some of the walls her childhood had built?

"How come we never talked about this before?" he asked, moving to the bureau to look at the photographs there.

"I guess for the same reason we never talked much about your growing-up years as a welder and carpenter— we just plain never talked much."

He had the sense that she could have said more on that subject, but she didn't, and he didn't pursue it. He didn't know why she was being open with him now, but he was glad and didn't want to scare her away from more of it.

He took a picture from the bureau top and studied it. In it, Beth was eight or nine years old, covered in mud, holding an equally grimy piglet under one arm and displaying a blue ribbon in the other hand. The grin on her face was so big, so proud, it helped to dispel some of the harshness she'd just shown him of her childhood. It hadn't been all bad.

Or maybe not so much bad as tough. Or toughening.

"This is great," he said, smiling over the photograph.

She came up beside him to see which picture he was looking at. "Cheyenne Frontier Days. I was the fastest kid to catch and keep a greased pig. I even beat out my brothers."

Still holding the photograph, Ash glanced at the others. There were two of her mother—one just a portrait, the other of her feeding a baby he presumed to be Beth. There were pictures of Beth and Linc, of Beth and Jackson, of the three of them, of her graduation. "Why didn't you bring these with you when you moved in with me?" She hadn't brought anything besides clothes.

"It was your house," she said simply.

"We were married. That made it your house, too."

Again she shrugged. "It always just seemed like your house."

He stared at her, at her delicate profile and the shine of her dark hair, and realized in that moment just how little he really did know about her. "If you didn't feel comfortable there, why didn't you tell me? What did you think would happen? That I'd make you live in the garage until you could appreciate it?"

"It was your house," she repeated with emphasis. "You liked it and it was a perfectly nice place. What I felt about it wasn't a big deal."

But how many things had she felt and kept bottled up inside, he wondered, telling herself they were no big deal when they really were? Maybe, all together, they'd chipped away at their marriage, at their relationship, at her love for him.

"It's not important," she insisted, and he could see she was shying away from the subject, so he let it drop.

He replaced the picture on the bureau and then pointed

an index finger at it. "I would have liked to have that picture in our home."

He knew there wasn't really anything for her to say to that and wasn't surprised when she didn't respond.

He leaned an elbow amidst the photographs and turned his full attention to her, wishing all over again that he could take her into his arms, that he could change the difficult parts of the way she'd been raised and put a little tenderness and understanding into those years, that he could comfort her for them, even belatedly.

But he only reached a fingertip to brush her hair back slightly from her face, just to be touching her in some way. "Is the baby kicking today?"

"It was quiet all day, but earlier tonight it seemed to be having a party of its own."

"Can I feel?"

She hesitated, and he knew why. They were alone behind closed doors and there was intimacy in the air all around them. There was the intimacy of the room, the intimacy of the insights she'd given him into her past and what made her tick, the intimacy of their bodies only inches apart. And somehow he knew she sensed that, as much as he wanted to feel the baby move, he wanted the intimacy of contact with her, too.

"It seems to have gone to sleep now," she finally said in a rush, as if she'd argued with herself about it and worried that if she didn't hurry with a denial she might surrender.

It was in his mind to do it anyway. To press his palm to her stomach. To circle her small shoulders with his other arm and pull her closer still, to kiss her properly, thoroughly, without holding back all he'd held back until now.

For the first time he began to wonder if the force with which she'd rejected his kisses was more because she *did* want him than because she didn't. Could it be her need to hide that fact that had made her so vehement?

It would certainly account for her responding one minute and shoving him away the next.

That thought strengthened his willpower and he kept his hands to himself. If she cared enough about him to hide it, she must care a lot. But he had to be cautious not to set off the mechanism that caused her to strike out to protect that hiding place.

And he wasn't exactly sure how to do that, except that it seemed better to heed the warning of her refusal to let him feel the baby kick, and let her come around in her own good time.

"I'd better get back downstairs," he said.

She nodded, but he could have sworn her agreement was reluctant, and he wondered if what flashed through her expression before she hid it could actually have been disappointment.

"Jackson and I have to finish the roof tomorrow, but I'll come out and get you for the wedding in the evening."

"I'm going over in the afternoon to help Kansas get ready. I'll just see you at the church."

"Okay," he said, though he envisioned spending the day without her and then losing her in the crowd of the wedding, too, if they didn't go together. None of it pleased him. Not any more than the thought of leaving her right then did, but he knew he had to.

He straightened away from her bureau and went to the door, not looking forward to rejoining the revelry down below. He hadn't realized Beth had followed him until he stepped into the hallway and turned to close the door.

But there she was, standing in the opening, looking soft and beautiful and just the slightest bit rounder with his baby.

His resolutions wavered and he couldn't resist reaching a hand to the bulge of her belly, after all—just for a split second when he said good-night, as if he were saying it to the baby at the same time.

But as his hand slipped away again, he nearly brushed her hand. Had she been about to cover his and hold it there the way she had the night before, or had she meant to stop him?

''Good night,'' she said, sounding slightly embarrassed and making him hope for the better of those two possibilities.

But then, from the party, he heard Linc calling his name, and the uncertainty in Beth's eyes reminded him to let well enough alone. For now, at any rate.

So he merely repeated his instructions to shut her door and keep her windows open against the smoke, and then he headed for the stairs.

He didn't go all the way down, though. He stopped at the second step, waiting until she closed and locked her door again.

Even after that was done, he hesitated, staring back at the hallway behind him, at all those closed doors down its long length. He couldn't help thinking about how difficult it must have been for a little girl growing up here. In a house without a mother and with a father who raised her not only to be a man, but to be a hardened one.

It made his heart hurt for her.

But it also made him wonder if there really was any hope of scratching the surface and finding her feelings for him ready to be rekindled.

Because now he knew just how tough that surface had had to be.

And yet, as he finally forced himself to go the rest of the way down those stairs, he knew he had to give it a try.

Chapter Seven

White candles wreathed in tiny baby's breath flowers and tied with satin ribbons provided the only light in Elk Creek's church the next evening. The flames cast an elegant, intimate glow within the high-ceilinged chapel. There were so many white roses and additional baby's breath all around the altar that when Beth let her vision blur, the candlelight might have been glittering on pristine snow.

But she didn't let her eyes blur for long as she sat in the first row. She needed to see clearly to be on the lookout.

The church was nearly full by the time she took her seat, and she hoped that anyone who noticed her frequent glances over her shoulder would think she was checking out the guests or watching for the bride.

But she'd been with Kansas most of the afternoon, had helped her dress and left her only moments before to have her picture taken.

No, much to her own dismay, she was looking for her former husband.

Most of the small town's residents had been invited, and with each look up the aisle, Beth saw more faces she knew—some she'd become reacquainted with since she'd been back, others she recognized from when she'd lived here as a girl.

Everyone who caught her eye smiled or waved a little and she returned them all, but among the crowd she didn't see Ash, and she felt conspicuously alone—the only person on the whole front bench while all the rest of the pews were close packed.

Even across the aisle, Kansas's brother-in-law was being kept company by his parents and sister so he wouldn't be by himself, even though Della was the matron of honor and all four of their kids were in the wedding.

Not that Beth knew for sure that Ash would sit with her. But still…

Then, on what seemed like her hundredth glance back, she saw him.

He was dressed impeccably. He wore a dove gray suit, white shirt and a mauve silk tie she'd bought him for his last birthday. He looked wonderful, but no matter how often Beth saw him dressed like that, she never failed to think there was something about him in the more formal attire that seemed slightly incongruous.

It was his hair, she knew. Even though it was neatly pulled back into a tight ponytail at his nape, the jeans and T-shirts he'd been wearing lately seemed more in keeping with those renegade locks.

Still, to her, he was the best-looking man in the place, and her heartbeat kicked up a notch at the same moment the baby just plain kicked, as if it were glad its father was coming to be with them.

And he *was* coming to be with them.

Shunning the usher's aid, he'd scanned the church until he spotted her and then started down the aisle. He didn't seem to notice the heads he turned as he did; instead, his gaze was trained on Beth as if he were hungry for the sight.

And though it shouldn't have, it pleased her very much.

"I wasn't sure you were going to make it," she said in a hushed voice as he stepped in front of her to sit down, leaving her closest to the aisle.

"I worked until the last minute so I could get that roof finished," he explained, bending near and inadvertently giving her a whiff of his clean-smelling after-shave.

Then his dark gaze studied her, starting with her hair, in its usual side-parted, curly, bob style. His eyes slipped over her face to her dress—a black sand-washed silk that fell loosely to her hips, where it was cinched to form a slight bubble over the figure-skimming skirt that reached to just above her knees.

"You look terrific," he said when he was finished taking it all in.

"Thanks. So do you," she answered before even realizing she was going to return the compliment.

Music began to play from the choir loft just then, and Linc and Jackson stepped from a side door to position themselves as a procession of two flower girls—Della's daughters—and three tiny ring bearers—Danny, and Della's two sons—started things off.

Everyone in the church stood to watch them coming, all five children very serious about what they were doing, but still wandering a little if they saw someone they knew along the sides.

Next came Della, dressed in yellow and looking slightly teary-eyed already, but working at keeping a smile on her face.

And then the opening bars of the wedding march heralded Kansas.

Her hair was sprigged with flowers and she looked beautiful in the gown Beth had made. The bodice conformed to her body from the narrow waist all the way up the high collar and down her arms to her elbows. The satin skirt was floor-length and ended in a slight train in back, all of it edged in the lace that had been Ash's contribution.

Beth was proud of both her creations, and for once it seemed that the feminine hobby she'd initiated to spite her father so long ago had been worth the battles Shag had waged over her squandering her time sewing.

Linc had stepped to the corner of Beth's pew, eager to meet his bride. When Kansas reached him, she gave him her hand, and he took her up the flower-lined steps to where the minister waited for them.

It wasn't anything at all like Beth and Ash's wedding, but somehow Beth couldn't help thinking about their own ceremony as everyone sat down again and the service began.

Shag had been opposed to her marrying an Indian, as well as being appalled that she and Ash had known each other only a matter of weeks. He'd refused to even attend their wedding, so they'd decided to have a private ceremony with only Ash's grandfather, her brothers and a very few friends in attendance.

They'd held it in the backyard of Ash's house on the reservation, and while everyone had been dressed in church clothes, there hadn't been a fancy wedding gown or tuxedos. Beyond the bouquet she'd carried, the only flowers had been in the garden, which didn't really come to life until after she'd married him and spent some time on it.

Still, she'd been so in love with Ash that the trappings

hadn't mattered. And as she sat there now, seeing her brother's feelings for Kansas in every line of his face, her clearest memory was of Ash looking at *her* that way, once upon a time, too.

How did they come from that to this? she wondered.

And though she was happy for her brother and Kansas, the sadness that washed through her with the thought was almost unbearable.

"This shindig isn't easy on you, is it?" Jackson asked when he'd insisted Beth share the first dance with him some time later.

The reception was in the church basement. There were food and drinks galore, a live band, and once everyone had made their way through the receiving line, the party began in earnest.

"It's a nice wedding. Beautiful," she answered, maintaining the smile she'd pasted on her face as soon as the ceremony ended.

But Jackson studied her in his quiet way, and she had the sense that while she may have fooled everyone else, she wasn't fooling him.

"Seems to me a wedding can't be high on the list of things a person would want to do right after gettin' divorced."

She knew he was itching to add something about it being especially distasteful when the person was pregnant with her ex-husband's baby. She appreciated his restraint. Still and all, she could see her brother was worried about her, and so she was honest with him. "I'm trying to think of it as any old party."

"How're you doin'?"

"Not good," she admitted under her breath.

"We could say you weren't feelin' well or were tired out and I'd drive you home."

For the first time that evening her smile was genuine. Beneath Jackson's gruff, no-nonsense exterior was an observant, sensitive man, and the concern in his offer was very sweet. Beth even considered taking him up on it.

But as he led her around the dance floor, she caught a glimpse of Ash sitting patiently at their table, and she knew a lie about being tired or sick would worry him unnecessarily.

Besides, as difficult as it was for her to be here, there was another part of her that didn't want to end the evening before she'd really gotten to spend any time with Ash.

"That's okay," she told Jackson. "I'll be fine."

Her brother followed her gaze all the way to her former husband and then looked down at her again. "Can't say I understand this."

Beth started to explain about a lie upsetting everyone, but Jackson stopped her. "I mean, I don't understand what the hell's going on between you and Ash. You're havin' a baby together, he's hankerin' after you and you're hankerin' after him—unless I miss my guess—but you just keep at this divorce thing."

The way he put that made her laugh. "Divorce isn't something you *keep at,* like training a stubborn quarter horse."

"Yours has that feel to me. And it just doesn't seem right when neither of you is happy about it. Ever think that maybe this divorce just didn't work out?"

Beth laughed again but had to admit to herself that her brother wasn't too far off the mark—so far, her divorce didn't seem like a great success. Not when she was still so attracted to Ash, not when she couldn't stop thinking about him, not when she craved being with him and had to fight her feelings with forced reminders that she wasn't supposed to be experiencing any of that anymore.

"I'm also thinkin' that you still have a tender spot for him," Jackson said as if he'd read her thoughts and found something she'd left out.

"That's what you think is it?" she asked without committing herself to anything.

But whether or not she admitted it, he'd hit close to home, and denying it didn't make it go away. Or apparently hide it either, if Jackson had seen it.

A tender spot...

Yes, she definitely had a tender spot for Ash.

What she wasn't sure of was if it was more than that.

Or how much more.

Or if she could deal with it.

"He's a good man, you know," Jackson said, just in case she might have overlooked it.

Beth glanced up at her brother from the corner of her eye. "That's a switch. You're the one who hit him in the jaw that first night," she reminded him.

"Only because I thought he wasn't intendin' to stand up to his responsibilities. But he is. I think he'd do right by you if you'd just let him."

"Are the two of you in cahoots or something?" she teased.

"Now don't get me wrong," he said, ignoring her joke. "You know that house is as much yours as it is mine, and I'm happy to have you and the baby with me. Hell, it can get damn lonely there all by myself sometimes. And I don't mind at all bein' as much of a daddy to this child as you want me to be. It's just that you don't seem happy with the way things are, Beth, and I'm wonderin' if you should rethink it."

As if she'd been thinking of anything *but* Ash and this situation lately.

But to rethink the divorce itself? That seemed downright crazy.

"There were good reasons for Ash and me to split up. It doesn't need to be reconsidered," she finally assured her brother.

But as the song ended both their dance and their conversation, she didn't feel as certain as she sounded.

In fact, the longer she was divorced from Ash, the more uncertain she felt. And confused.

And unhappy…

But as her brother led her back to their table, she held all those thoughts and feelings at bay.

After all, it could be the wedding had just gone to her head.

And then, too, there were those hormones….

The reception lasted well into the night, and even when all the guests had gone and all the gifts had been loaded into Jackson's truck, Beth still didn't feel as if she'd seen much of Ash.

They'd sat at the same table and danced twice, but the wedding was the first social occasion she'd attended since she'd come home to Elk Creek. And that meant that all the people she hadn't seen yet used the opportunity to say hello. To catch up. And—in not just a few instances—ask questions to satisfy their curiosity about the rumors around town that she was expecting.

She'd talked to more people than she could remember, but she and Ash could never manage even a few sentences before someone else interrupted.

So she didn't mind that there wasn't really room for her to ride home with Jackson, what with Danny stretched out sound asleep across the truck seat and gifts spilling over into the cab. Instead she and Ash said good-night to him, and to Della and her family, and stayed to close up the church basement by themselves.

"Who cleans this place?" Ash asked as they checked to make sure no one had left anything behind.

"The ladies' auxiliary will do it in the morning."

"Good. I was afraid you'd signed up for it."

Neither of them had found anything significant amidst the general debris that littered the hall, so they locked the delivery entrance, made their way to the front and turned off the lights that were controlled by a main panel near the door.

"Nice wedding," Ash commented as they stepped out into the cool summer night.

"Mmm," she agreed as she locked up behind them and then hid the key in a small box that gripped the doorjamb magnetically, out of sight of any but those who knew it was there.

"Did you enjoy yourself?" Ash asked.

"Sure. Did you?"

He didn't answer right away. His car was back at the lodge and they began walking in that direction before he said, "I did a lot of thinking during it."

"I wonder if anyone who's divorced sits through a wedding without thinking about the hopes and dreams they had when they stood in front of a minister themselves. And how they didn't pan out."

Ash had long since taken off his jacket and tie, rolled his sleeves to the elbows and unfastened his collar button. He carried the suit coat slung over his shoulder. When she glanced up at him, curious about his silence, she found him staring beyond the tops of the buildings they walked past, at the sky.

Finally, in a deep, quiet voice, he said, "It occurred to me as I sat there that our backgrounds weren't the only thing we didn't talk much about."

"I suppose that's true enough," she agreed airily, hoping to lighten what sounded like a serious subject he was launching.

"And the biggest thing we didn't delve into was why you wanted out of the marriage."

So much for keeping things light.

"All you said," he went on, "was that you just didn't want to be married to me anymore."

There was accusation in that but he was right. She hadn't explained herself. To give him reasons when she told him their marriage was over would have meant telling him how he'd hurt her, how lonely she'd been. So she hadn't said anything at all then, and she didn't now, either.

Ash continued anyway. "Part of it is my fault. I didn't push for reasons, because I assumed you'd realized you just didn't love me and I didn't want to hear that in words—even if I could have gotten you to say it outright. But as I listened to that wedding ceremony, I decided that it's time I stop assuming or guessing and know for sure."

That wasn't a direct question, just a statement of what he'd decided, so she danced around it. "It's late," she said. Late at night. Late for them…

Though she wasn't looking at him, she could feel the heat and intensity of his gaze on her.

"I won't push it now if you're tired. But we *are* going to talk about this," he warned.

She knew that tone of voice. It meant his tenacity had kicked in. The same tenacity that found funding for difficult projects, lawyers for impossible cases, solutions for insurmountable problems. He meant what he said. He wouldn't let this rest until he was satisfied.

Beth stopped walking and took off her high-heeled shoes. His hand snaked out to her bare arm to steady her and she tried to ignore how good the strength and warmth of it felt as she took the course of offense as the best form of defense. "You never told me why you wanted the divorce, either. Just that you'd been considering the same thing and maybe it was a good idea." And her own voice was unsteady with the harsh memory of that, and the anger and hurt it had caused her.

"We'll get around to talking about that, too," he assured her. "But you're the one who initiated the split, so you can tell me why first."

They'd reached the lodge by then, a semicircle of ten small cabins built around a centrally positioned office. Ash took his key from his pants pocket and opened the heavy wooden door to his cabin. "My car keys are inside. Do you want to come in and talk or shall I get them and take you home and we'll wait until tomorrow?"

She'd rather not have discussed this at all. "Are those my only two options? Right this minute or tomorrow?"

"That's it."

Beth sighed impatiently to let him know just how much she didn't appreciate this. But when she weighed the choices he'd given her, she decided the late hour now could work to her advantage by at least keeping the discussion brief.

She stepped into the cabin. "I'm not sure what you want to hear."

The close space was lit only by a chain lamp hanging over a small table to the left of the entrance. The air smelled of his after-shave, his soap, him. It was difficult for her not to be carried away by that and by being in a dim room alone with him and a bed that looked much too inviting.

Not wanting to get too comfortable, she put her shoes back on and perched atop the table. Letting her feet dangle, she clamped the edge with both hands in a white-knuckled grip.

Ash tossed his jacket across the back of one of the two chairs she'd ignored. Then he planted a foot on the seat, a forearm on his raised thigh, and met her eyes on an almost equal level, crowding her a bit as he made it clear they were about to get down to business. "I want to know why you divorced me."

She shrugged. "It wasn't a good marriage," she answered simply, as if that said it all.

"We didn't fight. I didn't drink or abuse you or cheat…did you?"

"Cheat? You know I didn't or you wouldn't have come here so sure the baby was yours."

"Okay. That's true. I didn't really think there was someone else, though that would at least be something concrete to explain why you wanted the divorce. So what made it a bad marriage for you?"

She hated this. She absolutely hated it. There was no way she could talk about her feelings and not hate it. "It wasn't that it was a *bad* marriage. It just wasn't much of a marriage at all."

"It didn't live up to those hopes and dreams you mentioned earlier?"

"Actually what it didn't live up to were my expectations. Not that I had a whole slew of them. My mother died when I was so young that I never had much of an up-close example of what marriage was supposed to be. But the one thing I did think was that we'd be together. At least some of the time. And we weren't," she said flatly, as if there hadn't been any emotion involved then or now. As if, like two bottles bobbing separately in the same sea, they'd just drifted calmly apart. No big deal.

Ash breathed out a short, mirthless laugh. "You know, my grandfather made a remark about my being away from you too much. Does he know something I don't?"

She shrugged again, only this time it felt so stiff she had to force her shoulders back down again. "I think there just isn't enough of you to go around. Your work with the foundation is time-consuming. But it's also important, so it has to take priority. What's left over isn't enough to maintain a marriage, too," she said as if she could accept the reality without a problem.

Ash's bushy brows dipped together in a frown. "Are you telling me that you felt neglected?" he asked as if he couldn't believe it.

Beth didn't like the word *neglected*. Not at all. To her way of thinking, it made her sound weak and needy. And her tone toughened in response. "It was just very frustrating to compete with your work, with the foundation, and with the demands of a whole nation of Native Americans," she finished with a flourish of exaggeration.

"You felt like you were in competition with all of that?"

"I *was* in competition with all of that."

"No, you weren't."

"Oh, come on," she said with a roll of her eyes.

"You weren't. The foundation is work. You were my *wife*. Two completely different things."

"Please."

"You weren't competing with it," he insisted.

"Okay. I wasn't competing with it, because I chose not to compete. Because I just stayed in the background and let it have you. Until I decided I didn't want my whole life spent in the background while everything else took priority over me. That's when I suggested the divorce.''

He looked stunned. He sounded stunned. ''Without so much as telling me you felt like this first? Without giving me a clue? My God, Beth, you always acted as if you couldn't care less how much my work kept me away, as if you were busy and wouldn't even know I was gone. Sometimes I had the feeling you were glad to be rid of me. Why didn't you *tell* me this?''

''What should I have said? I'd like to go to the movies tonight so don't spend the time to find a family that will take in the fourteen-year-old unwed mother, or an Indian home for that baby suffering fetal alcohol syndrome? Don't raise money for the homeless?'' she asked wryly.

''How about just saying you'd like it if I was around more? If I could rearrange things so we could see each other?''

''As if I couldn't live without you? As if I depended on you?'' she demanded, appalled.

''As if you loved me and wanted to be with me. And maybe even needed me just a little.''

Her spine straightened reflexively. ''I do all right on my own.''

''Sure you do. At least that's how you always made it seem. You encouraged me to spend all the time I needed to at the office. To go to every meeting. To see to all the details of everything that came up. To travel when I needed to. You didn't mind. You said you had paperwork of your own. Or you'd go to the movies with my grandfather. No problem. Except that you damn well divorced me because I believed it and did do it all.''

He looked as if he wanted to shake her.

''Would you have liked it better if I'd whined that we didn't see each other enough? Or begged you not to do what someone else depended on you for? Or pouted when a business trip took five days instead of three?''

''There's a difference between whining, begging or pouting, and just letting me know you want me around.''

But the difference was too subtle for her to see. ''It should have gone without saying that two people who were married to each other actually spent time together.''

''Not when you were pushing me out the door most of the time.''

''Oh, please. As if I invented all the things that called you away or needed your attention. I was just being supportive in the face of the inevitable.''

''Supportive?'' His voice had risen, apparently with the level of his disbelief, and he actually laughed.

Beth didn't know what he found funny.

''Hell, all that support made me think you could only stand me around in small doses.''

''Sure. I didn't want to be with you, so I worked on your causes and joined your groups just to catch a glimpse of you, or kept bending over backward to lure you home when I didn't think it would do any harm to what you were doing somewhere else.''

He pointed a long index finger at her and said, ''Boat!'' as if it had just occurred to him that that was the purpose of the game.

''Yes, Boat,'' she said, embarrassed to have admitted even that much.

He sighed and shook his head. The anger of moments before seemed to have evaporated, along with his need to discuss the reason for the divorce, as more pleasant memories took over. ''Boat was one of the few times I honestly knew you wanted me. You'll never know how much that meant.''

"You stopped coming home even for that," she said quietly, suffering anew the rejection she'd felt at the time.

He laughed wryly. "That's because I started to worry that it was only my services in bed that you were interested in." Again he sighed away the tension in the room. "Some of the best memories I have are of Boat," he said, his voice a deeper, huskier timbre, lost suddenly in the past. "Remember the rainstorm last year?"

Oh, she remembered all right. It sent shivers along the surface of her skin just thinking about it. "It's a wonder we didn't catch pneumonia." She pretended to chastise him for what had really been a delicious addition to the game. "Opening all the windows so the rain and wind could come in, as if we really were out in a storm at sea."

"Making wild, abandoned love to match it," he reminisced in a near whisper that brought him close enough for her to feel the warmth of his breath against her cheek. He shook his head and laughed yet again. "The marriage wasn't all bad."

She ignored that tie-in to what they'd been talking about, glad for any distraction from the more serious subject of before. "That was the coldest rain…" But even as she tried to make it sound bad, her tone gave her away.

"God, that was a great night," he said, with a groan that matched some he'd made in the act. "If ever there was a time I thought you might get pregnant even using birth control, it was that night."

"We *weren't* using birth control after a while. We ran out, and even that didn't stop things."

"There aren't any drugstores on boats cast asea in a storm. And as I recall we couldn't help ourselves."

"Carried away like two hormonal teenagers." The intended rebuke sounded more like a sweet remembrance.

He leaned forward, his beautifully boned face just inches

from hers. "You needed me to keep you warm." He placed a brief peck of a kiss on her lips.

"I needed you to shut the windows."

"That's not what you said at the time," he reminded with a smug grin before he kissed her again, holding it a moment longer this time.

"I expected icicles to grow from my ears."

He moved just enough to gently bite one lobe and then pressed slow kisses down the side of her neck to the spot where it dipped to her shoulder. "I'd never have let that happen. But I do remember some pretty great goose bumps." He laughed. "Yeah—like those. I didn't know you could do it on demand."

The goose bumps were hardly voluntary. They came in response to his kisses.

At any rate, her resistance was low, and so the sparks he rained through her went unchecked. The best she could manage was another phony complaint about that earlier event. "Not to mention that the neighbors could probably see what we were doing, since the curtains were open to let in the weather."

"The electricity was out and there wasn't even a moon." He reached behind her and turned off the wall switch so his room—like theirs that night—was lit only by milky light from outside.

He laid his palm against her cheek. "What a night that was," he said again, just before covering her mouth with his, completely, firmly, insistently.

His lips were parted and he urged hers open, too. Not that it took much persuasion. Beth let her head fall back and answered his kiss, the parting of his lips, even the first meeting of his tongue and hers.

He still smelled faintly of after-shave, and she breathed

deeply of it, enjoying it, for once savoring what it did to her senses instead of fighting it.

On its own, one of her hands reached inside his collar to the side of his neck, thick and corded and strong. His skin was smooth, warm, and she had much too vivid a memory of what it had felt like to have the whole length of his naked body against hers.

She raised her other hand to his chest, telling herself to push him away. But that wasn't what she did. Instead she just left it there, wishing in her heart of hearts that his shirt wasn't between them.

His kiss turned more insistent, as if answering the need she felt. Her back arched her closer to him.

He helped that along by wrapping an arm around her, pulling her more to the edge of the table where her knees just brushed the hard ridge of his desire for her.

Aware of that, she told herself to stop this. Now.

But she didn't pay much attention. Too many wonderful things were awake inside of her, awake and crying out for Ash.

She felt his hand slide from its caress of her cheek to her back. Slowly, slowly, he pulled her zipper down, and as he pulled it, her dress inched lower on her breast, stopping tantalizingly near the hardened crest.

She meant to stop him. She really did. But her body, her breast ached for his touch, cried out to know the feel of his hand against her, and rather than moving away from him, she arched even more seductively toward him.

His mouth left hers, nibbling, kissing, following the curve of her throat, the hollow, with his tongue.

And then he very carefully covered her breast with his hand.

It felt good. Great. Terrific. But, oh, how she wanted that dress out from between them!

She rolled her shoulder so it would fall further. Or maybe so he'd realize that if he didn't push down that silky fabric soon, she might go crazy.

He chuckled, a soft, barrel-deep sound from inside his chest, but he got the message, because he slipped the dress lower and finally, gloriously, bared her breast to the air, then to his palm.

Incredible. The feeling was like nothing she'd ever known before. Never in her life had she reached the level of sensation she did then.

"You are bigger," he whispered, as if confirming her need for those larger bras he'd pretended not to watch her buy, and for the first time she found pleasure in what before had only been a nuisance. She was bigger. And better. Much, much better...

As if he sensed that every touch, every caress, every kneading of her flesh was intensified a hundredfold, he explored this change slowly, tenderly, carefully. Almost too carefully, for she craved the touch she'd known from him before—firm, strong, possessive.

But more than that she yearned for his mouth there, covering that engorged crest, nibbling, teasing, tormenting as only he could...

She slipped her arms over his shoulders and buried her face in the side of his neck, kissing him, teasing him, urging him to go further.

But he didn't, and the frustration it raised in her began to remind her of the frustrations she'd felt when they were married, those same frustrations he'd just moments before insisted she tell him about.

And in the instant of that thought, and the flood of unpleasant memories it brought with it, she heard what almost sounded like her father's voice echoing through her mind, telling her that only idiots were slaves to their emotions and that they always paid dearly for letting anyone see the weakness those emotions caused.

She recoiled from Ash, sliding her dress back between her breast and his hand.

"This is Linc and Kansas's wedding night, you know, not ours," she said, trying to make a joke out of the abrupt ending she'd put to what was happening between them.

But it didn't come out sounding humorous, and from Ash's raised eyebrow and tone of voice, he hadn't taken it that way, either. "I didn't think it was."

She seized a better excuse, the one she'd already used tonight. "It's late."

"Too late?"

She knew he wasn't asking about the time. He was asking if it was too late for them. And in that moment she didn't know if it was too late for them or not. So all she said was, "It's been a long day and I need to get home."

"You don't *need* to," he challenged, as if to get an answer out of her that way. "You could stay here." He nodded in the direction of the bed.

Tempting. It was much, much too tempting. But the cooler her ardor got, the more vivid was the memory of so many other frustrations and unmet needs that had pushed her to divorce him in the first place, and she knew she couldn't give in to that temptation.

"No, I can't," she said, both in answer to his suggestion that she stay and as an order to herself.

Ash's black eyes searched hers in the moonlight for a moment before his hands came to cup the sides of her face. "Tell me what you're feeling," he demanded, sounding almost angry.

"Frustrated," she answered the same way. "Just like I felt when we were married."

For a moment he continued to stare down at her from

behind a fierce frown, but then his expression eased and he actually laughed, though there was only irony in the sound of it. "Damn it, Beth, that's not what I wanted to hear."

What had he wanted to hear? That maybe she still loved him? That she definitely still wanted him? That any of it made a difference to the way things were between them? Because it didn't.

"I need to go home," she said, pulling out of his grip. "Are you going to drive me or shall I walk?"

He stared off over his shoulder at nothing in particular and then looked back at her and sighed in what sounded like no small amount of frustration of his own. "I'm not going to let you walk all the way out to the ranch."

She slid sideways on the table until she was clear of him and could get down. "Then let's go."

He didn't follow her immediately. He left her waiting in the doorway while he stayed where he was, shaking his head again as if to say *I give up.*

And something inside of her cried out for him not to. Not to give up on her. Even as she stood there ramrod-straight, in control once again, and every inch Shag Heller's daughter.

Finally he grabbed his car keys from the bureau top and joined her at the door, holding it for her to go out ahead of him.

Neither of them said anything on the ride to the ranch. Once they arrived there, Ash walked her up to the house in spite of her insistence that he didn't need to.

Beth unlocked the door and opened it, but before she could step inside he took her by the shoulders, turned her to face him and kissed her again, soundly, firmly, passionately.

Then he let her go so abruptly she rocked on her heels.

"It isn't too late," he said then. "Not when I want you so much it hurts. Not when you want me. But maybe if you could just admit it—to us both—that might be the first step." He finished with a gentle jab of his index finger against her collarbone.

A first step toward what? she wanted to ask.

But she didn't.

Instead she said nothing at all.

He turned and left then, as if to stay one moment more might cost him the control of the passion that had resurfaced in his kiss.

And as Beth watched him go, she couldn't help wishing he wasn't leaving her. Wishing he'd kept her in that cabin, taken her to his bed, made love to her all night long.

But even as she wished it, she hated herself for the weakness she thought it shouted of.

Chapter Eight

The next day was the Fourth of July, a holiday Elk Creek celebrated with gusto.

Beth helped Jackson with a few minor chores that morning to speed things up. Then she took a quick shower, pulled her hair into a curly topknot at her crown, applied a slight dusting of blush and some mascara, and got dressed.

Her choices of what still fit seemed to be getting fewer every day, but she finally settled on a navy blue trapeze sundress with a tanklike top. There were twenty tiny buttons down the front and, in a burst of daring, she left the top three unfastened, showing a hint of her new cleavage that would no doubt scandalize Elk Creek. And tantalize Ash, though she pretended that had nothing to do with it.

She'd made no plans with him but still expected to find him waiting by the time she went downstairs, certain that he'd show up to insure they attend the festivities together.

But only Jackson and an excited Danny were in the kitchen when she got there.

Not for the life of her would she let her brother see her disappointment, so she hurried them out the door as if she didn't feel they were missing one vital member of the party.

They took Jackson's truck into town, her nephew sitting on her lap on the high bench seat. But Beth was barely aware of the little boy's fidgeting. Instead it was Ash she was thinking about.

She told herself he'd probably figured on meeting up with her in town, but still it was in the back of her mind that something might have finally called him away.

It was bound to happen and she knew it. She'd wished for it.

But just the thought that today might be the day twisted her heart into a knot and made her realize that she didn't want him to leave.

Lord help her.

The truth was, she woke up every morning anxious to see him—in spite of all her claims to the contrary—and went to bed every night consoling herself in her lonely bed with the thought that she'd be with him again the next day. And only when they were together did she feel content, happy, complete....

Riding along in her brother's truck, she closed her eyes as if to block out what she knew that meant. The same thing it had meant the first time she'd ever had those same feelings.

It meant that she really did love him.

Still.

Again.

Whether she wanted to or not.

And she didn't want to, because it didn't change anything.

Sure, being married to him would have been good if it had been the way things were now, the way they had been since he'd come to Elk Creek—seeing each other every day, spending time together, getting to know each other.

But that wasn't the way it used to be. It wasn't the way it would be forever. This was just a blip in the reality of life with him. A blip that could right itself and be back on course any minute. And she'd best not forget it.

She opened her eyes and stared past Danny's at Elk Creek as they drove into it, lecturing herself that these were only feelings. And Shag had taught her well that feelings could be ignored. That they never needed to be acted on.

And if Ash wasn't here anymore?

It would be just fine. For the best, actually. And she'd deal with it. She wouldn't let it devastate her. She just wouldn't...

Jackson found a parking spot in the school lot and they walked the three blocks farther to the town square. The street around it was closed off to traffic so booths could be set up to sell food and crafts, and offer diversions like shooting galleries and a number of games of skill and chance.

The park itself was turned over to picnickers, while the pavilion in the center of it was the site of contests in pie eating, arm wrestling, singing, dancing, cake baking, hog calling, and a half-dozen events designed for the kids of the community to compete in. This year there were even a few carnival rides brought in to operate beside the courthouse to keep everyone busy until after dark when the fireworks display would fill the sky.

The first order of business was to claim a spot in the

park and that was where Beth and Jackson headed, Danny riding on Jackson's shoulders.

Somewhere between only partially buttoning her dress and reaching Elk Creek, the stuffing had gone out of Beth's anticipation for the day, but she put a good face on it as they worked their way through friends and neighbors eager to say hello.

And then she spotted Ash.

He was standing beneath a huge old elm tree waving and shouting to them.

Run! Run the other way! that voice of caution shouted in her mind.

And her feet were moving, all right.

But not away from Ash—to him, as her spirits rose again and all of those dark thoughts lost their hold on her.

"You must have been here at dawn to get this place," she said when she, Jackson and Danny joined him. He'd spread a large blanket in the armlike roots of the tree that would shade them during the day but still leave them a clear view of the fireworks in the opposite direction that night.

"I didn't want you getting too much sun," he explained, shrugging off what had to have been hours of waiting for her.

His pampering was one more thing she knew she shouldn't allow. Her father would have considered it fostering weakness, and while she agreed that it would be a mistake to become accustomed to it, she couldn't help being pleased by it.

It would eventually end anyway, she reasoned. Just like this time they were having together. But what if, for this one day, she indulged? What if she turned off the negative voice in her mind and let go a little? It was a holiday, after all, and what harm could it do if, for such a short time, she reveled in Ash's company? In his attentiveness? In Ash himself?

Maybe all these mood swings had made her a little light-headed and frivolous, but she decided that the future would take care of keeping them apart. And even though she'd have to deal with the disappointment and the hurt and the myriad of other harsh emotions that would come with his leaving, at least she'd have this time.

Besides, it was already too late to think she could avoid any of those bad feelings—she'd felt enough of them on the ride into town at only the thought that he might be gone. They were just waiting to rise again when he finally left, no matter what she did or didn't do. So why not make the best of what she had for the moment?

Jackson set their picnic cooler on Ash's blanket and then glanced in the direction from which Rick Meyers, the Heller Lumber foreman, was calling his name. He waved at the tall redhead but turned to Beth rather than immediately accepting the other man's invitation to watch an amateur boxing match in a ring just beyond the booths.

"I'll take Danny," he offered.

"That's okay," Beth declined. "He wants to go on the carnival rides. We'll take him there." She finished with a glance at Ash. "You don't mind, do you?"

He was wearing those faded, low-slung blue jeans and a red T-shirt with a few of his buttons undone, too, exposing the arrowhead that hung around his neck. The shirt had long sleeves and, in answer to her question, he pushed them up above his elbows as if he were about to dig in to work. Then he held out his hand to the three-year-old. "I've been itching to get on those rides myself."

Danny took his hand without hesitation, having apparently warmed up to him while Ash worked with Linc at the honky-tonk, and that settled that. The three of them headed off in one direction while Jackson went in the other.

If Danny missed his dad and Kansas as the day went on, he hid it well. In fact, he seemed to have developed a fondness for Ash that bordered on hero worship. It was Ash he chose to take him on the Ferris wheel, and Ash he looked to for advice about whether or not to venture a ride on the children's roller coaster.

And when one of Kansas's nephews made a derisive comment about Ash's long hair, Danny set him straight, announcing with a full measure of awe and pride in his voice that Ash was a real live *In'ian.*

They met Jackson back at the park for supper as the sun finally began to relent and drift behind the Rocky Mountains, but it was hardly a peaceful meal, as a number of Elk Creek's single women kept happening by to say hello to Jackson.

"I never realized how popular you are with the ladies," Beth teased, unable to resist.

"Only with the ones lookin' for a husband," he said, as if they didn't count.

"I didn't know you were a confirmed bachelor."

"I'm not. Just not interested in faces I've been looking at since I was born. It'd be like marryin' you," he told her. "I know every little thing about 'em. It's boring as hell."

"Oh, come on," she cajoled, nodding at what looked to be the third return of one woman, whom Jackson had dated in high school. "I'll bet you don't give them a chance to surprise you."

Jackson caught sight of Suzy Teaton making her way toward them again and seemed to suddenly have had his fill. Though whether of food or aggressive women, Beth couldn't be sure.

He wiped his mouth on his napkin, tossed the remnants of his meal into a grocery sack they were using for trash and got to his feet in a hurry.

But before he left, he bent down to Beth. "How about I give 'em a chance to surprise *you* and remind 'em all that I'm not the only available man sittin' on this blanket?" he goaded back as he took off in the direction least laden with admiring females.

Beth glanced at Ash to find a Cheshire-cat grin on his face.

"Want an introduction?" she challenged with a nod toward the now-retreating blonde. But she wasn't feeling quite as unaffected as she wanted him to believe. In truth, with the exception of the brief worry she'd had in Margie Wilson's café about not wanting her baby to see him with anyone other than her, she hadn't thought about Ash being available to other women, just free to devote himself to the foundation. And she was coming to realize that the idea didn't sit well.

Actually, it rankled something fierce.

There was some consolation, though, in the fact that Ash seemed to have eyes only for her.

He was sitting with his back against the tree roots that rose up from the earth, his legs stretched out, but he sat up and crossed them in front of him so he could lean nearer to her. "It's not an introduction to someone else that I want," he answered, his tone dripping with insinuation that secretly delighted her.

Danny spared her having to respond to it, though, returning from his meal with Kansas's nieces and nephews to sneak up behind Ash and yank the ponytail he'd previously defended.

"Who's that back there?" Ash pretended to be surprised and outraged, grabbing the giggling little boy to roll him over his head and into his lap. "You know what I do to kids who pull my hair?" he demanded once he had him there. "I tickle them."

And that was just what he did.

Beth watched as the big man tormented her nephew only enough to elicit squirms and shrieks of delight. She appreciated how much attention he'd given the little boy all day, and it occurred to her that she'd never really seen how he behaved around kids for any length of time.

But he'd been good with Danny. Patient, kind; just firm enough to let the three-year-old know his limits, and as relaxed as someone who was not only experienced, but who genuinely liked children.

He'd be a good father, she realized with a new certainty, and it gave her heart such a tug to think that she might not be around to watch him play like that with their own son or daughter. That some other woman he was now available to might be the one to witness it. And never in her life had she wanted so badly to stamp her own brand on him.

"Maybe all that tickling isn't such a good idea right after he's eaten," she suggested, and even though it was true, it was also an attempt to ease her own discomfort. She'd *divorced* the man, for crying out loud. How could she suddenly be feeling so possessive?

She couldn't. She no longer had the right.

Ash stopped, held Danny upside down for a split second and then let him do a somersault onto the blanket.

"More," the little boy hollered, jumping into Ash's arms for a second round. But this time Ash diverted his energies into shooting trash into the sack, like balls into a basket.

By the time they had the whole supper mess cleaned up, Danny had something else on his mind. He frowned very seriously at Beth.

"Is there a baby in yer tummy like my cousin Billy says?" he asked dubiously.

"Yes, there is."

"An' can it talk and tell you secrets?"

Both Ash and Beth laughed.

"I don't think so," she answered.

"Yep, it can," he insisted, as if he knew something she didn't. "Billy says."

"You know," Ash added devilishly, "he could be right. I think I read something about that not long ago. Maybe we should have a listen," he suggested to the child, all the while grinning at Beth.

"Can we?" Danny asked, his green eyes wide with wonder.

"Sure we can, can't we?" Ash challenged her.

Beth ignored him and instead spoke directly to her nephew. "You couldn't hear anything, sweetheart. Babies can't talk until a long time after they're born."

"Let's see," he insisted, encouraged by Ash, who was clearly enjoying putting her on the spot.

Beth made a face at her former husband and then leaned back on her hands far enough to make her mounded middle available. "Okay, go ahead," she told Danny.

The three-year-old knelt down and put his ear to her stomach, listening intently. "I hear'd it!" he said after a minute.

Again Ash and Beth laughed.

"What did he say?" Ash asked, as if he honestly believed it.

"I dunno, but it was sum'thin'."

"Let's see if I can tell," Ash suggested, stretching out on his side and leaning his weight on one elbow.

"You can't do that," Beth said under her breath.

"We have to know what he's trying to tell us," he protested as Danny made way for him.

"Ash—"

"Shh…"

Beth glanced around nervously to see if anyone was looking but her concern was quickly replaced by a jolt of sensation as Ash's head pressed to her stomach. He cupped his hand around it, as if to hear better, but he was really giving her a subtle massage that only the two of them knew about.

Warm honey sluiced through her and made her forget that they were out in public. She couldn't resist watching him, drinking in the sight of his chiseled profile as she fought the urge to caress his head the way he caressed her belly.

Then, as if to say hello to its father, the baby gave a solid kick.

"Hear it?" Danny demanded at about the same time.

"I do," Ash assured him.

"Wa's it said?"

"Something about letting him out of there so he can see the fireworks."

"Well, let 'im out, Aunt Beth," Danny chastised.

"Sorry. I can't do that. The baby has to stay awhile longer, I'm afraid. Next year it can see the fireworks." Then she wiggled a little to let Ash know his time was up. "Now it's saying it needs to go to sleep," she added pointedly, because the longer Ash stayed like that, slowly, sensuously rubbing her, the more things he was awakening inside of her, things that she should absolutely not be feeling at that time and in that place.

He finally sat up, but his hand remained, still working its wonders.

"We better has ice cream now," Danny said very solemnly, and as if there had been some segue into it.

Beth was grateful for the suggestion of anything that would save her from herself and from Ash's arousing touch. "Ice cream?" she asked.

"I promised," Ash explained, finally dragging his hand away, though clearly with reluctance.

Or was it something else that caused him to slide his hand so lazily across the whole mound of her middle before actually letting her go? Maybe he was *trying* to turn her on.

Ash stood then and turned to help her to her feet. But what she needed more than ice cream was time to gather her wits. "I think I'll just wait here for you guys. Don't be long—the fireworks should start soon."

After finding out if she wanted something, Ash lifted Danny to his shoulders the same way Jackson had earlier in the day and headed across the park to the booth where ice cream was being sold.

Beth's gaze followed Ash the whole way.

And as she watched him, a shiver danced up her spine at just the thought of how right it had felt to have him touch her.

At how much more she craved.

And at just the idea that there could ever be someone else taking her place...

The fireworks were spectacular. By the time they began, Ash and Danny had had their ice cream, and Jackson had rejoined them all. To make room on the blanket—or so he claimed—Ash pulled Beth very close beside him, casually keeping his arm stretched along the tree's unearthed root behind her and urging her to lie back with him to more comfortably see the display.

She probably shouldn't have, but she did. And as beautiful as the lights bursting in the air were, the longer it went on, the more her senses tuned in to Ash lying next to her instead of what she was supposed to be paying attention to.

The lean, hard length of him was pressed ever so slightly to her side. His arm pillowed her head. His hand did a slow massage of her shoulder and reminded her of the more subtle one he'd given her stomach earlier. His deep, rich voice washed over her every time he praised a particularly impressive explosion. His after-shave lingered faintly to drift to her like the scents of a far-off forest.

What she wanted, she realized with the rapid rise in her heartbeat and the feeling that all her nerve endings had risen to the surface of her skin to tingle to life, was for them to be the only two people there at the moment. She wanted to turn to him, wrap her arms around his neck, meld herself to that exquisitely masculine body of his and make love with him for hours and hours....

"That's it," Jackson said just then, interrupting her fantasy.

Beth hadn't even seen the end of the fireworks; she hadn't realized she'd been lost in her own thoughts and imaginings for so long. But the sky was quiet and smoky, and all around them blankets and picnic gear were being gathered, letting her know it really was over.

Then she heard Ash say to her brother, "Go ahead and get that boy home to bed. Beth and I can collect all this stuff and I'll drive her back."

Forcing herself to sit up, away from Ash and his effect on her, she glanced at Jackson, who was holding a very sleepy Danny on his lap.

"You don't have to do that," her brother answered Ash's offer. "It'll only take a minute to clean up, and then you won't have to come all the way out to the ranch."

But Ash wouldn't have it any other way, and even though Beth knew it was dangerous to accept his offer when she was all churned up inside, she finally ended the debate by siding with him.

Jackson accepted her decision without any more protest, said good-night and carried Danny off. But he'd been right about it not taking any time at all to gather their things, shake out the blanket and join the weary exodus from the park, because he was barely out of sight by the time they had finished.

"We could have packed up in the time we argued about who I was going home with and saved you the trip," Beth mused as they walked to the lodge to get Ash's car.

"What makes you think I wanted to be saved the trip?" Ash asked in a husky voice for her ears only.

Not much more was said after that. Unlike the previous evening, they didn't have the street to themselves, but even if they had, Beth would have been a little uneasy about pursuing an explanation of his intentions and discovering his train of thought was on the same treacherous track as hers.

As they reached the lodge, the crowd around them thinned. Beth wondered if Ash would again invite her into his cabin.

And if he did, if she'd go.

Because if she went, she knew that this time it wouldn't be for just a half hour of conversation.

But her wondering was all for naught, because Ash went straight to his car, pulling his keys from his pocket this time instead of needing to go inside to get them.

"Are you tired?" he asked when he'd put the picnic things into the back seat and they were both in the car.

Tired? No, she wasn't tired. Her wandering imagination during the fireworks had left her wide-awake. "It's not really late," she answered a little vaguely.

He tossed her a rakish smile and a sidelong glance that seemed to say more than words. "Are you in a hurry to get home?"

Something purely sensual skittered up her spine. "No," she said in a voice three octaves higher than normal. She cleared her throat. "Did you have something in mind?"

"As a matter of fact, I do."

He didn't offer any more information, and once again she was afraid to ask for fear of appearing too eager. What if she was misreading his intentions based on her own thoughts and feelings during the fireworks? After all, his room would have been a better choice if he was thinking and feeling what she was.

Neither of them spoke as he drove out of town, and when he reached the road that led up to the ranch house, he went past it, going about half a mile farther out before he turned onto a dirt path that would take them to a small, secluded lake on Heller property.

"I'm surprised you remember this," Beth said when she realized where he was headed. "I brought you here only once, the first time you came to meet Shag."

"It's one of my better memories of your old hometown."

That surprised her. She'd have guessed just the opposite.

The lake was a mile across and two wide, surrounded by a soft, loamy beach and pine trees that grew all the way to the water in some spots. Their relationship had been new that single other time they were there. And Beth had been embarrassed by what had happened just before they'd come. She didn't remember anything else about it, and she certainly couldn't think why it would be memorable for him.

Ash stopped the car at the end of the road and turned off the engine. He removed his shoes and socks, leaving them on the floorboard, then grabbed the picnic blanket from the back seat and got out.

Beth expected him to do or say something that included her. But he didn't come around to her side or so much as invite her to go with him, and she had the sense that she was being given a silent choice.

To leave the car and join him was to accept that tonight there would be no stopping short when passion flared between them, as surely it would. If she didn't want it to happen, she knew she'd better not get out.

She watched Ash in the distance, spreading the blanket near the water's edge. He sat in the center of it, his legs stretched in front of him, his upper body braced back on his hands. Then he tilted his face up to the star-filled sky as if greeting the moon.

And the moon answered by christening him in a silvery glow, reflecting off the sharp crests of his bones and leaving deep shadows in the hollows. He looked regally primitive, elemental, so in sync with nature's beauty and grace that it was difficult to picture him ever sitting behind a desk or dressed in an expensive English suit.

And what he was waiting for, she knew, was for her to shed all of her own self-imposed restraints to let nature take the course it had been so strongly striving for since he'd shown up here.

But could she do that?

Letting go to enjoy his company in the middle of a whole town full of people was one thing. But this was very different. To do this she would have to ignore what

was in their past. To forbid herself to think of the dark
tunnel of their future. To allow him to see that she really
did still care for him…

If she stayed in the car, she felt sure he'd just come
back. That he wouldn't say anything. That he wouldn't act
as if she'd rejected him.

But they'd both know she had. That she'd closed a door
he'd opened for them again.

That he really wasn't hers anymore…

A single click and the car door opened.

She kicked off her shoes and left them on the floor, just
the way Ash had his, swinging her bare feet to the ground
and getting out. She closed the door behind her carefully,
as if not to disturb the night, and went to join him on the
blanket.

Sitting down with her legs curled to the side, she studied
his profile. He went on looking at the sky in stone-statue
stillness, as if he were hardly aware of her. Though she
knew that couldn't be true, because why else would he be
smiling that small, pleased smile?

"How can this place have a good memory for you when
we came out here after Shag had blasted our getting married?" she asked, as if no time at all had lapsed in their
conversation.

His handsome face turned to her then, that smile stretching a bit wider. "It was the only time you ever said you
loved me. Not directly, of course, you never did that. But
in the process of railing about your father and his poorly
concealed prejudice, you said that no matter what he
thought, you loved me and were going to marry me."

"I said it other times," she claimed, though without
much conviction, because she knew she hadn't been very
forthcoming with those sentiments. It just wasn't her way.

"No," he corrected evenly, "you said 'me, too' when

I said it. Or 'same here.' Or 'thanks'—that was the worst,''
he added, but with enough levity to take the sting out of
it. ''But you never looked me in the eye and said 'I love
you.'''

And apparently that had had an impact on him, on their
whole marriage, since he'd believed the reason she wanted
the divorce was because she not only didn't say it, but
didn't feel it, either.

''I'm sorry,'' she said, unsure how else to respond. But
she could sense that it was inadequate. ''I did, though,''
she added in a barely audible voice, staring out at the lake
over her shoulder because she was too uncomfortable to
venture it while she was looking at him. ''Is that why
you'd been thinking about divorce yourself—because you
thought I didn't love you?''

''That, and because I was so damn frustrated with the
fact that you never let me in—emotionally. When your
father died and you wouldn't come out of that bathroom,
when you wouldn't let me comfort you…I guess I just
started to wonder what the hell we were doing together at
all.''

His words hung there between them as Beth let them
sink in, as surprised by this as he'd been by her reasons
for wanting to end the marriage. Not only was it nearly
impossible for her to let anyone see her weaknesses, but
she'd believed she was doing him a service by sparing him
the sight.

Then Ash interrupted her thoughts. ''So, if you honestly
did love me then, what about now?''

''Now everything is confused,'' she said without having
to think about it, because she was so lost in just that.

She could feel him watching her, waiting. She knew he
wanted her to say more. That he wanted her to say she
loved him, that she always had.

But she couldn't, especially not now when they weren't even married, when everything between them was so ambiguous, so uncertain.

After a moment, he seemed to let her off the hook. "I know for a fact that I want you," he said with a note of hopefulness in his voice, as if maybe he could get her to admit that much.

But still the best she could do was, "I guess that's what we're doing out here, isn't it?"

"I guess it is."

Then stop all this talking, and—

He raised a palm to her cheek and brought her face back to him. He searched her eyes with his, captured them, held them, conveyed with the solemnity of that gaze that he meant business here, that she'd better be willing to go the distance this time.

But she didn't need to think about it any more than she already had. She'd made that decision before she got out of the car. So she merely reached up and covered his hand with hers.

He waited another moment, as if wondering if she'd pull his hand away. But when she didn't, he brought her toward him and pressed his mouth to hers in the sweet nectar of the kiss she was craving.

His lips parted over hers, urging hers open, too, so his tongue could unite them, and before she knew it, she was lying on the soft, blanket-covered earth with Ash beside her, his big body partly over her, lost in the hungry, yearning play that told her she hadn't been the only one having fantasies this evening.

He crossed a heavy thigh over her lap and Beth let her hand rest on it, reveling in the feel of the power there as wanton images flitted through her mind.

Somewhere deep down, she'd known this night would end like this. Or at least hoped it would.

Her back arched toward Ash's chest, and she let go of his thigh to wrap her arms around him, to pull herself up to him and feel the pressure of her breasts against that solid expanse.

But that was apparently not what he had in mind, for his hand left its caress of her face to slide down her neck to her shoulder, and on to her breast, outside of her clothes.

Much better, she had to admit as he began to work his magic there. Better still when he finally slipped inside to cup her bare skin and let her nipple grow taut in his palm. In fact, it felt so good, it took her breath away. She tore from their kiss and let her head drop back, inviting him to occupy his mouth in other pursuits.

He kissed his way down the column of her throat as he made quick work of the buttons of her dress, exposing her heated flesh to the night air and then to his seeking, moist mouth.

And even though she'd known that was where he was headed, the sensation was almost too glorious to bear.

Teasing, tormenting, sucking, circling her nipple with his tongue, even gently nipping and tugging with his teeth. Every stroke tightened a cord of pleasure inside her, a cord he strummed at just the right moments, with just the right touch.

She needed him to be closer, so much closer....

Suddenly their clothes seemed to be a barrier Ash couldn't abide one moment more, either. He abandoned her to tear off his shirt, to fling his jeans away, and then to undress her in the same flurry of impatience. When he came back to her, it was to press his warm, taut, naked body to hers with a new urgency....

Urgency in his mouth on hers again, briefly, before it

reclaimed her breast. Urgency in his hand exploring her belly for only a moment before he reached below and found the core of her yearning for him. Urgency in his long, hard shaft finding that same spot to slip inside her in what, by then, they were both straining for—that one perfect union, which would join them so completely that nothing that had ever separated them would matter.

Slowly, carefully, his thrusts spoke of his concern for her, for her condition, until Beth met and matched him and showed him how much more she wanted. How much more she needed.

His hands were in her hair, his mouth savored hers, until passion ignited into flames too consuming for anything but riding the storm.

And when it crested, her climax was so incredible she cried out as she never had, clinging to the solid wall of muscle that was Ash's back, wrapping her legs around him to hold him buried deeply inside of her as wave after wave of the most intense pleasure lifted her higher and higher until she thought she might burst.

Then, just as the waves began to settle her back to earth, Ash's whole body tensed above her, inside her, plunging in deeper still, forcefully, giving her not only more of the seed that had already sprouted in her womb but a second tremor of ecstasy to ripple through her until each thrust grew slower, calmer, and finally exhausted itself and them along with it.

Ash settled atop her. Keeping some of his weight on his arms braced on either side of her head, he looked down into her eyes again, holding them as surely as he held her.

And somewhere far out on the periphery of the pleasure he'd given her, the contentment she felt, she waited for him to complete it all by saying he loved her, the way he usually did at that moment. Not only because she craved hearing the words, but because if only he'd say it, she thought *she* might be able to, too.

But he didn't.

And without it, she couldn't.

Instead he slid his arms beneath her as his body slipped out of hers and he rolled to his back, holding her close to his side.

"Are you all right?" he asked, his breath a hot gust in her hair. "I didn't mean to be so rough, but—"

"I'm fine. You're never too rough," she assured him quietly.

He cupped the back of her head and held it to his heart, cherishing her even without the words, and she felt each of his muscles relax in turn, the way they did when he was falling asleep.

But somehow, even as wonderful as their lovemaking had been, it seemed incomplete. It was the words that were missing, she knew.

She waited, but those words never came. And then she heard his breathing deepen and knew that hole would not be filled. Not by him. Because he really had gone to sleep.

The stars glittered in the sky above them. The water moved just beyond them in a soft ripple. The moon bathed them. The soft earth cradled them. And she had the odd sense that all of nature was waiting, even if he wasn't.

"I love you, Ash," she whispered so softly even she barely heard it.

And as she finally drifted toward sleep, she wondered if he'd always felt what she did at that moment laying bare her feelings and getting nothing in return.

Because it was a loneliness as painful as any she'd ever known.

Chapter Nine

Sometime during the night Beth had rolled to her other side and Ash had apparently followed, because she woke to the feel of warm, early morning sunshine and him curved perfectly behind her.

That wasn't what lured her from sleep, though. What did that was his hand, moving in a slow caress of her stomach. And the sense that she was being watched. Or studied, actually, from where he'd propped his head up on his hand to peer over at her.

And while the changes in her body were not enormous or unsightly, and had some positive aspects, she wasn't comfortable having them all so openly assessed in broad daylight.

She reached for the edge of the blanket and pulled it around her as she turned to glance at him. "Looks like we camped out."

"Looks like it," he agreed, his smile mischievous, as if

he knew how uneasy she felt and was enjoying her modesty. He didn't do anything to stop her from covering herself, but he also didn't stop his sensual exploration of her middle underneath the blanket. "I was enjoying myself, you know."

"When?"

"Just now. Looking at you. There are some interesting things happening to you."

She glanced further over her shoulder and downward at him, and even though she couldn't really see anything, she said, "You look the same," with enough impudence to hide her own discomfort.

"Is that bad?"

"No," she admitted, unable to suppress an appreciative grin at just the thought.

Before she realized what he was doing, Ash flung the blanket away and pressed her to her back. "Your changes aren't bad, either. In fact, I'd say they're pretty terrific."

She tried to retrieve the blanket again, but one long arm shot out across her, caught her wrist and held it captive while he sat up some, still braced on his elbow but with his head raised, the better to see her. He began a slow scrutiny that seemed to memorize every new curve.

"They're all very sexy," he said in a quiet, husky voice that relayed his admiration. "And this…" he went on, his gaze dropping to the evidence of his baby. "This is what we made together. I could look at it forever," he said, finishing in awe, just before he bent over and placed a kiss above her navel.

Then he let go of her wrist and, in one lithe movement, sat up, swung a leg over her to straddle her, and cupped her stomach with one big hand on either side of it. "Incredible," he whispered, exploring, kneading, learning every inch of that small, firm mound with his hands and eyes as if to convince himself it was real, that what was growing inside of it was real.

Embarrassment warred in Beth with the rekindling of desires she thought had been well sated just hours before. She reached his thighs with both hands, considering whether to push him away. But once she felt those solid, muscular legs, the decision made itself and she did some caressing of her own instead.

"We should get dressed before somebody happens out here," she said, but it was a feeble suggestion that Ash didn't even seem to hear.

Instead his eyes had returned to her breasts, and a devilish smile played on his lips as he raised his hands from her middle and filled them with her new voluptuousness. "Oh, yeah, this is *very* nice. And would you look at that— all I have to do is say hello and they perk right up for me."

"You have no room to talk," she countered, finding the advantage to the situation in her own view of his body in broad daylight. He was gloriously, magnificently naked, wearing only the arrowhead tied around his neck and a clear indication much lower down that he wanted her. Again.

She slid her hands to midthigh but let her eyes go farther up his body to that long, thick shaft; to his flat belly; to the widening V of his torso; to his broad, powerful shoulders; to his exquisitely masculine face.

And, heaven help her, she wanted him, too. Again.

She paused for a moment. "In case you've forgotten, we're not far from the house, where at this moment, my brother and any number of ranch hands are getting ready to go to work. Depending on the direction they take, that could mean they'll pass right by here."

"I guess we'll have to hurry then," he answered with a sly smile that said he wasn't worried.

But then, neither was she. Not really. Not when he cradled her face and kissed her, setting aflame the passions that were so eager to be reignited it was as if they hadn't been satisfied at all.

Neither Ash nor Beth moved with any haste. They made love slowly, as if they had all day there in the sun, relearning the sight of each other the way their hands had already relearned the feel.

Beth's inhibitions about her body melted away. How could she stay self-conscious when Ash found such delight in it and in turn raised her own levels of pleasure to new heights?

He kissed her everywhere, following the path of his hands to trail every inch of her skin, awakening her nerve endings and bringing them all to the surface to sizzle to life. And along with the smooth, unbroken line of his exploration there was a playfulness, a teasing, a delicious torment that had her writhing in response.

In the light of day and their rediscovered familiarity, Beth gave as good as she got. He was a physically incredible man, and while it was easy to forget that in the cloak of darkness, now she feasted on it.

Her hands slid along the taut, burnished flesh of his shoulders, so wide her arms could hardly span them. She rode the bulge of his biceps with her flattened palms and kissed her way from one hard pectoral to the other while her hands rounded his narrow waist and slipped down to that derriere that caught her eye whenever his back was turned.

He was ticklish and she knew just the spot on his side to tease with her tongue to make him squirm, not minding at all when he got even with the flick of his own tongue in secret places that drove her wild.

And this time when passion grew too great to bear, she reached for him with both hands, reveling in the feel of that thick, hard shaft for a moment before guiding it home to fill the gaping emptiness as only he could.

She surrendered to the intensity of his thrusts then, letting him take her higher and higher, climbing until they reached their peak together, their breaths mingling, their bodies melded into one in an ecstasy so intense Beth could only cling to him, welcoming the full length of him so deeply inside of her that more than their bodies were joined—their spirits and hearts seemed to be, too.

But as much as she wanted it to go on forever, nothing that powerful could last, and finally they both crossed over the crest, slowly, slowly floating back to earth. To reality.

"I love you," Ash said into her hair in a ragged voice.

Beth smiled, truly feeling replete now, as she hadn't the night before. "I love you, too," she whispered back.

Ash pushed up on his hands and stared down at her. "What did you say?"

He wasn't going to make this easy for her. And it *wasn't* easy for her. Especially not if she had to look at him and repeat it or discuss it. Why couldn't he just let it lie?

"Beth?" he coaxed.

But she didn't know if she could say it again. If she could let him scrutinize her emotions the same way he'd studied her body.

She swallowed with some difficulty and tried. "I said I love you, too," she managed, though so softly it was a hushed whisper this time.

His supple mouth stretched into a leisurely smile that stretched into a full-fledged grin. "I'll be damned. I didn't think I'd ever hear that from you."

Then they were even—sort of—because she'd been afraid she might not ever hear it from him again, either.

He laughed wryly. "It's all the wrong way around, you know," he said, slipping from her and rolling to his side to prop his head on his hand once more.

"What is?"

"Everything about us. We got married before we really knew each other, and only after we divorced are we having a baby and are you finally telling me you love me. We should have met, gotten to know each other, *shared our feelings,* married, *shared our feelings,* and had a baby. And maybe skipped the divorce altogether."

His repetition of the sharing their feelings part nettled her as nothing in the soft earth under the blanket had. But she didn't want to fight, so she ignored it. "We certainly seem to have jumbled everything up," she agreed.

"Maybe it's time we straighten them out," he suggested in a quiet voice of his own, as if venturing into dangerous territory.

"Have you mastered the art of time travel to send us back to do it over?" she joked, for some reason feeling terribly vulnerable and pulling her side of the blanket over her again.

"I'm talking about making it right from here on," Ash said.

An odd mixture of feelings bubbled inside her at that moment. She had a pretty good idea what he was leading up to, and a part of her hoped she was right.

But another part of her hoped she wasn't.

With the blanket held tightly in place across her breasts, she sat up and looked at him, lying there in all his glory, staring past her out at the lake, as if he were gauging whether he really wanted to say what he was about to.

Then he turned his sharp-boned face up to her. "Maybe we should take a second stab at marriage."

Was he unsure of the wisdom in it? Or how she might react to the suggestion? Or was it that he didn't really want to? Because there was clearly uncertainty in his tone.

And that uncertainty fed the portion of her that had hoped a proposal was *not* what he'd been leading up to.

But she cared for this man and she was having his baby. And those two things kept her from doing or saying anything rash.

What they couldn't keep her from was voicing her own doubts. "I'm not sure that's a good idea."

He chuckled a little and sat up, raising one leg to brace an elbow on. "Well, at least that isn't a no. Let's talk about it."

Beth couldn't feel easy about either the idea of remarriage or the discussion of it. "I think we ought to get dressed first."

"You're stalling," he said, doubts creeping into his voice. "Surely this is something you must have thought about."

Not in a way that actually considered it. But she didn't say that.

And before she could say anything at all, he went on. "What worries you most about the idea of our getting married again?"

"What worries *you* most?" she countered. "You didn't exactly propose with gusto. And if the only reason you did was because you feel some sort of obligation—"

"I'll meet my *obligations* to the baby whether we're married or not," he cut her off. "I'm not talking about some shotgun wedding here. I'm talking about our getting back together because we both want to."

"All right then, what worries you most?" she repeated.

His frown was dark enough to let her know he was indeed worried, about more than whether or not she might reject his proposal. When he finally answered, it was as if he were choosing his words very carefully. "I can't say I'm comfortable with the fact that we'd be going back into something we already failed at."

She understood that well, because she had the same trepidation. But she could tell by the deepening of the lines between his bushy brows that there was more to it than his generalization. And that the details carried the most weight. "Go on," she urged and challenged at once.

He shook his head dubiously. "I, uh, don't know if you'll ever really be able to open up to me, to let me know what I need to know—good and bad—before just up and bailing out altogether."

He was being honest, and she knew she should be grateful for that. But what she wanted—deep down in that woman's heart her father had taught her to hide away—was for him to sweep her off her feet the way he had when they'd met. To tell her he loved her too much to live without her, no matter what had gone wrong before. To swear there wasn't a doubt in his mind that they could make it this time. That nothing would come between them. And she wanted him to do it all with so much conviction that even she would be convinced.

What she didn't want was a complaint that felt as if he were blaming her for the failure of their marriage.

But that's what she was getting.

Then, as if he read her mind, he reached over and took her free hand, rubbing the back of it in small circles with his thumb in a gesture that was soothing and sexy and sweetly romantic at the same time. "But we do love each other," he went on. "And it wasn't as if our marriage was horrible. There were a lot of good things about it. Good things between us. Good times.''

That was all true. She couldn't dispute it.

''And there's the baby now, too,'' he added. ''I'm not feeling I have some duty to marry you because you're pregnant, but the baby's a factor here. I want us to raise this child together. I don't want to be alone in the joy of it and feeling bad that you aren't there to see or experience something terrific. And I sure as hell don't want to be wondering what's happening that I'm not a part of. We've created a family, Beth, and I think that's what we should be. It's what I want us to be.''

She agreed with that, too. But still, that woman's heart was tweaked. ''If there wasn't going to be a baby, though, you wouldn't be here right now. You wouldn't even be thinking about our remarrying.''

''Don't be too sure. I wasn't happy about the divorce.''

''Oh, really? You seemed more than willing to me.''

''It was you who said you wanted it.''

''And you who said you'd been thinking the same thing. And then moved out of the house so fast you made my head spin.''

He was still holding her hand, but he wasn't rubbing it anymore. ''I thought that was what you wanted. Was divorce just a ploy? Are you telling me I called your bluff?''

''No, of course not.'' But it might have hurt less if he'd hesitated even a little. If he hadn't seemed so eager to be rid of her...

''Just don't pretend that you didn't want the divorce, too, when you made it very clear that you did.''

He took a deep breath and sighed it out. ''I couldn't have made it very clear that I wanted the divorce, because I *wasn't* very clear that I did. I said I'd been *thinking* about it myself.''

"And then you hurried to move out," she repeated.

"You wouldn't talk to me about it!" he nearly shouted, his frustration sounding. "And if you'll recall, I also suggested marriage counseling before we actually filed for divorce, but you refused that, too. You said talking wouldn't do anything and you weren't letting some perfect stranger poke around in your psyche. What choice did that leave? You wanted out and that was that. But it doesn't mean I was happy about it. And I've been even less happy about the reality of it."

"Meaning?"

"Meaning that I've missed you, damn it! I've missed coming home late at night and finding you all soft and warm in bed. I've missed Sunday mornings—making love, having breakfast together, reading the newspaper. I've missed being able to call you when I start craving the sound of your voice. And knowing you'll be there waiting for me when I get back from someplace. And knowing you're my wife and picturing us growing old together. I've missed…hell, I've missed just about everything."

Just about everything. But not everything.

Well, she'd missed a lot of things, too. But missing Ash wasn't anything new to her. All those same evenings he was so happy to come home and find her soft and warm in bed were the evenings she'd spent alone and lonely before she'd fallen asleep.

And how many Sunday mornings wasn't he there to make love to her and have breakfast with her and read the newspapers, when he was either out of town or already up and gone to the office or taking care of something else that needed him? She'd missed him then, too. Just the way she had through all of that time he'd been so happy to know she was waiting for him.

And even being married to him hadn't allowed her to

simply call to hear the sound of his voice when she craved it, because at the other end of the line would be either no answer or an intimidating Miss Lightfeather telling her he was unavailable.

Unavailable.

He'd missed her not being available to him since the divorce, but he hadn't been available to her in a long, long time.

"And I've missed playing Boat," he interrupted her thoughts, smiling at the memory and apparently overlooking the fact that she was not feeling lighthearted at the moment. "Not to mention making love to you the way I did last night and just now."

She smiled, too, but just for a moment. Finally she blurted out what was on her mind. "Would it be any different?" And her woman's heart listened very carefully, hoping that having let him know two days before why she'd divorced him had given him the clue to what to say, to what she wanted—needed—from him, and that he'd tell her everything would be better, that he'd make her and the baby his first priority...

"What do you mean?" he asked.

"A second marriage. What would change to make it work now when it didn't before?" she prompted.

"That's what we'd have to hash out, beginning with your being up-front with me about what's going on inside that head of yours."

Beth's heart took cover even as she prompted again. "Okay, let's say I start blathering about every little thought or feeling I have. What then?"

He frowned. "Then we work on what's wrong."

"I already told you what was wrong. You were gone all the time. I was just a pit stop in your life. How will you fix that?"

"I can't give you a blanket answer for what I'll do. It'll have to be something I deal with as each thing comes up."

"And how would that be any different from before? Except maybe that as you're leaving, you'll know I'd rather you weren't?"

"What are you saying? That you'd want me to turn my back on the foundation? On my other responsibilities? On my work?"

Beth just stared at him, wondering why it was so important for her to lay bare all her feelings when doing it didn't accomplish anything.

"No, I'm not saying I want you to turn your back on the foundation. I know what you do is important," she finally answered him. "But don't you see, Ash? The demands on you will be the same. And I think your response to them will be, too—you'll meet them all. And that will leave the baby and me at the bottom of the list."

He looked as if she were asking the impossible of him. "Maybe I could set aside some specific time for us—like a standing appointment, if that's what you mean," he finally said. "Or I could bring some work home so I can be available to you if you need me. Or try keeping the traveling to a minimum…"

But there was so much hedging in what he said, he didn't sound confident enough to convince himself, let alone her.

He'd have good intentions, Beth thought. He'd make a stab at putting their marriage before the foundation work, but demands would press in on him. Crises would happen. And he'd be off again.

"Remember," he put in, "you'll have the baby, too. You'll be busier than you were before. Part of the time you won't even notice I'm gone."

There was something about that that rubbed her the

wrong way. Something that she thought made her sound so needy and weak and dependent that he had to be pointing out what could occupy and entertain her.

She let out a mirthless little laugh. "So let me see if I have this straight. You believe that the real problem in our marriage was that I didn't announce what I was thinking and feeling every minute—"

"It isn't as if I'm blaming that for everything," he amended with no small amount of heat in his voice. "But I'll repeat what I said the other day—I can't fix what I don't know is broken. When you don't tell me what bothers you, how the hell am I supposed to know you're bothered?"

"But I *let* you know what bothered me. And the best you can do with it is say you'll try to be around a little more, but you're warning me even as you say it that nothing is likely to change, except that the baby will fill my time like a hobby."

"I don't know what else I can say except that I'll try to spend more time with you," he said impatiently, angrily.

Beth cringed. He sounded as if he were answering an old harridan's nagging. And she didn't like being cast as the nagging old harridan.

With her dignity stiffening her spine, Beth let go of the blanket and found her clothes to put on as if they were armor to bolster and protect her. "I just don't think so," she said then.

"You don't think what?"

"That our getting married again would work. It wouldn't be any different than it was before, except that there'd be the baby. What was wrong would still be wrong."

"And we'd have to work to make it right," he said in measured tones that announced he didn't like her answer.

"All the work in the world won't change the fact that you're constantly needed elsewhere. That there will always be something bigger and more important to take care of, something that can be dealt with only by you. And you'll be gone. And I'll be there. Waiting. Putting things off—putting off my whole life—until you have time for me."

"Damn it, Beth—"

"You know it's true. You've just said it yourself, in so many words."

"I said I'd try—"

"But trying won't change the fact that you need to do the work of three people. That you just plain don't have room in your life for marriage." Her voice cracked and it took her a moment to fix it before she could finish. And even then the sadness tinged it. "I won't marry you again, Ash."

"You're ignoring the good things. What about last night and this morning?" he demanded angrily. "What about the baby? The fact that we care about each other?"

"It isn't enough," she answered in a near whisper, because she wished it was.

Then she went to the car, put on her shoes, and began walking in the direction of the house.

"Where the hell are you going?" he shouted to her.

"Home," she called, salvaging what was left of her pride by not looking at him. She couldn't bear even the thought that he might see all the emotions that were tearing her apart.

"Damn it, Beth!" he said again. "Come back here and talk to me about this!"

But she just kept going, telling herself that no matter

how much she didn't want it to be true, there was no future for them together.

And she could only assume that in spite of Ash's protestations, he knew it, too.

Because he didn't follow.

Chapter Ten

What the hell did she want from him? Ash railed silently as he drove to the lodge in the glare of morning's first sunshine after watching Beth walk away from the lakeside where they'd spent the night. And made love. And argued...

She said that she didn't want to interfere with his work, that she knew it was important. But then she crucified him for it.

She didn't expect him to turn his back on the foundation. But anything short of that and she wouldn't marry him again.

What more could he do than promise to try to cut back some?

And what had she offered to change?

Had she said she'd try being more open about her feelings so he could know what was going on with her? So he could be warned when she felt as if he hadn't been around enough? So he could be alerted that he'd done something wrong?

No, she hadn't, not in anything more than a hypothetical scenario.

And what about the positive things she might be feeling? Had she said she'd work at letting him in on those, either?

No, she hadn't.

This was just like her—walking away from a problem rather than hammering at it until it was solved. Was that what she thought he should do with everything the foundation had to deal with—give nothing more than a lame attempt to fix it and then forget it? If it was too tough, too complicated, too messy, just bury it and leave?

Because he couldn't do that.

And he wished to God she couldn't, either, so that maybe they'd still be at that lake, figuring out a way to deal with their problems, to get back together, to be a family.

But no. She'd left. Basically, the same way she'd bailed out of their marriage.

He barreled into the lodge parking lot so fast the turn was nearly on two wheels and his tires squealed when he came to a stop in front of his cabin.

For a moment he considered backing out again and heading for the ranch. But it wouldn't do any more good to go after her now than it would have when she'd first taken off, and he knew it. Not when she was on her high horse like that, all closed off and impervious. She was never easy to reach, but when she put up that wall to hide her feelings behind, it was useless to even think about breaching it.

Besides, he was too frustrated and irritated to be rational or reasonable himself. He'd only make things worse.

So rather than retracing his tracks, he jammed the car into park and turned off the engine.

But he still didn't rush to get out. Instead, he sat there, staring at the small rustic cabin and wondering what the hell he was going to do.

He loved her.

He wanted her.

He wanted the baby.

He wanted them both in his life full-time.

But the foundation and all it entailed was a part of that life.

"Damn it!" he shouted, hitting the steering wheel with both hands.

He was disgusted. With himself. With Beth. With everything.

He finally shoved the car door open, got out and slammed it shut again. Hard.

Not that it made him feel any better, but if he didn't vent some of his anger and frustration somehow, he was liable to drive out to that ranch the way he was itching to and vent it at Beth.

He stabbed his key into the lock on the cabin door and threw it wide. In the gust of air that went with it, several small sheets of paper rose up from the floor like leaves in the wind, scattering back down to the nubby gray carpet.

He bent over to gather them, realizing as he did that they were phone messages that had been slipped under the door.

They were all from his grandfather, and with a wave of alarm he read through them in a hurry.

The time each call had been received was noted. All but one of them had come in late the day before and into the evening. The last was marked just half an hour ago.

Each one relayed a little more information, a little more urgency.

Serious charges were being levered against the drug and alcohol rehabilitation center the foundation had built and overseen.

An impromptu investigation was under way by hostile officials.

There were threats to close the place. To have the director arrested.

His grandfather thought he'd better get back there on the double....

"Perfect," Ash muttered to himself. "Absolutely perfect."

And he could have sworn the gods were laughing at him.

Beth had fallen on the walk from the lake to the house that morning.

Lost in thoughts of Ash and how stubborn he was, she missed spotting a gopher hole, stepped into it and gone down. Not hard. At least she hadn't thought so. Just enough to scrape a knee. Certainly not like some of the spills she'd taken as a kid, working the ranch.

She'd gotten to her feet, brushed herself off and walked the rest of the way, counting herself lucky that she hadn't broken or sprained anything.

It wasn't until that afternoon that the cramping started.

At first she hadn't even connected it with the fall. Then, when she remembered it, she thought maybe it had just caused some muscle spasms, because that's all it felt like. Nothing serious. And it would disappear. It was so mild she didn't pay it any mind.

Then, at four-thirty, she started to spot. Lightly, but unmistakably. And that was when she began to consider that the fall had been more jarring than she'd realized and she wasn't just having muscle spasms. She also finally admitted to herself that she wasn't just a kid coming in from chores with a scraped knee.

She was a pregnant woman who might be having labor pains.

Ash had been on her mind all day, but when it occurred to her that the baby could be in jeopardy she forgot about their fight. She just plain wanted him by her side.

After notifying the doctor's office of what was happening and telling them she was on her way in, she dialed Ash's cabin at the lodge. But there was no answer and when even her call to the front desk wasn't picked up, she was afraid of spending any more time trying to track him down.

Instead, she left a note letting Jackson know there was a problem with the baby, that she'd gone into town to the doctor, and asking him to please try reaching Ash to tell him.

Then she got in her car and headed for Elk Creek's medical facility without even considering that maybe she shouldn't drive.

That only dawned on her when it began to seem as if the pains were coming stronger and closer together.

Or did it just seem that way because now that she knew what they were she was alert to every twinge?

What if she lost the baby? she started to wonder.

Oh, Lord, she couldn't think about that. It made her heart beat even faster than it was, her hands shake more. Her whole body turn into an even tighter cord of stress.

What have I done? What have I done? she kept asking herself, wishing she'd never stormed off with no thought to anything but her pride and getting away from Ash be-

fore he could see how much she'd wanted him, how hurt
and sad and disappointed she'd been.

Please don't let anything happen to the baby. Please.
And please send Ash. Send him right away....

Because she was more afraid than she'd been in her
whole life, and if ever she'd needed anyone at any time,
it was Ash right then.

Ash didn't reach the reservation until late that afternoon.
He went straight to his office, finding Miss Lightfeather
closing up for the day.

She paused long enough to fill him in—a teenage patient
at the rehab center had convinced his parents that atrocities
were being committed by the director. The parents had
pressured authorities to look into it and at that moment
state investigators were at the rehab center in the second
phase of their inquiry.

"My grandfather?" Ash asked in a kind of shorthand.

"He's at the center, too, though I don't know what he
can do. It's *you* who needs to be there," the dour-faced
woman pointed out.

"I'm on my way," he answered, turning toward the
door he'd just come through.

"It's good that you're back," she called after him.
"There's an awful stack of other things that have to have
your attention, too. ASAP."

Ash waved a hand in the air to let her know he'd heard,
but he didn't pause to respond.

The rehab center wasn't far from his office. He made it
there in five minutes and was told where he needed to be
by the volunteer at the admissions desk without even having to ask.

He found the team of four investigators in the basement
with his grandfather and the center's very worried looking

director. Both men's faces showed relief when they caught sight of Ash, and within moments he had taken over, doing what he did best—dealing with the problem.

And immersing himself in work without another thought to anything else.

"You're looking tired, old man," Ash said as he poured himself and his grandfather coffee in the doctor's lounge while the investigators went through the director's files and journals later that night.

"Humph. Tired of waiting," Robert answered, accepting the paper cup as Ash joined him at a round table.

His grandfather's long hair—like his—was tied in a leather strap at his nape, but unlike Ash's, it was a shock of pure white. And while they resembled each other, Robert Yazzie's face was lined and creased like a river bottom in a drought.

"It's past ten. Just because I persuaded these people to work late doesn't mean you have to stay. Why don't you go on home?" Ash suggested.

His grandfather ignored him. "Did you settle things with our little Beth?" he asked instead, clearly seizing the first chance he'd had since Ash had arrived to satisfy his curiosity.

Ash let out a mirthless half chuckle, half sigh. "I don't think you could call anything between us settled, no. I had a big fight with her this morning—I asked her to marry me again and she turned me down flat."

"Why?"

Ash explained, trying to keep the anger out of his voice. And failing.

"I'm surprised at Beth wanting you to give up the foundation," his grandfather said when he'd finished.

"She didn't say that in so many words. But I sure as

hell can't see where she meant anything else. I said I'd cut back where I could, and she still wouldn't even consider our getting together again.''

"Could be she doesn't believe you can do it.''

Ash wasn't so quick to respond to that, because the tone in his grandfather's voice said the old man didn't believe it, either. "I know it'll be a hard promise to keep, but—''

"Or an impossible one. Over the years I've seen how much you've taken on for yourself through the foundation. Saw it even clearer being in your shoes since you went after her. You're a very busy man.''

"There's always a lot of work. A lot of problems,'' Ash confirmed with a glance around them, silently citing their present situation as an example.

"And somebody has to see to it all,'' Robert put in.

"And that somebody is me,'' Ash finished. He'd been wondering all day and through the evening if this particular crisis was fate's way of telling him he was a fool to think he actually could reduce his work load or avoid being drawn away by emergencies in order to devote more time to his personal life.

"Guess you *could* close down the foundation,'' his grandfather said, as if he were ruminating on the idea.

"You know I can't do that.'' And Ash knew his grandfather wouldn't want him to.

Neither of them said anything for a moment. Then Robert broke the silence with a change of subject. "I've been wondering about you, you know.''

"What have you been wondering about me?''

The old man shrugged. "Too many nights I played gin rummy with Beth while she watched the clock and looked out the window at every sound, hoping it was you. Too many times I watched her send you away with a smile, only to see that smile fade when you were gone. Too many times she trumped up excuses for me to visit just to keep away the loneliness. Too many times, Ash, and they all added up to the same thing—she didn't see enough of you. She missed you. But I never had the impression that you were missing her. Not until she ended the marriage. And I'm wondering why that is. If the little you saw her was all you really wanted of her.''

Ash couldn't believe what his grandfather was implying. ''You're wondering if I *liked* being away so much?''

Again the shrug, as if Robert thought it was possible. ''*Did* you miss her when you were gone?''

Ash started to answer that, but then stopped, because an honest response wasn't as easy to come by as it should have been. ''I was busy when I was gone and—'' But again he stopped short at the sound of his own words. And the words he hadn't been able to say—that yes, he had missed her when he was away from her during their marriage.

Because for the most part, he hadn't.

Not then.

Staring into his coffee cup, he thought about what his grandfather was getting at.

He'd been missing Beth something fierce since they'd separated. But before that?

Before that he'd always known she'd be there whenever he managed to get home to her, and that had made him feel good. Great. After all, he'd had other things on his mind while he was away, and knowing where she was, what she was doing, that she was capable of caring for herself and he didn't need to worry about her...

Had made him take her for granted.

Wasn't that what it all amounted to?

He didn't want it to be true, but as if a light had been turned on in a dark room, he knew it was.

Now he suddenly wondered if the way he'd felt since he'd lost her was how she'd felt throughout their marriage.

Because if it was, it was no wonder she'd divorced him.

And it was also no wonder she'd been protective of herself and her feelings before that.

He'd put all the blame on her for being closed off emotionally. But if they'd just seen more of each other, if she hadn't been left feeling bad and hiding it behind assurances that she didn't mind his being gone so much, would she have eventually opened up to him in other ways?

He couldn't be sure, but it seemed possible.

It also occurred to him now that the simple fact of spending time together might have allowed him to feel closer to her whether she wore her heart on her sleeve or not. And that should have been something that came naturally with being married.

What had she said when she'd finally told him why she'd wanted a divorce? That it should have gone without saying that two people who were married to each other actually spent time together?

And she'd been right. She shouldn't have had to complain about rarely seeing him in order for him to recognize that it was a problem. To get him not to take her for granted. Not to neglect her. Because he *had* neglected her, he saw that now.

"I've been a first-class jerk, haven't I?" he finally said to his grandfather, who had sat silently through his soul-searching as if he could see the process.

Still the old man didn't say anything. He just stared at him the way he had when Ash was a boy, as if waiting for him to see the whole picture for himself.

"You knew, didn't you? You knew that I really had just made her a pit stop in my life the way she accused me. That all the while she was missing me and unhappy, I was too wrapped up in work to feel the same way. The divorce and what I've suffered since she said she wanted out was what I had coming, wasn't it? Because it was just what she suffered, and I was blind to it. I barely took it seriously when she came right out and told me about it a few days ago." Ash shook his head in self-disgust.

"Some lessons aren't easy to learn," Robert said.

"The trouble is," Ash added, feeling as fatalistic as he sounded "even if I got a second chance to appreciate her, the rest of the problem hasn't changed. There's still the foundation and all the demands on me."

"Guess you could close it down," his grandfather repeated.

"Why do you keep saying that?"

Robert shrugged once more, this time in a way that said *figure it out*. "Something has to give, Ash."

But before he could mull it over, they were interrupted by the center's director. The man poked his head through the lounge doorway and asked them to rejoin him and the investigators in his office.

"Think I'll go on home after all, and let you take it from here," Robert said as they stood to follow the director into the corridor.

But there was mischief in those old eyes and Ash saw it. He just couldn't explore it right then. "I'll call you when I get through here and let you know what happens," he said instead.

"Do that," Robert answered pointedly, heading for the front door.

Ash watched him as the old man made his way out of the building. There was nothing about the sight of that big, broad back, still straight and strong in spite of all the years it carried, to make him think his grandfather was up to something.

But Ash sensed that he was.

And that before too long, he'd find out about it.

The lights were on in his two-story adobe house when Ash got there after midnight. For one split second he had the unreasonable thought that it was Beth who was inside, the way she used to be.

But of course that was just wishful thinking.

The kitchen and side porch light of his grandfather's house next door were also on, and it was a pretty good bet Robert was who waited for him.

Ash put the car in the garage, grabbed his garment bag and briefcase from the back seat and went in through the door that opened into the laundry room.

There were no sounds coming from anywhere inside, but out in his backyard he could see a fire burning. Just a small one. At the end of a brick path that wound through the garden.

And there, standing nearby, was Robert, looking very pleased with himself. "Come on out," he called when he saw Ash.

None of the patio lights were on, but as Ash went into the yard, his grandfather moved to a pottery bowl on the ground not far from the main fire and lit another one inside it to flame to life, too.

"What are you doing, old man?" Ash asked.

Robert just smiled, moved to yet another spot and set a fairly large pile of kindling ablaze. Then he pointed to the pottery bowl. "Better put that out," he suggested. As Ash did, he said, "How'd things go at the center?"

"The investigators didn't give us a final verdict, but I think we're in the clear except for some overcrowding problems. Since they didn't find naked women chained to beds or torture chambers in the basement or records of sadistic experiments and tortures on inpatients, they were finally convinced that that boy was just stirring up trouble because he hadn't liked being sent to us. We're clean, and they saw that. Now I just have to come up with the funds for expansion or turn people away,'' he finished with a weary sigh for yet another major problem that he'd have to deal with.

''Ah, a new fire,'' Robert murmured, but Ash didn't know if he was referring to the one he'd just lit or to the need for more funds.

Robert brought to life three more small conflagrations, and now he pointed to two of them. ''Better put those out.''

Ash knew the old man well enough to know this was what had caused the glint in his eye earlier that evening. He just didn't know what the hell it was all about.

He smothered the other fires, but when he moved to snuff the main one at the end of the garden path, Robert stopped him. ''Don't pay any attention to that one. Let it go.''

And by then there were four more blazes.

The old man was really prepared.

''Are you trying to burn this place down?'' Ash asked.

''I may unless you do something about those,'' Robert answered with a serene smile and a nod at some of the new fires.

Ash again did as he was told, but when he turned from it, he found half a dozen more infernos illuminating his yard, some of them large and much too near the house for his comfort.

''Damn it, Pap, what the hell are you doing?'' he said as he rushed to where flames licked at the woodpile against the garage wall, while another crawled ever closer to the dry timber of the toolshed.

Robert stood in the midst of it all, looking satisfied with himself.

"We're going to have the fire department here any minute," Ash grumbled as he ran from throwing dirt onto a small fire to finally pull the hose out to spray the bigger ones.

But even though he was rushing around the yard and Robert had stopped lighting new blazes, there were so many burning already Ash couldn't keep them all under control himself.

"Don't just stand there," he told his grandfather. "This is getting out of hand and we're going to have real trouble here if you don't pitch in."

Robert stayed put. "You can do it all if you only work a little harder."

"Just put out that fire near the toolshed. The mower is in there and there's gas in it. The whole thing will explode."

"You can handle it. You're the only man for the job."

"Pap!" Ash shouted impatiently. "Put out that damn fire!"

"Are you sure about that?"

"Yes, I'm sure!"

Robert grinned broadly, then walked to his own yard next door and brought his hose over, joining in until together they had them all out.

Then he went down the garden path to the fire neither of them had touched and stood over it, staring at the few embers that were left of it.

"Okay, what's your point, old man?" Ash asked in a much calmer voice when he joined him.

But Robert only laughed, clapped him hard on the back, turned and walked away across the yards to disappear into his own house.

Alone in the night with the smell of smoke all around him, Ash glanced at his grandfather's handiwork and rubbed the sweat from his brow with the back of his arm. Then his gaze settled on the scant orange glow of the last few unattended embers smoldering at his feet on the garden path.

He stared down into those embers for a while, thinking about what his grandfather had done. And said.

Then he looked past them, at the garden beyond.

And only in that moment did he realize he was standing in the exact spot he'd stood five years before.

Where he and Beth had been married.

Chapter Eleven

"She doesn't want to see you, Ash," Jackson said. "And right now I don't think she should be upset. The doctor said she needs to rest."

But Beth wasn't resting. She was standing at the top of the stairs, listening to her brother doing as she'd asked—barring Ash's entrance at the front door.

It was barely seven in the morning and she'd been awakened first by the doorbell and then by Jackson informing her Ash was outside—before he'd even answered it—so he'd know what she wanted him to do.

It was Ash's voice that came next, in an even but deadly serious tone. "The last time you and I faced off at this door, Jackson, I took a punch I didn't have coming. That means I owe you one. Now I'm going to see Beth. Even if I have to repay that punch to do it."

Jackson stood his ground, as Beth knew he would, but she couldn't be the cause of a physical fight between the two of them. With a full, disgusted sigh preceding it, she said, "It's okay, Jackson, I'll see him if I have to."

Her brother didn't budge from blocking the doorway except to turn his face to her as she started down the steps. "Are you sure?"

"Yes."

With an expression that relayed neither approval nor disapproval, Jackson headed for the kitchen, freeing the way for Ash to come in.

From the entryway, Ash watched her descend the steps, his expression almost dangerous, his black eyes faintly shadowed and bloodshot. He looked like a man who hadn't slept in a long time, which was no doubt the case since he'd driven from one side of the state to the other and back again in less than twenty-four hours, in spite of the fact that Beth had had Jackson tell him not to come at all.

And yet, even though he showed evidence of how bone weary, worried and, once again, unhappy with her he was, she still had the urge to cross the entrance to him, slide her arms around his waist, lay her head against his chest and feel him envelop her with the strength and security of his body to reassure her everything would be all right.

But she didn't do any of that, because during the previous night she'd done a lot of thinking. Thinking that hadn't been fogged by her blinding love for Ash, by the feelings that had reawakened since he'd followed her here. Thinking that hadn't been distracted by the pure power of his presence.

And what she'd finally decided was this: Her baby deserved a full-time father. A loving home where its needs would always come first. Anything less just wasn't enough.

And even though she was having to battle the power of

Ash's presence at that moment, she refused to lose sight of the way she knew things had to be between them.

"Why'd you come back?" she asked flatly, letting her tone convey that she wished he hadn't.

Ash ignored both her question and her attitude. "How are you? How is the baby?"

"Everything is fine," she answered almost airily, as if she hadn't been out of her mind with fear through it all. "I thought Jackson explained that on the phone last night."

Something in what she said seemed to anger Ash, because he closed his eyes tight and pinched the bridge of his nose. She saw his jaw clench as if he were working to control his temper.

But Beth wasn't sure what there was in such a simple statement to make him mad.

Jackson had arrived at the medical facility just after she had the evening before and had begun trying to locate Ash. Ash had left word at the lodge's front desk that an emergency had called him back to the reservation. But her brother hadn't been able to reach him there and he had ended up leaving several messages on the answering machines at the foundation office and at Ash's house.

Apparently Ash hadn't been at either place until the middle of the night, because when he'd received the messages at home at one this morning, he'd called right away.

But by then Beth had made up her mind, and she hadn't wanted to risk talking to him, afraid she might have broken down or wavered in the decisions she'd made. So she'd pleaded fatigue and had Jackson fill him in, which her brother had done. Thoroughly.

So what was there for Ash to be angry over? They'd done everything they could to let him know what was going on and had accepted a middle-of-the-night phone call from him, during which he'd been told all there was to tell.

Including that there was absolutely no reason for him to come back to Elk Creek.

After a moment, he took a deep breath and opened his eyes to her again. "Tell me yourself what happened."

"I think you ought to go to the lodge and get some sleep. You look awful," she said, rather than answer him, because even talking about the events of the previous evening put knots in her stomach.

Again his jaw tightened. "Tell me what happened," he repeated.

His tone and expression said he wasn't going anywhere until she did, so she figured she might as well get it over with.

Sliding her hands into the pockets of her bathrobe, she leaned against the banister, wanting to appear nonchalant about the whole thing. "I fell on the way home from the lake yesterday morning. Not bad, just a little tumble. I didn't think I'd hurt anything, but I guess it was enough to tear the placenta away from the uterus slightly, and that caused some pain and then some spotting. The doctor is sure there was no real harm done, though. The spotting and cramping stopped, the baby's heartbeat is great and an ultrasound test showed it doing just fine, so I was sent home to rest by about eleven last night. I'll go back in a couple of days to check on things, but there doesn't seem to be any problem." And there wasn't a single note in her voice that betrayed those knots in her stomach she'd been trying to avoid.

"Then this didn't happen from making love?"

"No, it didn't," she answered in a hurry. She certainly didn't want to discuss *that* subject. Just his saying the words raised goose bumps along her arms and much too vivid memories of pleasures she'd never have again.

"If you're supposed to be resting, I don't want you standing here," he said then. "Should you be in bed?"

"No, I only need to take it easy."

He nodded toward the living room. "Then let's go in there and sit down."

"Now that you know what happened and that the baby is fine, why don't you go get some sleep yourself?" she tried again.

He merely pointed a long index finger in the direction of the living room and stared at her as if the intensity of his eyes alone could move her through space.

Maybe it could, because even though she sighed impatiently, she went and sat on one of the sofas. "What was the emergency on the reservation?" she asked along the way.

Ash explained the crisis at the rehab center, but Beth paid only scant attention to what he was saying as she reminded herself that it had been a good thing he was called away. It had hammered home to her that in spite of the time they'd spent together in Elk Creek, in spite of the feelings he could raise in her, nothing had changed.

"If I'd have known everything wasn't all right with you and the baby, I wouldn't have gone. But as it was, I thought a little time for us both to cool off and think over the idea of our getting married again would be a good thing," he added when he'd finished.

Beth glanced at him where he stood not far away and wondered idly if even the threat of a miscarriage would have really kept him from the call of duty.

She knew he wasn't that unfeeling; he would have stayed with her at the doctor's—or at the hospital, if she'd needed to go.

But what about once the doctor had sent her home? When the worst of her jitters hit? When the adrenaline that came with fear finally waned and the full impact of what might have happened left her quivering in her bed?

After five years of experience she knew the answer to that. She knew that he would have been itching to get to the other crisis. And she knew she would have pretended everything was fine, that there was no reason for him to stay.

And that he'd have gone.

"I wish you would have thought to call Miss Lightfeather at home so she could have told you where I was or gotten hold of me herself sooner," he said then.

"It wouldn't have mattered," she lied. "There was nothing you could have done."

He let out a derisive, mirthless breath. "And you didn't need me or want me here, is that it?"

She raised her chin as if confirming it, all the while inside she was reliving just how much she *had* wanted and needed him. Too much. *Think of the baby,* she coached herself. *What kind of father do you want him to have?* "It was no big deal. I did okay on my own."

Ash sat on the coffee table in front of her and captured her eyes with his. "I don't believe that," he told her flat out and sternly. "I don't believe that you weren't scared to death that you'd lose this baby. I don't believe you didn't care that you were alone to face it. I don't believe that you didn't want me to be with you. What I can't handle is that you seem to think it's so damn bad to let me know it."

"It wouldn't have changed the fact that you were hundreds of miles away at the time," she pointed out. It would only have shown she was vulnerable and pitiable for having needs that wouldn't be met.

"No, it wouldn't have changed the fact that I was gone," he admitted. And with that, some of the steam seemed to go out of him, surprising her. "I'm sorry, Beth," he said then, taking her hands in his.

"Sorry for what?" she asked in a squeak of a voice as she worked to block the sparks that skittered up her arms at his touch.

"I'm sorry I wasn't here for you yesterday. I'm sorry I wasn't there for you through our whole marriage. I'm sorry I didn't see just how much I really did neglect you." He laughed a little wryly this time. "When I got home last night—before I saw the light on the answering machine and discovered Jackson's message—my grandfather was waiting for me, to point out a few things."

"Like what?"

"Like the fact that no matter how hard I work, I can't put out all the fires myself. And that I'm not the only one who can try. And that the price I paid for thinking I was, was losing you."

Beth didn't know what to say to that, so she didn't say anything at all. She just waited and watched him. And went on pushing hard against the wall that dammed her feelings for him behind it.

"I know I said before that I'd do what I could to cut back on work if you'd marry me again. And I know you didn't believe it could be done. But it can be, if I hire some help and delegate some of the work and responsibility."

"That costs money that's more needed other places," she parroted what she'd heard him say himself over the years, and then added the other reasons he'd always used against it. "And no one else carries the kind of clout or has the kind of connections you do after all your years of experience, or the drawing power to drum up funds and support. Plus, when you leave things to other people, they either get fouled up or at the very least are not done as efficiently or thoroughly or as well as when you do them yourself.''

"Don't stab me with my own sword, Beth," he said, and she saw him waver in his belief that he could, indeed, successfully share the load. "I'm not saying it won't take time to find good people and teach them the ropes and introduce them around and build confidence in them. Or that I'm handing over the helm. What I'm saying is that if I hire some help, I can put this job more into the perspective it should be, and actually have a life with you and the baby.''

Beth stared at him, loving him so much it hurt, memorizing every sharp plane of his handsome face and wanting to smooth away the lines that creased it with fatigue and stress. She knew he meant well. She knew he even believed that if he tried hard enough, he could do what he was proposing. And she believed he'd truly try.

But she knew him, knew how much he cared about his people and their plights, how responsible he felt, how duty bound to help, to make a difference. Those weren't the kinds of things that were just delegated, even to competent, capable people.

Beth shook her head and fought tears that threatened at the thought that no matter what he promised or how hard he tried, she and the baby still wouldn't be his first priority. They'd just be what kept him from doing what he felt he should. And she couldn't live that way. "It wouldn't work," she said very softly. "I know you want it to. I know you'd try to make it. But I also know that it won't. It can't.''

"It can with the right people," he insisted. "And if you meet me halfway and let me know if I'm getting too caught up in work and neglecting you or the baby, if you just speak up—'' But he curbed the criticism and tried a different tack. ''What about the time I've spent here? I've had Miss Lightfeather and my grandfather taking care of things, and until a major crisis came up, you and I were doing pretty well, weren't we? In fact, I was around more than you wanted me to be.''

Again she shook her head, this time more vigorously. ''But you were *here,* Ash, not in the thick of it. You and I both know that it's different being on the reservation, different when you haven't just temporarily postponed things to be away for a little while. And when you're right there, in the hub of what you care so much about, you are not going to be able to close your eyes to what needs attention. Or if you do you won't feel good about it, because I've whimpered or whined or nagged you into keeping your distance. And I won't feel good about it, either,'' she added quietly.

''Why is it that you always describe letting me know what you're feeling in such derogatory terms?'' he shot out, clearly frustrated.

''I'm just calling it the way I see it. Besides, that's what it would sound like. And I couldn't do it any more than you could allow anyone else to put out one of those fires you knew was burning.''

''Well, we could sure as hell give it a try, Beth.''

He was angry again.

But then so was she, for his wanting to force her back into the same position that had made her leave him. ''It just wouldn't work,'' she said again.

''Let's just try,'' he suggested as if soothing a skittish colt, squeezing her hands at the same time. ''Come back to the reservation with me. We don't even have to get married right away if you want to wait until I've proven to you that we can work through it all, that I can cut back. And maybe once we have more time together like we have while I've been here, you'll see it isn't so tough to open up to me, too.''

But as tempting as it was, she still shook her head against it, maintaining her denial. ''I just don't believe either of us could pull it off. Old habits die hard—I've heard you say that a million times over the years. And no matter how honorable your intentions, I know you'll be drawn back into it all. And even if I could live with it, it isn't fair to the baby. The baby deserves more than that. It deserves a father who's there for it.''

Too vivid in her mind was the memory of the past night, of letting herself think he would arrive any minute when the truth was he was gone, that in spite of his claims that he wanted to be a part of her pregnancy, a part of everything that was going on with her and the baby, he'd left at the drop of a hat.

Much as she loved him, she couldn't risk it happening again.

''I don't understand,'' he said harshly. ''Are you saying it's better for the baby if its parents aren't together?''

''In this case, I'm afraid that's so. Not the way we'd be together.'' Beth willed herself to keep from crying.

''And that's it? Your final answer? To hell with me. To hell with your own feelings for me. To hell with being a family.''

His words made her shudder internally. But all she could say was, ''For the baby's sake, if not my own, I just don't think I have a choice.''

This time it was Ash who shook his head. Clearly disgusted. Frustrated. So furious his jaw clenched once more.

But he didn't say anything. It was as if he couldn't trust himself to.

Instead, he stood and walked out, slamming the front door hard.

And the sound of that slamming door toppled the bricks of the dam that held her feelings contained, and they all suddenly came flooding out to drown her.

Chapter Twelve

"Are you all right?" Jackson asked Beth as he came out of the kitchen a moment later.

Beth didn't know her brother hadn't left the house after letting Ash in, and the realization that he was about to witness her falling apart jolted her back into control. She sat up straighter, squared her shoulders and blinked away the tears so perilously close to the surface.

"Sure. I'm fine," she managed.

But Jackson didn't seem convinced. He perched on the arm of the sofa, hooked a boot on the edge of the coffee table and frowned at her. "Shag would have been proud of you," he said, though it didn't sound like a good thing.

"You were listening?" But of course he had been, she thought. It was just like Jackson to be on the alert in case she'd needed him.

But all he said was "Voices carry."

Once more she found herself under a man's steady, unrelenting stare. And she was getting tired of it. "You look like you're busting to say something, Jackson. If that's the case, spit it out," she said peevishly.

That was all the invitation he seemed to need. "I don't mind tellin' you, Beth, I was worried that Ash wasn't doing right by you. But the truth is, it's you who's doing wrong. By Ash. By the baby. By yourself."

"Overhearing one conversation doesn't give you a complete picture."

"Gives me enough of it. Don't forget, I was raised by the same man, in the same way you were."

"That doesn't have anything to do with this."

"Maybe," Jackson allowed. "Then again, maybe it does."

Beth frowned back at him, wishing he'd leave her alone with her misery.

No such luck.

Jackson went on in that slow drawl of his. "Listening to Ash's side, it seems to me that Shag taught you too well to keep things to yourself."

Beth rolled her eyes at that, but began to be grateful for the rising anger that helped block the pain of having made what she believed to be the right decision against marrying Ash. Somehow it hurt even more than her earlier decision to divorce him. "Don't tell me you're advising me to turn into some simpering fool."

"Me?" he asked, shocked. "I'm the last one who'd do that. I'm just sayin' that when keeping your feelings to yourself means it costs you what you want most, it can't be all good."

She looked away from him and said flatly, "What makes you think I want Ash?"

Jackson blew out a derisive breath. "I was with you last night, remember? I was the one you kept sending to call him every five minutes. To find out anything I could about where he'd gone, if he'd be back, how to get hold of him. I was the one who watched you wishin' he was there so much you were nearly comin' apart at the seams. Now I hear you telling him to get lost for the baby's sake. But you and I know that's not what it's really about.''

''It's all more complicated than you think, Jackson.''

''Sounded pretty simple to me. Ash finally sees that he worked too much and is willing to hire some help so he can fix that. You're not willing to give him another chance because you're terrified of what it will do to you if he fails.''

''That's an oversimplification.'' But was it?

Jackson ignored the comment. ''Seems to me old Shag would have whupped the tar out of you for sitting back like some martyr and just being the silent, long-suffering wife. *Speak up for yourself* is what he'd have said.''

Jackson sounded so much like their father when he mimicked him that it made her smile in spite of herself.

But he wasn't finished saying his piece. ''Hell, Beth, even old Shag gave in to feelings for the opposite sex. You know he had a soft spot for Momma, and then there was Margie Wilson over at the café. And what about his lady friend in Denver those last years? He even left a full quarter share of everything to her, he must have loved her. You didn't see him counting it as a weakness and fighting against it the way you are.''

Beth didn't have a comeback for that because it was true. It just hadn't ever occurred to her before.

Jackson stood then, apparently drawing his lecture to a close. ''You have a baby to think of now,'' he said firmly. ''And a whole life of your own stretchin' out ahead of you. You may think you're doing this for the child's sake, but are you? Have you considered that a second marriage *could* work? Have you considered the fact that Ash *could* change, that you might be depriving your child of a damn fine daddy after all?'' He finished with a clear note of challenge in his voice, leaving her to think about it.

And she did think about it, because her brother's last comment rang in her ears.

Was she refusing to believe Ash could change because she was worried how she could bear it if he let her down again? Was she afraid of expressing her feelings to him and still coming up empty-handed?

But what had been accomplished by hiding them? she asked herself suddenly.

Sure, as a kid it had kept her from her father's wrath and harsh punishments. But as an adult it had cost her her marriage. It had caused her to walk from the lake so Ash wouldn't see her heart break and that had caused the fall that had put the baby in jeopardy.

Lord. She'd never thought of it like that before. But there it was now, frightening her to realize just how high a price she'd paid, how much more she could have paid.

And what about Jackson's perception that she wasn't standing up for herself?

That made sense, too.

But recognizing it and doing something about it were two different things.

Could she do it? Could she voice her needs to get them met if she and the baby began to slip down Ash's list of priorities? What if they got back to the reservation and being there, in the thick of the foundation's works and the problems that went with them, pulled him back in just as thoroughly as he'd been before? Would she really be able to pull him out again with complaints that would always ring in her ears as things she shouldn't be saying?

She didn't know.

And yet, when she really thought about what Ash had promised, she also realized that she should consider the kind of man she knew him to be. A man of intense pride and honor. A man who always kept his word. And he'd given her his word that he would do all he could to be a better husband. In fact, he'd given his word again and again that he'd try. If only she would...

Sitting there on that couch where Ash had left her, Beth had never felt so desolate.

She was facing the rest of her pregnancy and the birth of their baby alone—the way she'd been the night before.

She was facing raising the baby on her own.

But worst of all, she was facing the rest of her life without Ash. Without his love. Without his touch. Without sharing their child.

What she wanted, what she needed, was Ash as her husband. And as an active, full-time father to their baby. And there was only one chance of having that—if she met him halfway. No matter how tough that might be for her.

"Jackson!" she shouted in the direction of the kitchen, hoping her brother hadn't left the house.

Because she wasn't supposed to drive just yet.

And she needed to get to Ash before he really did give up on her.

One advantage to living in a small town was that Beth had no trouble getting a key to Ash's cabin at the lodge once she'd showered, dressed and fixed her hair and Jackson had driven her there.

She expected Ash to be asleep by then, so after assuring her brother he could go, she slipped quietly into the small, rustic room.

Ash was in bed, on his back, one arm across his eyes,

the other over his bare chest, a sheet covering his lower half.

He'd taken a shower himself before he'd gone to bed. Beth knew because there was a faint lingering of steam from the bathroom. The smell of his soap was strong in the air, and the towel he'd used to dry off was on the floor beside the bed.

She wanted to crawl in with him, curl up close to what she suspected was his completely naked body under that sheet, and content herself with lying with him while he slept. But she knew she'd disturb him, so she merely sat in one of the chairs at the table, intent on waiting until he woke up.

No matter how long that might be.

Just being able to look at him helped her feel that it wasn't too late for them. That she could rescind the rejections and mistrust and doubts she'd heaped on him recently and make everything all right again.

"What are you doing, Beth?" His deep voice came then as he lifted his arm enough to let her see that he'd been watching her from beneath it.

"I'm sorry if I woke you."

"I wasn't asleep yet. I was having trouble getting there. For some reason I seem to have a lot on my mind."

"Like why in the world you ever thought you wanted to remarry someone so worried about being a fool for love that she was just a plain fool?"

"Like how I was going to prove to you I meant what I said about putting work into line behind you so I could convince you to marry me again."

"And how were you going to do that?" she asked, her curiosity piqued.

"I'm moving to Elk Creek, for starters," he said without anything hypothetical in it.

That surprised her. "What do you mean?"

He sat up in bed, raising one knee under the sheet at the same time to brace an arm on. "I've been thinking about what you said earlier this morning, and you're right. As long as I'm in the thick of things on the reservation, I'll be drawn into everything in spite of the best intentions. But I can run things from here if I hire some help, and then I won't be tempted to rush to every little fire that starts. And when I do need to leave to take care of something, you'll have your family and Kansas and—"

"But you'd be leaving your grandfather, your home, your roots, your traditions."

"In my tribe," he said with a tired smile, "it's the custom for the man to join the wife's people when they marry. I may be a little late, but I'll be upholding tradition to move here."

"But Ash," she persisted, still as if this whole idea was just conjectural, "what about ceremonies, the community, being a part of your heritage—"

"I can still go back for special occasions and participate. Being here won't make me less an Indian. Just more of a husband." His expression sobered then and he pinned her with those black eyes of his. "Because that's what I want to be, Beth. So if you came here to run me out of town on a rail, you'd better know you're going to have some trouble." Which led them back to his unanswered question about her being there. "Is that why you sneaked in here—to try to get me to leave?"

"No, it isn't," she answered quietly.

He nodded his approval of that and made a sound that was part sigh, part laugh, as if that were the most he expected to hear from her in the way of an invitation to stay or a statement of her commitment. "Tell me you love me, Beth," he said, sounding as exhausted as he looked. "If you never do it again for as long as we live, tell me now. Tell me that's why you're here and that it's enough to work out our problems.''

"I do love you," she obliged, finding it easier than when she'd said it before. "Jackson gave me a good talking-to and pointed out a few things to me, but that was the one thing I knew even without his help."

The more she said, the higher his eyebrows arched, as if he couldn't believe she was speaking so freely. "Jackson's a good man, but what did he say that I didn't?" he asked, as if testing to see if she really was going to open up to him.

"Among a lot of things, there was one that really struck home—that I was so busy hiding my feelings from you I was refusing myself what I really wanted. I was so afraid of being disappointed again that I was denying the possibility that things could be different."

"An excellent observation. So here you are," he said then, tossing the ball into her court again.

"So here I am."

"And what happens now?"

She took a deep breath, shoring up her strength. "I decided that I'd like to give marriage a second try after all. That I know you'll do your best to keep your promise about not being swallowed up by the foundation—especially if you move here—and that I'm willing to wrestle with whatever I have to to do my part."

She stood and went to sit on the edge of his bed, facing him. "Because I really do love you, Ash. More than you'll ever know. And I want us to be together when this baby is born and through all the good and bad that comes with raising it, and—"

He reached up and cupped her cheek in his big palm

and she lost her train of thought as she melted into his touch.

"You know, I've been pretty dumb myself, missing out on all we had together by not putting you first," he said. "I don't plan on letting that happen again, so there shouldn't be a need for you to do much complaining about my not being around. But there can never be enough of this kind of talk."

"You want me falling all over you, is that what you're telling me?" she joked through her third flash of tears, though now they were from happiness and the swell of love for him that rose from her heart to her throat.

"Physically you can fall all over me anytime," he joked back, caressing her face. "But verbally? Just a little will do. Just a periodic *hey you, I'm glad you're my husband.*"

"Will you be?"

"Will I be glad or your husband?"

"Both."

"Is that a proposal?" he asked in mock surprise.

"I thought you had one coming since I've turned down so many of yours."

"Yes, I'll gladly marry you and be your husband, a real one this time. And the best father I know how to be."

He pulled her to him then, capturing her mouth with his in a long, slow, deep kiss.

"I love you, Beth," he said when he ended it.

"I love you, too." She looked into his tired eyes and smoothed a finger along the dark shadow beneath one of them. "But you'd better get some sleep." She kicked off her shoes and raised the sheet, trying not to notice just how naked he was, and slipped into bed with him.

"I suppose sleeping is all we can do?" he asked, sounding resigned.

"For a few days, until the doctor gives us the go-ahead again."

He wrapped her in his arms and they lay back together, Beth curved to his side, her head on his chest.

"Then I guess we'll have to plan our second wedding around when we can have our honeymoon—as long as it won't be too far-off," he said.

"And in the meantime," she added, snuggling in very close to his gloriously naked body, "we can make the best of resting."

Except, at that moment, the baby gave a kick hard enough even for Ash to feel against his side.

"Looks like we're the only two who need it," he said with a laugh. "My son is ready to play."

"Or your daughter," Beth amended.

Ash slipped his hand between them to just the spot where the baby seemed to be dancing a jig, and Beth watched as his eyes closed and his face relaxed into an expression of pure contentment.

He couldn't go to sleep any too soon, because the wonders he was working at her middle were making it difficult to follow doctor's orders.

But she managed to conquer her rising desires by reminding herself that they'd have their whole lives to satisfy and delight in them.

The divorce just hadn't worked out.

* * * * *

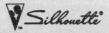

**Like a spent wave,
washing broken shells back to sea,
the clues to a long-ago death had been
caught in the undertow of time...**

Coming in
July 2003

Undertow

Cold cases were
Gray Hollowell's specialty,
and for a bored detective
on disability, turning over
clues from a twenty-seven-
year-old boating fatality
on exclusive Henry Island
was just the vacation he
needed. Edgar Henry had
paid him cash, given him
the keys to his cottage, told him what he knew about
his wife's death—then up and died. But it wasn't until
Edgar's vulnerable daughter, Mariah, showed up to
scatter Edgar's ashes that Gray felt the pull of her
innocent beauty—and the chill of this cold case.

Only from Silhouette Books!

Where love comes alive™

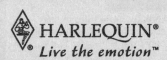
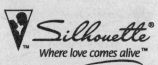

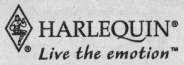